Advance praise for *A Buisness of Ferrets*

"An engaging cast of characters plunge into a deadly court intrigue that masks a supernatural intrigue more dangerous still. From the slum kids to the Scholar King, Hilgartner creates heroes both great and small that drew me into her tale."
—Lois McMaster Bujold

"A group of slum children take on scheming nobles in this entertaining fantasy thief adventure. Apprentice-thief Ferret has some pretty flexible ethics regarding property rights, but she firmly believes in loyalty to her friends. When pretty beggar-by Owl is sold as a slave to scheming nobles, Ferret investigates, drawing in other friends and gaining allies that include a prince in disguise, an artistic urchin, seers, a high priest, and a goddess. They ultimately uncover and foil a plot against the new emperor, an idealistic scholar willing to entertain unusual notions about the rights of the lower classes. A fun, fast-paced romp full of delightfully distinctive characters."
—*Locus*, April 2000

A Business of Ferrets

by

Beth Hilgartner

Meisha Merlin Publishing, Inc
Atlanta, GA

A BUSINESS OF FERRETS

An MM Publishing Book
Published by Meisha Merlin Publishing, Inc.
PO Box 7
Decatur, GA 30031

Editing & interior layout by Stephen Pagel
Copyediting & proofreading by Teddi Stransky
Cover art by Charles Keegan

ISBN: 1-892065-18-5

Printed in the United States of America
First MM Publishing edition: April 2000

0 9 8 7 6 5 4 3 2 1

http://www.MeishaMerlin.com

Library of Congress Cataloging-in-Publication Data

Hilgartner, Beth.
A business of ferrets / by Beth Hilgartner.— 1st MM Publishing ed.
        p. cm.
"An MM Publishing book."
    ISBN 1-892065-18-5 (alk. paper)
    I. Title.
    PS3558.I384375 B87 2000
    813'.54—dc21
                        00-008664

For my most adventurous friends:
Marjorie, Susan, Beth,
and
Neil

Table of Contents

A Business of Ferrets

Dramatis Personae

In the Slums

Ferret –	an apprentice thief
Owl –	a beggar
Kitten –	a beggar
Donkey –	potboy at the Trollop's Smile
Mouse –	a flower seller's daughter with a talent for drawing
Squirrel –	an errand boy
Sharkbait –	a trouble maker and longshoreman, currently trying to organize dockworkers into a guild
Arkhyd –	Innkeeper at the Trollop's Smile and Donkey's uncle
Zhazher –	Owl's brother; an addict
Khyzhan –	a Master in the Thieves' Guild and Ferret's mentor
Ybhanne –	a rival Master in the Thieves' Guild
Anthagh –	a slaver

In the Temple District

Kerigden –	High Priest of the Windbringer
Anakher –	Bishop of the Horselord's Temple
Dedemar –	a foreign mercenary in the Temple Guard

At the Court

Arre – a Seer and bard from the Kellande School in Kalledann; the Emperor's lover

Emperor Khethyran Anzhibhan (the Scholar King) – Emperor of Bharaghlaf

Venykhar Ghobhezh-Ykhave – Councilor for House Ykhave

Adheran Dhenykhare – Councilor for House Dhenykhare

Bhenekh (Commander) – Commander in the Imperial Guard

Ycevi Ghytteve (Lady) – Councilor for House Ghytteve

Cithanekh Anzhibhar-Ghytteve – possible heir to the throne and Ycevi's cousin

Myncerre Ghytteve – Steward for House Ghytteve

Elkhar Ghytteve – chief of Ycevi's bodyguard

Cezhar Ghytteve – a Ghytteve bodyguard

Rhan Ghytteve – a Ghytteve bodyguard (Cezhar's brother)

Cyffe Ghytteve – a Ghytteve bodyguard (Elkhar's sister)

Zhotar Ghytteve – a Ghytteve bodyguard

Alghaffen Ghytteve (Duke) – Duke of House Ghytteve (Ycevi's son)

Mylazhe Ambhere – Councilor for House Ambhere

Enghan Mebhare – Councilor for House Mebhare

Rhydev Azhere – Councilor for House Azhere

Zherekhaf Azhere – Prime Minister and Rhydev's uncle

Ymlakh Glakhyre – Councilor for House Glakhyre
Dharhyan (Master) – Master of the Caravan Guild
Falkhan –   a Watchman who also works for Rhydev Azhere
Ghorran –   an Azhere bodyguard

Council Houses:

Anzhibhar –   the Royal House
Ambhere –   Mining
Azhere –   Silk
Dhenykhare – Shipbuilding
Ghytteve–   Coffee, Sprits (drugs)
Glakhyre–   Wool
Mebhare–   Farming
Ykhave–   Artisans
Ythande–   Woodsdwellers/timber
Khyghafe–   Nomads/horses

Places:

Slum/waterfront taverns:
        Trollop's Smile
        Beaten Cur
        Ivory Comb (waterfront)
        Replete Feline (waterfront)

Yrkhaffe –   the capitol city of the Bharaghlafi empire
Kalledann – a politically progressive island realm off the coast
        of the Bharaghlafi empire
Amarta (the Federated States of…) –
        kingdom North of Bharaghlaf

Gods:
(Those with temples in the Temple District.)

The Windbringer
The Horselord
The Dark Lady

Chapter One
The Foreign Witch

The Yrkhaffe waterfront churned with activity. The *Metara Kentis* was in port. Even the stifling heat wasn't enough to still the grunts and curses of the longshoremen as they unloaded barrels and crates: the fabled wine of Kalledann; wheat from Mebharev; and liquor from the shipmaster's home port in Amarta.

Ferret watched the bustle with a shrewd and practiced eye. A plenitude of marks milled among the laborers, but members of the Watch were intermixed, like leaven in a loaf; and Ferret had no desire to lose a hand to one of them. She let her breath out in an almost soundless hiss. She didn't even want to think about facing Master Khyzhan empty-handed at day's end.

A ripple of disturbance drew her attention to the *Metara Kentis's* berth. Ferret frowned. It wasn't like Shipmaster Kentis to carry passengers—and a *woman!* The woman coming down the gangplank was thin, taller than most, dressed in a man's tunic and breeches which suited her lean frame well. As Ferret watched, the stranger waved farewell to the shipmaster; then, with the confidence of a fool or a fighter, she joined the throng on the shore.

Ferret lost interest. From her nest of shadows between waterfront taverns, she scanned the crowd like a predator. Too many Watch; her quick eyes counted easily three *hentes* of them. If she were caught with her fingers in someone's pocket, they'd run her down for sure. It was one of Khyzhan's maxims that caution was the best defense; but that wouldn't make him any easier to appease if she spent another day fruitless.

Ferret's wandering attention snagged again on the woman from the ship. As she approached, her eyes moved with an alert restlessness familiar to Ferret. Then, the woman's gaze crossed Ferret's—and snapped back, eyes widening in recognition. Her lips parted, as though she caught her breath. Ferret's heart tripped, then began to sprint.

"You. Lass. Come here!" the woman hailed her.

Ferret's instinctive fade into the shadows was halted by the appearance of a Watchman at the woman's shoulder. She took quick stock, decided on a role to fit the situation: youthful innocence. She was small for her age; it was usually easy to make people think her far younger than her sixteen years.

"Trouble, Lady?" he rumbled.

Ferret forced herself into the light, playing the injured innocent. "I've not done aught."

"No trouble, good sir," the woman assured the guard. "I thought I recognized a friend."

The guard moved on; as he passed Ferret, he growled, "Mind your step, Wharf-rat. I've an eye on you."

Despite her training, Ferret wet her lips nervously. "What game're you playing?" she warily asked the woman.

The woman smiled. "What's your name, lass?"

"Why do you care? I'm naught to you."

There was something compelling about the stranger. Her eyes—odd colored: one green and one blue—held Ferret as firmly as any Watchman's grip; and she seemed really to see her, to see *Ferret*, not the child she acted. Her rich voice spoke the Bharaghlafi tongue with a lilting accent. "You're mistaken," she said quietly. "You *are* something to me, though I'm not quite sure what. My name is Arre; I am a Kellande Seer. I have dreamed of you." She smiled again, gently, seeing the naked fear her words produced. "It's nothing to fear. I'd never harm you."

Ferret managed a skeptical look. "Gods and fish," she swore. "You tell me I'm deep in your heathen witchcraft, and then say I've naught to fear."

The woman said an exasperated word in her own language. "What's your name? Where do you live?"

With a bravura Ferret didn't feel, she lifted her pointed chin and eyed the foreigner insolently. "I'm Ferret. I live in the Slums. I'm a thief."

The stranger's gaze grew distant; the shadow of concern touched her brow. "Don't steal today, Ferret," she said softly.

"Oh, aye," Ferret said sarcastically. "Heathen witchcraft makes you high-minded, but what am I to eat at day's end?"

The stranger opened her purse and poured a stream of coins into Ferret's palms. "Don't steal today, Ferret," she repeated.

She left Ferret staring at the coins in her cupped hands. When the pickpocket looked up, Arre was gone. "Praise to the Windbringer," Ferret whispered as she hid the coins. "Yon woman's clean daft." There had been more silver in the clutch of coins than copper—three Guilds would more than satisfy Khyzhan. As her mind spun plans, she eased through the wharf crowds, heading for her burrow in the Slums.

The Yrkhaffe Slums filled a wedge of territory between the waterfront and the forbidding walls of the Temple District: a warren of streets and alleys, rife with violence, filth and the stench of despair. Dilapidated tenements leaned over ramshackle huts and hovels; abandoned warehouses did duty as market, counting house, tavern or flophouse. Beggars thronged the waterfront border and the Temple Gate, but the poor were everywhere. The Masters of the Slum-Guilds ruled with iron fists, but the Watch kept their distance. As long as the contagion of poverty and crime was contained, as long as the streets of the "respectable" districts of Yrkhaffe were reasonably safe, as long as (it was said) the bribes were paid on time and in full, the Watch left the Slums' inhabitants to their own, brutal justice.

Ferret had never known any other home. The broader streets of the respectable districts, into which she occasionally ventured in pursuit of her living, left her feeling dangerously exposed. She made her way to the rooftop shelter where she currently slept; her ascent involved several questionable railings and a stretch of very treacherous tiles, but she was small, whippet thin and agile as her namesake. She had made a rough shelter of some rotted beams and a tattered piece of canvas, and had carefully fashioned a place to store things beneath a loose roof tile. Her worldly possessions consisted of two changes of clothing (neither in good shape), a ratty blanket, a small clay brazier, several scavenged jars which contained her meager stores, a battered pot, a large stoneware bowl, an assortment of mismatched, chipped crockery, four wooden spoons and a good, sharp knife. Now, as she swiftly sorted the coins, her eyes widened in renewed amazement: a Half-Noble; twenty silver Guilds; twelve copper Commons. She chewed the inside of her cheek; too much, and Khyzhan would be suspicious: too little, and he would be angry. In the end, she wrapped the Half-Noble, all but two of the Guilds, and eight Commons in a rag, and tucked the fortune into her hidey hole. Then, she eased her way to the street and made for the Temple Gate. She'd do as the foreign witch advised, since the woman had paid her handsomely, and keep her hands in her own pockets; but to lie low the whole afternoon would be to invite suspicion. It was hard to mislead Khyzhan if he took it into his head to ask questions. With luck, Owl or Kitten would be begging at the Gate.

There were actually two gates at the Temple Gate. The first gave onto a huge open courtyard, paved with the ubiquitous silvery slate which was quarried from The Spine, a range of tired mountains at the city's back. The first gate was set in a chest-high stone wall, more a symbolic boundary than a real one, which kept the crowding Slum buildings at a distance. It was often called the "Waiting Wall"— an allusion to its role as a central meeting place for all but the most elevated of Yrkhaffe's residents; and today, as most days, it was the haunt of beggars, gamblers throwing *ysmath* bones, loiterers, small vendors, and the *khacce* players with their portable game tables. Across the square the second gate, through which one gained entrance to the wide boulevards and manicured lawns of the Temple District, was guarded by two *hentes* of Temple Watch in gray and scarlet tabards. Ferret gave the guarded gate wide berth as she searched the crowds for her friends.

There! Owl. He was attached to the sleeve of an avuncular merchant; Ferret knew better than to interrupt. Even from this distance, she could see how Owl's soulful eyes drew concern from his mark. She nodded to herself as the man dug into his pockets to find coins for the waif.

"Happen it's not fair to put the touch on him," remarked a voice which quivered with the edge of laughter.

"Ho, Kitten," Ferret greeted her friend.

"I got him on his way in," she went on, mischief glinting in her hazel eyes. "He gave me a whole Guild. And happen his Temple took him for something. If Owl doesn't pry a Half-Noble out of him, I'll be surprised. How's pickings, Ferret?"

"I've done for the day," she told the younger girl. "I'd a good haul, but there's naught of sense in straining luck."

"'Caution is the best defense,'" Kitten quoted.

Ferret looked at her sharply. "Dinna let yon kite Khyzhan get his talons into you."

"*Fret!*" Kitten protested, using her nickname for Ferret. "Happen I'd best learn a trade. I willn't be small and cute forever."

"Learn a trade—but not from Khyzhan. I'll teach you what I know, if learning's what you want, but he's a scavenger—and hard. Please, Kitten: wait on it."

As the spark of her rebellion dimmed, Kitten smiled wryly. "I'd the same lecture—nearly word for word—from Squirrel this morning. Happen you're both right."

Just then, Owl joined them. "Ho, Ferret; ho, Kitten."

"How'd you do?" Kitten asked eagerly.

He slapped his fist into his open palm in a gesture of enthusiasm. "Half-Noble, and two Guilds. If I'd caught him on his way in, happen I'd have gotten a whole Noble out of him."

"Listen, Owl," Ferret said. "You should hide that Half-Noble away. Give Zhazher the Guilds, and your other pickings, but save the bounty; he canna expect it—and he'll only buy Dream's Ease with it. You'd best have a thought for the future."

Owl's face clouded. "Happen you're right," he admitted. "But Zhazh always knows when I hold back. Lately, he's begun to say he thinks I'd be of more use crippled or blind."

Ferret shuddered, but Kitten's reply was matter of fact. "Not blind," she said firmly. "It's your eyes that make the difference between the Guild I got out of yon fat merchant, and the Noble you'd have gotten if you'd hit him when I did."

Owl actually laughed. "I'd best take you along to talk to Zhazh. Crippled I could probably face, but *blinded*...Lady of Sorrows, that scares me."

The warning clash of cymbals made the three friends run for the Waiting Wall and vault onto it. A cymbal-bearing herald and a *hente* of Temple Watch cleared the way for a litter borne by four men. The crowd quieted as necks craned to catch a glimpse of the personage who caused the disruption. The litter's blue and white curtains were tied back revealing a man with flaming red hair, dressed in gray robes, a harp in his hands.

"Windbringer priest," Owl murmured. "I've seen this one before. He usually walks."

"*Kerigden!*" The shout—a voice accustomed to making itself heard—cut over the desultory crowd noise. The priest's head turned. The children were close enough to see his expression change.

"*Arre!* Praise to the Windbringer! What breeze brings you hither?" He held up one hand to stop the litter, but Ferret was no longer watching him. Her mysterious stranger strode confidently toward the priest.

The three friends—and most of the crowd—watched while the priest and the woman spoke quietly. Then, the woman bowed and the priest sketched a blessing before he waved his bearers on. As Arre turned away, her watchful eyes touched the trio on the wall. She froze for an instant, staring at them all in startlement. They stared back. Then, with an apologetic smile, she shrugged and went about her business.

Kitten looked from Ferret's stunned face to Owl's frightened one. Annoyance brushed her features. "What's the matter?" she demanded. "Fret, you look poleaxed, and Owl—" She broke off in alarm as Owl dropped his face into his hands. His shoulders began to shake, as though he were weeping.

"*Owl,*" both girls exclaimed, "what *is* it?"

He raised tear-brimming eyes to theirs. "Sweet Lady of Sorrows," he whispered. "I must be going mad."

"What do you mean?" Ferret demanded.

He gestured vaguely in the direction Arre had gone. "Yon woman: *I dreamed of her.* She was on a ship, standing near the prow with the wind in her hair. It was..." His voice was oddly flat, his gaze unfocused. "It was the *Metara Kentis.*" He shook his head roughly, as though to shake loose the things he had seen, and managed a weak smile. "I'm sorry. I dinna mean to alarm you."

"*Ferret*," Kitten said, noting the expression on the older girl's face. "What's the matter with *you?*"

"This is the oddest nest of coincidences," Ferret said. "But we'd best not talk here. I've a bit of coffee in my lair. I'll share it with you and tell you the whole tale. Happen the three of us can make sense of it."

Chapter Two
Conversations

The taproom at the Trollop's Smile was quiet; it was early for the supper crowd. A pair of weathered drunkards snuffled and muttered to themselves, but the rest of the trade had moved on. Donkey swabbed down the last table and inched out of Arkhyd's notice into the kitchen.

A girl crouched near the hearth, sketching on the smooth slate with a blackened chip of wood. "Arkhyd said to tell you there's pots from the noonings to scrub," she told him.

Donkey turned calm brown eyes on her. "Always are, Mouse," he drawled, finally. Moving with measured slowness, he set about his task. Mouse watched him for several moments, then returned to her sketching. The deliberate clank and splash of Donkey's work lulled her as she envisioned the scene she recreated; the waterfront, lavish with courtiers, glinting with Watch; mounted heralds, Imperial Guard; and in their midst, the Scholar King: the Emperor Khethyran. She scrunched her eyes closed as she tried to summon his face: young, handsome, lordly. She sighed in vexation. It was like a story that wouldn't come alive; she could see the panoply in her mind, almost hear the clatter of hooves and the bright shiver of the trumpets; but the Emperor's face stubbornly remained hidden behind a stiff gloss of expectation. She opened her eyes. Donkey leaned over her shoulder. He pointed to one of the wild-eyed horses.

"I remember yon," he said. Then, as his scanning eyes took in the missing parts of her picture, he added, "If someone gave you a Royal, you could copy his face from that."

"A *Royal?* Oh, Donkey! If someone gave me a Royal, my parents could buy a shop in the merchant's district, and we could leave the Slums forever."

"They say the Emperor's face is on the Royal," the boy persisted.

Mouse scuffed her hands across the drawing, blurring all the lines into meaningless smudges. "It's probably the old Emperor's face, anyway."

"The *old* Emperor," Donkey repeated. "Hadn't thought of that. Happen you're right. So no use to find you a Royal." He gave her a damp cloth. "If you've done, wipe the hearth."

Mouse complied. Just as she finished, the door to the taproom swung open and Arkhyd bustled in. He smiled when he saw her. "So you're still here; good. There's a fellow—" he gestured toward the taproom—"wants a message taken. You'll do it, Mouse?"

"I'd go," Donkey offered.

A look of irritation crossed the tavern keeper's broad face. "He's in a hurry. Mouse?"

"Yes sir; thank you, sir," she said. As the door swung closed behind her, she heard Arkhyd's interrogation begin.

"Have you finished with the pots—" The door cut off his words.

"Sir?" Mouse asked the fellow who stood by the bar. "Did you want a message taken?"

He nodded shortly. He was better dressed than most Slum dwellers—not flashy, but his clothes were of good quality, and they were clean. Mouse summed him up while he fished in his pockets for a small, leather-wrapped bundle. "I want this taken to a man you will find at the Temple Gate. Here's a Common; there are five more for you, if you're back here in a quarter hour with an answer."

She took the package and the coin. "How will I know your friend?"

"He's a foreigner; has yellow hair and a mustache. And he's Temple Watch; he's on duty at the Gate until sundown."

Mouse gaped at him. "You want me to talk to a Temple Watchman on *duty?* For a *Common?*"

"No one would hurt a harmless little girl like you. Tell him it's from the Sea Hawk. He'll know what you mean."

Mouse shook her head. "I want three in advance."

The man hissed in irritation, then gave her two more Commons. "Go on. Hurry."

Mouse hurried. The Temple Gate was crowded. She watched the guards until she was certain which to approach. She masked her stuttering heart with a winsome smile and held out the package. "The Sea Hawk sent this for you," she said.

He snatched the packet and stuffed it under his tabard. "Run off," he ordered.

"Is there an answer?" Mouse asked, thinking of the three Commons waiting at the Trollop's Smile.

"*Run off*," he repeated, shoving the butt of his pike in her direction. Mouse dodged and ran. She reached the Trollop's Smile out of breath, but well within the quarter hour. The man who had sent her was gone.

Ferret *hated* the Beaten Cur, where her master Khyzhan held court. It was a filthy tavern, always hot, noisy and rank with the smell of sour ale and unwashed bodies. Khyzhan had a table in the dark inner reaches of the common room; as usual, he was surrounded by the pick of his bravos, as his apprentices and journeymen came to settle up. Ferret, chin high, ignored the sneering comments of Khyzhan's men.

"Why, it's my sweet Frycce," Khyzhan greeted her. He looked a little drunk, but Ferret suspected it was a snare for the unwary. She assessed the gathered thieves quickly—that one: he looked like one of Ybhanne's. She resolved to get away as fast as possible; she had no desire to be caught in any factional fighting among the Thieves Guild. "Did you do well today, apprentice?"

"Better than yesterday," she told him as she spilled the coins onto the table before him. "The waterfront was infested with Watch, but the Temple Gate wasn't too bad."

Khyzhan surveyed her offering. "Indeed, Frycce, it is better than yesterday. Tell the others what you brought me, yesterday."

Ferret grit her teeth. She hated Khyzhan in this mood. He would mock her, then take her entire offering and send her away empty handed. "I brought you naught yesterday, Master, as well you know. So today, of course, I expect naught from you—unless it be the beginning of a return to your good graces."

It was a foolish piece of bravura, she knew. Khyzhan was unpredictable; this would delight him, make him angry, or send his sharp wits off hunting answers. But she wanted to be out of the Beaten Cur before Ybhanne's man started his trouble.

Khyzhan's eyes narrowed. "Why the hurry, sweet Frycce? I'd almost think you dislike my company."

Inwardly, she cursed. Questions: dangerous territory with Khyzhan if one had aught to hide. With a silent prayer to the gods of foolish thieves, Ferret embarked on the greatest gamble she could think of. She didn't like to show too much cleverness; she usually played young-and-stupid for Khyzhan, but she needed to distract him. So she leaned closer to her master, speaking in a voice she hoped would not carry. "It is not *your* company I shun, Master; but in this gathering, I smell Ybhanne's perfume —and I've no liking for her heavy musk. And I'm not built for brawling."

The master thief's eyebrows rose as the mockery in his expression vanished. He shoved her entire offering back to her, a faint smile playing over his mobile mouth. "So. You have a wit or two after all. Happen I'll make something of you yet. Take it all and go."

Ferret paused, amazed, for perhaps two heartbeats. Then the coins disappeared into her clothing. "Thank you, Master." She started away.

Khyzhan's voice followed her. For the second time in as many minutes, amazement held her motionless. "Ferret!" Khyzhan had called: he *never* called her 'Ferret.' Recovering, she looked back. "I much prefer this. You *do* understand me, Ferret, no?"

"Yes, sir," she said. And she did. Young-and-stupid wouldn't work with Khyzhan any longer; it made Ferret a little nervous.

In the kitchen at the Trollop's Smile, the tide of the evening had turned, slowing to ebb. The door to the taproom was propped open, so Donkey could hear if someone shouted for a torchbearer. The last of the empty stewpots was scrubbed; Arkhyd served at the bar, leaving Donkey to his scullery realm. Mouse had gone back to the vendor's cart her parents and she called home. She had left another drawing on the hearth; Donkey knew he should clean it off, but it made him smile to look at it. Mouse had caught Ferret, exactly as she so often stood, her chin up to hide the uncertainty in her eyes. Donkey half expected the drawing to speak, so he barely twitched when Ferret hailed him from the back door.

"Ho, Donkey. Alone?"

"Ho, Ferret. Yes. Hungry? There's some fish stew yet."

Ferret slipped indoors and perched on a counter out of the sight line from the taproom. "Should I pay for it? I dinna want to make you trouble."

"Pay?" Donkey repeated, in his slowest, most obtuse voice. "Na. If my uncle asks, I'll say I got hungry again."

"So: aught happening?" she asked around a mouthful of the strong flavored fish.

"Mouse was here."

Ferret's eyes went to the hearthstone, then widened as she laughed. "That's *me!* Willn't you get in trouble for leaving it?"

Donkey shrugged. "Thought you might be in." He took a rag. "Seen it?" At her nod, he wiped the drawing off the stone.

"Have you seen Squirrel?"

"Not since morning. Sharkbait was in, though, hiring day workers for the morrow. Ice ship's due, and the shipmaster said he'd pay treble rates if they'd unload his wares first and fastest."

Ferret shook her head. "Yon willn't best please the other shipmasters."

"Na. But it's good for the longshoremen. Taverns will be crowded tomorrow night."

From the front room, someone shouted for a light. Ferret wolfed the last of the stew.

"You're busy and I'm off," she said. "Thanks for the food." She slipped out into the shadows without waiting for a reply.

Picking up one of his pitch-soaked torches, Donkey went into the taproom. The night was wearing old, and the roisterers wanted help home. He schooled his features to the pleasant blankness he found so useful. It never did to let either contempt or cleverness show.

* * *

The Royal Palace was a vast stone structure, with great arching windows and delicate, spired towers. There were hallways wide as galleries, great banquet halls and ballrooms, cloistered suites and terrace gardens; there were private inner rooms, which hid secret walkways; and there were spyholes, and listening places woven throughout the ancient stone fabric. It was a place built for intrigue, not for war; for stealth instead of siege. But it was beautiful: the graceful stonework, the carefully planned windows, brought to the Palace the illusion of simplicity. And this night, with the pale shield of the moon reflected in the waters of the harbor, the view from the Emperor's library spoke of serenity.

Arre leaned into the stone shelter afforded by the wide arch of a window. Her hands drew a whisper of music from her lute as her eyes dwelt on the moon's cool road, paved on the surface of the sea. Her face was calm, the watchful shifting of her eyes lost in the peace of the scene below her. She didn't even stir when footsteps approached her from the shadowed library behind her.

A pair of hands touched her shoulders, massaging her tight muscles. She smiled, but the music did not falter.

"Are you planning to sit there all night?"

"I might," she replied, still gazing outward.

"Are you fleeing your dreams?"

She turned then. The lute fell silent. For a moment, she searched the dear, familiar face: the planes of his face as clean as sculpture; the tawny smoothness of his skin beneath the sweep of sable hair; the eyes, almond shaped, the color of amber; and the impossible understanding, the compassion, for which she loved him with her whole soul. "In a way," she admitted at last, her wry smile a quirk of acknowledgment. "Mostly, I'm thinking."

With ink stained fingers, he brushed a strand of her fine, dark hair out of her face. "Tell me?" he invited.

She leaned her cheek against his hand. "Oh, Kheth. There's so little to tell: a thief, a young woman, who holds the world at bay with the tilt of her chin; a boy, with eyes full of visions; a sweet little girl, a chip of charcoal in her fingers. It's been with me since before I left Kalledann; bits and pieces, like beads in a box. And I'm looking for the thread, the strand to make it cohere." She drew away from his touch, studied his face for an instant. "It has to do with you. I'm sure of that. But it doesn't take a Kellande Seer to know that your Council Houses are spinning webs and setting snares. It's been—what? —four months since you were crowned. I'm surprised there hasn't been an attempt on your life, already."

"My father—" grief shadowed his eyes— "my father said the first year was the worst. But then, he was in his eleventh year when he was murdered."

She took his hand, mute comfort. "I wish I had more to offer than fragments of my worry. I wish I could *make* the pattern clear. I wish my gifts were stronger—or far, far weaker. This foreboding, these vague hints; they are wearing, but not very useful."

"Do you think you can make the pattern come clear by sitting up all night?"

"No," she admitted with a smile. "But I don't know what else to do."

He was silent. Then, he kissed her brow. "Will it distract you if I keep vigil with you?"

"Of course not; but surely you need your rest?"

"'Thou art my rest and my hope,'" he quoted, "'my shelter and my dreams. Thou hast cast thy mantle 'round me, and I am wrapped in joy.'" Then he shrugged. "I can sleep during the audiences tomorrow. That's the only advantage to my cursed rank: no one dares wake me if I drift off."

His impish expression made Arre laugh. "How is it, Kheth, that you can always make me laugh?"

"I know when you need to."

"Wait," she said, as he turned away. She hopped lightly down from her window perch. He raised eyebrows. "I've thought long enough; maybe if I give it a rest, clarity will visit."

He waited while she stowed her lute away; when she reached his side, he laid his arm across her shoulders. Guided only by the fickle glimmer of the oil lamp he carried, they left the library to its moonlight and silence.

Chapter Three
A Chip of Charcoal

The freighter, its bowels full of ice, creaked against the wharf in the pre-dawn grayness. Longshoremen gathered on the pier, like a flock preparing to migrate. On the vessel, two men spoke softly in the charthouse.

"I can't help but feel I'm setting you up for trouble, A—"

"*Sharkbait*," the other interrupted, with a feral smile. "The past is dead, Shipmaster Kharren. As for trouble, I like trouble." He looked as though that were true, too, with his scarred face and work-battered hands. "Truthfully, I need to be able to show my longshoremen that I can deliver if they'll cooperate."

"But the Dhenykhare are set against a Longshoremen's Guild. They'll fight you, Sharkbait; and they've a Council House's resources."

"That doesn't make them *right*, Khar. Justice—" He broke off. "Don't get me started," he added in an ironic drawl, "or we'll be here 'til your cargo melts."

The shipmaster was young, ambitious and eager to seize an advantage; but as he gazed at the longshoreman, he looked troubled. "You're different—and it's more than the scar. I'm not sure I've done you a favor."

Sharkbait raised a cynical eyebrow. "Did you do this as a favor to me, or to steal a march on your competitors? Let's do business, Shipmaster Kharren. You owe me for twenty men at fifteen Guilds each, plus my commission—a Half-Noble. Will you pay up front, or half in advance?"

When they had concluded their business, the shipmaster watched from the charthouse doorway as Sharkbait deployed his men. They were ruthlessly efficient; the shipmaster was impressed. This run, he would lose only a small fraction of his sawdust-and-sacking-wrapped blocks to the heat; and at this rate, he'd be out of the harbor with the noon tide. There was a maxim in this somewhere, he thought. Something about paying for quality, or spending a bit more to reap better profits. He watched a moment longer before he returned to his charts and ledgers.

Donkey stood, as stoic and patient as the name Ferret had given him, while Arkhyd's tirade seethed around him. "Wretched boy...lazy...useless...clumsy..." Donkey had heard it all before. He schooled his face to contrition, and fought back his own impatient defense. It never, *never* did any good to argue.

He caught movement at the edge of his vision: Squirrel. He stifled any betraying flicker of interest and hung his head a little lower.

"I swear it, Thantor, if I weren't so softhearted, I'd beat you for this morning's clumsiness: if it weren't enough you spilled on a customer, you had to break the dish as well! You'll have to fend for yourself, today: Tibhe will scrub your pots— and have your food! I willn't feed a clumsy, lazy boy. Get out of my sight—and if you dinna mend your ways, boy, late or soon, I'll cast you out on the streets for good, and not just for the day!"

"Good morrow, Master Arkhyd," Squirrel cut in brightly. "I dinna mean to interrupt aught, Master, but I've a message from the tavern keeper at the Anchor."

"Give your message, lad," Arkhyd instructed, pausing only to give Donkey a rough shove. "Run along, Thantor—and dinna let me see you again until nightfall."

"Master Rhenn wonders whether you could spare him two barrels of your small ale; he'd trade eight bottles of Thedezh red for it."

"I have no use for Thedezh wine," Arkhyd growled; in the face of Squirrel's alert attention, the tavern master's irritation began to ebb. "It's too expensive for my trade. Go back to Rhenn and tell him I'll sell him the ale, but he'll have to trade me three barrels of stout, or two Nobles. Here, lad." He flipped a scatter of Commons at the boy. "Hurry."

Squirrel darted outside; he clapped Donkey on the shoulder. "It's the Anchor," he whispered. "I'd best run 'til I'm out of sight. Catch me up." He sprinted off.

Donkey plodded after. Once he was out of sight of the tavern, he stretched his legs into a faster pace. He caught up with Squirrel, who was walking again, a block or so further on.

"Ho, Donkey. Sounded like ol' Arkhyd was really on you."

"Ho, Squirrel. He gets like that once a week, whether I deserve it or not. What's up?"

"Owl's brother beat him again last night; he looks a mess, but he doesn't complain."

"Does no good, complaining. Zhazher's a brute. Poor Owl."

"Look, Donkey: he's by the Waiting Wall. Why dinna you trot off; happen you could cheer him up. I'm apt to be running twixt the Trollop and the Anchor all morning. Rhenn hasn't *got* three barrels of stout—and *two Nobles* is a ridiculous price for that swill your uncle sells."

"You didn't mention Rhenn hasn't the stout," Donkey noted.

"At five Commons a trot? Course not. Ho! I just carry the messages; advice is extra."

Donkey smiled slowly. "See you at the Wall."

"Around noon," Squirrel agreed. "I'll buy you and Owl something to eat."

Owl wasn't alone, Donkey found. Mouse was there. Owl bore obvious signs of his brother's mistreatment: a purpling shadow across one cheekbone; a pinched expression on his face; and he moved like an old man. Mouse was trying to amuse him. They made such an appealing pair that several people had actually veered from their course to pass close enough to toss the children a coin. Donkey watched for a moment before he joined them.

"Ho, Donkey," Mouse greeted him.

"Ho, Mouse, Owl. I'll spoil your takings."

"Why would you?" Mouse asked.

"I'm not cute."

Owl grinned, then winced. "Just look half-witted—"

"More half-witted than usual," Mouse interjected.

"—and I'll look long suffering and responsible," Owl went on, ignoring her, "and Mouse can look worried."

As Donkey's face grew blank, he fished in one pocket. After a moment, he produced a lump of charcoal. He studied it stupidly until Mouse noticed what he held.

The little girl suddenly grew avid. "Oh, give it here, Donkey. Please, Donkey. I'm sorry I teased you. Oh, *please* Donkey; didn't you really bring that for me?"

Hiding all his amusement, Donkey feigned puzzlement. He let slow comprehension dawn, then pushed the blackened lump toward the girl. "Want?" he asked, and beamed in imbecilic gratification when she snatched it away.

A few more coins came their way before they forgot their charade as the drawing under Mouse's fingers came alive. She drew the scene around them; and in the crowd she was drawing, here and there a face would spring to sudden life: the bitterness in a harlot's painted smile; a robed Healer, compassion shadowing his dark eyes; a foreign merchant, with hair like cornsilk; two *khacce* players, intent on the stiff figures on their game table; a bargaining vendor; a nobleman, in silk and lace, with an ebony cane. It was magical, the way the drawing grew; but long before the boys were tired of watching, or Mouse had drawn all she could see, the lump of charcoal crumbled to nothing. Mouse sat back on her heels with a sigh. Then, and only then, did the three realize the attention they had attracted. They were surrounded by people.

The watchers were silent; awed or frightened. One sooty hand stole up to cover Mouse's mouth. Her eyes were wide. Owl had stopped breathing, expecting someone momentarily to raise the cry of 'Witch.' Only Donkey maintained his placid blankness—though his mind searched desperately for some way to ease the situation. Then, the nobleman Mouse had drawn stepped forward. Mouse had caught him perfectly: his shrewd eyes, his sardonic mouth, and the elegance of the narrow hand which held the cane. He planted the brass shod tip of his cane next to his portrait.

"Impressive," he said. "Very impressive indeed." With a languid gesture, he sent a shower of coins to the flagstones. As if his action were a signal, other coins followed his. Stunned, but not paralyzed, the three children scrambled to gather them. In their scuffling, the drawing was smudged beyond recognition.

"Sweet Lady of Sorrows," Owl murmured. "There's more money here than I see in a month."

"Dinna ask me to do it again," Mouse pleaded.

"Na," Donkey agreed. "Too near a thing."

"What can we do with the money?" Owl said.

"Take my share," Donkey offered. "You need it most."

Mouse nodded. "My parents would only ask *questions*— and they'd never believe I didn't steal it."

Owl was clearly terrified. "No. I mustn't have it. Zhazh— If Zhazh ever finds out—*Gods*, he'll think it's the *beating*."

"Ferret," Donkey offered. "She'd hide it."

"So she would." Relief warmed him; his face lost its waxen look. "So who wants to find her? Donkey?"

"Me. I'll go," Mouse said; and then, she was gone.

Mouse returned to the Waiting Wall with Ferret only moments after Squirrel showed up with a loaf of bread and a sausage. Squirrel grinned cheekily at the thief.

"Trust *you* to turn up where there's food," he greeted her.

"Ho, Squirrel, Owl, Donkey. So what's up? Mouse can barely squeak, she's so rattled."

"I want you to hide some money for me," Owl said. "If you're willing."

Squirrel's eyebrows shot up. "You're going to hold out on Zhazher?" At Owl's tight nod, Squirrel pounded his palm with a fist in a gesture of enthusiasm. "And high time."

Owl had torn a good sized bit from his ratty tunic, and had stowed the coins in the knotted fabric. Casually, he tossed the wad of cloth to Ferret. She was unable to suppress an instant's surprise at the weight. "Count it?" she asked.

He shook his head. "There's a deal of silver—and a lot of people."

"What happened?"

It was Donkey who told the tale, around a heel of bread and a chunk of savory sausage. Though his face was placid, it was clear that the others were still badly shaken. Despite the heat, Mouse huddled against Owl as though she were cold. When Donkey fell silent, they each remained pensive, until Ferret spoke. "Khyzhan says there's no figuring nobles."

"A pearl of great wisdom—and from a very unlikely source," a voice commented.

They all jumped. It was the longshoreman, Sharkbait. Ferret thrust her chin up and glared at him; Sharkbait made her a bit uncomfortable. Ferret disliked contradictions, and Sharkbait was full of them. He spoke like the gentry, though with his knife-scarred face and callused hands, no one could mistake him for anything but a worker. He had a reputation for shrewdness bordering on ruthlessness, but he was unfailingly kind to her and her friends; and Owl, who was quite good at assessing people, liked and trusted the man.

"Sharkbait!" Owl greeted him. "What are you doing here?"

"Eavesdropping," he told them. "Actually, I was commissioned to make a delivery." From somewhere about his person he removed a flat, rectangular package, which he gave to Mouse. "From an admirer."

Mouse regarded Sharkbait for several heartbeats, worry scoring her brow, before she untied the string and unwrapped the parcel: a nicely tooled leather case which contained a stack of creamy sheets of paper, several charcoal sticks, two small pots of ink, half a dozen quills, and a small, silver knife. The girl stared at the treasures in her lap, then she looked up at the longshoreman. His expression was strange, haunted.

"I've never used—" she gestured helplessly.

Sharkbait's lips twisted in a painful smile. "I'll drop in at the Trollop tonight and show you how to cut a quill."

"Who's it from?"

"Venykhar Ghobhezh-Ykhave. The nobleman with the cane. Shall I convey your thanks, Mouse?"

"Wait," she said firmly. "I'll make him a drawing."

Sharkbait leaned against the wall while she took one of the charcoal sticks and began. It was a portrait drawn from memory: her benefactor—looking down at something which interested him. Owl almost fancied he could hear the man saying 'Impressive,' in his dry way. When Mouse was done, she gave the drawing to Sharkbait. She held the stick out to him. "Write: 'Thank you from Mouse' on the bottom."

"Write?" Sharkbait repeated. "You think I can *write?*"

Mouse locked gazes with the man. "You said you'd teach me to cut a quill."

He brushed his forehead with two fingers in a gesture of concession, then took the charcoal and carefully made letters across the bottom of the page. He handed the stick back to Mouse, and with no further comment, melted into the crowd.

"Venykhar Ghobhezh-Ykhave," Ferret repeated softly, rolling the name over her tongue as though she could discern some important information from the taste. "I wonder who he is."

"I wonder how he knows Sharkbait," said Squirrel. "And how Sharkbait—*Sharkbait!*—learned to *write.*"

"I wonder," Mouse mused, "what Sharkbait would look like if he didn't have that horrible scar."

They fell silent; Ferret looked around and got to her feet. "I'm off. I've fish to fry—and a Master to appease. Will you lot be at the Trollop later?"

"After nightfall," Donkey answered. "I'm in disgrace."

Ferret grinned at him. "Is that again—or still?"

He shrugged. "Comes to the same thing. 'Til later, Ferret."

Chapter Four
Journeyman

Ferret had had a good day. Owl's secret hoard, which she had counted in the privacy of her lair before she hid it away, amounted to an unthinkable total: four Nobles, six Half-Nobles, fifteen Guilds and fifty-two Commons. On top of this amazing stroke of fortune (which, after all, had to do with her friend and not herself, for all that it was a wonderful thing), there had been crowds of incautious people loitering on the waterfront, and not many Watch. By late afternoon, Ferret had more than enough to appease her Master. Buoyed by her high spirits, she began to play little games with herself—shadowing this Slum denizen, spying on that one. Usually, Slum dwellers left one another alone. For one thing, it deterred one from stealing when there was a fair chance one's mark might turn out to be important in the Thieves' Guild. As Ferret made her way to the Beaten Cur, she noticed a man on the street: he was better dressed than most Slum dwellers; it wasn't that his clothes were flashy, but they were of good quality, and clean. On an impulse, she tailed him. He didn't move like a Slum dweller. He carried his head with the unconscious arrogance of gentry. She smiled slowly. If he was a merchant or some petty nobleman slumming, he was more than fair game. Carefully, she sidled closer.

Ferret's theft could have been a demonstration, it went so smoothly. One moment he had all his possessions; the next, an elegant leather purse rested inside Ferret's shirt. To make her escape, she scaled the wall of a decrepit warehouse; she watched the man saunter away, unaware of his loss. When he was out of sight—and after a careful scan of her rooftop perch—she slipped out his purse and opened it. Ferret nearly fell off the roof. In the purse were five, heavy yellow Royals, a lozenge shaped ivory miniature of a nobleman, and a gold and onyx signet ring. A wave of dizzying panic swept over her. This was no ordinary purse: it was the payment for a murder.

Ferret tried to catch her breath, tried to think. She slipped the miniature out of the purse and stared at it. Five Royals was a *fortune*; if this was the target, he'd have to be important. The miniature showed a young man in profile: tawny skinned like most of the people of Bharaghlaf; light brown eyes; classically sculpted features; black hair. It was a very good portrait, Ferret judged, for he looked as though he were about to turn to speak to her. Ferret stared at it, trying to memorize the face; then with a sigh, she made a move to return it to the purse. Instead, she found herself tucking the miniature away separately, and she recognized that she intended to keep it, and to keep it secret, regardless of consequences. She shivered. After a moment, she inspected the signet ring. The onyx was carved with a seal which was meaningless to her: a spread-winged butterfly prisoned within the lines of a six-pointed star.

After several minutes of intense inward debate, Ferret climbed down from the roofs and made her way to the Beaten Cur. At least, whatever else happened, Khyzhan couldn't accuse her of another fruitless day.

The Beaten Cur was crowded, noisome and loud. Khyzhan, sporting a bandaged arm, was holding court. There were no sniggers or comments from his bravos as Ferret approached. Khyzhan raised one eyebrow inquiringly.

"What happened to your arm, Master?" she greeted him.

"Nothing to worry over, Ferret: a mere brawl. But Ybhanne's man had a knife. In the end, we used it on him. A bit of poetic justice. And how's your hunting been, Ferret?"

"I think I've overreached, Master." She tossed the leather purse onto the table. "I lifted that off a mark I took to be flash slumming."

Khyzhan spilled the contents out onto the table. The gold chimed softly, then lay gleaming like a dragon's hoard.

"Holy gods," one of the bravos breathed.

Khyzhan picked up the signet. "House Azhere. Did your mark see you, Ferret?"

She shook her head.

"Are you certain?"

"He didn't even twitch, Master." The watchful stillness in Khyzhan's face made a horrible possibility occur to her. "He

could have known I was there and been shamming—but it
makes no sense. A trap for *me* would hardly be baited with
Royals."

Khyzhan was silent so long Ferret began to fear that he
was too angry to speak. He'd *warned* her to leave Slum deni-
zens alone—and clearly, she'd disobeyed him. "Well, Ferret,"
the master thief said, when the silence had grown nearly un-
bearable. "You dinna leave me much choice. I shall have to
promote you to journeyman, for all that you're young for it."
He gestured to the Royals on the table. "You've paid your
Guild dues through the seven years of your journeyman service." He put the things back into the purse, then rose to his
feet. "Come with me; I'd best take you down to Guild headquarters and register you."

"It's kind of you, Master, but dinna you think this a case
of dumb luck?"

Khyzhan pinched her chin. "Dumb luck or not, Ferret,
I've no choice. Even if I wanted to give you your apprentice
share, I haven't the coinage. At two fifths, Ferret—which is a
thin reward for an impressive haul—your share would be two
hundred Nobles; or four hundred Half-Nobles; or twelve *thou-
sand* Guilds. So let's be off, Journeyman Ferret."

Sharkbait didn't like the Ivory Comb; it was on the upper
fringes of the waterfront district, the haunt of gentry who imagined themselves daring. The prices were high, the ale was
inferior (though the wine was good), and he always felt con-
spicuous there. But Venykhar Ghobhezh-Ykhave hadn't asked
for Sharkbait's preference—and at least the old man hadn't
expected him to come up to the Palace.

He scanned the trade in the taproom; it was a bit thin, but
there was no one who looked like trouble. Venykhar Ghobhezh-
Ykhave had taken a table by a side window, where they could
see anyone close enough to overhear. He joined him.

"Here," Sharkbait began, handing him Mouse's drawing.

The old man smiled. "She's a wonder. What can you tell
me about her?"

"Her parents are flower-sellers. Too poor to be respectable, I suppose, but hard working. They're fond of her—which

means, in the Slums, that they don't beat her and she usually has enough to eat. Ven," he added, noting the other man's abstracted expression. "What are you thinking?"

"Such talent deserves to be trained. It's almost a pity she has kin. It might be easier for House Ykhave to acquire her if she were an orphan."

Sharkbait laughed mirthlessly. "Approach her parents. In the Slums, everything's for sale."

Venykhar Ghobhezh-Ykhave eyed him coolly. "That's not exactly what I meant. By the way, An—"

"*Sharkbait.*"

"Whatever. I heard Adheran Dhenykhare muttering imprecations against 'that damned troublemaker of a longshoreman.' It seems that two of his vessels didn't get unloaded before the noon tide and he was displeased."

"I'm not surprised." He smiled, suddenly. "And I'm not sorry. If that tightfisted bastard won't pay my men a decent wage, his wares can rot in his hold for all of me."

Venykhar sighed. "You certainly have a gift for making enemies—and not enough sense to pick ones who fight in your league. Are you trying to get yourself killed?"

"It's one answer," Sharkbait said bleakly.

The older man reached across the table and gripped his wrist. "It's not an acceptable answer. Why don't you go home?"

"Home? *Home?!*" He laughed bitterly. "I don't have a home, Ven; I have a cage. And I'd rather die trying to do something useful than live out my life as an exhibit in some damned nobles' zoo."

"But *is* it useful—or useful enough to risk your life at it? Better wages for a handful of unskilled workers?"

"I know what it seems like," Sharkbait retorted. "A noble's dicing bodyguards lose more in an evening than we're talking about; but do you know what a difference it makes in their lives? It means having enough money to buy both food and clothing; it means living somewhere better than in the shell of a burned out tenement. It means a little dignity, and hope— things which even in the Slums can't be bought or sold."

"It means," Venykhar countered crisply, "plenty of money for drink, drugs and prostitutes—but be idealistic if you like."

"Thank you, great lord, for your permission," Sharkbait retorted with scathing sarcasm. "And have you the slightest whim, the vaguest need, that I, with worm-like servility can hasten to gratify?" Something in Venykhar's expression deflated his anger. "You did that on purpose," he accused.

There was a glint of acknowledgment in Venykhar's eyes. "Well. You seem so different. I had to see if you'd really changed. Keep an eye on little Mouse for me, while I consider how to proceed. And—Sharkbait: be careful."

By the time Ferret reached the Trollop's Smile, the supper crowd had gone and the trade ran to serious drinkers. Donkey and Squirrel were out lighting people's ways, but Mouse, Owl and Kitten lurked in the shadowy scullery.

"We washed the supper pots," Kitten said, "so Arkhyd willn't complain about us. Mouse is waiting for Sharkbait. What's up, Fret? You're big with news."

"I'd rather not discuss it. Zhazh going to miss you, Owl?"

Owl shook his head. "He's full of Ease. So much for yesterday's takings. You'll feel better if you tell us."

"No, I willn't," Ferret insisted. Kitten and Owl were marshaling their persuasive forces; Ferret dreaded staving them off, but she was too uneasy to relate the events—and she didn't dare tell *anyone* about the miniature until she'd had a chance to *think*. Fortunately, Sharkbait chose that moment to sidle into the scullery and the conversation turned to desultory banter while the longshoreman taught Mouse how to cut and shape a quill. It wasn't as easy as it looked, and it took even more practice to be able to use the fickle implement for drawing. Sharkbait was surprisingly patient. As Ferret watched him, she found herself wondering what chance there was he would teach her the trick of writing. Before she could ask, Squirrel burst in, out of breath and extremely pale.

"You'll never *believe* what just happened," he panted. "The man I was escorting—we were attacked. At least five men—armed: knives; I think he was killed, right off. And then—and then the *Watch* showed up."

"The *Watch?*" Kitten and Owl demanded.

"In the *Slums?*" Ferret added.

Squirrel nodded. "We weren't three streets from the Temple Gate. Two *hentes*: one Watch, one Temple Watch. I dropped the torch and ran. I dinna like it."

"Your mark: what was he like?" Sharkbait asked.

"Flash slumming, I *thought*," Squirrel said. "Good clothes, clean. Naught remarkable, except he moved like gentry."

Mouse frowned at Squirrel. "Would you know him if you saw him again?"

"Happen you didn't hear, Mouse: he's *dead!*"

She dipped her quill in the inkpot and began to sketch. "Is this him?" She drew the man who had called himself Sea Hawk, and sent her on an errand to a Temple Watchman. Squirrel's eyes widened. So did Ferret's. Sharkbait swore.

"That's him," Squirrel breathed.

"How did you know, Mouse?" the longshoreman demanded.

"Guessed. He paid me to take a message for him, yesterday. To a Temple Watchman. He cheated me," she added primly.

"The Temple Watchman: was he a foreigner?" Sharkbait pressed. "Blond? Mustache?" At her nod, he swore again. Then he rounded on Ferret. "And why do you look like you've swallowed a hive of hornets, *Journeyman* Ferret?"

Ferret forced herself to breathe; somewhat to her surprise, her voice was steady. "You've a keen ear for rumor."

"Is that your mark?" Sharkbait persisted, eyes hard.

Ferret nodded. "Who was he?"

"What did you lift off him?"

Ferret's lip curled. "What? Didn't rumor say?"

"Rumor lies. *What did you lift?*"

The look on Sharkbait's face froze her blood. For an eternity, she considered—and he waited, coiled like an adder. Finally, seeing no alternative, Ferret answered him. "A purse, containing five Royals, a gold signet ring with a black stone, and this." She reached into her shirt; as her hand closed around the ivory miniature, she hesitated. "I've not told Khyzhan— or anyone else, for that matter—about this, if you're looking to get me killed." She spun the miniature across the stone floor to Sharkbait's waiting grasp.

His face lit with recognition, then clouded with puzzlement. "What was the signet?"

"A butterfly in a six-pointed star. Khyzhan said 'House
Azhere.' Who was the mark? And who's the portrait?"

While Sharkbait sat, thinking, Mouse snatched the miniature out of his hand. "It's *him!*" she crowed. "It is. *It is!*"

"*Who?*" Ferret demanded.

"*Him!* The Scholar King: Khethyran."

"The Emperor," Kitten, Ferret and Owl breathed.

"Who was he?" Ferret asked again. "The man hired to kill
the Emperor: who was he? And who hired him? House
Azhere?"

Sharkbait got to his feet, took the miniature back from
Mouse and shoved it into Ferret's hand. "Keep this hidden."

"*Sharkbait!*" Ferret's snarl halted him halfway to the door.
"You'd best explain."

"Or what? I recognize a threat when one's offered."

"Or I'll go to Khyzhan."

"All right," he growled. "This could get you killed—and
it's all surmise. I'm *trying* to protect you." When he saw no
compromise in her eyes, he sighed explosively and came back
to her side. "I *think* someone intended to implicate House
Azhere, make people think they hired your mark to kill the
Emperor. I can't imagine any other reason anyone would be
stupid enough to put a recognizable portrait and a signet ring
in the same purse. Now—"

"Wait!" Mouse cried. "*Is* someone trying to kill the Scholar
King?"

Sharkbait laughed mirthlessly. "Someone's *always* trying
to kill the Emperor. Now, don't speak of this to anyone."

"Dinna be silly," Kitten said firmly. "You must know we'll
tell Donkey."

He rolled his eyes. "Don't tell anyone else, then; and be
very careful you're not overheard. *This isn't a game, children.*"
Then, he disappeared into the night.

No sooner had Sharkbait gone, then Donkey stepped
through he door, smiling in his habitual manner. As he turned
to Ferret, his blank facade cracked into awe. "Did you really
lift a purse with *five Royals* in it?"

She nodded solemnly. "Khyzhan made me Journeyman over it. Were you outside the whole time?"

He shrugged. "Nearly. I heard the commotion the Watch made over Squirrel's customer. They weren't half angry; seems he was supposed to have something on him and didn't. I cut along when I heard them say 'search the streets.'"

"So what do we do?" Kitten asked.

"Naught," Ferret replied. "Wait. Lie low."

"We have to warn him," Mouse said.

"Dinna be silly," Ferret snapped. "Who'd listen to us?"

"No," Owl said. "No. Mouse is right. We have to warn the Emperor—but we must know more, first…" Owl's eyes were wide, desperate, unfocused.

"*Owl*," Kitten protested, shaking the boy's arm. "We're only *Slum-rats*. There's naught we can do!"

"*But he needs us!*" Owl wailed; then, he burst into tears.

Chapter Five
Slave

Much later, Owl crept into the dilapidated hovel he and his brother used as living quarters. He heard Zhazher's heavy breathing, interrupted by an occasional muttered word. Owl stifled a sigh. Zhazh must have taken the whole Half-Noble's worth of the drug in order to be so deeply under after all this time. His mouth quirked in a pained smile. At least he could stop creeping around quite so carefully. Zhazh was in no shape to notice if the Emperor and all his heralds marched through, cymbals clashing.

Going by feel, he located the flint and steel. A moment later, the hovel was warmed by a friendly pool of lamplight. Then, Owl froze. Light caught on a glitter of eyes in the shadowy corner; not rat's eyes: human's. Owl clamped his teeth on his startlement and by force of will, made himself set the lamp down with a steady hand. Then, he turned, making a pretense of looking for something while he edged toward the doorway. Whoever lurked there meant no good— else why not greet him?

Owl nearly made it; but as he ducked through the opening, muscles coiled to sprint for the Trollop, someone grabbed him, enveloping him in a smothering piece of canvas. He was thrown heavily to the cobbles. As he lay, trying to get breath back into his lungs, he heard voices.

"Got him?" That voice came from inside the hovel.

"Aye."

"Good. Truss him—but gently. Zhazh marked him; don't make it worse. When he's tied, I'd like a good look at him."

They bound his wrists and ankles, then removed the canvas. One of the men approached, carrying the lamp. By its light, the boy and the man studied one another. Owl saw a man in his late thirties, better groomed and fed than any Slum denizen; his round, gray eyes, and the thick fringe of beard along his jaw gave him an exotic look. As Owl studied him, the man smiled; the expression called to mind a cat faced with a very full dish of cream.

"For once," he murmured, "I'm not disappointed. You have amazingly beautiful eyes, boy, even with the bruises."

Owl turned his face away as an overpowering wave of cold despair churned through his innards. Now he knew who this was: Anthagh, the slaver. The two men were talking again; Owl made himself listen.

"—in no shape to take the agreed price, Sir. Do you want to leave it?"

"And risk a dispute about the pay? No. Stay until he wakes, then pay him. Twenty Guilds and a *fentarre* of Dream's Ease."

"You *canna*," Owl pleaded. "You canna give Zhazh that much Ease all at once. He'll take it all—he canna help himself—and that much would put him under for *days*. Someone's sure to steal the money from him, if they dinna *kill* him."

"Your wretched brother *sold* you, boy. You can't possibly care what happens to him." The slaver frowned, seeing tears on Owl's cheeks. "But you *do* care. Gods. He doesn't deserve you."

"I dinna deserve this," Owl said softly.

"No," the slaver agreed. "You don't." He stooped, and picked Owl up.

"If you untie my feet, I'll walk," Owl suggested.

The man laughed. "If I untied your feet, you'd run."

"Sir," the other man interjected. "Shall I fetch Thalen?"

"No. I'll manage." He set off into the night, carrying Owl like a child.

"What are you going to do with me?" Owl asked, watching the man's face.

"I'm going to sell you, boy. I've a client who's been looking for something like you."

"I've a friend in the Thieves' Guild who owes me a favor. Happen you could sell me to her."

"I doubt your friend owes you a favor big enough. If you interest my client, we're talking a price in Royals. And even on the open Block, without any training or talents, I daresay you'd fetch sixty Nobles." He looked down at Owl with a flicker of compassion. "Look: someone who pays that kind of money for you won't let you go hungry."

Owl's face crumpled into tears. "But—but I dinna want to be a slave."

He set Owl on his feet and wiped the boy's eyes with a handkerchief. "It's too late, lad. You are a slave. I have the documents, and your brother's been paid. Even if you got away from me, it wouldn't change that. You can scream, weep, plead—and none of it will help. Or you can walk beside me and try to make a good impression on my client. I think you'd be happier there, than sold on the Block to one of the pleasure houses."

"Not to mention," Owl put in sourly, "that you'd rather get a price in Royals, than a mere sixty Nobles. But go ahead and untie my feet. I willn't run away."

The slaver fixed a leash of rope to Owl's bound wrists, then cut the boy's feet free. The man took them out of the Slums, through the waterfront district into an area of wide streets lined with shops and good inns. There, he hired a litter. Owl had never ridden in a litter, and though he would have liked to see where they were going, the curtains were pulled shut. When the litter came to a halt and the slaver and Owl climbed out, they were in a courtyard. To Owl's surprise, a soldier in the colors of the Imperial Guard and two of his men came over to them.

"Ah," the Imperial Guard commander said, with faint disgust. "Master Anthagh. Plying your trade, I see."

"Indeed, dear Commander Bhenekh," the slaver replied with a tight smile. "As you are yours. Truly, there is no rest for us dedicated servants of the nobility. Come along, boy," he added, hurrying Owl though the courtyard and into a long, wide hallway.

Master Anthagh threaded his way through a maze every bit as complicated as the Slums—though far cleaner. They had been walking for several minutes before Owl realized they were in the Royal Palace. His heart sank; he remembered tales of the dissolute habits of the nobility. As suddenly and unexpectedly as hope, Owl heard music; it was coming from an open doorway: the subtle voice of a lute—

and then, impossibly sweet, a cascade of notes from a flute. He froze. With the music came an image: the foreign woman of whom he had dreamed, with a lute in her hands; beside her, the nobleman Mouse had drawn, his shrewd eyes half-closed, an ivory and silver flute against his lips.

"Come along," Anthagh prodded.

"Please, sir." Owl put years of begging experience to use. "Canna we go in and listen? Just for a moment? It's so very beautiful." When the slaver hesitated, Owl allowed a faint shade of his very real despair to color his voice. "Please. What difference will a minute or two make?"

The slaver looked down at Owl, and the pleading, the pain in the boy's wide, golden eyes got through his hard armor of self-interest. "What harm can it do?" he murmured, almost to himself. "Very well; a minute only. But don't disturb them." Master Anthagh and Owl slipped into the room. The musicians were seated between two banks of tall, white candles. They faced the doorway, not ten feet away, exactly as Owl had pictured them. The music surged around them, perfect and tender; then the lute player broke off. The nobleman opened his eyes to look reproachfully at his partner; then he followed her gaze.

Master Anthagh swept a bow. "Forgive us for troubling you. Come *on*, boy," he added.

"Wait," the woman said.

Spurred by panic, Owl dragged the nobleman's name to the surface of his mind. "Lord—Lord Ghobhezh-Ykhave!"

The flute-player approached, his cane tapping on the stone floor. "Of course," he said. "Mouse's little friend, no?"

He nodded. "Owl."

"Yes. Owl. Indeed." He turned to Master Anthagh. "Is he for sale? What's your price?"

"I regret, my lord, that the boy is already spoken for."

"But you s—" Owl began, before the slaver's hand crushed a painful warning into his arm.

"Perhaps I could pay for your client's disappointment," Venykhar Ghobhezh-Ykhave suggested.

"Ah, but disappointment is so very costly."

He turned his free hand palm upwards. "How much?"

Master Anthagh shrugged apologetically. "Fifty Royals."

Regret touched the nobleman's face as he looked at Owl. "I fear we of House Ykhave aren't equipped to buy off disappointment on such a scale. I'd go as high as five Royals for the lad, but I'm not in a position to offer more."

Master Anthagh bowed again. "If my client should decide he doesn't suit, I shall return."

"Good. I'll be here until midnight; or come to my rooms."

"Very good, Lord Venykhar. Come on, Owl."

Owl stopped paying attention to where they were going. Hopelessness overwhelmed him. Only the insistent pressure of Master Anthagh's hand on his arm kept him moving. When they finally reached their destination, a servant answered the slaver's knock and led them to a lavishly furnished room, its walls lined with shelves of leather-bound books. In one corner stood an inlaid *khacce* table, the exquisitely carved game pieces poised for play. After several minutes, a woman entered. Her silvery white hair spoke of age, but the dark eyes in her seamed face shone with vivid life.

"Ah, Anthagh," she greeted him.

To Owl's surprise, the slaver sank to one knee. "My Lady Ycevi. See what I brought you: will he do, do you think?"

"Come here, boy," she ordered imperiously. When Owl was in reach, she took his face in her hands, turning it this way and that. "Who beat you?"

"My brother."

"And did you deserve the beating?"

"He thought I did," Owl replied.

She removed a slender knife from her sleeve and cut Owl's bonds. "He's filthy," she commented as she examined his hands. "Where did you find him?"

"He begs in the Temple Gate. I saw him there; I thought he might have what you need."

She darted a shrewd look at the slaver. "Is he legally yours? I want no trouble."

"I bought him from his brother."

"Good." She turned back to Owl. "What are you called, boy?"

"Owl."

"You ought to know, Lady Ycevi, that Venykhar Ghobhezh-Ykhave is interested in the boy."

Lady Ycevi arched one eyebrow. "Really? I didn't think he was—susceptible. How did you learn this—and how interested was he, Anthagh?"

"We passed him in one of the galleries. He was making music with the Emperor's foreign mistress. The boy called him by name. He offered me seven Royals for Owl."

"Five," Owl corrected.

Anthagh pierced Owl with a poisonous look, but his tone was mild. "You need to learn to hold your tongue."

Lady Ycevi laughed. "No! That's his appeal. He's innocent, honest, forthright—and vulnerable. Surely an irresistible combination for the purposes I have in mind. My congratulations, Anthagh. What's your price?"

"Twelve Royals."

"Are you worth twelve Royals, boy?" the woman asked Owl.

"They paid my brother a *fentarre* of Dream's Ease and twenty Guilds. Twelve Royals seems an indecent profit to me."

"To me, also," she agreed. "But the good will of one's business associates is an important consideration." Her gaze sought the slaver's. "I'll give you ten." At his bow, her lips quirked in a rueful smile. "I daresay you'd have taken seven."

He spread his hands. "I'd have taken five—but you've bought quite a lot of good will, most gracious Lady."

"Find Myncerre on your way out; she'll see you're paid," she said by way of dismissal; her attention focused on Owl, calculating. "Yes. Oh, yes." Her avid smile chilled him. "You are—*irresistible*. That poor bastard doesn't stand a chance."

Chapter Six
Councils

Ferret and her friends didn't start to worry about Owl until the second morning after the slaver had taken him. It was Kitten whose insistence drove Ferret to seek out Zhazher. They went together. Kitten had wanted to bring Donkey with them, but he, having returned to Arkhyd's good graces, wasn't free to leave the Trollop.

"This isn't *like* Owl," Kitten said for the thirtieth time. "What if Zhazher really hurt him?"

When they reached the hovel, Ferret turned to Kitten. "You wait out here—whistle if anyone comes. Happen Zhazh isn't here, but if he is, he's apt to be surly."

Kitten nodded. As she positioned herself, alert for trouble, Ferret went inside. The hovel was dim; she waited inside the doorway for her eyes to adjust. The place stank of Dream's Ease and filth. Her quick ears caught no sounds of breathing. When she made out a huddled shape beside the rude table, she hurried to his side. It was Zhazher—dead. She cursed softly, then examined him. There were no wounds, no signs of struggle. Too much Ease. She searched his clothes. She found an oily paper wrapper which reeked of the drug—a scrap large enough to wrap a whole fentarre of the stuff. She folded the paper and tucked it into her shirt, then went on with her search. Her hand closed on a clutch of coins. "*Gods,*" she said aloud.

"What?" The younger girl appeared in the doorway.

"Dinna come in—I'm coming out," Ferret said. She joined her friend on the street; she was pale. Ferret showed Kitten the fat handful of Guilds. "I fear I've a notion what happened to Owl. Zhazh is dead. He must have taken a whole fentarre of Ease. I found these in his clothing."

Kitten pressed her hands to her heart. "Oh, no," she breathed, anguished. "The bastard must have sold him!"

Ferret nodded somberly. "Happen it's so—but we must find out for sure; and Kitten, if it's possible, we'll buy him back."

Kitten nodded solemnly.

"Let's go back to the Trollop and gather everyone. Happen together we can decide what we'd best do next."

Sharkbait was late. He arrived at the Ivory Comb half expecting that Venykhar would not have waited for him; but the old lord was in his usual place, nursing a glass of wine.

"I had almost given you up," he greeted him.

"Sorry," Sharkbait replied. "I didn't check your message drop until a few minutes ago; I didn't expect you to need me again, so soon. What's wrong?"

"You know little Mouse's friend, Owl, don't you?" At Sharkbait's nod, the lord continued slowly, "I saw him at the Palace, last night. He was in the company of Master Anthagh."

Sharkbait paled. "Sweet, weeping gods. That bastard Zhazher must have sold him. Do you know who bought him?"

"No; not yet. The slaver told me he was already spoken for when I tried to buy him; but he didn't say who his client was."

Sharkbait looked surprised. "You tried to buy him? Why?"

"I don't know. Because he was mutely begging me to do something. It didn't do any good. I offered Anthagh five Royals for him, but he wasn't interested." He went on before Sharkbait could overcome his astonishment enough to speak. "I'm worried. Arre says the boy's important, that there's something brewing at Court and Owl is a piece of it."

"Wait. Who is Arre?"

"The Kellande Seer."

"Oh. The Emperor's foreign witch," Sharkbait responded. "And she thinks Owl's *involved* in some plot?"

"She has dreamed of him. She thinks he's a mere piece on some Council House's *khacce* board."

"But which Council House?"

The old man shrugged. "Does it matter?"

"Ven!" Sharkbait cried, exasperated. "Yes, it matters! You offered to *buy* the boy; that's enough out of character for you to cause comment at Court, even if Owl's not an important part of some House's gambit. If your friend Arre is right, whoever bought Owl is going to wonder why you're interested in him."

"You're seeing ghosts in the shadows, my boy," Venykhar tried to reassure him. "How will anyone know I offered for him? There was no one there but Arre, and she'll keep her counsel."

"And the boy; and the slaver. *Anthagh* will tell his client, if only to drive his price up." Sharkbait sighed. "Don't you have any pressing business in Khavenaffe?"

Venykhar eyed Sharkbait indignantly. "You think I'm going to make a hash of this."

"Ven, intrigue is hardly your element. Why did you really offer to buy Owl?"

"I told you: he's little Mouse's friend, and I was sorry for him."

"*Five Royals* worth of pity? None of the other Council Houses will believe *that.*"

"So what should I do?" Venykhar snapped. "Spend the next few months leering at little boys until my reputation is an utter shambles?"

"*That* has possibilities," Sharkbait replied, snidely. "In the meantime, try to figure out who bought him—but *don't* ask any questions; just watch, and notice what color livery Owl shows up wearing." The longshoreman sighed. "I'll have to tell Mouse and Ferret and the others. They'll take this hard."

"I've thought of sending to Khavenaffe—to ask the Duke for permission to commit enough House resources to acquire the boy, but I doubt the amount of money Ykhave could raise would tempt Owl's purchaser; and I really can't justify the kind of concessions I'd need to grant in order even to pique their interest." He raised a sardonic eyebrow at Sharkbait's surprised approval. "Intrigue may not be my element, my boy, but I'm not an utter fool."

"I didn't mean to imply you were," the younger man said smoothly. "I'm just worried for you, Ven; I know what sharks some of the other Councilors are, and I'd hate to see you hurt. You'll tell me what you manage to discover about Owl, and whether he looks well and reasonably happy?"

The old lord smiled faintly. "*You'd* spend five Royals out of pity for him."

Sharkbait smiled sadly. "I'd spend fifty, if I had it; but then, I risk my life and spend my energy agitating for better wages for a pack of illiterate commoners." He rose. "Good night, Ven."

It was very late that night, when Ferret and her friends gathered in the scullery of the Trollop. The last of the revelers had been lighted home, and even Arkhyd had gone to bed. They were a sober group. Mouse had been crying. Squirrel and Ferret were angry; and Kitten had gnawed her fingernails to the quick. Donkey refused to show any emotion, but sat with deceptive placidness among his friends.

"I did some snooping this afternoon," Ferret began. "Anthagh bought Owl from his brother; and according to rumor, he sold him right off. I decided to find out who bought him, but when I went to Anthagh's headquarters, his toughs warned me off. I visited several pleasure houses, but no one would tell me aught. So I went to Khyzhan. I had to argue with him; at first, he'd have naught to do with my inquiries. He said Anthagh's the closest thing the Slum has to a Council Lord—independent and untouchable. So I told him if he wouldn't help, I'd go to Ybhanne—that's one of his rivals—and see if *she'd* be more use. I half expected him to call my bluff, but he didn't. He went rather still, then said if I was that stupid or that desperate, happen he'd best go along to minimize damage. He took me to some contacts he had in the Slave Market. They were abuzz with hints about a beggar child who had been sold to one of the Council Houses, for an outrageous sum. We heard everything from five to twenty Royals."

"*Lady of Sorrows,*" Kitten whispered. "Oh, Fret; we'll never raise *twenty Royals.*"

"It's not fair!" Squirrel burst out. "Owl was worth a hundred of that brute Zhazher."

"He's not dead," Mouse protested. "Dinna speak as though he were."

"Did you leave word for Sharkbait?" Donkey asked. "Happen he'll have some ideas."

"I didn't," Ferret began; but then, the kitchen door opened and Sharkbait slipped in.

He took one look at their faces and sighed. "You've heard about Owl, then. I'm sorry. It's an evil place, this empire where they sell children."

"What would a Council House want Owl *for*, Sharkbait?" Mouse asked, tearfully.

"How did you find out he was bought by a Council House? Do you know *which* House?"

Mouse gestured to Ferret, who shrugged. "Khyzhan introduced me to a couple of his contacts in the Slave Market; but they didn't know (or wouldn't say) which House bought Owl."

"*Khyzhan* helped you," Sharkbait marveled.

"You haven't answered my question, Sharkbait," Mouse pointed out.

"No," he agreed.

"*Well?*" she demanded.

He spread his hands, helplessly. "How can I say? To some extent, it depends on which Council House bought him. But Venykhar—who told me about Owl, by the way; he'd seen him at the Palace—Venykhar has promised to try to find out who bought him, and whether he's well." The longshoreman studied each of them in turn. "It needn't be disaster for Owl, you know. Think: he'll have regular meals; and he won't have that brute Zhazher beating on him. Maybe it's good luck for Owl."

"And happen he's been sold as catamite to some disease-ridden nobleman?" Ferret asked, bitterly. "I canna imagine that even Council Houses pay twenty Royals for a page boy. If it's good luck, Sharkbait, we'll wish him well in it; but we must know. Surely you see that?"

"I see," Sharkbait said sadly. "The only scrap Ven could offer was something the Emperor's foreign witch—Arre—said: she's dreamed of Owl; she thinks he was bought to be used in some Council House scheme; and she says that there's something brewing at Court. There always *is* something brewing (usually poison), so that's not very helpful."

Mouse caught her breath. "The plot on the Emperor! Owl spoke of it."

"And he dreamed of Arre," Ferret added. "He told us."

"You know," Sharkbait warned, "there's not going to be anything *we* can do about Owl's situation, no matter what Venykhar tells us."

"Nevertheless," Ferret said firmly, "we would know the truth."

"Very well. It will probably take a few days." He looked around at them all. "I am sorry; Owl doesn't deserve that treacherous brother."

Ferret looked at him sharply. "Zhazher's dead. An overdose of Dream's Ease, I think."

Sharkbait grunted in surprise. "That's poetic justice, if you like." He rose. "I'll talk to you when I know more. Good night, children."

They watched him go, all but Donkey, who was studying the young thief's face. "Ferret," he said at last, "what are you thinking?"

Her face was inscrutable. "That Sharkbait's wrong when he says there will be naught we can do. I predict we'll be up to our ears in this mess."

"We're Slum-rats!" Kitten protested.

"Happen that's so," the thief responded. "But when Arre met me on the wharf, she knew me; and she said she had dreamed of me, too."

Owl fingered the slave band they had fastened around his left wrist. The silver bracelet, locked on, was engraved with the symbol of House Ghytteve: a stooping hawk, its cruel talons extended, circumscribed by a diamond. It wasn't that it was uncomfortable, but he hated what it stood for; it was the bars of his cage, and he carried it with him always.

He had already learned how the bracelet marked him. As he trailed in the wake of the Ghytteve steward, Myncerre, he saw the dismissive looks other servants gave him. He knew, cleaned up and dressed in the new clothing Lady Ycevi had ordered for him, he didn't look like a Slum dweller; but the fine lawn shirt he wore under his tunic was cut shorter in the left sleeve than the right, so that the sign of his bondage would be instantly visible.

Myncerre looked back and clucked her tongue to hurry Owl along. She was a quiet, capable woman—neither unkind, nor warm. It had fallen to her to take Owl in hand, teach him how to go on in the vast, complicated Palace. Firmly, she drilled forms of address and endless rules of protocol; and she dragged Owl with her in all her duties, so that he could observe and mimic. Noting the glint in her eye, Owl hurried to catch up.

"Now," she said. "Say you were to run across one of the Council Lords. What would you say?"

"Naught—"

"*Nothing*," she corrected.

"Nothing unless spoken to," he replied dully.

"Yes. And if he spoke?"

"I would answer politely, and if I were *certain* I recognized him, I would add 'most gracious Lord of' and give his House name. Else, I would simply call him 'Your Excellency.'"

"No! 'Your *Eminence*.' 'Your Excellency' is for Bishop Anakher or the Prime Minister. Now, say you were sent with a message for House Ambhere; how would you tell their steward?"

"I would make the small bow and say, 'Esteemed sir, I bring word for your most gracious Lady Mylazhe Ambhere from my respected mistress the Lady Ycevi Ghytteve.'"

"Yes," Myncerre said; before she could pose another question, someone hailed her.

"Why, my esteemed Myncerre."

She and Owl both turned. The man who had spoken was richly dressed, a Council Lord's chain of office bright against the deep blue of his tunic. A small, pointed beard accented the narrow elegance of his features. His dark hair had silvered at the temples, lending an air of age and wisdom. His tone was dry to the point of insolence.

"Most gracious Lord of Azhere. How may I be of service?" Myncerre's answering tone was almost flippant.

"So—mmm—*formal?* I've told you to call me 'Rhydev.'"

"Yes, your Eminence; but I must set a good example for the boy."

Rhydev Azhere's attention shifted to Owl. "Ah," he said. He took Owl's left arm and looked at the engraving on the bracelet. "A new—mmm—*acquisition?* So, boy: what role do you suppose you're to play for House Ghytteve?"

Owl appraised the man frankly before he responded. "Your Eminence, I suspect I'm intended as bait."

Myncerre rounded on him in outrage. "*Owl!*"

But Rhydev Azhere laughed. "Very likely. But for whom?"

"I dinna—I don't know yet, your Eminence."

The Azhere Council Lord brushed Owl's cheek with his fingertips. "When you find out, Owl, I'd like to know." Without waiting for a response, he sauntered off.

"How *could* you say such a thing, Owl?" Myncerre demanded.

"You said I was to answer politely."

"You should have politely said, 'I don't know what you mean, your Eminence.'"

"But I *did* know what he meant."

"The requirement is a *polite* answer, not a truthful one, you foolish boy." She shook her head, then smiled faintly. "But you made him laugh. Not many can say that. Hurry, now. We've wasted time enough."

Arkhyd came into the scullery after the noon rush and untied his apron. "I'm off to the market, Thantor. Finish the pots, and keep an ear to the taproom. There's a pair of customers, still. They've paid their reckoning, but if they want aught else, I told them to shout for you."

Donkey nodded slowly. As his uncle bustled off, he propped the door open. The pots were scrubbed, and the afternoon stretched ahead, stiflingly hot and boring.

To amuse himself, he began to eavesdrop. It was a common pastime for him; after he had overheard a few scraps of conversation, he would invent far-fetched situations to go with them. This pair was promising. The two men were whispering, but Donkey's ears were keen; and there was something furtive in their manner. He edged a bit closer to the doorway. He was instantly rewarded.

"...made the kill, just as planned; it couldn't have gone more smoothly—but the wallet wasn't on him. The Lady's angry—money for the assassins, not to mention the...evidence;

she wants some answers, and she wants them *now*." It wasn't a Slum voice; this man had a cultured accent.

"If only I had answers." The second man spoke the Bharaghlafi language as though it didn't quite fit his tongue. "It is—mysterious. The Sea Hawk had the wallet, for I gave it to him myself; why he did not have it when the assassins struck, I have no idea."

"Well, you'd better come up with an idea, Dedemar; the Lady has begun to wonder whether you might not have been unduly tempted by the...evidence."

"I swear not," he said. "Tell her, Elkhar: I keep my word. I tell no lies."

The first speaker laughed, with bitterness. "She'll never believe *that*. In her world, there's no such thing as honesty—only expediency and credulity. Look, Dedemar: she's not happy and it's in your interests to *make* her happy. Can't you throw her a bone?"

Donkey shifted carefully, trying to get a look at the speakers. There was a pause, as though the man called Dedemar weighed his words. Donkey caught a glimpse of the foreigner: a tall, pale haired man in the livery of the Temple Watch; but the other man was ought of sight.

"Tell her," Dedemar said at last, "her puppy is meeting Rhydev at the Replete Feline tonight, after midnight. If she is aware, well enough; if not, could it be her hound turns feral?"

"The Replete Feline? A tavern on the Slum edge of the waterfront? I know the place. Good. If she wants you to spy, how can I get word to you?"

"I'm on duty. If she wants him watched, she must send someone other."

Elkhar made an approving grunt. "So you're showing some sense. There may be hope for you, after all."

"I learn fast. Do you want anything else, or should we go?"

Donkey heard the scrape of chairs as they rose. He padded back to the sink, in case either of them looked in before they left. He would have liked a look at the one called Elkhar, but it wasn't worth the risk. They hadn't sounded like they would tolerate being overheard; and words like 'assassins' and 'kill' were enough to give even Donkey pause.

He chewed on the conversation most of the afternoon. That they were talking about Squirrel's murdered customer seemed certain; but he did wish he could identify a few more of the references.

Chapter Seven
Dreams

Myncerre pursed her lips. "Come now, Owl; you must eat."

"I'm not hungry."

"Nonsense. A growing boy like you?"

He sighed. He knew that look: totally unyielding. She wouldn't ease up until he'd done as she said. He took a piece of bread and chewed a corner of it. He wasn't hungry—or not terribly. Besides, the food was highly spiced and tasted odd. He ate another bite of bread; it was so soft and pale that it seemed almost tasteless, but that was preferable to the strange spices.

"Eat some of the meat, boy," Myncerre insisted.

Dutifully, he choked down a few bites. The spicing bit at the back of his throat, made his tongue feel thick and slippery. He shoved the plate away. "I dinna—"

"*Don't,*" the steward corrected.

Owl sighed. "I don't want any more."

Myncerre studied him, then smiled commiseratingly. "Tomorrow I'll ask the cook to make you something less highly spiced." She handed him a glass of wine. "Here; drink this."

"I'd rather have water," he told her. His head had begun to spin sickeningly.

"Drink it," she repeated.

He swallowed some of it. It was bitter; it choked him. As he coughed, he knocked the glass over. The red stuff pooled like blood on the creamy linen cloth. Owl stared at it as he caught his breath. Then, he noticed some small, dark granules, like dregs, left where the liquid had soaked into the cloth. He pinched a few off the table cloth and rolled them between his fingers; they were hard, sharp edged little crystals, and they were blue. His heart lurched as his vision blurred for an instant; he swayed in his chair, then caught himself. His frightened eyes fastened on Myncerre's face. "You've poisoned me," he said, reproachful; then he slumped forward, unconscious.

Myncerre sprang into action, sudden worry on her face. She lifted Owl and carried him to his bed; she loosened his clothing and wrapped him in blankets. It shouldn't have been *enough* to make him react like this! Fear tightened her lungs. How could she have miscalculated so badly? Lady Ycevi would *flay* her if the boy died. She rang the table cymbal to summon a servant.

"Fetch a pot of coffee," she ordered.

Before the servant returned, Owl began to moan. Myncerre felt a flicker of hope. It would be bad. The boy would likely spend the night thrashing and screaming; but in her experience, the ones who made noise didn't die of the drug.

Owl was trapped in his dreams. Images surged in his brain like storm wrack: Zhazher crumpled in their hovel, too still. Ferret, arguing heatedly with a tight-lipped Khyzhan. A man he didn't know, slight, dark-haired, with beaky features and fierce, speedwell eyes; he wore a ring with a great, green jewel on his long fingered hand. The Scholar King at the head of a long table, surrounded by the Council of Advice—and familiar faces: Rhydev Azhere, and beside him, Venykhar Ghobhezh-Ykhave. There was something important about this scene, something Owl had missed. He tried to cling to it, but the drug's undertow pulled him away. He fought for air; he was drowning! He thrashed and screamed, but the thundering surf pulled him down, down…

"How much did you give him?" Lady Ycevi's voice was deadly.

"Only a little, Lady. I used half an *anthitarre*—and he only had two bites of the stew, and not half a glass of the wine. It shouldn't affect him like this." Myncerre pinned Owl's shoulders with her hands as another spasm of thrashing took him.

Lady Ycevi looked from her steward to her slave, annoyance marring the arch of her eyebrows. "*Haceth* is a subtle substance. Keep him alive; if you can get him to drink some coffee, that would be beneficial—but don't drown him with it. Zherekhaf asked to speak with me this evening, and I'd rather not call his attention to the boy; so keep him as quiet as you can and don't come running to me with any news. I'll return once the Prime Minister leaves."

* * *

Arre sat up with a hiss of indrawn breath. Her hands gripped the edge of the table while her eyes grew wide and unfocused.

"Arre!" The startled edge in Khethyran's voice jarred words from the Seer.

"*Piantele Doma*," she whispered, forcing gasping breaths in and out of her lungs. As her eyes regained focus, she leaned her brow against one palm.

"Arre." Kheth grabbed her shoulders, shook her gently. "Arre, what is it?"

"*Haceth.*"

"*Haceth?*" Kheth's voice spiraled toward panic. "*Someone gave you haceth?*"

"Not me. Owl. They gave Owl *haceth.*" She managed a deep breath. "God, he's strong. I've got to help him."

"Owl?" He shook her a little harder. "Arre, for the love of the gods, make sense!"

She looked into Khethyran's strained face and forced herself to speak clearly. "They gave Owl *haceth.*"

He took her chin in his hand. "By the gods above and below, *who is Owl?*"

"A boy; the boy in my visions. He—begged—in the Temple Gate; now he's a Ghytteve slave. He has Sight Gifts, untrained, very strong. And someone gave him *haceth.*" She shook her head. "God, he's strong. He nearly pulled me in. Kheth, I have to help him."

"*Help* him?" the Scholar King whispered. "How?"

"I'll lead him out of his nightmares. Otherwise, he'll die—or go mad."

"Lead—? I've spent enough time at the Kellande School to know this sounds suicidal. You've no anchor; you're not in physical contact with the boy; *he's* untrained and strong."

"Two things you need to understand," she said gently. "One: I've dreamed of him; he's important. I'm not sure, yet, how he fits, Kheth, but he's part of something and we need him. Second: he nearly pulled me under with him, just now. I'm trained; I was neither tranced nor sleeping, but I nearly joined him. If House Ghytteve is determined to addict him to *haceth*, if they keep dosing him with it, he could take me with him into madness. I can't be on guard all the time; and if I had been tranced, or sleeping—or even *overtired*, Kheth! —I might not have been able to hold on. I must lead him out, Kheth; at least, I must try."

Khethyran took her face in both hands, studying her as though he would engrave her features on his mind. "Be careful, Arre," he whispered at last. "I couldn't bear to lose you."

Down, down...The drug swept Owl into nightmares: the wailing ghost of Zhazher, '...your fault...all your fault...' Kitten, terror on her face, hands around her throat, choking, choking...The Lady Ycevi, smiling as she metamorphosed into a screaming hawk, talons ripping at his eyes...The slaver, Anthagh, chasing him and laughing...

Then, he heard music: the ripple of a lute. He flailed after it, and the music shattered into meaningless fragments. He caught one, held it in his mind; he used the chip of sound to build the image of the woman, Arre: a hedge against his nightmares. He pictured her, pictured the brilliant banks of candles; and there...There was the music again. He followed more gently, this time. Claws of nightmares raked him, but he nursed the thread of lute music in his mind. The drug flung his deepest terrors into the sea of his dreaming, but he fended them off, like flotsam, while he let the lute music act as a current, pulling him out of danger.

His breathing eased. His dreaming mind was no longer awash in a storm churned ocean. The imagery changed: a vast stone building. Tree-like columns supported a ceiling of shadows. Light at the far end of the hall drew him. Owl walked toward it, as the peace of the place seeped into his soul. As he neared the source of the light, he saw it was a candle, and in its pool of light sat the woman, Arre. Her lute whispered under her hands, but when he reached her, she gently stilled its voice.

"Owl," she said.

"Arre."

"You have a very strong Gift," she told him.

"I din—don't understand."

"Your dreams, the visions you have; they are a special talent you have been given. In my country, we call them Sight Gifts. Sight Gifts are rare; ones as strong as yours are rarer still." Arre's face clouded. "My people would teach you and cherish you, not bind you as a slave to a cruel, ambitious old woman."

Owl was silent.

"We haven't much time," Arre said. "Listen: try not to let them feed you *haceth* again; it is the bitter stuff you tasted in the food and wine. Your Gift makes you too sensitive to it. If they force it on you, remember this place; do what you did to build the image of me to bring yourself here. This is a place of peace, and if you are able to shelter your dreaming mind here, you will be able to withstand the worst of the drug."

"Is everything I dream *true?*"

She shook her head. "Especially not with *haceth*. The drug unlocks your innermost fears, and then casts them at you as though they were truth. Owl, can you tell me what Ycevi Ghytteve intends for you? Do you know?"

"No. She said I was irresistible, and that 'the poor bastard doesn't stand a chance,' but I don't know what—or who—she meant. I told Rhydev Azhere I thought I was intended as bait; but I don't know for whom."

"Bait," Arre repeated, frowning.

"Arre, can we talk like this again?"

"I don't know," she admitted. "I don't think so. I hope you won't be given any more *haceth*, and without the impetus the drug provides, or proper training, I doubt you have the strength to touch my mind." Suddenly, the dream world shuddered around them. "No more time," she said. "Remember: no *haceth*."

Owl coughed and sputtered as someone poured warm coffee into his mouth. He turned his head away, struggled weakly with the encircling arms that held him in a sitting position—then blinked hard, trying to clear his vision. He was awake.

"Drink the coffee, Owl," Myncerre said. "It will help."

"Is there more *haceth* in it?" he asked. His throat hurt, and his voice was hoarse.

Myncerre started slightly. "No. There isn't. But tell me: how do you know *haceth*, Slum-rat?"

Owl thought fast. "My brother is addicted to Dream's Ease. Once, when I was little, one of his friends thought it would be funny to dope me up. He gave me *haceth*. I nearly died. Zhazher—that's my brother—said some people are very sensitive to *haceth*."

"I didn't give you very much," Myncerre said slowly.

"It wouldn't take much to kill me."

"Well, there's no haceth in that coffee; drink it."

Owl complied. The taste reminded him of the stuff Ferret occasionally brewed for him. He saw the thief in his mind's eye, laughing as she shared a joke with him. The memory brought sudden, painful tears.

"Owl?" Myncerre queried anxiously. "What is it?" There was more tenderness in her voice than she usually allowed to show.

"I want to go home. Please, Myncerre. I want to go home." At her pitying expression, Owl's control broke. He buried his face in the pillow and wept as though the world were ending.

Arre returned to awareness of her surroundings to find Khethyran holding both her hands. He was waxen.

"It's all right," she said quietly. "Sweet God, I'm weary."

"And this Owl?"

She shrugged. "He'll live."

"This time," the Scholar King added for her. "Arre, I could go to Ycevi and demand that she give the boy up to me. I'm not sure it would be politically wise—the Council Houses are jealous of their prerogatives, and I'm sure they'd cast my meddling in an unfavorable light; but if it will make you safer, Arre, I'll do it."

Arre's gaze went distant for an instant; her inner vision was hazed with the silvery shadows which meant she was seeing the future—or possible futures: swift images of trouble and Council strife. "No," she whispered. "He's important, our Owl; but he's important *where he is*. I think—I think he is meant to work against Ycevi." She worried a knuckle with her teeth. "Oh, I wish I could make it come clear!"

"Give it time," he suggested. "You're back safely; the boy's neither dead nor mad; let's concentrate on one miracle at a time."

"He said he was bait," she mused.

"*Bait?*" The Scholar King's attention sharpened. "Arre, have you seen him? Is he beautiful?"

"Well, yes, even though he was looking rather the worse for wear the night Venykhar tried to buy him."

"Venykhar did *what?*" Kheth nearly yelped. "I mean, he's so upright; he has quite a reputation for prudery among the other nobles—about slaves *and* boys. Why would he—?"

Arre was laughing. "Owl's a friend of that child, Mouse; the little artist. Ven *said* it would ruin his reputation, but he didn't seem very concerned."

"Bait," the Scholar King mused. "If we leave Venykhar Ghobhezh-Ykhave off the list of those for whom such bait might be intended, Rhydev Azhere's name springs to mind."

"No. There's more to this than Ycevi Ghytteve trying to lever concessions out of the silk clans." Arre was decisive. "I'd sooner suspect—" She broke off suddenly as an image crossed her inner eye: a fine-boned, manicured hand wearing a green-gemmed ring. "Who wears a green gem? Rhydev's is blue."

The Emperor shrugged. "You'd sooner suspect whom?"

"Oh. Zherekhaf. Your Prime Minister."

Khethyran raised his eyebrows. "Anything is possible. Arre, it's late. Let's go to bed."

Much later, after Owl had cried himself to sleep, Lady Ycevi returned. The scratch of Myncerre's quill, as she made notes in the household ledger, provided counterpoint to the boy's calm breathing. Lady Ycevi moved the lamp so a little light spilled onto the boy's pillow; his face was serene with sleep, despite the old track of tears. She turned to her steward. "Well?"

"You saw what he was like, earlier. That went on a long, long time. Eventually, he calmed down. I got some coffee into him and he woke. He drank another cup, and seemed much better. Lady, he knew the drug. He asked me if there was more *haceth* in the coffee. He told me he was very sensitive to *haceth*, and that even a small dose could kill him. Then he went to sleep."

Ycevi raised her brows. "And the tears?"

"He said he wanted to go home; and then he cried himself to sleep. 'Please, Myncerre,' he said. 'I want to go home.' I've never felt like such an ogre."

Lady Ycevi smiled cynically. "He's good."

"I'm not sure he's play-acting."

"Of course not. That's what makes him so wonderful. It's a pity about the *haceth*; I had hoped to have that extra control—but it isn't worth the risk. Will he be better tomorrow? It's time he met Cithanekh."

In the gray hours before dawn, Owl dreamed again of the thin man with the green ring. In the dream, the man sat at a table in a shabby tavern; another person joined him: Rhydev Azhere. The two were locked in serious conversation, but though he was curious, Owl could not make their voices come into his dream. Just before he woke, the scene shifted. The man with the green ring was still there, but now he was standing by the tall windows in Lady Ycevi's library. The man turned—as though at the opening of a door—and in the dream, Owl watched the changes in the man's expression, as he looked at someone for the first time. Then, Owl woke.

He was alone. On impulse, he rose and dressed. He crept to his door and tried the handle. It wasn't locked. Using all his stealth, he slipped through the servant's dining room, down a flight of stairs, through the empty library and into the entrance hall. Then he froze. Elkhar and Cezhar, two of Lady Ycevi's bodyguards, stood by the door. Cezhar started like a hound catching a scent and turned to the boy. Lamplight traced a scar like a whip cut across his cheek. At first, Elkhar took no notice of Owl. He lounged against the door while he cleaned his fingernails with the point of his dagger; then Cezhar looked a question at him—in the unmistakable attitude of a subordinate to a superior. Elkhar shrugged. As he raised his head to meet Owl's eyes, the single silver earring he wore glinted.

"Good morning, Owl," Elkhar greeted the boy.

"Good morning, Elkhar, Cezhar. I thought I'd go out for a walk before breakfast."

"Think again," Elkhar suggested.

Owl smiled ruefully. "I think I'll go back to bed until everyone else gets up."

"Much better."

Owl started away. Suddenly, he looked back at the men. "One of you could come out with me, to be sure I didn't run away."

"And leave our posts?" Elkhar shook his head. "The Lady might forgive you, but she'd flay us."

"Do you like her—the Lady, I mean?"

"Owl, go back to bed."

There was enough warning in Elkhar's tone to send Owl back upstairs. He crawled back into the mound of covers he had forsaken. Though he was sure he would be unable to sleep, the next time he opened his eyes, it was really morning.

Chapter Eight
Hints

Mouse was alone in the Trollop's scullery when Sharkbait
slipped inside. The noise from the taproom was deafening;
Donkey assisted with the rush. Squirrel was out, lighting
someone's way; and Kitten and Ferret hadn't arrived yet. Mouse
was putting finishing touches on a pen and ink portrait of Owl.
Sharkbait watched her work.

"I must show you how to sign your name," he said, striving
unsuccessfully for a light tone. "*Gods.* Poor Owl."

Mouse looked up at him, solemn. "How did you scar your
face, Sharkbait?"

"With a knife."

"In a brawl?"

"Drop it, Mouse," he advised.

Mouse studied him in the disconcertingly intense way which
made one certain she was storing the image for later use. Then
she opened her leather case, removed three drawings, and laid
them side by side on the dead hearth. Sharkbait's breath caught
as he looked at them.

"Oh, child," he whispered. "You play a dangerous game.
What *will* happen to you when you stop looking so sweet and
harmless?"

Silently, Mouse picked up the middle sheet and held its
edge to the lamp flame. The paper blazed up, curling and
blackening. She held it until there was only a corner unburning,
and then dropped the flaming sheet into the cold ashes in the
grate. "Did you scar *yourself?*"

A muscle jumped in his jaw. "Mouse," he warned.

"The scar distracts the eye, but it doesn't destroy the likeness. After all, I see it."

"*Mouse.*"

"Are you related? Why are you hiding?"

"*Mouse!*" He gripped the girl's shoulders, his amber eyes
fierce and desperate. He lowered his voice. "It isn't safe for

you even to ask those questions, much less to know the answers. Let it go. My past is dead—and deadly. Leave me as
Sharkbait. Please. *Please*, Mouse."

Mouse slipped the two remaining drawings into her leather
case. Then, she took out one of the charcoal sticks and handed
it to Sharkbait. "Show me how to make my name."

They were still at it when Kitten and Ferret came in.

"Any word from your noble friend?" Ferret asked the longshoreman.

"Not yet," he replied. "I'm here because Donkey sent
word that he wanted to talk to me. Do you know what he
wants?"

Ferret shrugged. "I've no idea. Sounds like the crowd's
thinning; if it is, Donkey will be along, soon."

At that moment, Squirrel came through the door; almost
immediately, Donkey slipped in from the taproom. "What's
troubling you, Donkey?" Sharkbait asked him.

"Sharkbait, do the names Elkhar or Dedemar or Rhydev
mean aught to you?" Donkey asked him calmly.

Sharkbait's face went still as an effigy. "Why?" he whispered, his lips barely moving. "Donkey, why?"

"I overheard Elkhar and Dedemar speaking, this noontime. They talked about someone they called 'the Lady,' who
was displeased because…" He faltered as he sorted the original conversation from the overlay of conjecture he had fashioned. "Because a wallet had gotten lost. The one named
Elkhar called it 'evidence,' and all but accused the other man
of making it disappear. There was a kill, which went smoothly:
the Sea Hawk was murdered, but he didn't have the wallet
when the watch found him. So the Lady was angry about the
wasted money: money for the assassins, for the evidence—
happen it was a great deal of money."

"Was that everything?" Sharkbait grated.

"Na. Elkhar told Dedemar he'd best throw her a bone—
the Lady. And Dedemar said to tell her her puppy is meeting
Rhydev tonight, after midnight, at the Replete Feline."

"The Replete Feline?" Kitten repeated. "That's where Magpie works—used to be the Fat Cat. Come on; it must be getting on toward midnight. Let's go!"

"No!" Sharkbait snapped. "Kitten, this isn't a game; or if it is, the stakes are too damned high!"

"Did that lot make sense to you?" Donkey asked.

"Enough of it did to convince me that this is no matter for children! It's Council politics; and there's nothing more vicious than Council Houses engaged in intrigue."

"So this has to do with the plot on the Emperor's life?" Squirrel asked. "Who's the Lady?"

"Don't you *listen?*" Sharkbait demanded. *"This is too dangerous!"*

"We listen," Donkey said placidly. "Happen we dinna agree."

Sharkbait studied their uncompromising faces. Pain and worry twisted his features and he raked his fingertips through his dark hair. "Gods," he murmured. "How will I live with myself if I let any of you get killed? Ferret." He focused on the thief, pleading. "Council intrigue is worse—far, far worse —than the infighting in the Thieves' Guild. It's no place for any of you, but think of Mouse and Kitten."

Ferret regarded the longshoreman levelly. "Happen I'm thinking of Owl."

"But this hasn't a thing to do with him!"

"Owl thought it did," Ferret said, her voice quiet, almost gentle. "And he said the Emperor needs us."

"I don't give a damn about the Emperor!" Sharkbait cried.

"You should," Mouse put in, primly.

"The Emperor's *always* a target, or a pawn, or a puppet. It goes with the crown; a warning isn't enough to save him. But if you get mixed up in this mess, someone's bound to get hurt."

"Give it up," Donkey suggested. "We're in it already. You willn't convince us otherwise. And if you refuse us your help, we're even more vulnerable. So who's the Lady?"

Sharkbait wrestled with his conscience, but finally, he sighed, turning one palm upward in a gesture of defeat. "Lady Ycevi Ghytteve—I'd guess; at least, Elkhar is a Ghytteve man. Ycevi is the Councilor for House Ghytteve. She's vicious, and she's always scheming. Rhydev is the House Azhere Council Lord. Azhere and Ghytteve are usually at each other's throats."

"Who's the Lady's puppy?" Squirrel asked.

"That I don't know." Sharkbait sighed again. "Though I daresay I could find out for you."

"Good," Ferret responded promptly. "I'll come with you."

"No."

"Then I'll follow you."

"*No*," Sharkbait repeated firmly. "I go alone, or I don't go at all."

"Very well," Ferret replied. "Who wants to come with me? Squirrel? Kitten?"

"*Ferret!*" Sharkbait cried, outraged. "What purpose would that serve? You wouldn't recognize the Azhere Councilor."

The thief shrugged. "You think I canna identify flash slumming?"

Sharkbait stared at her, then laughed mirthlessly. "And to think I wondered how you persuaded that tough scavenger Khyzhan to do what you wanted." He made an elaborate bow to her, then motioned her to precede him through the doorway. He looked back at the others. "And *you*, for the love of the gods, *stay here.*"

"So who's Magpie?" Sharkbait asked as they lurked in the shadows outside the crowded tavern.

"Goodness. Aught you dinna know," Ferret retorted. "The rest of the world knows her as Adyce. She's a barmaid here."

"Oh. Her. Why do you call her Magpie?"

"She has a fondness for small, round shiny objects," Ferret said dryly. "Preferably silver. Shall we go in?"

"What? You're not planning to scale a wall and climb in a window?"

The thief ignored his biting tone. "The door's open," she pointed out, bland.

"Why, how observant you are. How *have* I managed without you?" He took her arm as they started inside.

The Replete Feline was crowded; there was no chance of securing a table commanding a view. Instead, they joined the press at the bar, and Sharkbait bought them mugs of ale. They nursed their drinks as they scanned the crowd covertly, all the while shamming a flirtatious conversation. When Ferret's cup was empty, she set it on a passing barmaid's tray and looked up through her lashes at Sharkbait.

"Let's go."

"What? Already?"

She smiled dazzlingly and nodded.

His answering expression was so wolfish, Ferret was hard put not to step back. "So you think he's here?"

She batted her eyelashes. "The table by the door; the man with the pointed beard, sitting with the skinny fellow with the green ring."

Sharkbait chucked her under the chin. There was something dangerous in the back of his eyes and in the grit in his voice. "My clever infant. Let's go."

They had to walk past the men's table in order to get out. As they drew abreast, the younger man hailed them. "I say, my good man: isn't she rather young?"

"*Have you taken leave of your senses?*" his companion hissed.

Sharkbait looked him up and down, with insolent attention, before he replied, "She's old in experience."

"It's barbaric—"

"My friend's had rather too much to drink," the man with the pointed beard began.

Ferret cut them both off. "Leave it," she said, firmly. "I must eat."

The thin fellow rose, pulling a purse from an inner pocket. "If it's money—"

"Cithanekh, *sit down!*" The older man made a grab for his companion's wrist.

What Ferret saw put real conviction in her voice. "Put that away! If you flash a Royal in here, you're apt to get us all killed." They stood, frozen like one of Mouse's pictures, until with a sigh, the man returned the purse to his pocket. "Look," Ferret patted his arm, consolingly. "It's kindly thought of, and I'm grateful; but you canna eat gold. Not in the Slums." Then she turned back to Sharkbait. "Come on, lover."

Sharkbait stopped walking once they were through the door and out of the spill of customers and lamplight. Ferret pulled him on. "Move," she urged.

He hesitated.

"Come on; let's run."

"Run?" he repeated, starting to move. "Gods, Ferret. You *didn't!*" Then, they were pelting for the twisting alleys of their home ground.

When they had put some distance between them and the tavern, they slowed to a walk. In the pallid light of the waning moon, Ferret saw the glint of Sharkbait's watchful eyes on her. She grinned, unrepentant.

"Yes: I picked his pocket," she answered his look. "So? I'm a thief."

"So much for being inconspicuous."

She hunched a shoulder. "He was going to remember us, in any case. Who is he, this Cithanekh?"

Sharkbait shook his head. "I'm not sure," he said slowly.

"Does that mean, 'I have a guess I'm not telling you?'"

"Yes." A deadly silkiness invaded his voice. "And you've pushed me as far as you will tonight, my sweet thief. Go back to the Trollop and send the others home."

"While you do what?"

But Sharkbait had already melted into the night.

Much later, Rhydev Azhere sat in his comfortable study, nursing a solitary brandy and thinking. He thought he had all the pieces, now, if he could just construct the puzzle… The boy, the beautiful Owl, was bait. The obvious inference was that Ycevi meant to use the boy to leverage some concessions out of *him*; but somehow, that was too obvious, too crude for a woman of her subtlety. So if not him, then who? He'd heard the rumors: Venykhar Ghobhezh-Ykhave offering five Royals for the child; but Ycevi had nothing to gain from House Ykhave. She wouldn't need expensive bait to lure the Council Lord of the artisans. The boy *could* be aimed at the Prime Minister; but if so, he doubted her ploy would work. Old Uncle Zherekhaf was truly unlikely to sacrifice his eternal, convoluted scheming for a fleeting passion, be the boy ever so appealing. No. He had another theory—and he thought he was right. Ycevi's young kinsman, Cithanekh, had the proper bloodlines; and—judging from his behavior this evening at that tavern—he was compassionate enough to be vulnerable, whatever his proclivities. Unless he was very much mistaken, the boy was aimed at Cithanekh.

It was a beautiful plan; it might even work. But if it would work for Ycevi, it would certainly work for him. The ticklish part was how to get the boy. After that, it would be a fairly simple matter to eliminate rival claimants and engineer a disaster for the Scholar King. The whole would take *delicate* conniving, but Rhydev was confident of his ability. He smiled very slowly. If he were *particularly* skillful, he might even enlist his uncle's support—and that truly would be an elegant piece of deviousness. Pleased with himself, Rhydev tossed off the rest of his brandy and went to bed.

Chapter Nine
The Lady's Puppy

Owl sampled, with elaborate caution, the breakfast Myncerre served him—a fact she couldn't fail to notice. After the third time he broke one of the savory cakes into tiny pieces, Myncerre clicked her tongue.

"The Lady forbade me to dose you with more *haceth.* You might as well enjoy your meal."

Owl nodded. "And if she *had* given you orders to poison me again, no doubt you'd say exactly the same thing."

Myncerre winced. "I daresay I deserved that."

Owl went back to dissecting breakfast cakes with great attention. After several silent minutes, Lady Ycevi herself swept into the room in a swirl of pale blue silks. Owl froze in outrage as she swooped over to him, and planted a scented kiss on his brow.

"How are you feeling, my poor, sweet boy? Why, you've hardly eaten *any* breakfast."

"Do you blame me?" Owl demanded.

Lady Ycevi's mouth hardened. "I paid ten Royals for you. I'm unlikely to poison you intentionally. If you hadn't proved sensitive, the *haceth* wouldn't have been harmful."

Owl did not reply, but the skeptical assessment in his clear eyes flustered even Lady Ycevi. She picked at the hem of one flowing sleeve. "Have you finished your meal?" she asked, then at his nod gestured for him to follow her. He obeyed, trailing the requisite three steps in her wake.

At the door of the library Lady Ycevi paused and said, with a little moué of irritation. "I've left something in my chambers. Go amuse my guest until I return."

"May I not fetch it for you, most gracious Lady?"

"Do as I say," she instructed. She opened the door, sent him through with a gentle push, then she shut it behind him; he heard the scrape of a key as the lock snicked home. A man stood by the tall windows, looking out across the sheltered gardens; as he turned toward the boy, Owl's breath caught.

He had dreamed of this man: young, thin, with aquiline features, a green-gemmed ring on his hand. As they studied one another, the man's expression ran the series of changes Owl remembered from his dream. With a very faint smile he gestured for Owl to approach. The man put fingers under Owl's jaw and turned his face to the light, much as the Lady had done. He brushed the greening bruise.

"Did Ycevi do that? Or order it done?"

"No. My brother beat me."

"Brother?" Surprise widened the man's impossibly blue eyes; his gaze darted to the slave band on Owl's left wrist.

"Before he sold me."

"What are you called, boy?"

"Owl."

"Owl? Why Owl?"

"Ferret named me. She said I had owl's eyes." Unbidden, the whole memory surfaced: a younger Ferret, brash, laying out the rules. *If you're to be one of us, you need a new name. Like me: I'm Ferret, not Frycce. You're Owl. You've an owl's eyes—and you've an owl's vision, too. Owls see in the dark; you see into the soul's darkness. It makes you good at begging—you recognize those prone to pity.*

The memory stung. As his eyes swam with tears, he bit his lips together, determined not to cry. The man's face clouded with concern, and he smoothed a strand of Owl's tousled hair. "Oh, Owl," he murmured sadly.

It was the tenderness that undid him. As his tears spilled, the strange man drew Owl gently into a comforting hug. Owl fought down his tears and pushed the comfort away. Without comment, the man handed him a handkerchief.

Owl wiped his eyes and blew his nose. "I'm not usually such a baby," he said with disgust. "Sorry."

Cynicism glinted in answer. "*I'm* not usually such a soft touch. My name's Cithanekh. How long have you been here, Owl?"

"Four nights and three days."

"Before your brother sold you, what did you do?"

"I begged in the Temple Gate."

His eyebrows rose. "You clean up nicely, for a Slum-rat."

A sneering edge sharpened Cithanekh's tone. "You must enjoy this newfound ease—enough to eat, new clothes, a comfortable bed."

"And such beautiful jewelry to wear," Owl retorted, displaying the slave band. "*I hate it!* Even when the food isn't drugged, it's too highly spiced; the bed's so soft, it smothers me; and the clothes itch. I'd far rather be at home, even with the filth and vermin. Happen life's hard in the Slums, but here, I'm naught but a piece of expensive Ghytteve property. And you think I *enjoy* it? *Gods!*" He spun away and stalked off. Halfway to the door, he stopped. "I canna even stomp out in a huff," he added, as wry amusement won out over anger. "She locked us in."

Suddenly, they were both laughing. "Oh, don't leave, Owl; and don't be hurt. I apologize. My cousin Ycevi is a gifted manipulator. I hate feeling used; I can't imagine why I thought you wouldn't mind." Cithanekh held out his hands. "Come sit with me, and tell me all about life in the Slums."

Owl took one step toward the man, then froze. He covered his mouth as he raised stricken eyes to Cithanekh's face.

"*Owl.* What is it?"

"Rhydev Azhere asked me what role I thought I'd play in House Ghytteve; and I told him I thought I was intended as bait. He laughed, and he said, 'Very likely; but for whom?' She must mean to use me against *you*."

He crossed to the boy, laid a gentle hand on his thin shoulders. "Heavens, Owl; *that* was obvious from the moment she sent you in here. But if you're not her willing tool…why, perhaps she's miscalculated."

Owl met Cithanekh's eyes, serious. "I'm not her willing tool—but I *am* her slave," he whispered. "And I'm frightened."

The young man's face softened. "So am I," he breathed. "Ycevi petrifies me—but it would never do to let it show. So come and sit down—and tell me about your friend, Ferret."

Lady Ycevi moved away from the spyhole, satisfaction molding her lips. It was progressing just as she had planned: the trap was set; the prey was nosing the bait. Now to wait, to proceed slowly; she must do nothing to alarm her prey. Late or soon, Cithanekh would take the bait, and then—*then*, he would be well and truly caged.

In a susurrus of silk, she moved into the hall where one of her bodyguard waited. "Elkhar."

"Most gracious Lady," he responded with a slight bow.

"Does Cithanekh know that he was observed with Rhydev Azhere last night?"

"I don't believe he saw me, most gracious Lady."

"I want him told—and I want him frightened. Filter the information through Dedemar. Also, see what you can uncover about Venykhar Ghobhezh-Ykhave. I want to know how he knows Owl, and why he's interested. Five Royals is a lot of money for House Ykhave—especially since they don't trade in slaves."

Elkhar bowed again. "As you command, most gracious Lady."

The Prime Minister Zherekhaf fingered his chain of office as he considered his nephew through narrowed dark eyes. The younger man bore the scrutiny calmly: Rhydev Azhere was no stranger to the game of intrigue.

"Let me be frank," the Prime Minister said at last.

Rhydev hid a smile; his uncle Zherekhaf was never frank.

"You recognize, I'm sure, that my first consideration is and must be the health and strength of the Empire."

"Indeed," Rhydev agreed, cynically amending the statement...*the strength of that bloodsucker's place in the Council.*

"Undue upheaval..." Zherekhaf frowned gravely. "There is little benefit in a change in leadership if the people suffer."

Meaning, of course, Rhydev thought, *that when one starts a purge, it's easy to get purged in the process.*

"I have, of course, heard some of the rumors and the rumblings; there is growing discontent with the Scholar King among certain Houses. But I am not convinced that the time has come to take direct action."

"Indeed not," Rhydev agreed quickly. "And I am not—mmm—*suggesting* anything of that nature. I am a cautious and—mmm—*restrained* player in this game. However, neither caution nor restraint are virtues I would necessarily—mmm—

ascribe to the dissident Houses. What I am suggesting is that we—mmm—*scrutinize* their actions with particular care. It might, then, be possible for us to—mmm—*anticipate*, or even forestall, their gambit. I, for one, fail to see the advantage of changing the hand at the helm unless we are—mmm—*certain* of our ability to dictate the course."

The older man's eyes glittered suddenly, as he shot an assessing look at the Azhere Council Lord, but his smile an instant later was patronizing. "That 'we' was a masterful touch, Rhydev—but I'm an old hand at this game. You and I both know that no one makes moves on the Council Houses' *khacce* table without enduring *everyone's* scrutiny and assessment. So: you want my cooperation in whatever you're planning. Very well; I'll hear your scheme. Tell me: what, exactly, do you hope to gain from this ploy?"

Rhydev hid his satisfaction; it was rare to lure so much directness from his uncle. Now for the gamble. "Personally," he said, allowing a hint of vindictiveness to lurk beneath the surface of his bland tone, "I should like to see Ycevi Ghytteve fall."

The older man's eyes widened. "Do you think it likely?"

Rhydev lifted an elegant shoulder. "Perhaps. Yes, if she decides to do more than—mmm— *complain* about Khethyran."

"You're talking about trapping her in treason."

"My dear Uncle Zherekhaf," he said in a voice poisonous with malice, "I'm talking about trapping her in any snare that will hold her."

"Well," the Prime Minister said; then he added, as though thinking aloud, "But who would succeed her? Her wretched son?"

"Duke Alghaffen has no interest in Council politics. If he did succeed to Ghytteve's seat, I doubt he would prove a force with which to be reckoned." He managed to sound disinterested; he *needed* Zherekhaf to take the false trail he'd laid. He had to convince his uncle he was acting on emotion, not intellect.

Conjecture roiled behind the Prime Minister's unrevealing eyes. "Whatever did Ycevi Ghytteve *do* to earn such enmity?"

Rhydev's nostrils flared as he feigned suppressed anger. "I'd rather not discuss it," he grated, setting the hook.

The Prime Minister eyed his nephew sternly. "If I am to cooperate with you in this, there are to be no secrets."

His jaw muscles bunched. "She stole a boy from me—" His even tone frayed, and he burst out, "Do you really need all the sordid details?"

Enlightenment dawned in Zherekhaf's face. "I've seen a boy, trailing after Myncerre."

"Owl," Rhydev said, as though he couldn't help himself.

"You'd bring Ycevi Ghytteve down over a slave?"

Rhydev turned one palm upward. "You've seen him. It's the only way I'll ever get him back, Uncle."

Zherekhaf nodded slowly. "How long will it take?"

"Perhaps a couple of months. Will you help me, Uncle?"

The Prime Minister considered, then nodded decisively. "But if we're to settle personal scores, I have one I'd like to set your agile mind to work on."

"You have only to ask," Rhydev responded gallantly.

Every bit of suave oiliness was stripped from the Prime Minister's voice as he gritted out, "Come up with a way to rid us of the Emperor's foreign witch."

Rhydev bowed. "As you wish, Uncle. As you wish." Then he excused himself. On his way to his quarters he was hard put to keep his raging inward battle between unease and jubilation from showing on his face. Zherekhaf had bought the story—at least, he *appeared* to have done. *Now pray all the gods I've guessed right,* Rhydev thought. Owl was bait; the boy had said so, and Myncerre had been aghast. If Rhydev could get the boy, he could bring Cithanekh to heel with him. But what if he were wrong? And what if the Prime Minister had outguessed him? Zherekhaf was a shrewd player; one didn't survive twenty years as a power in the Bharaghlafi Court without both luck and consummate skill. The game was always deeper than the surface ripples. Rhydev would be foolish not to expect Zherekhaf to play at least a double game. The Azhere Council Lord was many things, but no fool.

* * *

Zherekhaf watched his nephew's departure, questions shifting behind his inscrutable eyes. How *satisfyingly* ironic if Rhydev had really set aside his incessant calculations for some beautiful boy. Of course, he distrusted satisfaction; Rhydev was capable of guessing that such a turn of events would appeal to him.

The Prime Minister turned the situation like a gem in his mind, catching light in every facet. Regardless of Rhydev's motives, it would be a positive advantage if Ycevi fell—that woman was powerful and unscrupulous. And Rhydev's assessment of her son, Alghaffen, was on the mark. The Duke, as Ghytteve's Council representation, would lack both the skill and the ruthlessness of his mother; the influence of House Ghytteve would inevitably subside.

Of course, Rhydev would be there to fill the void. House Azhere would rise as Ghytteve set. Well enough; Zherekhaf could work with Rhydev. The Prime Minister pondered consequences of such political upheaval with satisfaction. When Ycevi fell, who would hold her puppy's leash? He thought of Cithanekh: a curious mix of cynicism and naiveté; astute enough to recognize political truths and *not*, if Zherekhaf were any judge, a partisan of his cousin Ycevi. Was he, perhaps, too practical to court martyrdom over principles? Was he, in fact, a man of more *malleable* substance than the one who now wore the Emperor's coronet?

Khethyran. The young Emperor's face rose in Zherekhaf's mind. Khethyran had been something of a disappointment. He had been so sure that the old Emperor's youngest son would be easily led—a *scholar*, for the love of the gods. Instead, Khethyran had proved intractable: an idealist, with courage; uncomfortably shrewd, for all that the game of Court intrigue was relatively new to him; and such a gift for making allies. Why, the foreign witch alone was worth—

He surfaced abruptly; he was no longer alone. Reflexively, he made a deep obeisance.

"Forgive me for interrupting," the Emperor said.

"Your Majesty," Zherekhaf murmured. "You must not apologize to *me*. I exist merely to serve you."

Khethyran's amused exasperation said as plainly as words: what sort of fool do you take me for? But his reply was mild. "Rank doesn't excuse one from showing common courtesy. Zherekhaf, I'd like your advice: Master Dharhyan has reported an increase in caravan losses: raiders. The Caravan Guild would like to raise carrying charges and hire mercenaries, but the wool clans have threatened to send their wares by sea if they do."

"Even if the Caravan Guild *doubles* their fees, it will still be far cheaper than ship transport."

Khethyran sighed. "So I told Ymlakh Glakhyre, and he accused me of favoring Dharhyan's Guild. He said he'd float his own fleet before he'd pay 'those thieving commoners' a Noble more."

"Float his own fleet?" the Prime Minister repeated. "Speak to the shipwrights. Adheran Dhenykhare is no fool; he *must* realize that Ymlakh could never pay for such an extensive project."

The Emperor nodded. "Thank you, Zherekhaf. I don't know Adheran well. If you say he's not unreasonable, I'll approach him. A libation of cold reality—spilled by someone other than *me*—might just be enough to quash Ymlakh's fuming." Then, with the energetic stride so at odds with typical noble languor, he left the Prime Minister's chamber.

Chapter Ten
Hunters and Prey

Even in the heat of noonday, the Temple Gate was crammed with people. Kitten worked the crowd, gleaning scant fistfuls of Commons and the occasional Guild. As she turned away from her latest mark, Kitten found herself face to face with a man, youngish, well dressed, impressively muscled. He looked her up and down in an unpleasantly appraising manner; returning his scrutiny, she noted the dangling earring he wore in his left ear: a silver disk etched with a stooping bird of prey.

"Please sir, pity me," she began, though his fiercely handsome face seemed incapable of a gentle expression.

"*Pity* you?" he repeated.

"I have no parents, no family, neither kith nor kin to care for me." Kitten knew it was useless, but Owl had taught her: even if you mistakenly approach someone unsympathetic, let the *mark* end the conversation.

To Kitten's astonishment, the man produced a coin. "At least you haven't a worthless Ease-addicted brother to beat you, then sell you into slavery," he remarked as he turned away.

Kitten grabbed the man's arm. "Owl? *Do you know Owl?*"

He spun back swiftly, gripped her wrists as he pushed his face toward hers. "Are you Mouse?" he demanded sharply.

"No: Kitten. Is he well? Did he ask you to look for us?"

"Us?" the man repeated. His grip on her wrists tightened.

"Me," she replied, half laughing. "And Mouse and the others. He must have told you about us. Is he well? Which Council House bought him? Are they kind to him?"

"He appears to be well treated," the man responded, watching Kitten intently. "He wears a page's livery: green and silver. Ghytteve, I think."

Kitten tried to keep the surprise off her face. Ghytteve was the bunch Ferret thought were plotting against the Emperor—and *they* bought Owl. "Does he like it there?" she asked. "Does he say?"

The man shrugged. "He doesn't complain to me."

"I *wish* I could *see* him," Kitten said passionately. "I miss him so much. Does he ever come away from the Palace?"

The man shook his head. "They don't let him out of sight. I'll tell him you miss him—and I suppose I could carry other messages between you. Are you here every day, Kitten?"

"Sometimes I'm on the wharves, instead," she responded.

"*Would* you? Would you *really?*" At his nod, she went on effusively. "Oh thank you, thank you *so* much—" She broke off with an apologetic laugh. "I dinna know your name."

His eyes chilled to watchfulness. "I'm Elkhar."

"E-Elkhar," she stammered, stunned by recognition, and flooded with sudden unease. Elkhar was a Ghytteve man, Sharkbait had said. As she recovered her wits, she feigned strong emotion. "O-Oh I c-canna begin to th-thank you enough." The tears she had summoned spilled. "I miss Owl so m-much." She covered her face to scrub away tears. When she looked up a moment later, Elkhar had gone.

Elkhar paused in the shade afforded by a traveling puppeteer's stage. He frowned. That little Slum-rat had *known his name*, or he was very much mistaken. Elkhar didn't like to be mistaken; but he *hated* the idea she had known his name. And how had she known to ask which Council House had bought Owl? Surely the private doings of the nobles weren't common gossip in the Slums. He didn't like it; she had far too much information. It simply didn't figure.

He had come to the Temple Gate in search of the Mouse Anthagh claimed Venykhar Ghobhezh-Ykhave had mentioned. Instead, he had met Kitten. Mouse, Kitten, Owl, and 'the others.' *What* others? He didn't like it; it looked like a pattern.

Intrigue was a deep game, Elkhar knew. Could little Owl be a piece on more than one board? He frowned. Anthagh. What were the slaver's motives, and where did his real loyalties (if he had any) lie? Owl *looked* perfect for the Lady's plan—but was he really harmless? Or was he subtle bait for House Ghytteve's Lady? Owl was quick, appealing, wise for his age; in spite of years of caution, the bodyguard found in himself a surprising level of sympathy for the boy. Now, it worried him. If Owl was a piece in someone else's game, whose? And was he aware?

A movement caught his eye: Dedemar; and an affirmative hand-signal. The Lady's puppy had been warned—and frightened. Elkhar would get a full report from the Temple Watchman later. In the meantime...In the meantime, he'd see whether he couldn't trap himself a Mouse—and find some answers.

Mouse sat in the shade of her parents' hand cart. Her deft fingers tied a thin velvet ribbon into a bow. With a sigh, she set the finished nosegay on the tray beside her: *ghenne* flowers trimmed with lace and ribbons, for the Ythykh-fair crowds tomorrow. Her mother handed Mouse more flowers.

"Happen you'd rather spend the day with your friends," she said, "but your father and I need your clever fingers, Amynne."

"It's not that. Mama, I miss Owl."

The woman stroked her daughter's hair. "Oh, 'Myn. Happen it's for the best. Think of it: for the first time in his life, he'll have enough to eat—and he willn't have to live in fear of a beating from his worthless brother."

"Some masters whip their slaves."

"Owl's too good a boy to earn a whipping," she soothed.

Mouse's eyes were bleak. "Some people enjoy inflicting pain and Owl is very stubborn. He willn't like being a slave, Mama, even for the food."

"He's practical. He'll make the best of it." Tears glittered in Mouse's eyes; her mother sighed. "There's naught you can do, Amynne; there's naught of sense in aching your heart."

Mouse blinked back her tears. "Sense," she retorted, with a determined sniff, "has naught to do with it." She pulled away from her mother and went back to making posies.

By the end of the afternoon, Elkhar was in a foul humor. He'd been touched by every wretched begging child in the Slums, but had found no sign of the elusive Mouse. Other than Kitten, no one had taken the careful bait he had offered about Owl—a clear enough reference to startle recognition, but also a common enough story to be unmemorable. As sullen as the thunder-heads gathered over the harbor, Elkhar left the waterfront district. He made for his appointed rendezvous with the Temple Watchman: the tawdry pub in the Slums known as the Trollop's Smile.

Dedemar was late. It figured, Elkhar thought sourly as he struggled with the bitter ale the barman served him. He couldn't imagine why the Temple Watchman favored this place; everything they served was awful. The rank odor of fish stew permeated the place and made Elkhar slightly nauseous. The tavern was quiet; must be the word had spread about the dreadful ale—or it was too early for the rush. He had chosen his table for the view it gave him of the main entry; but the spot was also near the door to the kitchen, which undoubtedly accounted for the overpowering presence of the fish stew.

The barman cast an appraising eye at his single patron, then slipped into the kitchen. Through the door, which was ajar, Elkhar heard the man giving directions, loudly and slowly, to someone within. Moments later, a boy shuffled out to position himself behind the bar. The boy cast slow, incurious eyes around the room; when his gaze crossed Elkhar's, he appeared to think hard, then said, "Wan' another?"

"Not yet," Elkhar responded curtly. A half-wit; what else could he expect from such a place. But a moment later, when Dedemar appeared, he was grateful for the boy's stupidity. There weren't people to cover their conversation. If the boy had any wits, Elkhar would have been nervous about being overheard.

"So?" Elkhar began, after the boy had brought the Temple Watchman a mug of ale and retreated to the bar. "You saw him?"

The foreigner nodded. "I saw him. I told him he had been observed with Rhydev Azhere; and I warned him. I said, 'The Lady gives, she can take away. And she is skeptical of innocent reasons.' He assured me it was happenstance he and Rhydev were drinking together. I reminded him he didn't have to convince me, he had to convince *her*. And he got very still, very white. Then he said, 'He's an attractive man, Rhydev.' And I said, 'To you, he's poison. If he poisons you, or Ycevi poisons you over him—both ways, we bury you. Don't be a fool.' And then I left him."

The taproom was silent while Elkhar considered this. At the bar with studied care and imbecilic concentration, Donkey dried the pewter mugs and put them away. He could hear every word; and only long practice kept interest and puzzlement from showing on his face. Rhydev; Ycevi; these were names he knew. And it was the same Temple Watchman: Dedemar. The men must be talking about 'the Lady's puppy.' Carefully keeping his face placid and stupid, he took another good look at the men, so as to be able to describe them later.

"Good," Elkhar said at last. "We have to keep that puppy scared. We can't have him making common cause with Azhere or any other House. Now, I have another task for you. Do you know the Ykhave Council Lord by sight?"

"The flute-maker? Walks with a cane?"

"That's him. Was he in the Temple District today?"

The Temple Watchman nodded. "He goes to the Windbringer Temple nearly every day." Something in the bodyguard's eyes drove Dedemar to continue. "He makes music with the priests. He's perfectly harmless, Elkhar."

"No one's perfectly harmless."

"No one's harmless, no one's innocent. Dear gods, Elkhar, you sound like the Lady. He's an old man who makes flutes."

"He's a good friend of the Emperor's foreign witch, and he knows a good deal more about Owl than I like," Elkhar snapped.

"Owl? Who is Owl?"

"Never mind. Tomorrow I'll send Cyffe to you; brief her on his movements." In response to something in the Temple Watchman's face, Elkhar's voice dropped to a dangerous purr. "Dedemar, you wouldn't be thinking of *warning* him, now, would you?"

"No. No, indeed, Elkhar."

"Good." The danger in his voice increased. "I'm glad you understand. Such a move would have *disastrous* consequences. If you're done with that slop they call ale, let's go."

As the men headed toward the door, Squirrel pelted through at a run, nimbly dodging them at the last instant. "Excuse me, gentlemen," he said, with a quick bob of his head. Then he tossed something through the air toward Donkey.

"Ho, Donkey," he cried. "Mouse sent you flowers."

To Squirrel's surprise and sudden alarm, Donkey merely stared brainlessly, first at the bouquet and then at Squirrel. "Wha?" he responded.

The dark-haired man's hand closed hard on Squirrel's upper arm, turning the boy to face him. "*Mouse?*" the man demanded, avid. "I have a message for Mouse from Owl."

Pieces snapped abruptly into a disquieting whole. Donkey only acted *that* stupid when there was real need; and the man who had such a painful grip on Squirrel's arm had the face of a predator. Squirrel chose his role and played it out. "What? You want a message carried?"

"I have a message for Mouse," Elkhar repeated.

"For who?"

"For *Mouse*." Elkhar's temper began to fray.

Squirrel opened his eyes wide and put on his best alert and willing face. "I'm happy to carry messages, sir. I charge five Commons a trot, and I'm fast. Just tell me how to recognize this Mouse person and where to find him."

Elkhar lifted Squirrel so that the boy's face was level with his own. "It's no good, boy," he said, with the careful diction of someone really furious. "I heard you, when you came in. You said: 'Mouse sent you flowers.'"

Squirrel's face lightened. "But I didn't say 'mouse.' I said 'Ma.' My *mother*. 'Ma sent you flowers.' She always does, for Ythykh-fair. No one else remembers, and he likes the smell, and the colors."

Elkhar didn't reply, only stared into the boy's face. Squirrel looked at the floor below his dangling feet, then raised his eyes to the man's cold scrutiny.

"Sir?" he said. "Do you…Do you think you could put me down, sir? Please?"

The bodyguard set the boy on his feet but didn't release him. "What's your name?"

"Effryn," Squirrel told him. *Definitely* not the time to tip the balance with the name Ferret had given him.

Elkhar regarded him silently for at least an eon; then, he let him go and strode out of the tavern. Neither Donkey nor Squirrel dropped the characters they had assumed for a solid five minutes. Then, Squirrel sidled over to the bar, raised an eyebrow and looked expectantly at his friend.

"Good thing you're quick," Donkey remarked. "That fellow's no *friend.* Name's Elkhar—Ghytteve's man, Sharkbait said. And it sounded like he plans to do Mouse's nobleman some sort of mischief. You'd best find Ferret—but be damned sure you're not followed." Suddenly, Donkey grinned. "'*Ma* sent you flowers,' indeed. Squirrel, you're a wonder."

"I willn't complain if I'm never dangled in the air like that again," Squirrel admitted with a shudder. "Gods. I thought he was going to break me into bits."

"Near thing," Donkey agreed. "Go on; we need Ferret."

Owl gazed out the window at the courtiers who strolled among the bright, scented shrubbery in the formal gardens. They were too far away for their voices to carry to the boy's ears, so he amused himself by inventing their conversations. Those two were flirting, he decided of an elegant pair by the hibiscus bushes; the three men by the fountain were discussing horse racing; the flock of lace trimmed ladies were gossiping about the lone young lord by the marble bench. Something familiar about the man by the bench struck him and he craned out the window to see better. He was right: it was Cithanekh. As though he sensed the touch of Owl's curiosity, the young lord looked up; Owl saw the flash of a smile and his cautioning gesture.

Owl drew his head back inside, still watching, as the ladies moved toward Cithanekh in a wave of dizzying color. Owl frowned slightly; he was convinced the ladies were teasing Cithanekh in that mannered way the nobles had. He was distracted, then, by another familiar presence: Rhydev Azhere, deep in conversation with an older man whose rich dress was all in shades of russet and brown. Affairs of state, Owl decided, wondering briefly who the other Councilor (for he could see the glint of a golden chain of office) was.

A movement caught Owl's eye, and simultaneously, a wave of stillness swept the garden; conversations everywhere broke off as people stared at the newcomer. It was Arre. She smiled and nodded to people; but no one returned her greeting. Owl felt a surge of kindred loneliness at the sight of her straight back and hard won unconcern. He leaned out of the window again.

"Ho! Arre!" he called, waving.

She raised her head at the sound of her name; as she caught sight of the boy leaning from the upper window her face eased to a smile and she waved back. Then, she continued on her way.

Owl came back inside and shut the window, suddenly thoughtful. She must have recognized him; and yet, she hadn't called his name. He wondered if he had done a foolish thing by hailing her. He lifted his chin. It didn't matter; he didn't care! She was lonely—and the courtiers were *horrible!*

But the watching game had lost its appeal. Owl flopped down on one of the carpets, and pretended to amuse himself by picking pieces of lint out of the nap. Misery pounced on him; his eyes were awash with unshed tears. Gods knew it was bad enough being a slave, but did it have to be so *boring?*

The sound of the door opening spurred him to batten down his feelings. He bit his lip and willed the tears away. Footsteps approached, slowed, stopped. Owl wouldn't look up. A gentle hand patted the center of his back. "Ho, Owl."

"Cithanekh!" He sniffed hard as he scrambled to his feet. "What were the ladies teasing you about?"

A flicker of surprise glinted in his cobalt eyes, but he merely shrugged. "The usual things. How do you know—Arre?" He said the name as though it had an unfamiliar taste.

Owl hunched a thin shoulder. "She's a friend of Ferret's."

"Your thief friend?" At Owl's nod, Cithanekh's eyebrows rose. "I suppose it would be pointless to inquire how *they* became acquainted?"

Ferret had told Owl the story of her encounter with the Kellande Seer, but he didn't feel it was his tale to share; instead, he smiled wryly. "Knowing Ferret, she probably tried to pick Arre's pocket."

"No doubt. But speaking of picking things, Owl, what *were* you doing to the rug?" He eyed Owl's collection of lint bits.

"Oh, that. Well, when I'd gathered enough, I was going to spin it into yarn, then braid the yarn into a rope, and climb out the window to freedom." The flight of fancy fell a little flat, and he smiled apologetically. "Truthfully, you have no idea how bored I get. They leave me here for hours at a time, and if I so much as venture to poke my nose into the hallway, Cyffe or Elkhar or Cezhar or Myncerre or Zhotar is there to chase me back inside."

Cithanekh scanned the walls with a disbelieving eye. "Bored, Owl, in a roomful of books?"

Owl's golden eyes widened as he stared at the young lord. Cithanekh returned his blank look. Finally, Owl sighed. "How many Slum-rats do you know who can read?"

A complex array of emotions skimmed across Cithanekh's face and resolved into determination. He fetched a thick volume, then settled on the sofa, motioning Owl to his side. "I know one who's going to learn how," he told the boy. "Come on, lad. I may not be able to do much for you, but I *can* teach you to read."

Later, when Myncerre looked in, they were still at it, heads bowed close over the page while the boy puzzled out words. The steward watched, feeling an odd catch in her own throat. She closed the door without even a click to disturb them.

Chapter Eleven
First Blood

Squirrel ran Ferret to earth at the Beaten Cur. When she had concluded her business with Khyzhan, he drew her aside to tell her about the afternoon's events.

She frowned, perplexed, when he was done. "I canna make it figure," she complained. "What do they want with Mouse?"

"*I* dinna know," Squirrel replied. "I canna figure why they're after Mouse's nobleman, either. Happen they think there's a plot where there isn't."

Ferret nodded; then her eyes narrowed. "Or happen we're part of a plot we dinna know about. We'd best gather—with Sharkbait, if we can. We must warn Mouse that Ghytteve's tracking her, and get word to her nobleman." Ferret considered. "I saw Kitten begging on the wharves; you fetch her and Mouse. Happen I can find Sharkbait."

They separated. The thief had been in and out of a dozen waterfront taverns before she noticed she was being followed. She pretended she didn't suspect and headed for the Star and Sextant. Instead of entering the common room, she slipped into the shadows of a side alley, to watch her back trail. For several minutes, no one came. Ferret began to fear her tail was aware of her subterfuge; but as deeply ingrained caution held her motionless, her patience was rewarded. Her shadow slipped out of hiding and made for the tavern door. Ferret got a good look: a slender woman with dark eyes, strong features, brown hair braided flat to her skull. She wore good clothes, breeches and tunic; a dangling silver earring hung from her left ear. She moved with a gliding grace that spoke of deadly intent and competence. As her long-fingered hand reached for the latch, a voice spoke out of the darkness at Ferret's side.

"Cyffe." Sharkbait. He moved past Ferret into the light, with only a quick hand-signal: *wait*, to show that he knew she was there.

Surprise sparked in the woman's eyes. "*Antryn.* So. I've wondered what became of you. I didn't expect to find you mixed up in Council House plotting."

"I'm not," he gritted. "And it's '*Sharkbait.*'"

Her eyebrows rose. "So *you're* the one organizing the long-shoremen. *That* I should have guessed. You've been busy. I don't like the scar, by the way. It ages you."

"Why are you here, Cyffe?"

She laughed. It wasn't a pleasant sound. "Why do you think? Don't look so *owlish*; I'm *ferreting* out your secrets."

"*Not* very cleverly," he whispered. His dangerous tone made Ferret shiver. "If I were you, Cyffe, I'd shriek for the Watch; that may be your only chance for getting out of here whole."

Her smile was half snarl. "I don't *like* the Watch." Then, with feline grace, she drew a knife and sprang.

Ferret held her breath. Though nearly silent, they fought ferociously. Knives glinted in the uncertain light, bright flashes like fish in murky waters. Circle, close, scuffle; lunge, strike, leap aside. Ferret heard Sharkbait's hiss of pain and muttered curse. A spatter of dark drops hit the wall by her head as the longshoreman dodged. The woman pursued, close—so close—to Ferret's hiding place. Ferret heard Sharkbait's labored gasps, in sharp contrast to the woman's even breathing. Understanding the risk, but unwilling to stand idly by while Sharkbait fought to his death, Ferret acted. She rushed the woman's unguarded back, hooked a leg around the woman's feet, planted both hands in the small of her back and shoved. It knocked Cyffe off balance. Sharkbait seized the moment. His desperate lunge sent both his opponent and his ally sprawling. As Ferret picked herself up she heard the unmistakable sound of a blade driven home and a faint, gurgling gasp. Sharkbait snatched Ferret's wrist and towed her along as he set off in a shambling run. They were out of the waterfront district and well into the Slums before he stumbled to a walk.

"How badly are you hurt?" the thief asked steadily.

"She marked me twice," he gasped. "Shoulder and thigh. I'll live if the wounds don't fester. I don't suppose you have any clean bandaging in that rathole you call home?"

"Happen you're not fit to climb up there," she retorted. "We'd best go to the Trollop."

"But Arkhyd—"

She snorted rudely as she flashed a clutch of silver. "Arkhyd is practical. Sharkbait, who—was—that woman?"

"Ghytteve," he said shortly. "Get me to the Trollop, and I'll tell you the whole."

The thunderclouds, which had brooded sullenly all afternoon, chose that moment to have their tantrum. The thief and the longshoreman struggled through pelting rain, he leaning heavily on her. They arrived in the kitchen doorway, silhouetted against a flash of lightning. The others were waiting; Arkhyd was minding the taproom. Donkey took in Sharkbait's condition—blood, rain, and pasty face—rekindled the cookfire, set water to heat, and began tearing several clean linen towels into strips.

"What *happened?*" Kitten breathed.

"Knife fight," Ferret responded, as she peeled torn clothing away from Sharkbait's wounds. They were messy but not deep. When the water was hot, she and Donkey ruthlessly washed the cuts and bandaged them. Sharkbait endured it, his jaw clenched and a glint of some appreciative emotion in his amber eyes.

"I promised Ferret an explanation," he said when they were finished. "But perhaps I should wait my turn?"

Ferret nodded. "Donkey, tell us about this afternoon."

With unhurried detail, Donkey repeated the overheard conversation, Squirrel's run in with Elkhar and the conclusions the two boys had drawn. When he had finished, Kitten spoke.

"Happen I've done a bad thing," she confessed, and related her encounter with the Ghytteve man. Sharkbait groaned.

"Well, he knows Owl," the girl defended herself.

"Of course he knows Owl," Sharkbait snapped, "since Ghytteve bought him. And he was looking for Mouse—but he'd never heard of you, Kitten. I don't like it. If Owl trusted Elkhar well enough to mention Mouse, he would have told him about the rest of you." He narrowed his eyes. "I wonder what he's thinking, now."

"Oh Sharkbait, you worry too much," Kitten said. "Why would he be thinking anything at all? He was looking for Mouse, and he didn't find her."

"No," Sharkbait responded, exasperated. "He didn't find Mouse, he found *Kitten*—who knew enough about *his business* to ask which Council House had bought Owl. That's enough to make Elkhar suspicious; and suspicious means dangerous." He looked around at their puzzled faces. "The Council Houses don't have to be certain before they take action; and their suspicious don't have to be correct to make them deadly."

They were silent for a moment, then Donkey asked, "So what happened to you?"

"Cyffe was tailing Ferret," Sharkbait began.

"You knew?" Ferret interrupted.

Sharkbait nodded. "I was shadowing you both."

"Wait, wait, wait!" Squirrel interjected. "Back to the beginning. Who is this Cyffe? Donkey, you said that Elkhar mentioned a Cyffe."

"'Tomorrow I'll send Cyffe to you,'" Donkey quoted. "He wanted Cyffe to know about Mouse's nobleman's movements."

"Cyffe was one of Ycevi Ghytteve's bodyguards," Sharkbait explained. "The Ghytteve bodyguards are almost legendary—a cross between House troops and spies."

"Was?" Squirrel demanded. "Cyffe *was* a bodyguard?"

Sharkbait hunched his uninjured shoulder. "She lost the knife fight, Squirrel." He looked around at their stiff faces. "Haven't I been telling you, all along? This isn't a game and it's dangerous."

Mouse answered for them. "You have, and we believe you. But Sharkbait, yon Elkhar is *already* looking for me; and he's planning some nastiness for Venykhar Ghobhezh-Ykhave. You canna imagine they'd leave us out of their schemes just for our asking."

"More's the pity, no," he responded grimly. "But back to the story: Cyffe came hunting on the waterfront; when I noticed her, she was tailing Ferret. So I tagged along, to keep Ferret out of trouble and to see whether I couldn't find out what scent Cyffe was tracking. Ferret made for the Star and Sextant, by which I guessed she knew she was being followed; there's such a convenient cul-de-sac there. So I slipped ahead of them and confronted Cyffe. We fought, and here we are."

"How do you know Cyffe?" Ferret asked.

Sharkbait shot Ferret a level, inscrutable look. "I used to spend time in the Palace; I had friends, like Venykhar, in House Ykhave; the Ghytteve assigned Cyffe to track my movements."

"You were important enough to follow," Ferret said softly. "Why? And you dinna seem very surprised that the Ghytteve are hunting Mouse and tailing me. Is it common practice, then, for the Council Houses to concern themselves with a pack of Slum-rats—*or are you using us?*"

"*Using* you? Gods! I'm *trying* to protect you. And as for not being surprised…Well, I know the Ghytteve. The pieces of your encounters fit together into a peculiar but coherent whole if one knows Ycevi Ghytteve bought Owl. That woman is *always* scheming; and Elkhar, the chief of her bodyguards, is one suspicious bastard."

Ferret said nothing. After a moment, Kitten broke the silence. "But I don't understand," she said, plaintively. "What possible use would House Ghytteve have for Owl? If it's nobles plotting against the Emperor, why do they need a Slum-rat beggar lad for a page? It doesn't make sense."

"Happen there are pieces missing yet from the puzzle, Kitten," Ferret replied. She fixed Sharkbait with a piercing look. "What do *you* think?"

"That there are too many pieces missing."

"What will House Ghytteve do when they find this Cyffe dead?" Squirrel asked.

"I don't know," the longshoreman answered. "But I'd wager we won't enjoy it. Ycevi is bound to be—displeased. Cyffe has been with her a long time, and was fanatically loyal."

"Would she really have killed you?" Kitten asked.

"If she'd meant to kill me, I'd be dead," Sharkbait said harshly. "She was trying to disable me—to take me prisoner."

"*Why?*" Ferret demanded.

"To question me; because *they* think I'm mixed up in some damned plot against them."

"And are you?" Ferret pursued.

"*No! Gods,* Ferret!" His face was haunted, anguished. "I ran away from Court because I couldn't bear the incessant conniving. I am neither a *khacce* piece, nor a player; so my only recourse was to leave the table. Whatever the Ghytteve think, the only 'plots' I'm involved in are trying to get the longshoremen organized into a guild, helping you find out about poor Owl's fate, and—against my better judgment, I might add—some random snooping on your behalf about 'the Lady's puppy.' But the nobles see intrigue in every shadow; the Ghytteve are adding things up and getting wrong answers." With an effort, he controlled his temper. "This is why I hate dealing with the Council Houses. If you're suspicious enough, *everyone* is a threat. That's why I'm worried about Venykhar. He really is harmless—and guileless. He would never imagine that anyone could think him dangerous. I would be very grateful if one of you would take him a letter from me, warning him that he's drawn House Ghytteve's interest. I'd go, but I'm not exactly fit…"

"To the Palace?" Kitten asked. "How would we get in?"

"Windbringer Temple," Donkey suggested. "Yon Dedemar said he was there every day. He makes music with the priests. Happen they'd deliver a letter."

"Very good," Sharkbait approved. "Mouse, may I have a sheet of your paper?"

Several minutes later, Sharkbait folded his note and handed it to Squirrel. "Give it to one of the priests, and be sure to tell them who it's for."

Squirrel nodded and started toward the door. Donkey picked up a torch. "Light you to the Temple Gate?"

"If you can keep a torch alight in this downpour, my good Donkey," Sharkbait drawled, "I'll be tempted to eat it."

"That hungry?" Donkey said, bland. "Rain stopped a while back. I noticed."

Their eyes met; Donkey's were placid and unrevealing. Approval gradually warmed Sharkbait's expression. "I'm glad you're on my side, Donkey," he admitted. "Be careful, Squirrel—and thank you. Venykhar is far more interested in his flutes than in the ceaseless Council politicking. He's very dear to me—and extremely vulnerable."

* * *

All it took, Squirrel found, was confidence and a Guild to get past the guard at the Temple Gate. The man looked him over, asked his destination, took his money and waved him through. Squirrel didn't notice the second guard—though the man saw him, and the sight made him frown.

The Temple of the Windbringer was a square, marble building, graced by a profusion of columns, like tree trunks supporting the gently pitched roof. At the peak of the Temple roof stood a statue of the Windbringer: a woman in a wind-blown cloak, holding a harp. Squirrel could barely make out the statue as a paler bulge against the heavy sky. The boy mounted the steps to the great double doors, standing open, which led into the main sanctuary.

He gained admittance without trouble. The sanctuary was lit by sconces of candles and several hanging oil lamps. By the fitful light, Squirrel made out the figure of a man, whom he approached.

"Excuse me, Your Holiness," he began.

The man turned. He was young, not very tall; and he had hair of a startling copper color. "What may I do for you?" he asked.

Squirrel produced the note. "Could you please give this letter to Venykhar Ghobhezh-Ykhave? I understand he comes most days to make music, and it is very important that he receive this."

The priest took the note, and with a bow and murmured thanks, Squirrel turned away. As he started across the shadowy hall, he thought he saw movement by the door; but the light was too uncertain. He hurried back to the Temple Gate where Donkey waited.

The Temple Watchman followed Squirrel back to the Gate, and watched the boy join his friend. He narrowed his pale eyes, and stroked his mustache. He thought he knew what was in the letter; and though part of him was well-pleased to have the old flute maker warned of his peril, the sight of the two boys made him wonder, rather uneasily, whether Elkhar might not have some justification for his suspicions, after all.

* * *

Silence fell in the Trollop's kitchen after Donkey and Squirrel left. After a minute or two, Kitten rose. "I'm off, then. You want to walk with me, Mouse?"

Mouse shook her head. "My father's coming for me."

"Ferret?"

But the thief shook her head, too.

With a shrug, Kitten said, "Goodnight, then," and slipped into the rain-washed streets.

"If you want to sleep," Ferret said to Sharkbait, "go ahead. I'll fix things with Arkhyd when he comes in."

"Ferret," he said. "Do you believe me? That I'm not using you?"

It was an odd question; and he asked it simply, without his habitual ironic armor, as though the answer mattered. "Should I?"

"Do you?"

She met his gaze, then, looking for challenge or mockery, but caught instead something vulnerable and pleading. It rocked her and she moved to his side. "Are you all right? Are your wounds hurting you?"

His mask snapped back into place: a faint, mocking smile. "No worse than expected. How solicitous you've become."

"How old are you, Sharkbait?" The question surprised them both. Ferret had never thought to wonder, before, and from his startled, wary response, she realized he was younger—*much* younger—than she had assumed.

"Old enough to resent your asking, child," he retorted, recovering himself, "though not quite in my dotage."

Mouse came over to them. Her intent, wise eyes had watched the entire exchange. "Council House politics steals childhood as surely as poverty," she said softly. "I never knew that."

"Mouse." It was a plea; it made Ferret shiver. But Mouse only smiled enigmatically and brushed her hand down the scarred side of his face.

"For what it's worth," the younger girl told him, "I believe you."

His haunted, amber eyes shifted to Ferret's face, and an unguarded question leapt at her. She nodded, then. "You should rest," she told him.

"Yes," he agreed, and for an instant, naked exhaustion showed in his face. Then, he rolled carefully onto his uninjured side and closed his eyes. Mouse returned to her corner while Ferret stationed herself near the doorway to await Donkey and Squirrel's return.

Chapter Twelve
Threats

The Watch had found the murdered woman's body at dusk. Identification had been complicated by the fact that one of the Watch had pilfered the silver earring which bore House Ghytteve's seal; but even so, it was only a matter of hours before the news of Cyffe's death was broken to the Lady. By midnight, the juicy tidbit was common knowledge, and the Palace rumor mill was grinding out reasons—each less plausible than the last—for the bodyguard's death.

Rhydev Azhere sat at his desk, facing a Watchman. He fingered the silver earring contemplatively. "A heart thrust and no—mmm—*other* wounds?" he mused. "And yet, you found a spatter of blood on the wall? What do you make of it, Falkhan?"

"I've sparred with Cyffe," he said. "She was damned fast. If she cut her assailant, she could as easily have killed him. It doesn't follow."

Rhydev considered. "No doubt she didn't want him dead. But why not—mmm—*summon* the Watch?"

Falkhan's laugh was harsh. "She hated interference. 'Sides, it's more than likely she *started* the fight."

"So: we're looking for someone who is wounded, whom Cyffe Ghytteve would have thought important enough to capture rather than kill. Anything else?"

Falkhan nodded. "I did some asking—on my own. Cyffe had been tailing a Slum-rat girl, reputed to be a thief."

"Guild connections?" Rhydev asked, interest quickening.

"Likely. No one would give me her name, though I flashed enough silver."

"You don't think the *girl* killed Cyffe?"

Falkhan shrugged. "Could be she helped—especially since the assailant was wounded." At the Azhere Council Lord's impatient gesture, the Watchman elaborated. "Cyffe—there aren't many good enough to best her. Even holding your own's more than most could manage. Her assailant was cut; wounds slow you down. And the heart-thrust; that's risky. Cyffe knew half a dozen lethal counters to that move. Her assailant would almost have to know she didn't mean to kill him, or else have her so badly off balance that he didn't fear her counter-strike."

"Or both," Rhydev mused.

"Aye."

The Azhere Council Lord sifted information. His face gave nothing away; he raised his eyes to the Watchman's. "Falkhan, catch me a thief. Ghorran will help."

The man looked doubtful. "The Guild won't like it."

"I'm more concerned with Ghytteve. I want that girl alive. I want to know who's moving against House Ghytteve, why, when, and how; and I want to know yesterday. Find the girl, Falkhan. Bribe the Guild if you have to; use my hold over Ybhanne, if nothing else will serve. Understand? *I want that girl!*"

"I understand, my lord. I'll find her."

Owl woke. The nightmare left him gasping; he smothered his tortured breathing in his pillow. This was one dream he *did not* want to explain to Myncerre. Another wave of terror and nausea pounded over him. Sharkbait, Ferret, Cyffe; an alley; knives; death. It *couldn't* be true—but what if it were? He fought his rebellious body. He hadn't liked Cyffe (who could have liked the cold, sarcastic woman?), but memory of Sharkbait's heart thrust, and Ferret—*Ferret!*—businesslike and deadly, turned his world inside out. Nausea surged back, stronger. He clutched both hands over his mouth, retched, then swallowed determinedly. No good. He rolled out of bed heading for the garderobe across the hall. As he entered the hallway, hands closed on his shoulders.

"Owl? *Owl!*"

Myncerre. He turned his head away before he spewed. She held him through the wracking heaves, wiped his face with her handkerchief.

"Oh, poor Owl."

The pity broke tears out of his fear and queasiness. He let himself cry; it was easier than talking. With the corner of his mind given to noticing things, he heard rapid footsteps, then voices. Elkhar.

"The Lady said no more drugs," the bodyguard accused.

"I swear there was nothing in his food but spices."

"Who has been alone with him, today?"

"Me," the steward replied. "And Cithanekh; but the puppy wouldn't poison him."

Elkhar drew Owl out of the shelter of Myncerre's arms and studied him. "What did you take, and who gave it to you?"

"Nothing. No one. I'm just *sick*." He tried to turn away, but the man held him firmly. "Leave me alone."

Elkhar's grip tightened savagely. Owl hissed in pain and shock. "Tell me what you know about Mouse," the man gritted out.

Real confusion clouded his face. "Mouse?" he repeated; his mind had been on Ferret, on Sharkbait. Seeing Elkhar's doubt, Owl clung to bafflement.

"Or Venykhar Ghobhezh-Ykhave?"

"The Council Lord for House Ykhave," he responded promptly.

Owl blanched as Elkhar's grasp tightened again. Myncerre placed a restraining hand on the bodyguard's shoulder. "I've been coaching him on the Council Houses, Elkhar," she said.

Elkhar glared at Owl but eased his hold to the point where it was no longer painful. Then, with a lift of his chin and hint of a sardonic smile, he looked over Owl's shoulder and said, as if in greeting, "Cithanekh."

With an irrepressible spurt of hope, Owl looked over his shoulder. There was no one there. As he turned back to Elkhar, the bodyguard released him.

"Send him back to bed," Elkhar told Myncerre. "I'll get someone to clean up the mess."

"Do you need anything?" the steward asked as she tucked the covers in around Owl. "A drink of water?" At his nod, she went out; when she returned with the glass, Owl's eyes were closed. She set the cup down and tiptoed out. Elkhar and the Lady were both in the hall. Myncerre eased the door closed behind her.

"Well?" Lady Ycevi demanded.

"He's asleep. It couldn't have been poison; there was no opportunity." She shrugged. "He isn't used to rich foods."

Ycevi turned to Elkhar. "And are you satisfied that he's free from the taint of association?"

Elkhar shrugged. "Judging from his reaction to your puppy's name, he couldn't dissemble well enough to fool me, if he really had connections to this mysterious Mouse. Of course, that means some of our other information is incorrect, for Anthagh reported that Venykhar Ghobhezh-Ykhave said the boy was 'Mouse's little friend.' Someone is lying—or mistaken."

Inside his room, Owl knelt beside the door, his ear pressed to the keyhole. What *could* they think Mouse was up to?

"Perhaps," the Lady mused, "Owl knows this 'Mouse' by some other name."

"That's possible," Elkhar agreed. "And I suppose it is also possible that he is not aware of the whole of this Mouse's scheme. It bears watching, though for the moment, I am inclined to think the boy is no immediate threat."

"Very well," Ycevi said. "But who killed Cyffe—and *why?* What was she *doing* on the waterfront?"

"I'd sent her seeking Mouse. She must have uncovered some trail, some connection. Clearly she found something more—*interesting*—than what I found in that child, Kitten."

"Kitten, Mouse, Owl," Ycevi mused. "It reeks of collusion."

"But children are like that," Myncerre said. "They make up stories and play games. Lady, it could all be coincidence."

"Except," said Elkhar, "that Owl doesn't *know* Mouse."

"In any case, I don't believe in coincidence," the Lady snapped. "Not where there's more than one Council House gathered. Elkhar, I want answers, and I don't much care how you get them. Try to be discreet—but if it comes to killing, I'll back you."

Some instinct warned Owl; he scampered across a mile of floor, dove under the covers, turned his back to the door and forced his breathing to slow. His ears, strained to aching, caught the click of the latch; quiet footsteps approached, a swish of silk, the breath of perfume: the Lady. He was sure she would

hear his thundering heart. He rolled over, with a little, murmured groan. The light from her oil lamp scorched across his
eyelids; he felt their betraying flutter, so with another sleepy
moan, he opened his eyes.

The lamplight cast Ycevi Ghytteve's face in odd shadows,
emphasized different planes than the kinder light of day. She
looked so sinister, so implacable, that Owl couldn't stifle a
whimper of alarm.

"Yes," she whispered. "You *should* fear me, boy. I hold
your life in my hands, and ever shall. Yet, there's room for
comfort, even happiness, if you serve me well. But if you
betray me, then—" the menace in her voice sent fear writhing
down his spine—"then I shall make you wish you had never
been born."

Owl found his voice; it shook with tears. "I don't even
know what you want me to *do*. How can I serve you well?"

A smile, more frightening even than her grimness, stretched
her mouth. "You will see. In time, you will see." Then, she
left him, closing him in darkness.

Against the pressing blackness, he saw a vision, vivid as
day: Kitten, eyes dilated with terror, looking back over her
shoulder as she fled through deserted, fog-shrouded alleys of
the waterfront district.

"No," he breathed. "Oh, no." Fear overwhelmed him. Visions pelted him, as wild and terrifying as the *haceth* nightmares. The images were hazy, indistinct, as though he watched
through a silvery scrim. He saw burning buildings; an angry
mob on the waterfront; Elkhar, his expression feral and trium-
phant; Arre, unconscious. *Arre!* He seized on that, remembered what she had said about finding the peaceful place, the
haven from his visions. He slowed his breathing, concentrating on the memory of music. The frantic rush of visions
slowed; he felt a hint of the peace of the haven place and a
rush of surprise. He didn't let the startlement shake him; instead, he used the peace like an eyelid for his inner vision. He
drew it closed, and in the vision-free stillness, he slept.

On the other side of the Palace, Arre came to herself with a
shake of her head. That was decidedly odd; someone had

called her name, mind to mind. Owl, she thought. But then, instead of talking to her, he had wrapped his mind—and hers, for a moment—in stillness. He hadn't felt desperately frightened, nor had she sensed *haceth* driving his visions; but Owl shouldn't be able to do anything so controlled—not without training. She *had* described what to do if they dosed him with *haceth* again, and it *was* the basis for a controlling trance; but she remembered how long it had taken her to learn the skill, even with constant coaching. If Owl was picking it up on his own, he must be fantastically talented. (Or someone had worked with him, though that seemed terribly unlikely.)

She shook her head again. She wanted to talk to the boy—needed to, in fact; but she didn't know how to manage it. She'd only seen Owl, once or twice, pacing solemnly behind the Ghytteve steward—and talking to him under those circumstances would only put him at risk. With a sigh, she picked up her lute and began to play.

Chapter Thirteen
Secrets

There were relatively few courtiers in the garden, that morning, as Arre made her way to the stone fountain where Venykhar Ghobhezh-Ykhave waited. She and the old flute-maker were going to the Windbringer Temple together, to make music with Kerigden.

As they left the garden, Arre noticed that the courtiers buzzed with some interesting gossip—so much so that they neglected their usual game of be-rude-to-the-foreigner. She speculated about what the news might be, but she couldn't guess; it was possible, she thought with jaded hope, they might simply have tired of making sport of her.

The King's City was full of people dressed in holiday finery; Ythykh-Fair was upon them. Arre and Venykhar made their way through the press to the haven of the Windbringer Temple. When they reached their destination, they were shown to one of the inner chapels, where Kerigden, the High Priest of the Windbringer, played quietly upon a small harp.

He was not a large man, but he was imposing nonetheless, with his fire bright hair, clear green eyes and his undeniable presence. Even in repose, his features were vivid, and his smile of greeting lit his face.

"Arre. Ven. Good morning." He reached into a fold of his robe and produced a folded piece of paper. "I have a note for you, Ven."

"What does it say?" the Ykhave Council Lord asked as he reached for it.

The priest smiled and gestured them to stools. "I didn't read it. Sit."

"It's not even sealed," Arre observed, laughing. "No wonder the Council Houses don't know what to make of you, Kerigden. What does it say, Ven?"

But Venykhar didn't reply. Instead, frowning, he pushed the note into Arre's hand.

As Arre's fingers touched the paper, her inward vision flared warning. She held the note gingerly, her eyes closed, while her mind pursued the images: a weathered signboard, crudely painted, with a smirking woman in a reddish gown; a boy with a still, placid face, but watchful brown eyes—briefly overlaid by the patient, gray muzzle and long ears of a donkey; the thief, Ferret, and a man, his scarred face mostly in shadow; one of the Ghytteve bodyguards, unmistakably dead. As the storm of visions subsided, she opened her eyes, remembered to breathe, and read the note. 'Please tell Venykhar Ghobhezh-Ykhave that he has earned the enmity of Ghytteve. They are at least watching, and possibly planning him harm.' It was signed with a symbol—neither a name, nor an initial—which was meaningless to Arre.

"Do you know who this is from?" she asked him.

"Yes."

"Do you know what it is about?" she probed, with an edge of exasperation.

"It must be because of Owl. The Ghytteve have no doubt heard that I was interested in the boy, and they are seeing counterplots in the shadows."

"Owl?" Kerigden asked; and between them, Arre and Venykhar told him what they knew about the former beggar, and his entrapment in Ycevi Ghytteve's schemes.

"Elkhar Ghytteve is the most intensely suspicious individual I have ever met," the High Priest mused. "But Ven, wanting to assassinate you for showing an interest in a slave seems extreme, even for him. What else could be contributing to the situation?"

"One of the Ghytteve bodyguards—Cyffe—is dead," Arre said in an almost toneless voice; her eyes grew unfocused as her inner sight was again assaulted by visions: the Prime Minister and his nephew, Rhydev Azhere, deep in conversation; Owl, Ferret and a third girl sitting on the Waiting Wall at the Temple Gate; Elkhar Ghytteve gripping the same girl by the wrists; a thin fingered hand with a green-gemmed ring resting on Owl's shoulder; the unknown girl again—overlaid briefly by a kitten's face.

She surfaced from her visions abruptly, a piece of the puzzle snapping into place. "It's the pattern which has Elkhar worried," she said, "as well as Cyffe's death. Owl; Mouse; Ferret. He doesn't like it."

"Mouse and Ferret?" Kerigden asked.

"Mouse is the little artist," Venykhar said. "I told you about her; Ferret's another friend, I think."

Arre nodded. "That's right. She's older than the other two, and she's a thief. She'd be enough to make Elkhar nervous, if he knows about her; and she's involved, somehow. I've dreamed of her. Ven," she added gently, "don't you have some pressing business in Khavenaffe? I'd hate to see you come to harm."

The old lord raised his eyebrows. "And are you going back to Kalledann? This isn't really your quarrel, after all."

She shook her head. "Actually, after we've finished here, I'm planning to go into the Slums. I'm looking for a tavern."

"There are taverns in better parts of the city," Venykhar pointed out.

"Oh, I know," Arre said easily. "I'm looking for a particular one." She smiled apologetically. "I'll tell you more when I've answered some of my own questions. Shall we play?"

The Temple Gate was more crowded than Arre's most pessimistic expectation. With merrymakers jammed like grapes in a winepress, it took skill and tact to get through. As Arre neared the low wall which bordered the Slums, she noticed a boy ahead of her. She watched with admiration as he weaseled neatly between a stout merchant and his equally stout wife. The boy darted an engaging smile at the couple as he slipped by.

"Lad!" Arre called; he looked like he'd know the Slums. As he glanced over his shoulder, she waved to him. He waited for her to catch him up. His bright eyes, and abrupt, quick movements made her think of a small woodland creature.

"I wonder whether you might be able to guide me to a particular tavern? I can't remember what it's called, but its sign has a smiling woman in a red dress." He caught the coin she flipped him with practiced ease.

"The Trollop's Smile," he said as he eyed her dubiously. "It's in the Slums. It's not exactly safe, lady."

She spun another coin toward him. "I'm not as feeble as I look," she told him dryly.

His expression hinted at mischief. "I'm *supposed* to be running an errand, but I might take a detour, *if...*"

She tossed a third coin to him; a Half-Noble. "Of course I'll pay for your inconvenience."

He nodded. "Come on."

Even in the Slums, where the crowds weren't as thick, Arre had to work to keep up; finally, he paused beneath the swinging signboard of her vision. She tossed him another coin and he hurried away.

Arre didn't go in, right away. The sign was right, but the door was somehow wrong. After a moment, she went looking for the kitchen entrance, which she found off the alleyway that ran along the far side of the building. The kitchen door was open. Arre peered in cautiously. It was a long, shadowy room; activity was centered at the front end, near the hearth. A graying man—judging by the leather apron stretched over his paunch, the tapster or the tavern master—inspected a cauldron of rank fish stew; a boy sliced bread and cheese at a plodding pace, setting the pieces on wooden trenchers. It was the boy from her visions. The man gave a final stir to the stew, then, with a muffled oath, bustled through the door into the taproom in response to several raised voices. As he went out, Arre came into the kitchen.

"Excuse me. I'm looking for Ferret or Mouse," she told the boy.

The boy ceased his methodical slicing to peer around the dim kitchen with painstaking thoroughness. "Not here."

"Are they apt to come in later?"

He repeated the performance, ending with a baffled stare in Arre's direction. "Might."

"May I wait here for them?" she asked pleasantly. "It's quite important."

The boy gestured toward the taproom. "Wait in there."

"I'd rather wait here, " she said, wondering how to put the boy at ease. He *couldn't* be as stupid as he acted; though there was no hint of it in his expression, now, she remembered his watchful intelligence from her vision. Before she could try another tack, the tavern master came in from the taproom.

"Thantor! I *need* that bread." Noticing Arre, he demanded crossly, "What're you doing here, besides distracting my nephew?"

Something about the name jolted Arre; she looked sharply at the tavern master and said, "What did you call him?"

"Thantor," he snapped. "It's his *name*. I dinna approve of the way that Ferret mocks him: Donkey, indeed. And now, happen you'll answer me: what are you doing in my kitchen?"

Arre forced herself to answer over her rising excitement. "I'm looking for Ferret—or Mouse."

The tavern master made a sour face. "On *Ythykh-Fair?* They'll be working, both of them, until after nightfall. Now, if you'd like ale or food, come into the taproom. Else, go away. This is a tavern kitchen, not a boarding house, or a meeting place!" He seized the trays of bread and cheese. When Arre didn't move, he huffed in exasperation. "Go on; away with you! Drop by this evening, but right now, Thantor needs his wits undivided." Then, he was gone.

Arre remained motionless as, with a feeling akin to a chord suddenly centering into tune, a series of disparate pieces connected. "*Donkey*; you're Donkey. Ferret. Mouse. Donkey. Owl," she said softly. "You're all part of it."

Arre had barely finished speaking when she was grabbed from behind by someone who'd learned to fight early and dirty. One arm was pinned painfully behind her, while a knife rested against her throat. "What are you?" a man's voice grated. "Some Ghytteve cur?"

"No! My name is Arre; I'm from Kalledann. Hasn't Ferret spoken of me?"

"No," he gritted, without slackening his grip. "Why should she? And what do you know of the others?"

Arre swallowed convulsively, felt the blade cold against her throat. "Ferret—I met Ferret on the waterfront. I've seen Owl at the Palace; and Venykhar spoke of Mouse."

Sharkbait sheathed his knife and released the woman. She turned to look at him; as their eyes clashed, recognition sparked in both their faces. Sharkbait spoke first. "The Emperor's foreign witch."

"Who are you?"

His smile was unpleasant. "I'm Sharkbait."

"You're *Anzhibhar!* The resemblance—"

"*No!*"

"Yes! Which collateral branch? Not Ghytteve—Azhere?"

"No! I'm *just Sharkbait!*"

Arre's eyes unfocused for an instant as an image overran the dim kitchen scene: the white rose badge of House Ykhave. She sent her bardic memory coursing along family trees. Her voice was almost singsong. "Zhanece Anzhibar married Khanyrr Ykhave and bore a son, Anzhyran who married—"

Sharkbait caught Arre's wrist and twisted until she caught her breath in pain. "No more—or I break it. Hear me: *I want no part of my past.*" With his free hand, he traced the scar on his face. "*None.* And if I have to kill to keep my secret, I will. I *refuse* to be a piece on the Council Houses' *khacce* table. Do you understand?"

Arre nodded; he released her wrist, which she hugged to her stomach, fighting nausea. "You're the one organizing the dock workers," she remarked after a moment. It was not a question, but Sharkbait nodded.

"I'd kill to keep that secret, too," he warned.

"You've made that point," Arre said waspishly. "But who *are* the game pieces? And where does Owl fit?"

Sharkbait's eyes glinted. "Does the name Cithanekh mean anything to you?"

Arre nodded slowly. "Antelle Anzhibhar—Ythkheff's sister—married Cithekh Ghytteve. They had several children; one was named Cithanekh."

"What an amazing memory," Sharkbait said, sardonic.

"Indeed. Courtesy of the Kellande School. And Owl?"

"Such tenacity: I admire that. Ycevi Ghytteve bought Owl for ten Royals; she must have a use for him."

"She said he was irresistible, and that the poor bastard didn't stand a chance," Arre murmured. "What do you know about Cithanekh?"

"I saw him in an tavern with Rhydev Azhere."

"Rhydev *Azhere?* Sharkbait, I don't like this."

Sharkbait hunched one shoulder. "'When you drink with nobles,'" he quoted an adage, "'watch for poison.'"

"Or 'Intrigue makes few friends, but many bedfellows.'"

Sharkbait laughed. "I've never heard that one; where did you get it?"

Arre smiled faintly. "I made it up." Then, she noticed the spreading, dark blotch on his shirt. "Good God, you're bleeding." As she made to look more closely, he twisted out of reach. "I'm only trying to *help.*"

"Donkey can tend me. You had better go; if Arkhyd comes back and you're still here, there really will be trouble."

Arre hesitated, but an urgent hiss of warning from the boy started her toward the door. "I'll be back—as soon as I may," Arre promised; she slipped outside just as the tavern master came back into the kitchen with a tray of soiled dishes.

Chapter Fourteen
Ythykh-Fair

The Ythykh-Fair crowds were a pickpocket's dream. Ferret eeled through shoals of folk, helping herself to the contents of other people's purses. Mouse and her parents were doing a brisk trade in nosegays and poseys, but mindful of the risk, Ferret didn't stop to chat. Once, from a distance, she caught a glimpse of Squirrel, darting through the crush like a minnow through weeds.

Toward noontime, Ferret made her escape. She bought a small round of cheese, a sausage and a loaf of bread to share with Kitten before she set off for her lair.

Ferret found Kitten asleep. With a smile, the thief waved the spicy sausage under the beggar's nose. Kitten woke promptly.

"Food! Oh Ferret, bless you!"

They shared the meal, then spent a quiet afternoon, napping and chatting. Toward dusk, Ferret got her day's take ready to settle with Khyzhan.

"Off to the Cur?" Kitten asked. At the thief's nod, she looked wistful. "May I come along?"

"Why not meet me at the Trollop? I'll go there after."

"I *know* you think the trade at the Cur too rough for me; I'll wait outside, but canna we walk together?" Kitten pleaded.

Ferret met the younger girl's hopeful eyes. To get to the Trollop, Kitten would pass a scant alley's length from the Cur. She acquiesced, and the two of them scrambled down to the streets.

There was still heavy foot traffic. Revelers would celebrate Ythykh-Fair until well after midnight; the ale houses and taverns would do a roaring trade, this evening. Secretly, Ferret dreaded the Cur. It was bad enough when it wasn't crammed with folk who had begun drinking early in the day. She left Kitten in the alley and slipped inside.

Kitten picked an inconspicuous place to wait, nestled in the doorway of a dilapidated tenement. As she waited for Ferret she idly noted the others who came and went at the Cur. Ferret was right: the trade was rough. Bravos from several rival factions of the Thieves' Guild; tough, foreign sailors, boldly carrying steel; pimps with their harlots—cold-eyed, all; a couple from the Watch—not uniformed, but unmistakable in their swaggering superiority; and there—that one: flash, slumming. Kitten's interest caught. One Watchman disappeared within, but the second, with the man she had marked as gentry on the prowl, melted into the shadows by the doorway. Odd. She strained her ears for their conversation, but either they were silent, or the background growl from the Cur covered them.

A knot of carousers roiled into the street, leaning against one another and singing raucously. Kitten nearly choked on the smell of sour ale as they passed her hiding place. Ferret came out—small, quiet, and watchful—behind them.

What happened next froze time. Kitten felt like a beetle in amber as the two men emerged from their hiding places and pounced. Ferret struggled uselessly. One of the men covered her mouth and nose with a wad of cloth and Ferret went limp. Then, the third man slipped out of the Cur. He bundled Ferret into a shabby cloak and slung her over his shoulder. Silently, they moved off into the evening mist.

Time unfroze; Kitten flitted after them. No use shouting for the Watch—even if the Watch *cared* about the Slums, Kitten would stake her ears that two of the three men *were* Watch. But it wasn't an arrest; it *couldn't* be. There had been no outcry of 'thief'—nor was there likely to be such, so deep in the Guild's territory. Kitten followed, easing closer as she tried to glean crumbs of their conversation.

The men lugged Ferret through the Slums to the waterfront district. As they left the Slums behind, wisps of evening fog, tangy with salt, rolled up from the wharves. The wider streets made fewer comfortable shadows in which Kitten could lurk; yet she pressed ever closer. What were they *saying?*

Suddenly, they stopped. "This is it," the one Kitten thought was gentry said. "In the name of all the gods, what keeps that *chair?*"

As if his words had summoned it, a curtained litter, carried by four brawny bearers, turned a corner and stopped before them. The flash mark climbed in and the Watchman handed him his burden.

"Meet us at the Palace. Azhere will want a complete report from each of you," the one in the litter said. "And stay out of the Slums; Khyzhan's apt to move against Ybhanne for this." He closed the curtains and the litter moved off.

Kitten, stunned by the implications, stood still a moment too long. One of the men nudged the other; they'd seen her. Swallowing a terrified squeak, Kitten fled for the twisting alleys of her home turf; if she could only make it, surely the promise of Guild infighting would warn the Watch off.

The men pounded after her, but fear lent her wings. She reached the borders of the Slum and vanished into its unsavory maze. The two men stopped, exchanged troubled and angry looks.

"Gods curse it, Falkhan. Ghorran will have our hides."

"I got a good look at her. I've seen the brat; begs in the Temple Gate. If Azhere wants her, I'll get her."

"You don't think we should go after her now?"

Falkhan shook his head. "I told Ghorran this; didn't tell you. The thief brat we nabbed—Ferret. She's a Journeyman: one of Khyzhan's. There'll be blood in the streets before morning."

The first man's jaw dropped. "Holy gods," he breathed, then turned brisk. "Let's get out of here."

Kitten reached the Trollop's kitchen pale as paste and utterly winded. Only Sharkbait was there, dozing in the shadows like a hibernating bear. He snapped alert at the sight of her.

"Get your breath, Kitten, and tell me from the beginning."

"It's Ferret," she gasped. "She went—to the Cur; I waited—outside. Three men—nabbed her. Two Watch, off duty; one flash. I followed them—overheard—the flash one said, 'Meet us at the Palace. Azhere—will want a full report.' And he told them to—stay out of the Slums. He said, 'Khyzhan's apt to move—against Ybhanne for this.'"

"*Gods,*" Sharkbait whispered.

"And Sharkbait," Kitten ended, despairing. "*They saw me.*"

Sharkbait's face had gone gray. "Are you sure they said Azhere, Kitten?"

She nodded.

"And would you recognize them if you saw them again?"

She nodded again.

"Think they'd recognize you?"

"The flash fellow didn't see me; but the other two got a good look," she replied, grim.

Sharkbait cradled his face in his hands. "So." His voice was muffled. "Against all custom and Guild law, Ybhanne betrays one of Khyzhan's Journeymen to House Azhere. This, after a *Ghytteve* cur is killed in the waterfront district. Of course, Cyffe had been tailing Ferret. Someone noticed that; Azhere, no doubt." Sharkbait raised his head: his eyes were bleak. "And it's such a short step from there to me." He sighed. "Mere grist for the Council Houses' mill." He fell silent. Kitten watched him anxiously; he caught her at it and managed a strained smile. "Ferret's clever, but she's no match for Rhydev Azhere. If I had any sense I'd run. It seems very clear: run, or be ground up. But you know, Kitten," he added, his tone edged with self-mockery, "I seem to have lost my survival instinct; I'm not running. It's a form of madness—it must be." He took a step toward the door, shaking his head. "I *should* flee, but do you know what I plan to do instead?"

She shook her head, her eyes wide.

"While you stay here—and *you will stay here*—I shall walk over to the Beaten Cur and start a Guild war."

"Sharkbait, why?"

"Why? Two reasons." He held up one long finger. "First: because I know I haven't any chance at all of killing Ybhanne myself; and—" another finger joined the first—"second: because a really vicious Guild war—as this promises to be—will keep the Watch and other strangers out of the Slums for a while. We may need some breathing room. Wait here; I'll be back." Then, he was gone.

Owl spent the most miserable Ythykh-Fair he could remember shut in the library under the vigilant supervision of

Myncerre, Elkhar and the other bodyguards. He tried to amuse himself by practicing his reading, but it wasn't much fun without someone to help him when he got stuck. Even the garden was empty of interest, for the courtiers had abandoned it to their servants. A patio had been swept for dancing, and candles in little colored glass globes were being set along all the walks and fountains. Clearly, there would be a wonderful celebration this evening—and just as clearly, Owl thought, glum, he wasn't invited. No one had even brought him a nosegay; he had never passed Ythykh-tide without a posey—gift of Mouse or her mother.

A painful wash of homesickness swept over him. He held his breath, blinking hard, while he waited for it to pass. It wasn't *safe* to think of Mouse, or Ferret, or any of his friends. With sudden, anxious worry, he wondered *why* Elkhar and the Lady were looking for Mouse—and whether Sharkbait and Ferret had really killed Cyffe. Arre had said not everything he dreamed was real; but surely his nightmare was too unexpected, too far-fetched, to have come from some secret, inner fear of his own.

He made himself turn the page of the heavy volume open in front of him. He knew of the spyholes and listening places which riddled the Palace; Cithanekh had pointed one out to him in warning. It was important, Owl had discovered, to act normally—apparently, boredom was acceptable, probably expected; but tears would bring Myncerre, and an angry tantrum would summon one of the bodyguards. With a heavy sigh, Owl closed the book and put it away; then, he curled up on the sofa. Perhaps a nap would make the time pass more swiftly.

He woke, some time later, as the door opened. He smiled welcome: Cithanekh. The young lord closed the door, then tossed something to Owl.

"Catch."

Owl's beggar reflexes plucked the posey out of the air. He buried his nose in the flowers to hide his sudden prickle of tears. Cithanekh ruffled his hair.

"I asked Ycevi if I could take you down to the Temple Gate this afternoon, but she said no. So I did the best I could."

He produced a sticky bun, carefully wrapped in oiled paper, a reed pipe festooned with braided ribbons, and a round package, wrapped in a piece of green silk and tied with a bow.

"Thanks," Owl said, his voice a little tight. "I was feeling sorry for myself."

His lips twitched. "I wonder how I knew you would be."

Owl scrabbled open the paper on the sticky bun and broke it in half. "Share with me?" he invited. "Or are you already full?"

The young lord took the proffered bun. "A fair isn't much fun if you're on your own."

"Don't you have friends among the other lords?"

Cithanekh's expression hardened, though he managed to keep his tone light, slightly mocking. "No. My acquaintance is neatly divided into those who think I will make a useful tool to their hands, and those who would like to be a useful tool in mine."

"Which am I?" Owl asked, troubled.

Cithanekh brushed a strand of hair off Owl's forehead. "You," he said at length, "are in a category all your own."

"Is that why they keep me locked in the library?" Owl asked dryly.

Cithanekh's unguarded laughter lit his face. "Must be," he agreed. "Now, won't you open the package?"

Owl did. Nestled in the shimmery green folds was a bracelet: ivory, carved very cleverly into a pattern of birds and grape vines. The birds were of two kinds, hawk and owl. The owls' eyes were chips of topaz, the hawks', jet; and nestled under the leaves were clusters of amethyst grapes.

"I've never seen anything so beautiful," Owl breathed.

"Two things: let me show you." Cithanekh's long fingers found the hidden catch, and the bracelet sprang open on a nearly invisible hinge. "This is one you can put on and take off at will, Owl; and then, there's this. First hawk, third owl," he said as he pressed them gently. With a faint click, a panel on the inside of the bracelet slid aside, revealing a narrow chamber. "It was so clever, and so beautifully made, I couldn't resist it; but I don't really know what you could use it for." He demonstrated how to close the compartment, then handed the bracelet back to Owl, who put it round his right wrist and pushed it up his arm so that it was hidden by his sleeve.

"I could hide poison," he whispered, fierce, "for Ycevi."

"You mustn't jest about that," Cithanekh warned. "It's damned tempting, but it's been tried—and never with satisfactory results."

"I wasn't jesting—I was *wishing*; I'll stop if it worries you. No one has ever given me a beautiful thing before. Thank you." His hand felt the hard shape of the bracelet through the fabric of his sleeve. "Will they really let me keep it?"

"If they don't," he responded, his brilliant eyes narrowing, "they'll regret it."

Cithanekh's threatening mien reminded Owl uncomfortably of Lady Ycevi. He shivered and looked for something to take his mind off the memory. "Show me how to play the pipe?" he asked, holding it out to the man.

Cithanekh demonstrated where the fingers went, and played a twittering tune. When Owl tried, it shrilled like a mad thing. He laughed. "It doesn't like me!"

"You're blowing too hard. Pretend you're whispering."

After some experimentation, Owl managed to coax a passable tone from the thing; he put it away, tucking it behind a row of heavy books, promising to practice when he was alone. "I'll drive them all crazy: Myncerre and Elkhar and all the rest who guard me—and it will serve them right."

As he turned away from the bookcase, he felt a swooping behind his eyes. The room disappeared. His vision was filled, suddenly, with the hot, red glow of coals: a brazier; and beside it, rows of wooden-handled silver implements. Elegantly manicured hands arranged the implements over the hot coals. A sense of menace grew in Owl like the need to scream. The winking of a sapphire ring tugged at Owl's memory. Then, the focus of his vision widened. It was Rhydev Azhere who sat before the brazier, intent upon the heating implements. As Owl watched, the Council Lord selected one and approached his victim...

"No," Owl whimpered, shaking his head from side to side as though physically to dislodge the vision. The victim would not come into focus: only a bared, thin arm, strapped to a chair. The glowing tip of the implement approached, appallingly; then it kissed the skin. "NO!" Owl cried and his vision went fuzzy.

Suddenly, the boy felt hands on his shoulders. Cithanekh was shaking him. "Owl?"

Owl lowered his hands and opened his eyes.

"Owl!" Cithanekh's worried face was inches from his own.

"Oh, gods," Owl whispered, white.

"*What?* Owl, are you all right? What frightened you?" He breathed the last three words.

"I don't dare tell you. What if they're listening?" Owl replied in a careful, dismayed whisper.

Cithanekh pulled him into his arms. "We'll tell them you're homesick," he murmured against Owl's ear. "Pretend to cry."

It was no pretense. Owl was so afraid and unnerved that when he loosed his control, weeping overwhelmed him. Cithanekh held him, let him cry. The door opened to admit Myncerre.

"Poor Owl," she said softly. "Is he sick again?"

"Homesick," Cithanekh said; then suspicion narrowed his eyes. "Sick *again*. What do you mean?"

"He was ill during the night," the steward explained. "He's not used to such rich food."

"*Haceth*. Oh, *gods*." His voice was heavy with pain. Suddenly it rose to an angry cry. "That *bitch!*"

"Cithanekh." Myncerre was urgent. "It's not *haceth*." She laid an open palm over her heart. "Blood and honor, not *haceth*."

Owl trembled in his arms. Cithanekh gentled him, pressed his cheek against the boy's hair. His gaze met Myncerre's, his face chill with bleak understanding. "She means to use him to control me," he stated. For a tense, watchful instant, neither of them moved. Then the young lord closed his anguished eyes and his shoulders slouched in defeat. "And it will work."

Owl pulled away enough to look into Cithanekh's face. "You mustn't *let* it work," he said, his voice rough with tears, but his expression determined. "She can't kill me; she'd lose her hold entirely. And I'm used to beatings."

"She's ruthless. If beatings don't serve, she'll use torture: hot irons and broken bones."

"You do what you must," Owl said steadily, "and I will bear whatever I must."

Cithanekh took Owl's face in his long hands and searched the boy's eyes. "And when she comes to me and says, 'You will do as I say, or I will pluck out his eyes,' what shall I do?"

"Do what is right, and I will bear what I must. I don't want to be blind, but still less do I want to be the knife at your throat."

"Oh, brave," Cithanekh murmured. "You shame me."

"I don't mean to *shame* you," Owl said, fierce. "I mean to give you hope."

As she listened, Myncerre's eyes, bright as jewels in the mask of her face, filled with tears. She turned away, so that neither of them would notice. Her movement drew Cithanekh's attention. "The Lady's faithful ears," he commented in a tone which flayed feelings. "What will you make of this, in your report?"

Almost against her will, she jerked back to face him. Tears streaked her cheeks; she saw his surprise. "I will answer what I am asked," she said, bland as milk, "as I must." Then, she stalked out, locking the door behind her.

In the silence the steward left, Owl murmured, "Why must she control you?"

Cithanekh looked unutterably weary, sad and bitter. "She means to make me Emperor, and she intends to hold the leash."

Doubt clutched his stomach with chill talons. "You don't want it, do you?" he managed.

"*Want* it?" Cithanekh demanded, with passionate scorn. "Gods, Owl, I'd rather die cleanly." The fire faded from his face, leaving misery. "I *need* to talk with you where we won't be overheard," he added in an undertone.

Owl nodded solemnly. For a moment, both were silent, then Owl managed a small, hopeful smile. "Will you help me with my reading?" he asked in a normal tone. "I tried on my own, earlier, but it's hard without a teacher."

Cithanekh fetched down a book. "Tomorrow," he said reflectively, "I'll bring writing tools with me. For one thing, it's easier to practice writing on your own—and it's a useful skill."

Chapter Fifteen
Interrogation

Ferret swam back to awareness through swells of aching dizziness. The light in the room pulsed in time to her head's throbbing. She focused on a candle flame and tried to adjust to the earth's slow spin. Her stomach rebelled with a wrenching heave. A hand steadied her head, another shoved a basin under her mouth.

"Spare the carpet," an ironic voice suggested.

When she was done, he wiped her face with a square of linen. As Ferret managed to sit up, she fixed the man with an accusing glare. He was handsome, his dark hair silvered at the temples; a neat, pointed beard accented clean features. And she recognized him: the man who had been in the Replete Feline with the Lady's puppy. She reached for his name; her mind felt thick; the spark failed to catch. She wondered if he remembered their brief, chance encounter. A score of questions assailed her but she bit them back. Let *him* ask, since he'd gone to this trouble.

He arched an elegant eyebrow, mocking, as though he read her resolve. "So. You're Ferret—the youngest Journeyman in the Thieves' Guild. Hardly what I'd expected, given your—mmm—*reputation*; but I suppose anyone would appear to disadvantage, vomiting over a basin."

"Reputation? I daresay it's naught but a pack of lies—to drive your Watch's price up."

"What makes you say they're Watch?" the elegant man asked, his calm slightly flapped.

"Any Slum-rat can smell the Watch thirty yards off." She raked him with scornful eyes, noting the heavy gold chain of office round his neck. She made out the device on the medallion: a butterfly within a six-pointed star. The piece clicked in her slow brain. This was Rhydev Azhere; Council Lord for House Azhere, Sharkbait had said. Azhere, not Ghytteve. And those two Houses were often at one another's throat. She wondered if this were cause for hope. "What do you want with me, Lord Azhere?"

The flicker of surprise her question caused was gone so swiftly, she wondered whether she had imagined it. "Rhydev," he corrected, suave. "You must call me Rhydev. We're going to be friends; we mustn't stand on—mmm—*ceremony.*"

"What do you want with me, Rhydev?" she repeated, refusing to be sidetracked by his hints of friendship.

"I'd like to know why you killed Cyffe Ghytteve."

"I *knew* this was all a mistake," Ferret said, disgustedly. "I'm a thief, not an assassin; I've never killed *anyone.*"

"I have testimony that Cyffe Ghytteve was tailing you. She was observed following you from the Whistling Pig to the Landlubber; after you left the Landlubber, she followed you toward another tavern: the Star and Sextant. She was found dead—knifed—in a nearby alley. You never made an appearance in the Star and Sextant. It seems a reasonable guess that you were the last person to see her alive. Believe me: it is to your—mmm—*advantage* to tell me what you know about all this. Even if you didn't kill her, it seems probable that you know who did. Mind, I have neither need nor desire to serve as an—mmm—*instrument* of Ycevi Ghytteve's revenge, but the Watch wants answers. The rule of law survives on the waterfront, where it doesn't in the Slums. If you won't tell me what you know, young thief, I will have no choice but to turn you over to the Watch and their—mmm—*ungentle* questioning."

Ferret shuddered. She had heard tales of the Watch's interrogation methods.

"On the other hand," he continued, turning a studious gaze on his neatly manicured fingernails, "there may be room for—mmm—*collaboration* between us. House Azhere is no friend of Ghytteve. I'm inclined to be grateful for Cyffe's demise—however it came about. If you were to confide in me, we might find one another of mutual use."

Ferret's mind churned ponderously through implications and shades of meaning. She didn't think she *wanted* to be of use to him, and she was determined not to implicate Sharkbait. "I canna tell you what I dinna know, Lord Rhydev," she said, taking refuge in feigned ignorance.

Rhydev Azhere tapped steepled forefingers meditatively
against his even front teeth while he regarded Ferret. Finally,
he sighed. "I'm too softhearted, I fear. It makes me quite—
mmm—sad to think of you with the Watch and their hot irons.
Their current Interrogator is rather a butcher—no finesse, and
such scars." He shook his head regretfully.

Ferret flinched. "How can I tell you what I dinna know?"

"Whom do you seek to protect?"

"Protect?" she demanded. *"Gods and fish!* I've no way
even to protect myself!"

"You could start by telling me what you know."

"I dinna know aught!" the thief countered indignantly.
"Happen you want me to make something up?"

"Remember," Rhydev Azhere warned, cool. "I have testimony. Cyffe Ghytteve was known to be following you."

Ferret kept her face impassive while conjecture heaved in
her sluggish brain. Testimony. That meant someone in the
Guild had betrayed her. She battened down her outrage, and
spun lies and truth together as fast as she could. "You've
been paid in tin Nobles, no mistake. I know naught of this
Cyffe Ghytteve, but I do know I've rivals in the Guild. No
one makes Journeyman as young as me without putting thorns
into some tender prides. If you got your information from
Ybhanne, or any of her people—or from Theffeth, for that
matter—they're just trying to make me trouble." She chose
her names with care: Ybhanne had a spreading organization,
and she *hated* Khyzhan; and Theffeth, as the Guildmaster's
right hand, held his cloak over a vast number of minor Masters and Journeymen. "It's true enough," she went on, "that I
was on the waterfront. I was doing an errand for my Master;
but I completed it at the Landlubber, and then went home. *No
one* was following me; I am a Journeyman, and I *would* notice.
Happen it was convenient I was there, for whoever's spun yon
yarn, but I *wasn't* this Cyffe's quarry."

Doubt knit Rhydev Azhere's brow—quickly smoothed
away. "Innocence is no defense against pain," Rhydev warned.

"Innocence is useless," she said bitterly. "And clearly, ignorance is dangerous. And pain…" She shivered. "Suffering
is stupid. Dinna you think I'd tell you if I knew aught?"

Rhydev Azhere was silent, inscrutable. Then he rose, went to the desk and struck the small table cymbal there. When in answer, a man in blue and silver livery appeared in the doorway, Rhydev said, "Bring a brazier, and send Ghorran to me."

The servant bowed. After he had gone, Rhydev removed a rectangular wooden box from a drawer in the desk and opened it. Slowly, he removed a series of wooden-handled silver implements. Some were long and thin, like darning needles; others had flat disks on the end; one was shaped like a tiny trident. As Rhydev laid them out on the desk in a ritualistic pattern to glint with candlelight, the servant returned with the brazier. Rhydev arranged the metal implements, one by one, over the hot coals. Sweat broke on Ferret's brow.

An unremarkable man, plainly dressed, entered then, and bowed to the Council Lord. At Rhydev Azhere's small nod, he took Ferret by the arm and propelled her to a wooden chair. With strength born of terror, she fought him, twisting and biting in his grip. But it was no use. In a trice, her wrists and ankles were lashed to the chair.

Rhydev Azhere removed a skewer from the brazier and approached Ferret. Her eyes seemed irresistibly drawn to the glowing tip of the implement.

"Now," Rhydev said softly. "Tell me what you know about Cyffe Ghytteve's death."

"I told you: naught!"

"You've told me nothing," he agreed quietly. "But you must tell me something." The glowing tip of the skewer descended toward her forearm. "Can't you remember anything?"

"I dinna know aught!" she cried, frantic. She could feel heat as the skewer hovered over her skin. It bit, searing. She gave a gasping cry. Rhydev withdrew the skewer and moved it half an inch toward her wrist. "I dinna—know—*aught!*" Ferret repeated unsteadily. It stung again and she shrieked.

"For whom are you working?" Rhydev asked, replacing the skewer in the brazier and removing one of the tools with a disk on the end.

She shot an apprehensive look at the glowing disk, then wet her lips nervously. "I'm one of Khyzhan's," she whispered. She could almost hear her Master's voice, advising: 'Misdirect with truth, whenever possible.'

"Against Ghytteve?" the Lord pressed.

"I know naught about Ghytteve!" she cried passionately.

The flat disk hissed against her arm; she screamed. After an eternity, Rhydev replaced the implement in the coals.

"What errand was it which sent you from tavern to tavern on the waterfront?" the Azhere Council Lord asked. His hand hovered indecisively over the handles of his silver tools; finally, he removed the trident.

"I was seeking one of Khyzhan's bravos," she said dully.

"Why?"

"I had a message: Guild business."

The glowing trident surged nearer. "What was it?" he purred, deadly.

"Khyzhan wanted his man to tail a fellow posing as a foreign sailor; the Guild suspected the stranger of operating within its bounds without sanction." It was a common enough tale. She hoped it would deflect the lord's questioning.

"And Khyzhan's man's name?"

"I canna tell you that," she protested, shocked. "It's a Guild secret."

Three pronged pain blazed up her arm; he had jabbed deeply. "His name?"

"Rakhazh!" she screamed.

The other man nodded. Rhydev withdrew the trident. Tears ran down Ferret's cheeks; she made no effort to check them. Rhydev studied her for several moments, then turned to his man with a shrug. "Well, Ghorran?"

"Could be true: it's a common enough story. And Rakhazh is one of Khyzhan's. But by the same token, it could be a clever lie." He picked up a skewer and brought it slowly toward Ferret's cheek. "So tell us about the girl who followed us after we nabbed you: the pretty little beggar lass who works the crowd in the Temple Gate."

Ferret's stomach did a slow, cold roll. *Oh, Kitten,* she thought. Then, she became aware of the glowing point of the awl, hovering in the air just below her eye. *"Gods."* It was whispered, a prayer. "She just tags along with me, sometimes," Ferret told the men. "I share with her when I've extra."

"And why was she with you, then?" he pursued, the hot, silver point shifting closer to her eye.

Ferret scrunched her eyes closed and flinched away. "I *told* you: she tags along."

"She didn't go into the tavern with you."

"Gods and fish!" Ferret's eyes snapped open to glare. "The Cur's no place for a little girl. I told her to wait outside."

"Really? You told her to wait for you? And where were you going, after you'd settled with your master?"

A simple, reasonable explanation presented itself. Ferret seized it. "Out fairing. I'd promised her a meat pie for Ythykh-Fair."

As he studied her, Ferret saw the shadow of his decision; he replaced his implement in the coals. "I doubt she knows anything useful, your Eminence. Shall I dispose of her for you?"

Rhydev considered. "I don't think she knows anything useful, either, Ghorran—but I could stand to have Ycevi in my debt. We'll throw the girl to the Ghytteve. Deliver her with my compliments, and convey the information that she's the one Cyffe was following when she was killed. That should suffice."

"Very neat, your Eminence." He cut Ferret free of the chair, retied her wrists behind her back and coiled his large fist lightly round her burned arm. "Come quietly, now," he suggested, with a slight—excruciating—tightening of his fingers. Ferret complied.

No one paid any heed to them as they wound through endless palace corridors. Ferret's arm throbbed, her ears buzzed and her head felt unpleasantly light. Rhydev's man left her to her muzzy, worried thoughts. It sounded as if Rhydev expected the Ghytteve to make rather short, unpleasant, work of her. She concentrated on ignorance; she *did not* have any useful information; she had never even *heard* of Owl or Sharkbait. It sounded unlikely that she would escape this tangle alive; at least she could try not to bring her friends down with her.

"Ghytteve!" Her captor's tone jarred Ferret alert.

The man so hailed turned toward them: a thin, young man with dark hair and brilliant blue eyes. Ferret's heart lurched with recognition. The Lady's puppy: Cithanekh.

"Compliments to your Lady from Rhydev, Lord of Azhere; this is the creature Cyffe was following when she was killed. He thought your Lady might be able to find a use for her."

The young lord bowed slightly. "Please convey my Lady's sincere thanks to the Council Lord of Azhere."

Ghorran pushed Ferret toward him. As the young man took her injured arm, she hissed in pain. Though his face remained impassive, his grip loosened instantly. "Come," he told her, and as Ghorran started back to his master, Cithanekh led Ferret in the other direction.

When the other's footsteps had faded, the young Ghytteve lord halted. He looked around carefully, as though seeking watchers in the shadows; then he gazed down at Ferret. "I remember you, from the Replete Feline. Whatever did you do with the Royal you stole from me?"

"I hid it away. I'm saving to buy a friend out of slavery."

Enlightenment broke in his sudden smile. "You're *Ferret*. Owl's told me about you." Sudden fear clouded his face. "I've got to keep you out of Ycevi's hands." He looked around him again. "Come on: hurry!"

He chivvied her through twisting leagues of corridors; they emerged in a long gallery. At the far end was a dais, lit by two sconces of candles; music swirled toward them. The young lord drew his knife and cut Ferret's bonds.

"I daren't spend any longer in your company. My cousin Ycevi doesn't trust me; she often has me watched. We may have been lucky so far." He gestured toward the musicians. "The woman with the lute—"

"Arre?" Ferret asked.

Cithanekh nodded. "She'll help. I must go." He strode away.

"Wait," she called softly. Then, when he did not respond, she called again, "Cithanekh, wait."

He spun back swiftly, his eyes wide and alarmed. "How *do* you know my name?" he demanded. "I didn't tell you."

Ferret thought her heart would stop in the face of his terrible, intense suspicion. She searched her mind for an innocuous explanation. "Rhydev Azhere called you that in the Replete Feline. I've a good memory for names."

His suspicion eased very slightly; then, his eyes narrowed again. "The man with the scar," he murmured, almost as though to himself. His gaze sharpened on the thief. "Who is he?"

"Another friend of Owl's; name of Sharkbait. Cithanekh, I have to know: is Owl all right? And what, in the names of all the gods, does Ycevi want with him?"

"For the moment, he's well. As for what she wants," his face turned bleak as winter. "I'm Anzhibhar; she plans to make me Emperor, and to use Owl as a hostage, to control me. Owl will be all right." He added, with self-loathing, "I haven't the courage to defy her. Ferret, go. Ycevi mustn't find you." This time, when he strode off, Ferret made no move to call him back. Instead, she staggered toward the pool of light and music.

There were three musicians: Arre, a fire-haired Windbringer priest with a harp, and Mouse's nobleman. They broke off at the sight of the disheveled thief.

"Ferret," Arre cried. "What are you doing here? Did Sharkbait send you? And how did you get through the Guild war?"

Ferret tried to answer, but her torpid brain refused to respond. With a sudden rushing in her ears, darkness crested over her and she collapsed to the floor in a dead faint.

Chapter Sixteen
Collaboration

Arre was first on her feet after Ferret collapsed. She felt for a pulse and saw the burns on the thief's thin arm. She cursed softly in her own language; Venykhar knelt beside her.

"What should we do with her?" the flute maker asked. "My quarters are closest."

Arre looked sharply at him. "And how better to convince the Ghytteve you are a threat than by sheltering Ferret?"

Venykhar made a face. "Antryn's a worrier."

"*Antryn*," Arre repeated. "Is he the one who sent you the warning, then?" At the old lord's nod, she said, "You ought to heed him; he's right. You are in danger."

A sudden gust of wind rattled the music on their stands and made the candles flicker. The wind carried the unmistakable tang of the sea, and the echo of harping. Arre jumped and looked at her friend, the Windbringer priest. He was sitting perfectly still, his head up like a stag scenting danger; his eyes were bright and wide in his white face.

"Kerigden?"

The next gust was stronger; several candles went out, and the harping was louder. The young priest shook his head once. The third gust appeared to follow immediately upon his denial; the harp notes played a recognizable melody, and Kerigden's music blew off his stand.

Arre frowned absently. She recognized the melody: part of a hymn to the Windbringer from the Canticles of Creation. It filled her mind, to the exclusion of all other thought, with a kind of muzzy purpose. As if obeying some inward directive, she fit the ancient words to the tune and sang softly:

"'Dost thou know wherefore shineth the moon?
Dost thou ask whither goeth the wind?
Dost thou see every heart's hidden dream?
Canst thou separate fate from doom?'"

"All right! *Enough.*" Kerigden's voice was tight. "I don't pretend to understand, but I will obey."

The muzziness left Arre's mind with a snap. She stared at Kerigden. "I didn't—I wasn't—" she began, but Kerigden cut her off with a gesture.

"What?" Venykhar asked, puzzled by the tension between them.

A shiver of awe began in Arre's stomach as the implications came clear in her mind. Her people followed the One God, but her schooling was thorough, and she had been taught the histories of other gods. "She used me," Arre said, between outrage and awe. "Talyene."

At the Windbringer's ancient name, wind swirled through the chamber, tossing Arre's hair into her face, and extinguishing all but one of the candles. And they all heard it—not harping, this time, but laughter: a woman's low laughter.

They were silent for a long moment; then, Kerigden lifted one hand, sang a phrase of music in his clear tenor, and the candles bloomed with light. Kerigden came to join the other two, beside the fallen thief.

"Arre's right, Ven," he said calmly. "It would be foolhardy for you to shelter Ferret. I'll take her back to the Temple with me. She'll be safe there."

"*You'll* take her," Venykhar exclaimed. "But you've spent *years* convincing the Council Houses that you're neutral in their constant scheming. If this gets out, it will destroy your carefully built reputation."

"Yes," Kerigden agreed.

"Ven's right," Arre said gently. "It's not really your quarrel."

"It is now," the High Priest said. "She has made it mine."

"*Why?*" Arre demanded. "What does the Windbringer care for the Scholar King and his courtiers?"

A strange smile touched Kerigden's face. "She hasn't told me. Perhaps it is the children; she likes children." As he gathered Ferret into his arms, Venykhar put the harp back into its case and slung it over the priest's shoulder. "I'll take care of Ferret; come tomorrow to see us."

* * *

Ferret returned to consciousness in a room full of sunlight.
Someone had cleaned and tended her burns and cuts; she had
been bathed, and she lay in a comfortable bed. She turned her
head at a faint rustling sound beside her; Arre sat in a chair at
her bedside, reading. Arre smiled at her.

"Back among the living, I see."

"More or less," Ferret agreed cautiously. Her head ached
and her arm throbbed dully. "Where am I? Is this the Palace?"

"No. This is the Temple of the Windbringer; we thought
it was safer."

"Oh," Ferret said, while inwardly, she was wondering, We?
The torn net of her memory had allowed several significant
events to escape. Ferret puzzled over the disjointed fragments
until Arre spoke again.

"Will you get up? There's a clean tunic, if you like; and
Venykhar and Kerigden are waiting for us."

"Kerigden?" she repeated. As though he were conjured
up by his name, he came through the door with a coffee pot on
a tray.

At the sight of the fire-haired priest, several bits of
Ferret's jumbled recollections connected. The priest had
been with Arre last night, when the Lady's puppy had left
Ferret in the gallery. And hard on that memory came the
knowledge that this wasn't just any Windbringer priest; it
was the High Priest, the head of the sect. She studied him
covertly as he set the tray down and poured her a cup of
coffee. He was very young, in his twenties, she thought;
she remembered that gossip said he was quite a prodigy:
the youngest high priest in the history of the Temple District—or some such. And there was something else. She
fished for it. Oh, yes: rumor had it that he was completely
disinterested in the political maneuverings of the nobles
and the temples. She wondered if that were true.

"I'll get up," Ferret said, realizing belatedly that Arre had
asked her a question.

"Good," the young priest said with an almost mischievous
smile. "Venykhar has had long years in which to cultivate the
art of waiting, but I am of an impatient disposition. He sent
me in here with the coffee to still my fidgeting."

A few minutes later Ferret was dressed and starting on her second cup of coffee. She, Arre, Venykhar and Kerigden sat in his study, a bright, spacious room with tall windows which overlooked the Temple District's beautiful park.

"As no doubt you have surmised," the priest began, "I am Kerigden, the High Priest of the Windbringer. Last night, after you interrupted us, we brought you here for safety's sake. We would all like to know what happened to you: how you were captured, and by whom; how you escaped; and how—or whether—we can be of help to you."

Ferret sighed. "Happen it's a tangle, but I'll do my best. Yesterday, I was captured by some men in the Slums. They were Watch, I think, but it wasn't an arrest. They took me to Rhydev Azhere, who wanted to know what I knew about some Ghytteve woman who was killed."

"Wait," Kerigden said. "Did you recognize Azhere, or did your questioner introduce himself as Rhydev?"

"I knew him: I'd seen him before. He told me who he was, too; he tried to convince me to be his friend, but happen I'm not so great a fool."

"*Did* you know anything about the Ghytteve's death?" Venykhar asked.

After an instant's hesitation, Ferret nodded. "But I didn't tell Rhydev that. I didn't kill Cyffe; but I helped."

"Who did kill her?" Kerigden asked.

"Happen I'd rather not say."

Venykhar frowned as he thought, then he said, "How badly is Antryn—*Sharkbait*—hurt?"

Ferret shot him an assessing look. "I beg your pardon?"

The old lord smiled wryly. "He sent me a *note* of warning; he would have come in person if he'd been able. So: how badly is he hurt?"

"He said he'll live if the wounds dinna fester."

"So," Kerigden said, "somehow Azhere guessed you were involved in Cyffe Ghytteve's death, and arranged to have you brought in and questioned. How did you convince him you didn't know anything?"

"I knew I'd been betrayed by a Guild thief; so I told him that I have enemies in the Guild. I'm a Journeyman—and

young for it. I said you dinna make Journeyman as young as
me without putting thorns in some tender prides. I gave him
the names of people who might do me mischief; and then I
stuck to ignorance. Eventually, he decided I didn't know anything, so he had his man deliver me to the Ghytteve. He
wanted Ycevi in his debt, he said. Only his man gave me to
Cithanekh, who figured out I was Ferret—a friend of Owl's—
and he let me go."

"And you recognized Cithanekh Ghytteve?" Kerigden
asked.

She nodded. "I'd seen him, too—with Rhydev Azhere."

"Gods above and below," Venykhar swore. "No wonder
the Ghytteve are jumping at shadows. For an innocent friend
of little Owl, you know an uncomfortable lot about Court
matters. Are you *sure* you're not working for someone?"

"I'm sure. But the Ghytteve *are* plotting treason, you
know; and happen I'd not weep if the Lady's scheming came
to naught. Cithanekh told me that Ycevi plans to make him
Emperor and to use Owl as a hostage to control him.
Cithanekh is not happy with this plan. He's to be Ycevi's
puppet; and if Owl is at all fond of him, he'll *hate* being her
strings. There's no one as stubborn as Owl. Happen he'll
push Cithanekh into defiance, even if it means pain and danger for himself. I'm not working for anyone; what yon nobles
do to one another doesn't make much difference to me. But
I care about Owl, and it seems to me I'd best foil their plan
somehow, to safeguard him."

"Make him Emperor?" Kerigden repeated, puzzled.

Venykhar nodded. "He's Anzhibhar. I'd forgotten that; he
lacks the resemblance."

"Anzhibhar?" Ferret asked, ears perking at the familiar
word. "What's that?"

"It's the family name of the Royal House," Arre told her.
"Cithanekh's mother was the old Emperor's sister."

Kerigden frowned. "But is he really close enough to be
construed as the Scholar King's heir?"

"Let me think," Arre said, running family trees in her mind.
"They're first cousins. There's Ancith—Cithanekh's younger
brother; then, let's see...There's an Anzhibhar-Azhere:

Morekheth; another first cousin, but he's younger than Cithanekh. And there's Antryn."

"He's a *second* cousin," Venykhar corrected.

"Yes, of course. So by age and degree, one might argue the descent as Cithanekh, Morekheth, and Ancith."

"Wait," said Ferret. "Sharkbait is the Emperor's second cousin? *Sharkbait?*"

Venykhar looked abashed. "Oh dear. You won't tell him we let it slip, will you? He's touchy about it."

But Ferret's mind had raced on without waiting for the old lord's comment. "If the Ghytteve are half as suspicious as Sharkbait says, then if they figure out Owl and I and the others all know Sharkbait, happen they'll think he's using us in some plot or counterplot." Ferret looked up at Arre. "Elkhar Ghytteve came to the Slums looking for Mouse; but he found Kitten. Just the pattern of our names makes him nervous. If he knew about Sharkbait, happen naught could convince him we were harmless."

"You're not harmless," Kerigden pointed out. "You are trying to save your friend Owl—which will foil Ycevi's schemes, no matter what your motives. So: how can we help you?" He turned to Arre. "Couldn't the Scholar King—appropriate—the boy?"

Venykhar drew breath sharply. "None of the Council Houses would accept that calmly. Many of Khethyran's ideas and policies make them nervous about their prerogatives, even without flagrant examples of interference by royal fiat."

"Besides," Arre said, "if Kheth took Owl, she'd just think of something else—even if it meant poisoning Cithanekh and starting over with Ancith. But if Owl stays where he is, I *think* he'll be in a position to help us bring her down."

"Yon sounds dangerous for Owl," Ferret put in.

"Ferret," Venykhar said gently. "There is no safety for Owl. You and Mouse and the others exist, and you all know Sharkbait. That connection alone could be enough to destroy Owl, if the Ghytteve learn of it. He's your friend and you love him; but to Ycevi Ghytteve, he's a minor *khacce* piece: expendable. And she'll sacrifice him without hesitation if it appears to be in her interests to do so."

"Happen that's so, but I willn't wring my hands and wait for the worst. What can we do?" She rounded on Arre. "Is there aught your heathen magics can do? Owl said he dreamed of you; did you cause that?"

"No. Owl has Sight Gifts of his own. He's far stronger than I," she added, for Kerigden's benefit, "and just coming into his power; but he is untrained."

"Can you touch his mind?" the priest asked.

"I have," Arre admitted, "but he'd been drugged. They gave him *haceth*. He's untrained; I'm not strong enough to hold him."

"If I helped?" At her shocked look, he hunched one shoulder. "We are taught mind work. We're not the Kellande School, but surely there is common ground."

Arre looked doubtful, but she said, "All right. I'm willing to try it. I need to talk to that boy."

Ferret eyed them dubiously. "I'd best go back to the Trollop and tell Sharkbait to keep his distance for a while."

"You can't do that," Venykhar said. "The Slums are aflame with Guild war."

"Guild war," Ferret repeated. "*Thieves* Guild war?" At their nods, she swore. "*Gods and fish*; it *was* Ybhanne—must have been. But that just means I have to go back. They're fighting over *me*, over who betrayed me, and all; happen Khyzhan will cool things if he knows I'm safe and not much damaged."

"We can't let you—" the flute maker began.

She cut him off with a feral grin. "You canna stop me, Lord Venykhar. See here," she added more gently. "I'm a Journeyman in the Thieves Guild. I know I play young-and-stupid most of the time, but I'm older and smarter—and a good bit more ruthless—than I act. A Guild war's dangerous; but I know the Slums, and I willn't be careless."

"She's right," Arre said, her gaze distant. "She's needed."

Kerigden touched Ferret's wrist. "Listen: if you or your friends need a place to hide, a place of safety, come to me here. Once the Guild war burns itself out, come anyway. If Elkhar Ghytteve is really bent on combing the Slums for you and Mouse, it would surely be wise to be elsewhere."

"I will, then," she said. She got to her feet, and including them all with her eyes, thanked them and bade them farewell.

Chapter Seventeen
Guild War

The streets were worse—far worse—than Ferret had antici-
pated. Not only were there knots of bitter factional fighting,
there were bands of hunting bravos bent on running down
anyone they could flush out of cover.

She wound deeper into the Slums, making for the Trollop's
Smile. As she slipped past the mouth of a shadowed alley,
warning came to her on a breath of fetid air. She turned just in
time to see movement, deep in the shadows; so she was sprinting for her life before the two men broke cover.

They were fast; she didn't think she could outrun them.
And her quick ears caught the noises of fighting all too close.
She darted down a side street and clambered up the scarred
face of an abandoned tenement. Her pursuers did not follow.

Before she could catch her breath, she realized she was
not alone: three men moved with deliberate menace toward
her perch. Ferret thought fast. They thought she was cor-
nered; they were between her and the side of the building which
leaned closest to its neighbors. On the clear side, there was a
ghastly long jump to a second building, fire-scarred and der-
elict. One of the men drew a knife; they were laughing. They
didn't expect her to try the jump—or to survive it.

Ferret sprinted away from them. There wasn't time to think,
just to leap, and pray she'd make it and that the roof tiles
would hold. She made the distance, but the agonized com-
plaint of the roof beams drove her on. She raced lightly over
the raddled tiles, made a second, easier jump to a sturdier building, and scrambled down a gutterspout to rest, panting, in the
space between a pile of refuse and a shadowed doorway.

From her hiding place, Ferret watched her earlier pursuers
running their current prey. He wasn't as fast as she had been,
but he was larger: a solid, blond foreigner who did not seem so
much frightened as affronted. He stopped with a curse, and
drew his knife. The two bravos circled in, intent and deadly.

Ferret recognized the thieves, though the foreigner was a stranger. The bravos were Ybhanne's; Khyzhan held grudges against both of them. They were good, and they often fought as a pair. The foreigner hadn't gotten his back to the wall, and though he certainly knew how to use his knife, one of his attackers was inching his way around to his back.

Sudden anger filled Ferret. Not only was it unfair, but when they killed the foreigner, they would be all too close to her hiding place; and even the rooftops weren't a safe haven, now. She didn't want to be trapped between death on the ground and death on the roofs. There was a loose cobble by her foot. She picked it up and hefted it, judging its weight. She chose her moment with care and flung the stone into the fray. It caught one of the bravos an ugly smack on the jaw. He staggered; and in the instant's surprise that gained him, the foreigner killed his other assailant. Then, he whirled and dispatched the second thief before he could recover.

Ferret heard more running footsteps. "Hsst! In here," she breathed to him; the foreigner was winded and bleeding. "Quick."

He dove into the shadows beside her an instant before a troop of hunters came around the corner. Ferret and the foreigner held still, not even daring to breathe, until they had moved on.

"It's my life I owe you," he whispered. "I thank you."

Before Ferret could reply, they heard cries: they had been spotted from above, and the ground hunters were being summoned to the chase. "Gods and *dead* fish!" she swore. "Split up—and go to ground." Without waiting to see whether he followed her advice, Ferret sprinted away.

Thankfully, the Trollop wasn't far. Ferret flew through the refuse-scattered streets to the kitchen door. She dove inside, slammed the door and leaned against it, panting.

"*Ferret!*" Sharkbait cried. He strode to her side and reached to grip her shoulders.

"Gently," Ferret warned, holding her bandaged arm out of the way. "I'm more than glad to see you, too." She swept the kitchen with a glance: Sharkbait, beside her; and Donkey, patiently slicing bread—but grinning in spite of himself. "Where are Kitten, Squirrel and Mouse?"

"Taproom," Donkey said. "Kitten and Squirrel are serving—I'm in disgrace—and Mouse is with her parents. Ferret, what *happened?* And how did you escape?"

She told the tale, leaving out only Sharkbait's relationship to the Emperor, and the details of her wild trip through the Guild war's lines. When she was done, Sharkbait spoke from his corner. "Donkey, don't tell the others."

"Why not?" Ferret demanded sharply.

"The Ghytteve are looking for you, for Kitten (whom they know by name and sight) and Mouse (by name). If they should chance to find any of you—may all the gods forfend—what you've just told us is enough to doom Owl. The Windbringer Temple, Venykhar, Arre, and I are all helping you; one doesn't need to be Elkhar Ghytteve to find that suspicious. You asked me once, Ferret, if I were using you; I said I wasn't, and I'm not. But there isn't a Council House noble alive who would believe me (or you) now, if they knew how many—and how disparate—are your allies."

"But—" Ferret began, before Donkey interrupted.

"No, Ferret; Sharkbait's right. Happen we'll tell them when this Guild war cools and we take refuge with yon Windbringer priest. But not yet. You kept Sharkbait out of it with Azhere; but do you honestly think Kitten could do the same? Or Squirrel?"

"Or Mouse?" Sharkbait put in.

Donkey looked at him, the shrewdness showing through his mask for an instant. "Mouse might. She's clever and stubborn."

"And brave," Ferret added. "All right; I dinna like it, but happen it's best—for the moment. Tell them I was here, and that I'm all right. Make something up, if you need to, about my getting away. I'm off to find Khyzhan."

"Wait," Sharkbait said. "I'll leave with you; I'd best be off to the waterfront."

"But you're hurt," Donkey protested.

"I'm better than I was. Besides, I'm a danger to you—and to Owl—if I stay." He came to Ferret's side; she noted that he was moving almost normally. "Ready?" At her nod, they slipped into the streets.

It took Ferret hours to find the Master Thief. When she finally ran him to earth, though he was glad to see her free and not permanently damaged, he would make no promises concerning the cooling of the Guild war.

"I want Ybhanne's organization destroyed," he said wolfishly. "She's overstepped; and from what you tell me, she's belonged to Azhere for a long time. The Guild willn't have it; we canna tolerate treachery. But Ybhanne knows that, and she's fighting for her life. There will be no quarter asked nor given until one of us is dead."

"May it be her and may it be soon," Ferret replied. "Guild war is hard on everyone."

"Indeed." Khyzhan looked at her suddenly. "Do you need a place to go to ground, Ferret?"

"Thanks, but no, Master. I have my own boltholes."

"Well, have a care for your skin, Journeyman."

She departed from the Master's temporary headquarters and made for the Trollop. But the bravos were thick in that quarter, so prudence forced her out of the Slums. Sharkbait had told her of one of his places: a waterfront warehouse. She arrived at the door just as the waning moon cleared the horizon.

One of Sharkbait's longshoremen let her in and sent her into a room full of bales of wool. Ferret made herself a nest and went to sleep. Much later, footsteps woke her. She jerked up to find Sharkbait, a small lamp in his hand, coming slowly toward her.

He stopped before her, studying her silently. Ferret stared back, while the last sleepy cobwebs were scoured from her mind by a deep unease. "Sharkbait?" she whispered; and when he did not respond, she said, "Antryn."

"They told you," he said, finally. "And don't say: 'What?' I can see it in your face."

"I haven't told anyone else," she said. "Not even Donkey. It's still a secret."

"Do you see why it matters? Think of Cithanekh."

"You dinna want to be used," Ferret said simply. "Happen I can understand that."

"When I was a child, my father often told me I had to live up to my heritage: 'Antryn,' he'd say, 'you must prove yourself worthy of the blood you bear.' But it wasn't true. The blood I bear is nothing but trouble. It makes the schemers see me as a tool or a threat, and the toadies see me as a master. And always—*always!*—it puts my friends into danger.

"Last night—*gods!* Last night was awful. I thought you were dead, Ferret, that Azhere would kill you. I started the Guild war; Kitten saw you kidnapped, but I reported it to Khyzhan. And through it, I kept thinking I should run, hide; you'd tell Rhydev about 'Sharkbait' and he would remember Antryn—and all my vain attempts to excise my heritage would be undone. But I couldn't do it; *I couldn't run.*" The lamp flame jumped as his hand clenched and trembled. "I thought nothing mattered to me more than freedom—survival on my own terms; I thought I'd safely cauterized all dangerous sentiments. But there I was, as helpless as I've ever felt—like a nightmare, where you see yourself doing stupid things but are powerless to stop." His head came up, then, and turned, listening. The gesture put the scarred side of his face in shadow; it made him look impossibly young, and very vulnerable.

"What hurt you?" she breathed. "Whom did you lose?"

He shot her an unreadable look. "How do you *do* that?" he demanded, exasperated. "Am I that transparent? He was nobody important—except to me: an Ykhave cousin. But someone put a stiletto between his ribs because his presence was inconvenient. I made a vow, after he died, that I wouldn't be used, that I would do *anything* to safeguard my independence, my anonymity."

"Happen I can understand that, Sharkbait, as long as you didn't also swear never to care for anyone else."

"Caring," he said bitterly, "weakens one."

"No. Sharkbait, you're wrong. Caring makes you strong."

Sharkbait was silent so long that Ferret wondered whether he would ever speak again. Then, very quietly, he asked "What is it that you care for, my sweet thief, that makes you so strong?"

Ferret laughed. "My *friends.* What did you think?"

Sharkbait turned away. "I didn't know. That's why I asked."

* * *

"'...And thus it came to pass that when the great lamps of heaven were completed, burning in the field of the sky by day or night as the gods had decreed, the Company of the Gods bethought upon what next to undertake. And strife arose among the Company over which aspect of their handiwork on the face of the world was most nobly done, and most fitly answered the challenges of Kherhane.'" Owl paused in his reading, his index finger stalled beneath the next word, and looked up at Cithanekh. "The Company of the Gods spends a great deal of time in strife."

Cithanekh smiled wryly. "Rather like the Council Houses."

"It seems a waste; and it slows down the story, rather. I saw the Canticles of Creation done by a traveling puppet troupe. It was much more exciting."

"What, are you finding this dull? When I was congratulating myself on having found something livelier than *A Treatise on Herbs and Their Properties?*"

"It *is* an improvement," Owl admitted. "Just not enough of one. But never mind. I'm told I'm terribly difficult to please."

"And I'm far too lenient," Cithanekh responded. "I ought to have brought a whip to crack."

Before they could return to the lesson, Lady Ycevi interrupted, Elkhar beside her. Though her elegant features gave no hint of her state of mind, Elkhar looked wrathful. Owl was close enough to hear Cithanekh's alarmed indrawn breath.

Ycevi looked down her nose at the two of them, the only hint of her temper the slow clenching and unclenching of her left hand. "Where's the thief, Cithanekh?" she asked at last, with as little emphasis as an inquiry about the weather.

"Thief?" he repeated, bland.

"From Azhere," she prodded.

"Oh. The lass. I let her go."

There was an inarticulate growl from Elkhar; the Lady restrained him with an upraised finger. The lift of an eyebrow goaded Cithanekh to elaborate.

"It was perfectly clear: Rhydev wanted you to do his dirty work. She couldn't have known anything useful. He'd never have parted with her if she had."

"Rhydev is known to be squeamish," the Lady said, cold. "He'd used force: I saw the burns," Cithanekh replied evenly. "My Lady, it seemed likely that Rhydev intended to use the girl to embarrass you. Tell me: how did you learn of her existence? Did he ask you about her publicly?"

She was silent, considering. "At Council," she replied. "He asked me if I had learned anything useful from Ferret."

Owl fought to stay calm. Ferret? And *Rhydev? And burns?*

"It's *possible*," she added grudgingly, "you had my interests at heart."

"*I wanted her!*" Elkhar burst out. "She was our link to Cyffe's murderer. You had no right to let her go!"

"You can't get blood from cheese, Elkhar," Cithanekh said, maddeningly reasonable. "She didn't know anything. You'd have taken her apart for nothing—and then, how would the Lady answer the Emperor's searching questions?"

"It *was* there, you treacherous bastard. I'd have found it."

"Or murdered the girl trying, no doubt."

"Murder?" Elkhar snorted. "She's a *Slum-rat*."

"Do you think that is a consideration which weighs with the Scholar King?" Cithanekh responded.

The bodyguard seized Owl by the front of his tunic and dragged him upright. "*What do you know about Ferret?*" he demanded. His barely contained rage terrified Owl. "And *Kitten? And Mouse?*" He shook him sharply. "*Answer me!*"

Owl was afraid to reply. He knew Elkhar would never believe that Ferret, Mouse, Kitten and the others were simply his friends, members of a childhood secret society who looked out for one another. So he held his tongue. Elkhar struck Owl a hard open handed blow across the face.

"I want an answer," Elkhar said, chillingly calm. When Owl did not instantly respond, he struck him again.

"*Leave him alone!*" Cithanekh leapt to his feet and rushed the bodyguard. Elkhar thrust Owl aside with force enough to send the boy sprawling as he took a fighting stance.

Ycevi's voice froze them all. "Stop. *Elkhar.* Cithanekh." She turned to Owl. "Now, boy; you will answer *my* questions—won't you?" She pinned him with a hawk-bright glance. "Owl, we know that Kitten knows you: she told

Elkhar she misses you. So tell us what you know about
Ferret, and Mouse, and Kitten."

"Ferret, Mouse, Kitten, Donkey, Squirrel, and Owl; those
are the special names Ferret gave us. We're just friends. We
live in the Slums. We look out for each other."

"Who is the leader?" Ycevi pursued.

"It was Ferret's idea—but we don't really need to be
led. We help each other out when we're in trouble—you
know: *friends!*" Owl caught Cithanekh's fleeting wistful
grimace.

"For whom do you work?"

"As a group? We don't work for anyone. Kitten and I
beg—or Kitten begs, and I used to; Squirrel runs messages.
Donkey is a potboy in his uncle's tavern; Mouse's parents are
flower vendors and she helps them. Ferret's a thief. We're just
friends—Slum-rat children."

"Donkey," Elkhar said. "At the Trollop's Smile? And
Squirrel's real name is Effryn?"

Owl's heart chilled, but he nodded faintly.

Ycevi turned to Cithanekh. "How old is this Ferret?"

He shrugged, prevaricating. Owl had said she was sixteen, but she was small. It would be a natural mistake, and a
younger age might allay some of the Lady's fears. "Thirteen;
fourteen, perhaps."

A movement by the library door snagged Owl's attention.
Myncerre was there, silent, observant; as their gazes crossed,
Owl thought he saw a smile flicker in her dark eyes.

Ycevi turned to Elkhar. "Well?"

"It sounds plausible," he replied. "But Cyffe is dead."

"Cyffe was not without enemies," Cithanekh put in.
"Surely it is possible that her murder had nothing to do with
Ferret."

"I don't like coincidences," Ycevi said tightly. "But you
are right: it is possible. Owl?"

"Lady?"

"Is there anything you are neglecting to tell us?"

"I don't think so, Lady," Owl lied with outward calm.

"What do you think your friends did, when you disappeared?"

"No doubt they worried, and asked some questions. Ferret's persistent. I wouldn't be surprised if she'd found out that I was sold to House Ghytteve. They're probably trying to raise money to buy me back."

She looked skeptical but said, "We must send them word you're not for sale—not at any price. Do you understand?"

"Yes. I understand." He saw the truth in her cold eyes. She would never let him go, never sell him; and if he failed to be useful, she would see him dead. Yes. Owl understood.

As though what she read in his face pleased her, the Lady smiled faintly. "Good. Cithanekh." Her voice hardened again. "If I find you have lied to me, you won't suffer for it: Owl will. Do I make myself clear."

"Yes," the young lord whispered.

"Excellent. Elkhar: send word to this Trollop's Smile. I want Ferret and her friends to know that I will never part with Owl."

"The Slums are aflame with Guild war, Lady. Is the message worth the danger?"

"Ah. No. I don't want to risk any of my bodyguards." She considered for a moment. "Send Dedemar."

Elkhar bowed, and at her dismissal, left the library.

Lady Ycevi studied them for a long moment, her bright eyes narrowed. Finally, she turned toward Myncerre. "Watch the boy," she instructed. "Cithanekh, come with me." And in a swirl of costly silk, she swept out.

After the Lady was gone, Myncerre came to his side. She gently probed the reddening welts on Owl's face. "You're in for more bruises, Owl. I'll get you some ice."

Owl hunched a shoulder. "Why bother? I'm used to beatings. Myncerre, what will she do to Cithanekh?"

The steward shrugged. "Threaten him, probably."

Owl's eyes filled with sudden tears, and he clutched Myncerre's wrist before she could rise. "*What should I do?*"

She gently pried Owl's fingers open. "Do whatever the Lady tells you to do—both of you." Then she got up and went out.

As he heard the key turn in the lock, Owl covered his face with both hands. "But it's wrong," he whispered.

Chapter Eighteen
Desperate Ventures

The taproom at the Trollop's Smile was full of people, but for all that, it was fairly quiet. People ate and drank but sparingly, and there was none of the roistering gaiety one associated with a tavern full of people. Mouse and her parents sat at a table, nursing cups of ale and picking at bread and cheese. Donkey—restored to his uncle's good graces by necessity—was behind the bar, while the tavern master bustled to and from the kitchen. From Arkhyd's sour expression, Donkey could tell that he was muttering imprecations.

The door swung open suddenly, and a large, blond foreigner stumbled through, slamming it shut behind him. He was pale and clearly winded; a makeshift bandage, soaked with blood, was tied around a forearm, and there was a crusted cut across his brow. But even under the blood, and without his uniform, Donkey recognized Dedemar.

Dedemar came to the bar. As Donkey passed him the mug of ale he ordered, he leaned casually toward him and pinned the boy's wrist with one hand. "Donkey," he said in a low voice; there was menace in his tone, though he kept his expression pleasant. "I know you are not as stupid as you pretend. I have a message for you, and for Ferret, Squirrel, Kitten and Mouse. It is from the Lady Ycevi Ghytteve, and it is about Owl. If I tell you, will you tell the others?" When Donkey remained silent, his face blank, Dedemar's grip tightened painfully in warning. "Answer."

Donkey nodded.

"Very well. The Lady bids me tell you that Owl is not for sale—not for any price. You must give up any hope you cherish of freeing him from House Ghytteve. Do you understand? Answer."

Donkey nodded again.

"Good," he said. Still pinning Donkey's wrist, he picked up the tankard in his other hand, drained it, and shoved it back across the counter to be refilled. When Donkey complied, Dedemar took the cup to a table near the kitchen door. He sat there, deep in thought, for several minutes before he took several objects out of his pockets and put them into a leather pouch. Donkey tried to see what he was doing, but the man was too far away. The next time Arkhyd bustled out of the kitchen, Dedemar stopped him. They spoke together, too softly for Donkey to hear; then, Arkhyd went back into the kitchen and Dedemar followed him.

While Donkey was receiving Ycevi Ghytteve's message in the taproom, Donkey's uncle Arkhyd grumbled around the kitchen. Squirrel had made himself useful and was slicing bread and cheese at the counter, while Kitten tried to squeeze into one corner of the room, out of the tavern master's notice.

"A bad business, Guild war," Arkhyd groused. "The place is full of people bent on staying out of the way of the bravos; they're not hungry; they willn't drink; and I canna turn them out." He glowered at Squirrel. "Slice that cheese thinner, boy: happen only the gods could say when we'll be able to get more from the market." He grumped into the taproom.

"Happen we could escape to Ferret's lair," Kitten suggested for the fiftieth time. "Arkhyd's getting—He'll never let us spend another night here."

"Kitten, he just *said* he canna turn people out; he'll let us stay. Besides, even if we made it to Ferret's, there'd be naught to eat—and no Slum markets are open. I hope my father is safe," Squirrel added. "Mouse is lucky; at least her parents are here."

Their desultory complaints were cut off by Arkhyd's return; he came through the door speaking over his shoulder. "...you can ask them—though if they've any sense, they'll refuse."

The tavern master came into the dingy kitchen, towing a stranger. "This gentleman is looking for a messenger. Happen none of you is fool enough, and so I told him, but he insists on asking." Then, as though eager to be free of the whole transaction, Arkhyd pounced on a tray of bread and cheese and returned to his taproom.

Suddenly, the kitchen seemed very close, very stuffy, to Squirrel. Anxiously, he regarded Arkhyd's gentleman. Tall, flaxen haired, with the muscular build of a fighter, he filled the kitchen with his presence; even without his Temple Watch uniform, Squirrel recognized Dedemar. Kitten, who had never seen him, was unaffected.

"I require the services of a messenger," he announced.

Squirrel found his voice. "In the midst of a Guild war? Thieves are out there, slitting one another's weazands and filling the gutters with blood. Happen you're mad!"

"Not mad," he contradicted as he spilled a chime of silver onto the scarred table top. "Desperate."

Kitten's eyes riveted on the pile of coins: mostly Nobles and Half-Nobles—more money than she would see in an entire year. "Where?" she asked. "You want your message taken where?" Squirrel trod squarely on her foot. When she glared in reproach, he shook his head. She pursed her lips in annoyance.

"To a tavern on the waterfront," the man replied. "The Star and Sextant. There will be three men there; one has a scarred face. They will sit at a table near the door. Give them this." He removed a leather pouch from his shirt.

"It's too dangerous," Squirrel hissed. "Even for the money."

"No one would harm a little girl, surely," Dedemar soothed.

"And I'm fast," Kitten said. "And the money...Yon—" she gestured to the heap of silver—"yon would pay my apprentice-fee to a real *trade*."

"What good's the money if you're killed?"

"I'll be careful," Kitten promised airily. "And once I've delivered the message, why, Sharkbait'll look after me."

"Dinna go," Squirrel begged. "Please dinna go."

Kitten ignored him. "The Star and Sextant; three men— one with a scarred face—at a table by the door; and you want me to give them yon pouch?"

Dedemar pressed the pouch into Kitten's hands. "Go. And hurry, for it is vital my friends receive this."

Kitten tucked the pouch away and pushed the silver coins toward her friend. "Look after the fee for me. Happen I'll breathe easier knowing it's safe." Then, while Dedemar looked on, Kitten slipped out into the dusky alley.

More than once, pure luck saved Kitten. On three occasions, she was forced to trust her slight weight to very corroded gutterspouts in order to elude bloodthirsty bravos; but the gutters and the questionable roof tiles held her. At long last, she reached the relative safety of the waterfront district and made her way to the Star and Sextant.

The tavern was packed. She scanned the trade for Sharkbait and his two friends. When she saw no sign of him, she wondered for the first time whether Sharkbait really was the scarred man to whom the foreigner had referred. On her second scan of the room, she noticed a man with a scar like a whip cut across one cheek. He was with two others, and though they were not seated, they had grouped themselves between the entrance and the nearest table to it. Kitten's breath froze in her lungs: each of the men wore a single, dangling silver earring—just like Elkhar's.

Kitten's heart drubbed her ribs as possibilities leapt and plunged. They *had* to be Ghytteve; and if they were, they might well be entangled with Owl, or with the plot on the Emperor's life. Kitten forced herself to behave casually as she slipped back outside. She *had* to know what was in the pouch. What if it were a clue, and she tamely handed it over? In the spill of light from the doorway, Kitten untied the drawstring. The pouch contained several delicately carved *khacce* pieces: a Sorceress; a Swordsman; a Clanlord; an Assassin, broken in two pieces; a Priest; and a Page; and four polished round stones. One was a deep blue, two were gray, the fourth, white. Kitten stared unhappily at the meaningless collection. She tipped the things back into the pouch, retied the string, then returned to the tavern to deliver the message. Perhaps if she got close enough to the men, she would overhear some clue.

The three men were exactly where she had left them. Kitten made a play of looking around the room, before she approached. She spoke to the man with the scar. "Happen I have a message for you, sir. Do you have a foreign friend, with hair like straw?" At his short nod, she produced the pouch. "He sent this."

"Ah." Interest sparked the man's eyes. "Shall we see what Dedemar has to say?" When he saw that Kitten still stood there, he tossed her a coin. "Run along."

Kitten could have screamed with frustration. *Dedemar!*
That must have been why Squirrel had tried to warn her off.
By reflex, she caught the coin, and with a little bow moved
toward the bar. Perhaps she could sneak back within earshot
if she made it look innocent. She bought a mug of foul ale,
then angled herself with apparent aimlessness toward the door.
Using the edges of her field of vision, Kitten watched the
men empty the *khacce* pieces and stones out of the pouch. She
edged closer, then closer still.

"I'm confused," one of them was saying. "The Priest?"

"And a white stone: Windbringer."

"That *can't* be right. That fop's *never* bothered with politics."

"Ded dealt us the witch. Could it be *she's* hooked him in?
They're friends."

"The Page, the Swordsman, *two* grays; what *is* he hinting at?"

"Dedemar should have come himself," the scarred man
said. "The message can be read too many ways. Zhotar, find
that child; I want to send word back to him."

Kitten's heart nearly stopped; she was far too close; surely
they would realize she had been spying on them! To cover her
terror, she buried her face in her tankard. When the man's
hand closed on her shoulder, she choked.

"Here, lass," he said, thumping her back. "We want you to
carry a message back to our friend."

She widened her eyes. "I'd not planned to go back into the
Slums tonight. The Guild war's hot. It's not safe."

"We'll make it worth your while, of course," the scarred
man said cynically. "Just tell him—"

"Why, good heavens," a new voice cut in. "It's *Kitten.*"

Kitten jumped. The new speaker was Elkhar. Her stomach rolled queasily, but she summoned a bright smile. "Elkhar!
Do you have a message from Owl for me?"

The scarred man snapped his fingers. "*Owl!* Of course.
That's the Page."

"I may have," Elkhar replied. "Come; sit with us." He
pulled her to the table and pushed her down onto the bench
beside him. "What's this?" he asked the scarred man.

"A message from Dedemar in the *khacce* code; but it's not
clear. It can be read too many ways."

Elkhar studied the pieces and stones on the table. While he was absorbed, Kitten edged to the end of the bench. Maybe she could slip away while he was occupied.

"You're right," Elkhar said. "It isn't clear; but I don't like it. If he means the Page for Owl, it would seem the boy's mixed up in Cyffe's death, after all."

Kitten slid off the bench, but Elkhar caught her by the scruff of her neck. "Not leaving us, were you?"

"I must go home. If I dinna get back soon, my people will worry."

"Your people? But I distinctly remember your telling me you have neither kith nor kin."

Kitten laughed. "That's beggar's patter. Surely you dinna take it all for fact."

"Wouldn't you like to see Owl?" Elkhar asked her.

Kitten swallowed. Though the man's words and expression were cajoling, there was an avid flicker at the back of his eyes that made her shudder. "Another time," she said firmly.

"No. Tonight. Now."

The man called Zhotar protested. "We were going to send her back to Dedemar; his message isn't clear."

Elkhar took Kitten by the arm. "Go yourself," he ordered. Come along, little one; we mustn't keep Owl waiting."

"Wait!" Zhotar insisted. "Child, where was Dedemar when he hired you to carry his message?"

"A Slum tavern," she replied. "The Trollop's Smile."

Then, as irresistible as the tide, Elkhar towed the little beggar out into the night. "You canna do this," Kitten said. "My people will worry."

Elkhar halted. "You have a choice, Kitten: walk beside me calmly and quietly; or I'll truss you up and carry you. Which is it to be?"

"I'll walk," she responded weakly.

"Very wise. This way." They sank into the shadows as Elkhar, ruthless as a current, dragged her toward the Palace.

Mouse gnawed the stale crust of her bread and scanned the taproom of the Trollop yet again. Her parents had succumbed to sleep, their heads cradled awkwardly on their arms; but

Mouse was wide awake. She longed to draw the people around her, to capture their worried faces, their fear—and by concentrating on their emotions, to escape her own. But she knew better than to call attention to herself in a tavern so thick with tension. She couldn't even chat with Donkey, since Arkhyd had sent him back to the kitchen a few minutes ago.

Her scanning eyes paused on the Temple Watchman, Dedemar. Out of uniform, he seemed furtive, more foreign. He hunched, morose, over a pewter tankard at a table not ten feet from Mouse's. As she watched him, she heard a commotion outside: the thud of running feet, a skirl of cries; then, the tavern door was flung wide as a man staggered in. The door slammed. He took two steps into the room, and like a tree falling, crashed to the floor. A knife's hilt protruded from his back.

Shock silenced the taproom. In the breathless hush, the scrape of a chair was loud as a drum roll. Dedemar ran to the fallen man's side with a cry. "Zhotar!"

"Ded?" The man lifted his head with effort; a silver earring glinted in the lamplight. He coughed. A spatter of blood stained his lips. "Elkhar sent me. Your message was unclear."

Dedemar found Arkhyd in the crowd, glared at him commandingly. "Fetch hot water and clean linen." As the tavern master moved to obey, he turned back to the wounded man. "I didn't think Elkhar would be there; but why did he send *you?* Wouldn't the child have served better?"

"Elkhar took her; seems she's a friend of Owl's, and he's been itching to question someone ever since the puppy let the thief brat go." He coughed again. Dedemar steadied the man, supporting him gently. "Ded?" His hand sought the Temple Watchman's, closed on it hard. "Did you really mean the *Windbringer* Priest?"

"Aye."

"But he has no interest in politics; he *can't* be in it. He—" Coughing interrupted him. Dedemar held his shoulders.

"Breathe, Zhotar; don't talk."

Arkhyd returned with a steaming basin and several clean towels. Under the directions of the Temple Watchman, a trestle table was cleared, and the injured man was lifted gently onto it. Then, Dedemar carefully removed the knife and tended the wound; Mouse watched him, absently admiring the competence of his clever hands, while she turned and sifted his words. *What* child? Surely none of *them* would have been fool enough to go out into the middle of a Guild war. But 'a friend of Owl's'? She was frantic for more information, but she dared not call attention to herself.

The one called Zhotar did not look well, despite Dedemar's ministrations. When the Temple Watchman had finished, he settled his friend for sleep. Zhotar's breathing was shallow, and his skin was very pale.

"Will he live, do you think, sir?" Arkhyd asked in a low voice as he loaded a tray with soiled rags and basins.

Dedemar's face was bleak as the moon. "I doubt it; the lung was touched. He is strong, but that is a dire injury."

The tavern master looked worried. "Here: be useful, Mouse." He gestured to the laden tray. "Take that out to Thantor, and bring in a tray of clean tankards on your way back."

Mouse obeyed, noting the sharpened interest in the foreigner's eyes. "You call her 'Mouse?' Like the vermin?"

Mouse escaped to the kitchen.

"Gods!" Squirrel greeted the sight of the bloody cloths. "What *happened?*"

"A friend of Elkhar Ghytteve and that Temple Watchman Dedemar got himself knifed."

"Is Elkhar Ghytteve *out there?*" Squirrel squeaked.

"No. Just Dedemar." Mouse searched the kitchen shadows anxiously. "*Where's Kitten?*"

"She took a message for Dedemar," Donkey said, grim. "Squirrel tried to warn her, but she wouldn't listen. Mouse, what?" he asked, seeing the anguish on the younger girl's face.

"Elkhar has her," Mouse told them; and then, before she could relate the rest of the overheard conversation, Arkhyd poked his head through the door.

"*Mouse!* I need those tankards!"

She snatched up a tray. "I'll be back."

Squirrel and Donkey exchanged worried looks. "So where's Sharkbait?" Donkey said.

"And Ferret?" Squirrel demanded. "I thought she was coming back after she saw Khyzhan."

Mouse returned with a tray of dirty mugs. As she and Donkey washed them, Mouse told her tale. When she had finished, Donkey relayed Dedemar's message about Owl.

"It worries me," he ended. "The Temple Watchman knew all our names, and made a point of using them so I'd know. Happen the Ghytteve put some pressure on Owl to make him tell them about us."

"But if Owl told them about us, he would tell them we're all just friends, and they wouldn't be so worried, surely," Squirrel said. "Why would Elkhar take Kitten, then?"

"Happen the Ghytteve dinna believe Owl," Mouse put in. "Happen they want to question Kitten to be sure he told them the truth."

"But he did tell them the truth."

Donkey nodded. "But Kitten knows who killed Cyffe Ghytteve: Sharkbait—*and Ferret.*"

They were silent as the implications unfolded.

"I'd best go back," Mouse said heavily. "My parents…"

"Be careful," Donkey said. "He knows you're Mouse; happen he means you mischief."

She nodded and slipped back into the taproom. A subdued hum of conversation had resumed, though there was an island of silence around Dedemar and his unconscious friend. Mouse slid into her chair; her parents eyed her anxiously but did not question her.

After a time, Zhotar groaned feebly. Dedemar hurried to help him.

"Ded?" His voice was thready with desperation. "Ded!" The Temple Watchman murmured soothingly.

"No, listen—I should know." Zhotar shook off the soothing. He whispered, in the sort of tone that carries, "Run! Flee! Escape while you still may! *She'll eat your soul.* She ate mine; chained—and then devoured at her leisure. This is a bad business, Ded. There's no good in it. Elkhar's killing children. Cyffe's dead—now me."

"Zhotar, Zhotar. Calm yourself. All is well."

"All's *not!*" he retorted, sharp. "The Windbringer's in it—

and the witch. Heh!" he laughed mirthlessly. "The witch. In *khacce*, the Sorceress moves sideways through time. They say the Emperor's witch sees the future. If that's so, surely the Lady will fail."

Dedemar laid fingers across Zhotar's mouth. "Be still; it tires you to talk."

"It worries you," he said, slightly muffled. "It should. You don't belong in this, Ded; you're too pure. The blood of children—" He coughed, rackingly. "Even the puppy," he gasped after a moment. "Even the puppy has conscience enough to find it filthy—and *he* stands to gain, if anyone does besides *her*." He fixed Dedemar with clear eyes and said with powerful intensity, "Do as I say: get out of it, before she damns you." Coughing convulsed him. With a last shudder, the breath rushed out of him. Dedemar held him a moment longer before he eased him gently back to the table. Zhotar was dead.

Dedemar folded Zhotar's hands on his breast and closed his eyes. With a long, speculative look at Mouse, he resumed his seat. Covertly, she returned his regard and vowed to keep him in sight. As the night aged, however, Mouse found it impossible to remain wakeful. When she woke, Dedemar was gone.

Chapter Nineteen
Danger

Elkhar hauled Kitten out of the waterfront, past the shuttered shopfronts of the mercantile district. When they reached wealthier neighborhoods, the avenues came to life. Litters and carriages conveyed merrymakers to and from parties; inns and gaming clubs catered to a variety of appetites; they passed a theater, where the evening's entertainment was about to begin. Kitten eyed the crowds, wondering whether anyone would be moved to help her if she made a scene. As though reading her thoughts, Elkhar's hand tightened on her arm. She hissed in pain.

"Please," she whimpered. "You're hurting me."

"It's a warning. If you make trouble, I'll break your arm."

"Trouble?" she queried innocently. "You're taking me to see Owl; it's tremendously kind of you. Why would I make *trouble?*"

Elkhar smiled sardonically. "You waste your breath trying to melt me, Kitten. I sold my heart for meat long since."

"Well, I hope you got a good price for it," she snapped.

He laughed, but the sound was bitter. "Not particularly. Tell me, Kitten: what is Owl to you, really?"

"He's my *friend*—if you know what that means. We used to beg together, before he disappeared."

"And did Ferret beg with you, as well?"

"Ferret's a thief," Kitten responded automatically; then doubt assailed her. "How do you know Ferret?"

"I don't know Ferret, but Owl has spoken of her—and of Mouse, Squirrel, Donkey—and you, of course. I'm very eager to meet you all; he speaks so warmly of his *friends*."

Kitten suppressed a shiver. There was something intensely menacing in the bodyguard's manner. Abruptly, he halted and swung her to face him, gripping her other arm.

"Tell me what you know about Cyffe Ghytteve's death," he gritted, cold eyes noting every fleeting expression on her face.

"Who?"

"My sister, Cyffe Ghytteve. She was killed on the waterfront: knifed. What do you know about it?"

"Naught! Not a thing! I never met your sister."

"Your friend Ferret killed her."

"Dinna be silly; Ferret doesn't go armed." Kitten's heart began its drubbing anew. The conversation was like a nightmare game of *khacce*: too much at stake, and not the faintest notion how even to move the pieces.

"But she has friends who do," he purred, dangerous, "no?"

"I dinna know as she does," Kitten replied carefully. "But happen I've not met all her friends."

He yanked her onward with angry energy. Kitten was out of breath by the time they stopped at a small gate in a stone wall beside an opulent house. Elkhar took her through a dark garden to a humble door—a servant's entrance, Kitten surmised. A man in green and silver livery answered Elkhar's knock.

"Where's the puppy?" Elkhar asked.

"Still at the Palace." He gestured toward Kitten with his chin; a silver earring glinted with the movement. "Mouse?"

"Kitten," Elkhar informed him. "Find her someplace *comfortable* to wait while I go report."

"Where's Owl? When may I see him?" Kitten asked, winsome.

Elkhar raised one eyebrow. "Surely you're cleverer than you pretend, Kitten."

"But you *said*—"

"Stow it. I'm out of patience." He shoved her roughly into the other man's hands. "Varhynn, deal with her." He went out.

"He *promised*," Kitten wailed, then burst into tears.

Unmoved, the servant herded Kitten up a flight of stairs into a small bedroom. "Are you hungry?"

She nodded. He locked her in. As his footsteps faded, Kitten hurried to the single window: barred. She grabbed the grill, tried to rattle it; it fit snugly. She leaned her forehead against her gripping hands and sobbed in real fear and despair. She was still standing there when Varhynn returned with a tray. Without a word, he laid out the meal on the small table and went away. It was a long time before Kitten, even hungry as she always was, could bring herself to eat.

When Elkhar arrived at the Ghytteve quarters, he was discomfited to find the rooms full of courtiers. The Lady was holding one of her impromptu gatherings. He scanned the gaudy crowd. Owl, in the green and silver Ghytteve livery, stood stiffly between Cithanekh and Myncerre; the Lady, exquisite in gold silk and pearls, chatted with the Prime Minister Zherekhaf. Elkhar noted the other Court powers present: Rhydev Azhere; Bishop Anakher, of the Horselord's Temple; Lady Mylazhe Ambhere; Commander Bhenekh of the Imperial Guard; young Enghan Mebhare, looking as though he'd be more at home with a herd of cows; Ymlakh Glakhyre, toadying up to Azhere as usual; a host of lesser luminaries. His eyes narrowed as he considered who was not present: Venykhar Ghobhezh-Ykhave; neither the Emperor nor his witch; no one from the other Temples, neither from the Windbringer (which didn't surprise him) nor from the Dark Lady's Temple (which did); no representatives from Houses Khyghafe, Dhenykhare, or Ythande. As he watched, he saw Rhydev neatly detach himself from the Council Lord of Glakhyre and approach Owl. Elkhar slipped closer to listen.

"Why, Owl," Rhydev began. He brushed a feather's touch across the boy's purple cheek. "You collect bruises. Are you—mmm—*overly* fractious?"

"I must be, most gracious Lord of Azhere," he replied, studying his feet.

The Council Lord ran one finger along Owl's jaw to his chin, which he lifted to make the boy look at him. "Rhydev," he insisted; the tone was charged with unspoken things.

Owl stiffened. He wanted to pull away, but Cithanekh put a steadying hand between his shoulder blades. The boy searched Rhydev's unrevealing eyes. Across the room, Owl saw the Lady and her companion, strangely intent on Rhydev.

Owl wet his lips. "Who is the man with the Lady, Rhydev. And why are you performing for him?"

Surprise arched his brows; then he smiled. "Ah, beautiful *and* clever. Does Ycevi guess? It's the Prime Minister, my uncle Zherekhaf. But are you sure I'm performing?" He released Owl's chin to caress his hair; then, after blowing the boy a kiss, he melted into the press. Owl followed him with troubled eyes before he turned anxiously to Cithanekh.

"What was that about?" Owl asked the young lord.

"*Bastard*," Cithanekh spat; then he eased his tone. "He's just playing his damnable games, Owl; pay no heed."

"He likes you," Myncerre offered, bland.

"*Likes* me?" Owl choked. "He makes me feel like a fish, and he's a very hungry heron. Cithanekh, must we stay? Couldn't we get away from all these courtiers?"

Cithanekh noticed Elkhar then, saw the bodyguard shake his head emphatically. The young lord sighed. "No, Owl. I'm sorry."

"It would be rude to leave," Myncerre added, "just as the Prime Minister is coming to meet you."

"Oh no," Owl breathed.

"Courage," Cithanekh whispered.

Elkhar caught the Lady's eye, then, and she nodded summons. He made his way to her side.

"My faithful Elkhar. You're big with news."

"Dedemar sent a very obscure message to the Star and Sextant—in the *khacce* code, and quite ambiguous. It seems he's trapped by the Guild war. But he sent the message with a little Slum-rat child: Kitten. I left her with Varhynn. I thought you might want to question her."

"Ah. Good. Anything else?"

"Lady, I know you think me—obsessed—with this, but you were watching Owl with Rhydev."

"I was. Were you close enough to overhear?"

He nodded. "Owl accused Rhydev of performing for Zherekhaf." At her startlement, he took courage. "Lady, he's too damned shrewd to be innocent. Intrigue is his *element*. Rhydev sees it. 'Beautiful,' he said, '*and* clever.' Please, Lady; he's dangerous, and I am charged with your safety. Get rid of him."

"Get rid of him?" Her tinkling laugh was brittle as crystal. "Don't be ridiculous. I paid ten Royals for him; he's *supposed* to be good."

Elkhar bowed. "And the girl?"

"I'll be by, after my guests leave. Now, go rescue Owl from that snake Zherekhaf, before he swallows him whole."

As it turned out, Owl didn't need rescuing; the Prime Minister, looking very thoughtful indeed, had walked off before the bodyguard was close enough to overhear. Cithanekh and Myncerre struggled to hide amusement, but Owl looked baffled. As Elkhar covertly studied him, the boy's face went blank, then contorted in pain. Fear bleached Owl as he turned toward Cithanekh.

"No, oh no," Owl whimpered, distraught.

Cithanekh shook him gently. "Get hold of yourself, Owl; it's all right."

Owl focused on his friend's face. "It's not: *not* all right," he said distinctly, through his strange abstraction. "Kitten's in trouble."

"*Not here!*" Cithanekh whispered urgently.

"No," Owl agreed. "Not here. In a room with a barred window, and a man in green and silver livery. *Green*—" he repeated, looking down at his own sleeve. "Oh, gods."

Elkhar's hands closed hard and insistent on Owl and Cithanekh's upper arms. "Shall we go someplace private," he suggested, deadly, including Myncerre with a look, "for a little *chat?*" Feral eagerness lit his eyes. "About *Kitten*—and where you get your information."

Owl stared, appalled, at Elkhar's terrible face. Darkness spun on the edges of his vision. Air did not reach his lungs; a deadening wave broke over him and swept his mind away.

In the Temple of the Windbringer, Arre and Kerigden sat opposite one another at a small table. Kerigden's open palms lay against Arre's, and between their joined hands sat a pale blue crystal on a silver stand. They had spent long hours discussing the theory of mind work and magic, before they had decided on this particular experiment. Both traditions taught the use of a focus stone; and they hoped that by working together they could raise enough strength to call Owl and then to hold his untrained mind.

They were breathing in unison, now: smooth, deep breaths, while their concentration deepened. Then their minds touched. Sweat broke on Arre's brow; the Windbringer priest's power glowed like a bed of embers, wanting only a breath of wind to stir it to fire. Arre opened her tranced mind to listen for a whisper from the boy; it was late. With luck, he would be sleeping, susceptible to their gentle touch.

Suddenly, like a towering wave, foreknowledge and terror swept over them both. Arre's hands tensed, and Kerigden gripped them in response. Something was wrong; Owl was desperate, panicked, and Arre felt her careful control swept beyond her reach, like a stick in a millrace. She would have cried out, but Kerigden was there, solid, steadying; a phrase of music echoed in their minds, anchor and safety. Then, the priest drew calm and darkness from their joined memories and wrapped Owl's torment in it.

The bright center of the boy's dreaming gift shone like a sliver of the sun. Arre touched him, felt his terror, his need. *The dreaming place,* she thought at him. *The safe haven.*

And he did it; he built the precarious shelter she had taught him. *Arre? Arre! Help me.*

I will; I am. What is it?

They've caught Kitten; and Elkhar knows that I know. But I can't know. I don't know how I know. He's going to kill me!

Then, something broke the contact; Arre and Kerigden were thrown out of their trance like storm wrack on the beach. They stared at one another, pale and breathing hard.

"Is he dead?" Kerigden asked.

"We'd have felt that—I think," she replied.

"What should we do? Try again?"

Arre's vision hazed with an image of the future: Elkhar with a knife; the child Kitten; and Owl, appalled and helpless.

"Later," she said, her voice thick with horror. "He's going to need us."

Chapter Twenty
Disaster

Owl choked and spluttered back to consciousness through the slap of cold water. He lay sprawled on the stone floor of one of the upper galleries. Elkhar loomed above him, empty bowl in his hand and retribution in his eyes. Cithanekh knelt protectively beside him; and Myncerre observed.

"Now," Elkhar growled. "An explanation."

Owl floundered helplessly, baffled. "What am I supposed to explain?" he asked meekly. Nausea writhed in his belly.

The bodyguard's words were clipped with sarcasm. "You might begin by explaining how you learned that your friend Kitten is in trouble, and how you are able to describe so accurately the place she is being held."

Memory and fear returned. Owl fought drowning terror, fought to *think*, to come up with an explanation to satisfy Elkhar; but no inventiveness answered his need. To buy time, he sat up and scrubbed his face with his hands. When he dropped his hands he was caught, like a bird before a snake, by the murderous look on Elkhar's face. "I just *know*," Owl gasped, desperate. "We're that close: I just know."

"You *just knew* about the room with the barred window and the man in the green and silver livery?" Elkhar asked, scathing. "You must do better than *that*, Owl."

"What will you do with Kitten?"

Elkhar's smile was unpleasant. "You'd be better served to ask what I intend to do with you. Owl, *I want an explanation.*"

The boy swallowed hard against his rising gorge; there seemed no choice but the truth. "I have Sight Gifts, Elkhar. Visions just—come over me, sometimes. About people I care for. I can't control it; it just happens. I saw Kitten in my mind, and I knew she was in trouble."

Elkhar studied Owl silently, then he turned to Cithanekh. "Have you anything to add? Did you know about these visions?"

"Yes," Cithanekh said calmly. "Owl's had these attacks before; they are very disorienting."

Elkhar looked from one to the other, his eyes narrowing. "Somehow, I don't think you're being entirely honest with me." He twisted Owl's wrist painfully. *"Are you?"*

"Ow! Yes! I've told you the whole!"

Elkhar levered Owl to his feet by the tortured wrist. "Now why don't I believe you?" he purred as the boy paled.

Owl's gut rebelled. In surprise, Elkhar released him; Owl collapsed to his knees as he retched. The bodyguard grabbed a generous fistful of Owl's hair and dragged him upright.

"What did you see, Owl, that night you were so sick; the night Cyffe was killed? *What did you see?* Tell me! *What?"*

Owl struggled with his fuddled mind; the whole story would *never* do. "My—my brother," he began; he remembered Ferret's advice: mislead with truth. "My brother dead of too much Dream's Ease." His eyes filled with tears. "I don't want it to be true."

"And is it?" Elkhar asked, cold.

"I don't know," Owl wailed. "How could I know for sure? Nobody passes me messages."

Elkhar frowned at Myncerre. "Well?"

She shrugged. "Do you suppose this Kitten would know whether Owl's brother were alive or dead?"

"What good would that do, knowing?" Elkhar demanded.

Myncerre replied with the toneless care of one explaining the obvious to the obtuse. "Judging from Owl's information about Kitten, his visions are accurate. If Kitten confirms the brother's death, it might be an indication that the boy has told the truth."

Elkhar's shuttered face revealed none of his thoughts. Finally, he turned to Owl. "Shall we go see Kitten?" He propelled Owl along. Cithanekh and Myncerre fell in behind him. The bodyguard took them through a concealed door which opened on a narrow passage; it was inadequately lit by oil lamps in metal brackets fastened to the cool, stone walls. Though Elkhar's painful grip disturbed Owl's concentration, the boy was vaguely aware of a number of branching corridors and a long, uneven flight of descending steps, before they finally paused in front of an iron bound door. Elkhar rapped: a distinctive rhythmic pattern. He was answered, after a few moments, by the rasp of a drawn bolt. The door was hauled open by the green and silver liveried servant of Owl's vision.

"The girl?" Elkhar asked.

The doorman gestured upward. Elkhar dragged Owl up a flight of stairs, trailing Cithanekh and Myncerre. He unlocked a door and thrust Owl inside, abruptly releasing his arm; the boy staggered as Kitten flung herself at him.

"Owl! Owl!" Her voice was frantic with tears. "Make them let me go!" Then she noted his bruised face. "Oh, *Owl!*"

Elkhar shoved Owl down on the bed while he seated Kitten at the table. "Answer some questions, Kitten," he ordered.

She gulped and nodded.

"Tell me everything you can about Owl's brother."

"Zhazher?" she asked, baffled.

"Is that his name?"

She nodded. "He sold Owl into slavery for a lot of money and some Dream's Ease. He—he—Owl, I'm sorry: Zhazher's dead. He took too much of the drug, right after you disappeared. Ferret and I found him."

Owl covered his face with his hands; the loss was still fresh enough that the tears were real. Cithanekh perched beside Owl, patting his shoulder consolingly. Elkhar looked from the boy to Kitten and back.

"Kitten," he said. "I asked you earlier about my sister Cyffe's death. Why don't you tell me the truth, now? What do you know of her murderers?"

"Naught," Kitten protested. "I told you: I never met your sister."

Elkhar drew his jeweled dagger and began meditatively to pare his nails with it as he leaned against the bedstead. "So you never met Cyffe; I suppose that *could* be true. And perhaps you didn't know her name. Nonetheless, I'd wager you *have* met her murderers—or is a murder such a common thing to your friend Ferret that she wouldn't mention it to you?"

He studied her narrowly, and she swallowed hard. "Ferret had naught to do with it!" she snapped.

"Are you *sure?* And are you sure that's what you should say? House Azhere questioned your Ferret, you know—and then, they sent what was left of her to House Ghytteve."

Secure in the knowledge that Ferret had escaped, Kitten managed a challenging tone. "If that's true, then why bother with me at all?"

Elkhar buffed his trimmed nails on his tunic then admired them. "It's common practice, in interrogations, to verify information through a second source."

Owl stirred uneasily; Cithanekh's hand tightened warningly on his shoulder. The silence was charged.

"But I dinna know aught," Kitten said.

Quick as a pickpocket, Elkhar seized Owl, laying his dagger against the boy's throat. "Then make something up," he advised, "or I'll kill him."

As Kitten hesitated, Elkhar changed the angle of the blade, and a thin line of scarlet beaded Owl's throat. He was intent as a bloodhound, suspicious; and Kitten teetered on the brink of a chasm full of damaging admissions.

"*Stop it*, Elkhar," Cithanekh cut in, forestalling Kitten's panicked revelations. "You know you can't really hurt him— the Lady would flay you. And as for Ferret, Rhydev didn't hurt her very badly and I let her go. They're just *children.*"

Elkhar released Owl; his narrowed eyes pinned Kitten. "You aren't surprised; you knew she was free. How?"

"She came back to the Trollop. I didn't see her; but Donkey said she was safe."

"Yes." Watching even more intently, Elkhar said with ominous clarity, "The Lady's puppy let Ferret go."

Kitten's face showed an instant's recognition at the name;her eyes darted to the young lord's face, before she thought to turn her expression to a puzzled frown. "The Lady's puppy? What an odd thing to call someone."

Owl wanted to slump in despair; he could almost hear fragments of conjecture meshing in Elkhar's brain.

"Odd, indeed," Elkhar purred. "And memorable. Where did you hear it before, Kitten?"

Kitten tried an airy laugh. "I dinna know what you mean."

"I think you do," he contradicted, softly. "Tell me."

With all his heart, Owl willed her to deny all knowledge, to stick to her pretended ignorance; he realized that if she changed her story *now*, Elkhar would push her on all her answers.

Kitten licked her lips, nervously. Elkhar's menace was like a sharp taste. He shifted toward her, toying meaningly with his dagger. "I dinna know," she squeaked.

Elkhar landed on her like a diving hawk; he splayed her left hand against the table, pinning her little finger just above the knuckle with his dagger. "Think again," he whispered.

"I dinna—" The blade bit; they all heard it snick into the table in the instant before Kitten screamed. Owl buried his face in Cithanekh's chest while the young lord held him tightly.

"Pay attention," Elkhar advised. His voice cut off Kitten's shrieks; she subsided to gulping sobs as his knife moved to her ring finger. "Who killed Cyffe Ghytteve?"

"Sharkbait."

"Who is Sharkbait?" Elkhar demanded.

"A—a longshoreman."

Elkhar and Myncerre exchanged speculative glances. Despair seethed in Owl's stomach. "Why did this Sharkbait kill Cyffe?"

"I dinna know!" Kitten wailed.

"*Why?*" He bore down slightly.

"I dinna know, I dinna know, I dinna—" Kitten's frantic denials peaked in a scream as the blade snicked through. Owl and Cithanekh clung to each other in horror.

"Why did Sharkbait kill Cyffe?" The dagger moved to the next finger.

"She knew him," Kitten gasped. "And she was trying to take him prisoner."

Elkhar frowned. "How did she know him?"

"He used to spend time at the Palace."

"With whom?"

"How would I know?" Kitten cried.

"Think fast," he warned, pressing. "With whom?"

Resistance left her. "House Ykhave," she said dully.

Myncerre's eyebrows arched in surprise; Elkhar nodded with grim satisfaction. "*Antryn*," they said, together. Cithanekh shut his eyes in pain.

"So explain," Elkhar instructed. "What is Antryn Anzhibhar-Ykhave to you and your Slum-rat friends."

"I dinna understand," Kitten told him, flat. "He's just Sharkbait. He helped us find out what happened to Owl; but he wouldn't do anything else. He said he didn't want to get mixed up in the Council Houses' endless intrigue."

"He's mixed up now," Elkhar retorted, vicious. "I'll kill him for this."

"You'll *try*," Cithanekh said, cold. "Cyffe was faster than you, Elkhar; and this Sharkbait is no child for you to terrorize."

For an instant, it seemed that Cithanekh's words would goad Elkhar to violence; but instead, he turned to the steward. "Take the puppy and the brat away. I have more answers to extract from our little Kitten before the Lady comes."

Myncerre moved to comply. Owl got up shakily, leaning on his friend's steadying arm. "Kitten," he whispered, pleading.

"Dinna leave me! *Owl!*" Terror rasped in her voice.

"*Kitten!*" he wailed. Myncerre took the boy by the arm and propelled him to the door. He flailed uselessly against her. "Kitten! Let me help her. Let me go! *Kitten!*"

Myncerre and Cithanekh herded him inexorably away. They were in the secret passage, probably half-way back to the Ghytteve apartments, when another wave of visions took Owl. Brutal images swept him like flotsam in a mill race; he clung to Cithanekh, weeping hysterically.

"He's going to *kill* her. *He's going to kill her!* Hurt her, and then kill her. Oh, *Kitten!*" Owl turned to the steward, then, struggling for calm. "Oh, please. *Please*, Myncerre. Stop him. Please. You must."

She studied him silently. As if eluding her conscious control, one hand reached toward him; but the hand dropped, like an abandoned tool, before she touched him. "Did your visions say that I *could?*" she asked.

Though Owl sensed some momentous resolve lurking in her, the import she gave his words bound him to truth. "No."

For an instant, Myncerre's face melted to apology, before it hardened to aloofness. "Lady."

"What's all this?" the Lady asked. With a finger cold as a talon she tilted Owl's face to the inadequate light. "Tears?"

"I'm sick," Owl told her. "No doubt Elkhar will explain."

The Lady's lips quirked. "No doubt he will. Put the boy to bed," she added crisply, "and one of you stay with him until I come."

Cithanekh stayed with Owl. For a long while, Owl stared at the ceiling in silence. Finally, he turned to his friend.

"I don't want to sleep," he whispered.

Cithanekh smoothed the hair off the boy's brow. "Oh, Owl. I feel so helpless. I wish there were something I could do."

Owl sighed. "We *are* helpless—*khacce* pieces in Ycevi's game, frozen into our stiff, unchanging roles. How I wish someone would come and overturn her board—even if it meant I were broken in the fall. Gods, I'm frightened, Cithanekh. She has such power over us. If we can't get free of her, then late or soon, we'll become in truth the *khacce* pieces she wants. Like Elkhar: blind to everything except the web of suspicion and intrigue Ycevi has taught him to see; or like Myncerre, who turns to stone before my very eyes. I don't want to be blind and lifeless, unfeeling as alabaster: a perfect little *khacce* piece, flattered by the touch of her hand. *No.*"

Cithanekh cupped the boy's bruised face carefully as he met his eyes. "That will never happen to you, Owl. *Never*. If you live here a hundred years, she will *never* freeze your heart. As soon chill the sun to ice. And Myncerre: it's not that she turns to stone before your eyes; she's been stone as long as I've known her, impervious as marble. Owl—my dear, amazing Owl—it's that she turns to flesh in your presence."

They searched each other's faces, beyond words; Owl's eyes swam with tears. "Kitten," he moaned. "Oh, *gods*, poor Kitten."

"Oh Owl," Cithanekh murmured. His own eyes stung as he held his friend gently and let him cry.

It was thus the Lady found them, when she came. Cithanekh saw her satisfied smile; with effort, he kept the despair and anger off his face. She gestured imperiously.

"Leave him and come with me, Cithanekh."

Owl's arms tightened, a wordless entreaty, and the young lord hesitated.

"You can come back when I've finished with you," the Lady said, knowingly.

"Courage, Owl," he murmured, and the boy let him go.

Owl listened to their retreating footsteps. When he heard the door close behind them, he closed his eyes, slowed his breathing, and built, step by painstaking step, the dreaming haven Arre had taught him.

Chapter Twenty-one
Night Work

The dreaming haven was a place of twilight, mysterious with shadows. Owl followed the pale glitter of distant light, and the faint music; but he didn't find Arre sitting in the candles' glow. It was a man: a fire-haired man in the gray robes of the Windbringer's sect. He remembered him: Arre's friend from that day at the Temple Gate. *Kerigden.*

Yes. Arre and I are working together. We want to help you.

Can you save Kitten?

There was grief in his mind voice. *No.*

Then what can you do?

I want to teach you something: a way to call me, or Arre.

It's not enough just coming here? Owl asked, surprised.

It is if we are listening for you, but if we weren't tranced together, we would not know you wanted us. Now, relax; think of nothing, and I will try to put this in your mind. It isn't words: it is more a feeling, a need.

It was hard to think of nothing, but Owl tried. After a long moment, he felt the thing Kerigden showed him.

Try it, Kerigden instructed; and Owl did, pouring into his attempt all his grief and fear and helplessness. Kerigden flinched slightly, and for an instant, his image wavered. *Yes. That's it exactly. If you need one of us, call like that; then, we can meet you in this dreaming haven.*

But you can't save Kitten, he said, with pain rather than accusation.

No. Owl, I'm sorry.

Then I shall have to find someone to avenge her, he said, grim with resolve; and he broke the tenuous contact.

When Owl opened his eyes, he found Cithanekh had returned. The young lord sat beside his bed; Owl took his hand but did not speak. For a long time, he lay thinking, trying to remember. When he was very small, before his mother had died, she had used to tell him stories. She had had a fund of tales and histories, and the ones he had loved best were about the Windbringer. She was an unpredictable goddess, who championed odd causes for obscure reasons. His mother had told him the goddess loved children, and every night it was her ritual to kiss her son's brow and to whisper, "Windbringer guard you."

Now, Owl considered. The ancient names of the gods were said to have power; he and Cithanekh had been reading about them in that dry book. Favrian; Vasgrifallok; Kherhane; Celacce; Talyene: strange names, some of them foreign sounding. But there were no use-names, no way to tell which (if any) of the names belonged to the Windbringer.

"Cithanekh, what is the Windbringer's ancient name?" he asked.

"Talyene," he responded. "Why?"

"Just thinking."

The young lord took his free hand and brushed Owl's hair off his brow. "You should sleep," he suggested, very gently. "I'll stay right here."

Owl's grip tightened for an instant. "I know. I'll try," he said, and obediently closed his eyes.

Arre found the Scholar King in his library. His welcoming smile metamorphosed into a look of concern when he saw how wan she looked.

"What *have* you been doing with that Windbringer priest?"

She sat down opposite him and shoved one hand through her hair. "Mind work. We wanted to try to touch Owl's mind— to see what he knows, and to find out how we can best help. We succeeded in contacting him, but in the process, we discovered that the Ghytteve have captured and tortured one of the children—Kitten. We don't know how much the child knows, but whatever information she has, no doubt the Ghytteve will have it by morning."

"Captured and tortured a *child?*" Khethyran demanded angrily. "By all the gods, they *court* my intervention!" He stood up with such energy that his chair scraped, protestingly, across the polished floor. Then, abruptly, he checked his temper. "Is it a trap for me, Arre? Am I intended to rush in to rescue the child, thereby incurring the other Houses' wrath?"

"I don't think so; though were you fool enough to do that, no doubt, Ycevi would use the opportunity. Kheth, I don't think they see the poor as people at all—just pieces to be used and discarded at will." She went to his side and put her arms around him; her tone was gentle. "Besides, even if you instantly sent in the Imperial Guard, it's too late. The Ghytteve move quickly, and we did not have any warning."

The Emperor was silent for a moment. "I hate this worst of all. I am the Emperor—and yet, my Council Houses hold me nearly powerless in matters like these. There should be *laws* to protect children like Kitten; *checks* on people like Ycevi Ghytteve. There should be justice for all my people; the nobles should *uphold* the rule of law, not rule by whim and caprice."

Arre's arms tightened as she whispered, fiercely, "You must *survive*, my dearest love, in order to *establish* such justice."

"Indeed," he agreed. "Dear gods, poor Kitten. She doesn't deserve to be sucked dry by those filthy leeches. Arre, this could put you in danger, if Kitten knew that you'd helped Ferret to escape. I suppose there's not much chance you'd agree to disappear until all of this is over?"

"None whatever," she replied with determined smile. "But we need to be thinking ahead. If Kitten knows much of anything, the Ghytteve will be after the rest of those children, especially Ferret; and they'll want Antryn. Kerigden will give them sanctuary—"

"*What?*" the Scholar King interrupted. "Why?"

She hunched a shoulder. "The Windbringer wants him involved, apparently. Don't ask me, Kheth," she added in the face of his puzzled astonishment. "Even Kerigden can't explain why she's interested. All the same, we need to *think*. We need a way to know what the Ghytteve are up to. I'd ask Owl to watch and report, but—" She broke off, shaking her head. "His position is so precarious."

"Are you *sure* I cannot intervene?" Khethyran asked. "Should I commandeer the boy—or are you still convinced the boy needs to stay where he is?"

"More than ever," she said. Her mind clouded with a string of her silvery future images: Kheth speaking with the Lady Ycevi; Elkhar Ghytteve with a garrote around Cithanekh's throat; the Ghytteve steward holding a silver cup to Owl's lips. "No. They'd kill him if you showed any interest." She smiled sadly. "Now, if you had a troop of fanatically loyal spies…"

"Spies," the Emperor repeated, musingly. "There's your thief, Ferret; and Antryn. He's rumored to be more than competent, if he's the one organizing the longshoremen. Arre, you know that the Palace is riddled with secret passages, spyholes and listening places."

"True," she agreed. "But we don't *know* the secret ways; and we can hardly ask that snake Zherekhaf to make us a map."

Khethyran smiled. "No. But Arre, there might be a map— or not a map, precisely; but we might be able to construct a map, if we could find the original architectural drawings of the Palace."

"But surely they were destroyed," she protested. "Weren't they?"

"Possibly," he agreed, rising. "But one of my Anzhibhar ancestors took an interest in architecture and building; his collection is quite extensive and includes a number of exceedingly rare works. He would certainly have *wanted* documents pertaining to his own house. It's not inconceivable that somehow, he acquired plans—or reconstructed them. I'll look; it should only take a few hours."

Owl built his dreaming haven. He drowned all extraneous thought in the mysterious shadows of the place; and then, he did what Kerigden had taught him. He poured his pain and rage, his grief and uncertainty, into the call. *Talyene. TALYENE!*

The name resounded through the dreaming haven like distant thunder, before the ageless silence returned. Then, on the very edge of Owl's awareness, there was a sound like a plucked harpstring which trembled in his mind. Stealthy as dawn, the sound grew into music, tender, infinitely gentle, and a woman appeared. Wrapped in a rain gray cloak, she played a small harp. Her wild, black hair was a mane lifted by phantom winds. She studied Owl out of silver eyes, inscrutable as fog, as the music spun webs around them both.

You called me? The question was amazed, not annoyed. *How?*

Owl replied, *I used the call that Kerigden taught me.*

Ah! Understanding lit her silvery eyes for an instant. *Then I have wagered well, and need not fear my brother, after all. Did he tell you to summon me?*

No.

No? Then why did you call me?

Owl answered, *I need you.* And then, without warning, his control wavered; his eyes filled with tears, and the images of Kitten's brutal torture surged into his mind.

Talyene extended a hand, inviting. *Owl,* she said. *Tell me.*

But Owl could not answer. Though he strained like a fish gasping for water, something held him mute. His memories burned like acid; tears scalded his cheeks. Anguished, desperate, he seized Talyene's hand. Her touch opened his heart. Memories streamed out of him: Kitten with Elkhar; Anthagh the slaver; the Lady Ycevi; the repetitive round of his life with the Ghytteve; Ferret and his friends. Anger, grief, fear spilled away as the Windbringer shared his memories, his pain. When the memory-flood had abated, the only sound in the universe was the slow plash of Talyene's tears. She caught one, opalescent, in her fingers, then pressed it into Owl's palm. It was hard as a gem and warm.

The sacrifice of children must not go unsung, nor unavenged. There is power in friendships, Owl; and power in you; and hopeless causes do not always fail. Tell Kerigden that. And remember: I keep faith, though my ways are inscrutable. Sleep, she ended, gentle, *and be rested.*

A surge of music swept the dreaming haven into darkness. Owl's breathing changed as sleep claimed him; the hand in Cithanekh's relaxed. No dreams troubled the boy, but later, he stirred in his sleep, slipping his cupped hand under his cheek; he did not move again until morning.

Exhausted though she was, Arre kept vigil while the Scholar King worked. The sweet ripple of her lute encouraged the breeze from the garden, drawing coolness and moonlight into air thick with the scent of old leather bindings. Arre watched him work, observed his peaceful intentness as though memorizing it: the crease of concentration between his brows—not quite a frown; the scratch of his quill as he made notes in his distinctive handwriting; the inkstained fingers raking his dark, unruly hair. So dear. The music under her fingers ached with longing. Khethyran looked up, met her eyes through the golden lamplight, and smiled tenderly.

"*Tears*, Arre?" he asked, rising. He took her face gently in his hands. The lute faltered to silence.

"I love you." She leaned into his touch.

He smiled sadly. "And yet, you refuse to be my Queen."

"Oh, Kheth," she replied, pained. "Your Council Houses would *eat* me. Surely we've been over this often enough."

"Indeed," he agreed. "Forgive me; I don't mean to wound. But Arre, there's you, whom I love and cannot marry; and there are the pampered darlings of the Council Houses—sleek as sharks, all of them—one of whom I *must* wed." His face clouded with pain and despair. "By the gods above and below, why, *why*, *why* did this come to me?"

She caught his wrist before he could turn away and pressed a kiss into his palm. "Because, my dearest love, you are strong enough to bear it."

He considered then said, with a wry smile, "I could wish that the gods had made me rather weaker."

She answered his look with tenderness. "And who would shepherd your people then?"

"The wolves of the Council Houses," he replied. "And yes, I realize wolves make very poor shepherds indeed. I know I cannot reject my destiny, Arre, but I do wish it were other: vineyard-tending, perhaps; or teaching at the Kellande School."

"I know," she whispered. As her eyes darkened briefly with the burden of her visions, Khethyran stroked her hair; he kissed her and went back to his research.

Much later, Khethyran's murmured exclamation roused Arre from reverie. "I've found it," he told her. "Come see."

She looked over his shoulder: an architectural plan of the Royal Palace—missing the accretions of later centuries, but recognizable—complete with the network of hidden passages.

Arre put her bard-trained memory to work as she tried to make sense of the intricate drawing. There: that would be the Ghytteve complex.

"Strange," she said, pointing. "That passage looks as though it leads beyond the Palace walls. I wonder if it's still usable; it would come out in the Upper Town, now, though it would have been park or forest when this plan was drawn."

Khethyran nodded. "It's probably not usable; I suppose the tunnel opening was destroyed when the Upper Town was built. Unless—"

Their eyes met. "Unless they built a house over it, to hide it," she finished for him. "Kheth, *does* Ycevi Ghytteve own a house in the Upper Town?"

"I've no idea. If she does, no doubt the Prime Minister knows of it; but I'm not sure I want to ask him."

"Or that he'd tell you the truth," Arre added sourly.

The Scholar King made a gesture to acknowledge her hit. "Shall I copy the plan for you?"

"What, tonight? Gods, Kheth; don't you *ever* sleep? Surely the morning is soon enough."

He directed her attention to the map, to the part depicting the library itself. "And if, by some mischance, *we* are observed?" he breathed.

She stifled a shudder; she felt as though the walls were leaning inward to listen. With a sigh, she picked up her lute again, while Khethyran began his painstaking copying.

Chapter Twenty-two
Salvage

A whispered breath of name roused Sharkbait. He leapt up, wolf-quick, to find one of his longshoremen keeping wary distance. The faint light seeping into the abandoned warehouse proclaimed it close to dawn.

"There's a thing you should see, Sharkbait." The man's voice shook. "Happen you'll not like it."

Sharkbait scrubbed hands over his face. "Show me."

As he moved to follow his man, Ferret joined him. On the weathered quay below the warehouse they found a clutch of longshoremen, focused on something by their feet. They moved aside for Sharkbait and Ferret. It was a body; a child's body, sprawled face-down. Premonition chilled Sharkbait; he knelt beside the child and with trembling hands, turned her gently over. It was Kitten.

He heard Ferret's sharply indrawn breath; he swallowed hard. Kitten's torturers had left brutal marks upon her—and something else: a silver brooch, etched with the stooping hawk of House Ghytteve, pinned to her ragged shift. Kitten had told the Ghytteve everything before she died. The way they had left her body like a flung gauntlet where Sharkbait couldn't help but find it left no doubt.

He looked up at the thief. She was still and white and cold; only her eyes glittered fiercely. There was nothing he could say to her. He bowed his head, and brushed Kitten's cold cheek with a gesture like apology; then he rose. With peculiar, dreamlike detachment, he noted the horrified faces of his men and their murmurs of recognition and distress. "Bury her," he commanded. "Ferret," he began, but the thief cut him off with a sharp gesture.

"Happen Kerigden should know; I'll go. And you: get down to the Trollop and take the others to the Temple. If Kitten told them about you, she told them about the Trollop. Get them out before the Ghytteve find them."

"Ferret," he tried again.

But she had turned away and didn't answer.

Someone produced a shroud of tattered sailcloth. Sharkbait watched them wrap her; their gentleness stung tears from him, dragged his feelings out of their numb shelter. "Oh Kitten," he whispered, fierce, "in the sight of all the gods this I swear: *the Ghytteve shall pay for what they have done!*"

In the gray dawn, Donkey rose. He lit the fire, set water to boil, then ground the coffee beans needed for breakfast. The rhythmic sound of the grinder, rather like snoring, didn't rouse Squirrel. While the coffee brewed, its aroma doing its work, he slipped outside to test the temper of the morning.

The streets were quiet, but it was a tense hush—a lull, not peace. The dead and injured had been carted off, as though the streets had been scoured by some avenging god; but groups of bravos, like hunting sharks, drifted by. The Slums were tinder, and clearly, Ybhanne and Khyzhan still struck sparks. He hurried back to the Trollop.

The scent of coffee had roused Squirrel, who filled cups and loaded trays for the tavern master. Stirring porridge, Arkhyd cast a stern glance in his nephew's direction as Donkey fell in with the breakfast preparations. When the tavern master went out with the last of the trays, Donkey dished out two bowls of porridge, while Squirrel poured coffee.

"Are the streets quiet?" he asked Donkey.

"Strung tighter than harp strings."

Just then, Mouse came in bearing a tray laden with soiled dishes. "Dedemar's gone," she said, skipping greetings. "He slipped out during the night."

"Did he take his friend's body?" Donkey asked.

Mouse shuddered. "No."

"No wonder your uncle's looking so sour," Squirrel remarked. "What will Arkhyd do with a body, Donkey?"

"Whose body?" Sharkbait asked harshly from the alley door. They all jumped.

"Why, good morning, Sharkbait," Mouse greeted him waspishly. "How nice of you to drop in. It was a friend of Dedemar's; a man named Zhotar."

Sharkbait came into the kitchen, fast. *"Zhotar?* Another Ghytteve bodyguard dead? *Good."* The word was vicious.

"Sharkbait, what's wrong?" Squirrel demanded, alarmed.

Rage died in his face, leaving sorrow like bitter ashes. "They killed Kitten." His voice caught, trembled. "They wrung her dry and cast her off like refuse; they left her on the waterfront, where I would find her. My men buried her."

The others exchanged stricken looks. Mouse's hand crept up to cover her mouth. Squirrel pounded the table with his fist.

"Kitten," Mouse sobbed.

Donkey wrapped the girl in a comforting hug; tears streamed like rain on his cheeks. For several moments, no one spoke. Then Donkey asked, "Where's Ferret?"

"She's taken word to the Windbringer's Temple. I'm to bring you there."

"To the Windbr—" Squirrel began. "Sharkbait, *why?"*

"My parents—" Mouse protested.

"All of us?" Donkey asked.

Sharkbait held up one hand. "Just the bones for now. Kit—" his voice caught on the name, "Kitten will have told the Ghytteve about the Trollop; your scent must be cold when Ycevi's hounds come hunting. Kerigden—the Windbringer's High Priest—helped Ferret to escape Azhere, and he offered to shelter all of you. So we're going." Suddenly, his gaze sharpened on Mouse. "You said Zhotar is dead. How?"

It fell to Mouse to relate the events of the past night, including Dedemar's message to all of them, and the conversation she had overheard between the dying bodyguard and his friend. When she had finished, Sharkbait looked thoughtful.

"And now, Dedemar is gone," he said softly. "I wonder whether he's taken his friend's advice—and how we can make use of this tangle." As Sharkbait narrowed his eyes in concentration, Arkhyd came bustling back into the kitchen.

An unwelcoming frown settled on the tavern master's face. *"You're* back? What do you want, now?"

Inspiration drew a bitter smile from Sharkbait. "I understand," he drawled, "you have a bit of a disposal problem. Perhaps you'd like my help with it?"

Arkhyd's expression teetered between relief and suspicion. Suspicion won. "Happen you'll explain why you're so helpful of a sudden."

"I've a score to settle with the Ghytteve. He was one of their bodyguards; did you know?" Sharkbait's words turned Arkhyd's face the color of putty.

"I run a respectable tavern," the tapster bleated. "Do you mean to *ruin* me?"

"No, merely to save your skin. The Ghytteve are full of rage and bloodlust; they believe they have reason to connect a number of us—Ferret and her friends—with foiling some scheme of theirs. It's nonsense, of course; but deadly nonsense. Arkhyd, they murdered Kitten; she was tortured. It's likely she mentioned the Trollop. You *don't* want to have the corpse of a Ghytteve bodyguard in your possession—no matter how innocently acquired—when Ycevi unleashes her hounds."

Arkhyd's gaze touched each of the children in turn. "Are they in danger?" he asked.

Sharkbait nodded. "And their presence here is a danger to you. Let me hide the children. I believe I can keep them safe."

"Mouse's parents—" Arkhyd began, but shouts and the clash of weapons from the street interrupted.

"*Explain* to Mouse's parents," Sharkbait suggested. "In private. For now, put the body in your wine cellar, and turn a blind eye to the fact that the children and I have disappeared from your kitchen."

The tavern master looked alarmed. "Happen that's the Ghytteve in the streets, now? What then?"

"*Whenever* you meet the Ghytteve, Arkhyd, remember this: they won't believe you're ignorant—or innocent. Your best course is to tell them—right off—yes, Sharkbait uses the Trollop as a meeting place—and pays you well to do it. Say you can't predict my movements, but invite them to post a watcher on the premises—*for a suitable fee*. The Ghytteve understand trade, and betrayal. And they don't believe in compassion, charity or loyalty. Offer them a business proposition, Arkhyd; it's safest."

The tavern master swallowed audibly. The noises from the street had moved into the distance. "Go. I'll explain to your parents, Mouse. Thantor—" His gaze reached through an illegible scrawl of emotion to touch his nephew's face. "I never knew what your father was thinking, either," he whispered. "Go, lest I start asking questions—and I'd best not know aught else."

They went. Sharkbait led them with a woodsman's skill past hunting bravos. At the Waiting Wall, he gave them a fistful of silver and sent them ahead to the Windbringer's Temple. Then, with a promise to meet them before the morning was over, he melted back into the Slums' labyrinth.

Ycevi Ghytteve regarded Elkhar over the rim of her shell-delicate porcelain coffee cup. "Let me be sure I understand you. The child, Kitten, told you that Cyffe was killed by 'Sharkbait'—whom you surmise to be Antryn Anzhibhar-Ykhave."

"By Sharkbait *and Ferret*," Elkhar corrected, "when I pressed her on it."

The Lady raised her eyebrows. "So the little thief was clever enough to dupe Rhydev—or this Kitten was fabricating things to appease you. What else?"

"She mentioned Venykhar Ghobhezh-Ykhave, but she called him '*Mouse's* nobleman;' she didn't connect him with Antryn (or Sharkbait) at all, and when I asked her why he was 'Mouse's nobleman,' she said he was impressed with Mouse's skill at drawing. She said that *Owl* had told her—before we ever saw him—the Emperor's life was in danger, and that he had dreamed of the Emperor's foreign witch. (She called her *by name*.) Even pushed—and I pushed hard, Lady: trust me—she maintained they were all just 'friends;' but this Sharkbait started a *Guild war* when Azhere kidnapped Ferret. There's more moving here than the child knew—I'm certain of it. Dedemar's message indicated that the Windbringer priest and the Emperor's foreign witch are somehow involved, but Kitten knew nothing about it."

The Lady frowned. "The *khacce* code is ambiguous; perhaps Dedemar didn't mean the Windbringer High Priest was involved. Kerigden has spent years impressing upon us his disinterest in politics. Might he have meant a priest of the Windbringer?"

"It's possible," Elkhar admitted. "I sent Zhotar to seek clarification of him—" Suddenly, Elkhar stiffened. "I sent Zhotar to the *Trollop's Smile*; and he hasn't reported in, yet."

"The Trollop's Smile?"

"It's the tavern where those children congregate. If harm has come to him, I'll—"

"Yes," she cut him off. "But Elkhar, what's the connection? What part do you suppose Owl is to play in all this—if any? What possible *value* can he have to people as different as Ghobhezh-Ykhave and the Emperor's witch? Not to mention Antryn and Kerigden, if they are in truth involved." She drank her cooling coffee with irritation.

"I told you about his visions. He *must* be part of Antryn's plot—or counterplot. Perhaps they are leagued to thwart us, Lady. For all that I can't bear the creature, I have difficulty imagining the Emperor's witch plotting *against* him." Elkhar fell silent as he sorted scraps of fact and surmise. "Get rid of Owl, Lady; that boy is dangerous."

"No. No." Ycevi's calm facade frayed. "We *can't*. If *fatal* harm comes to Owl, I won't have a prayer of holding Cithanekh—and all our work would be undone."

"Kill them both, then," Elkhar urged, "and start over with Ancith. He'll be of age in three years—and a Regency could work to your advantage." As the Lady began to shake her head, he gestured imploringly. "I know he ought to be perfect—but what use is 'ought' if your puppy turns out to be a wolf, after all? You've planned so carefully; don't throw it away."

"It's *Owl*," Ycevi snarled. "*It's always Owl.* He's the grit in the flour. He seems so innocent, and flawless for my purposes; but he's trouble—always trouble."

"Get rid of him," Elkhar repeated. "It would be a simple matter to poison…"

"Elkhar," the Lady's crisp tone recalled him to duty. "No. I do not wish to consider such measures. As for the rest, you've made a satisfactory beginning—but it is *only* a beginning. I want that thief: Ferret; and Sharkbait, if you can trap him."

"May I bait the trap with the boy?"

"No. Not if it will risk him. Go."

"As you command, Lady."

After Elkhar left, the Lady pondered for several minutes. Reaching some inward decision, she rang her table cymbal. When Myncerre answered the summons, Ycevi said, "Fetch Owl."

"I'm not sure he's up yet, Lady."

"Wake him."

Myncerre returned shortly with Owl who was wrapped in a silk robe too large for him. He was heavy eyed and pale. The Lady studied him silently for several moments.

"You remember, no doubt," she began at last, "that I said you were not for sale? Not at any price."

"Yes, Lady. I remember," Owl replied with flat politeness.

"I may have spoken too soon. Rhydev Azhere would pay a lot of money for you—*a lot* of money." She watched his face closely, saw his spasm of dread. "Wouldn't you like that?"

"Why?" Owl's question was faint as a breath.

Her smile reminded the boy of Elkhar—the same feral eagerness. "I don't trust you, boy. You're too clever. Clever tools make me uneasy. Come here. Give me your hands."

The Lady saw panic flash across Owl's face. As he struggled with the too-long sleeves of the robe, she reached over and imprisoned his wrists. At her touch, his face went stiff. She set his forearms on the table before she peeled back the extra inches of sleeve to reveal each hand. His left was clenched. She tapped it imperatively. When he opened his hand, the Lady caught her breath. In his palm lay an opal the size of a wren's egg: of blues darker than midnight, its heart of fire glinted, elusive, in its depths.

"Where did you get that?" the Lady demanded.

"I found it on the floor in the library," Owl lied. "It must have fallen off the *khacce* table; but it was so pretty I...Lady, I meant to put it back."

"That never came from my *khacce* table, boy," she said, holding out her hand. "Give it to me."

For a heartbeat, it seemed Owl would refuse. Then, resigned, he dropped the stone into her outstretched palm. A brilliant flash of scarlet made the Lady blink, bemused. Then she shrugged. "I suppose since you found it, there's no harm in your keeping it." She gave it back. "Why aren't you dressed?"

"You wanted him immediately, Lady," Myncerre offered.

"Of course." She was silent a moment longer, then she lifted the coffee pot. With a moue of irritation she set it down again. "Take him away, Myncerre; and have the kitchen send up another pot of coffee."

In the hallway, Owl and Myncerre exchanged looks. "Does she mean to sell me to Rhydev Azhere?" Owl asked, troubled.

Myncerre hunched one shoulder. "She only meant to frighten you. Owl, what did you have in your hand—and where did you get it? You didn't stop to pick anything up."

He showed her the stone. "Someone put it into my hand last night while I slept."

Myncerre smiled ruefully. "I wonder where Cithanekh came by such a thing. It's beautiful, Owl."

"You won't tell the Lady?"

The steward made a dismissive gesture. "I doubt she'll ask me. Go dress, lad; I must stop in the kitchen."

When he reached his quarters, he found Cithanekh, pacing anxiously. The young lord smiled at the sight of Owl in the borrowed dressing gown. "It's rather too large," he remarked.

Owl managed a smile. "I'm relieved. I thought I'd shrunk in the night."

"What did the Lady want?"

"She threatened to sell me to Rhydev Azhere: Myncerre said she only meant to frighten me." Cithanekh frowned; to forestall comment, Owl shook one hand free of its sleeve and touched his friend's wrist. "I need to talk to you," he breathed. "Is it safe?"

The young lord considered. "Keep your voice low; we'll act as though I'm comforting you. All the guards know what happened. It shouldn't cause any comment."

Owl nodded faintly. "Cithanekh, I—I dreamed last night."

With a wordless protest, the young lord wrapped an arm around the boy's shoulders.

"It wasn't awful. My visions were full of…of music; and then, the Windbringer came."

"The *Windbringer*," Cithanekh whispered. "How did you know it was she? Is that why you asked me her ancient name?"

He shook his head. "I asked you her name because I wanted to try to summon her; I didn't think she'd answer me, but—" His eyes filled, suddenly, and he struggled to whisper around tears. "*Someone* must avenge K-Kitten, and I don't see how I—I can. Anyway, she answered me. And she—she wanted to know about K-Kitten. It—it made her weep. And then she said, 'The sacrifice of children must not go unsung, nor unavenged.' And she gave me this." Cautiously, he opened his hand between them, so that Cithanekh might see the stone, but any watchers in the walls would not. He caught his breath, then, for the stone was different: the blues and greens of summer sky and sea; the fire in its heart gold, instead of brooding red.

Cithanekh's long fingers touched the stone, wonderingly, though he made no move to take it from the boy.

"It changes color," Owl added. "It was darker when the Lady looked at it."

"The La—She let you keep it? You didn't tell her about your dream?"

"No, I told her I found it on the floor in the library. I don't think she meant to let me keep it, but—and this was really odd—when she took it, it flashed red, and she acted confused, as though she couldn't remember what she was doing. She sent me away to dress before I'd have said she was done with me. Oh," he added, a little guiltily. "I *implied* to Myncerre you'd given it to me; I said someone slipped it into my hand while I slept. She assumed I'd meant you."

Cithanekh ruffled Owl's hair; then, conjecture and worry gathered in his eyes. "Owl, how much control do you have over your visions?"

"Over the visions, none, really; they just come. But—" He leaned toward Cithanekh, who gathered him into his arms so that Owl could whisper into his ear. "I can speak mind to mind, a little, with Arre and Kerigden."

The young lord drew back so he could see Owl's face. He bit his lips as he studied the boy.

"Have I frightened you?" Owl breathed, his eyes brimming with tears.

Cithanekh brushed his face, lifting his chin so he could look into Owl's eyes. He smiled crookedly. "A little," he admitted. "It isn't everyone who can converse silently with witches and priests—not to mention Talyene." At the name, the stone in Owl's hand blazed briefly with a multitude of joyful colors. They exchanged awed glances. "It knows her name," the young lord whispered, shivering.

"Don't be afraid of me," Owl pleaded. "Cithanekh, I need you." The tears spilled.

Cithanekh brushed them away, gently. "My dear, amazing Owl," he breathed. "I'm not afraid of you; but I am terrified *for* you. Ycevi would never let you live if she knew the extent of your gifts."

Owl nodded, but his tears didn't stop. After a moment, Cithanekh gathered him into his arms and held him.

Chapter Twenty-three
Stratagems

The Temple of the Windbringer looked very different, Squirrel decided, by daylight. For one thing, the imposing marble steps were crowded with people; well-to-do worshipers, and priests and acolytes in the gray of the sect, streamed purposefully in and out. No one took much notice of the three ragged children, until Donkey caught the gray sleeve of a tiny old woman and said, "We'd like to see the High Priest."

She fixed him with a penetrating dark gaze and said, "Are you Donkey or Squirrel? He said to expect you."

"Donkey," he replied. "These are Squirrel and Mouse."

She nodded greeting at them, then led the way up the steps, through the main sanctuary, and along a narrow corridor to a closed door. She rapped, and when the door was opened, she gestured the children inside.

Ferret was there, leaning over the shoulder of the dark haired woman Squirrel had guided to the Trollop on Ythykh-Fair. The woman was unfurling a roll of papers on the table. Beside her was Mouse's nobleman, and across the table was the red-haired Windbringer High Priest. The thief's head came up as the door opened, and almost before her friends had begun to move into the room, she had come around the table toward them. They flung themselves at her, and she gathered them into a hug which was more of a huddle. The contact made her eyes fill. She blinked hard, unready to indulge her grief. "Sharkbait?" she asked, noting who wasn't present.

"He had to help Arkhyd dispose of a body," Squirrel said. "He said he'd be along."

"Whose body?" Ferret demanded, but before they could begin the tale she said, "Wait. Introductions: Mouse, Squirrel, Donkey; Arre, Venykhar, Kerigden. Now, come sit down and tell us the whole."

Donkey related the events, warnings, and conversations while Ferret and the others listened attentively. When he finished, there was a short silence.

"In light of what you've told us, Donkey," Kerigden said, "I would like to know whether Dedemar has reported for duty, or not." He rang a table cymbal, and sent the person who answered off on the errand.

After the messenger left, Arre said, "On our side of events, Kerigden and I have tried to teach Owl how to control his Sight Gifts; we've touched Owl's mind, and together, we might be able to do it again. And Khethyran has made us a map—granted from an old source, so perhaps not entirely accurate—of the secret passages and spyholes in the Palace."

"Are we going to spy on the Ghytteve?" Squirrel asked.

"Perhaps," Arre replied. "It is crucial that we discover what they plan to do, and when. We know that Ycevi Ghytteve plans to murder the Scholar King and put Cithanekh Anzhibhar-Ghytteve on the throne instead. She plans to make Cithanekh a puppet by holding Owl hostage to her interests. But we don't know how they plan to murder the Emperor, and we don't know when they intend to act."

"We'll find out," Ferret said grimly. "Happen I said, once, the Ghytteve dinna matter to me; it isn't true any longer. They've killed one of my friends, *and they shall suffer for it.* How much proof do you need before the Emperor can charge Ycevi with high treason?"

Venykhar shook his head. "Treason is difficult to define: in the eyes of the Council Houses, it *isn't* treason if it works; and intention is almost impossible to prove. For every witness we could find to say Ycevi meant this or said that, she would have at least three who would defend her. It is probably a better plan to avenge your friend by foiling her scheme."

"So how do we do that?" Squirrel asked. "Spy on them? I'm fast, and quiet. Happen I could discover their plans."

"It's dangerous," Kerigden warned.

"Happen we know they're playing for blood," Donkey said. "It doesn't matter; we're in the game, whatever the stakes."

"Very well," Venykhar said. "We can use my apartments as headquarters; I'll provide you boys with page's livery, and Mouse—"

"Ven, wait," Arre began; and at the same moment, the door opened and Sharkbait came in. He was pale and sweating, his expression stony.

"Antryn, what's wrong?" Venykhar cried.

"If we were counting on the Guild war to keep the Ghytteve out of the Slums, we were dreaming," he said bitterly. "I got Zhotar's body dumped without trouble, but I've seen several brace of hunting Ghytteve this morning; and I overheard some troubling things. Ferret, they are looking for you—and me."

"Naught to surprise us there, surely," she interjected.

"No, but they also think you're involved, Kerigden—or someone in your Temple—and that I didn't expect."

"Dedemar must have seen us with Ferret—or someone who owed him a favor did," Kerigden sighed. "Well, it can't be helped—but it does render the sanctuary I've offered you something less than safe, I fear."

"Naught's safe," Ferret said, "until yon Ycevi's dead."

"Ycevi *and* Elkhar," Sharkbait corrected. "So: how to proceed?"

While they filled Sharkbait in on what they had discussed, Kerigden's messenger returned with word that Dedemar was, indeed, missing with no explanation. When the messenger had left, they began to debate the advantages and dangers of spying on the Ghytteve. Surprisingly, Sharkbait agreed with Venykhar that his apartments should become the headquarters for any surveillance within the Palace; but he argued against either Mouse or Ferret helping to watch the Ghytteve.

"They want you, Ferret; and there are enough people— like Azhere—who know your face to make it too dangerous for you to be in the Palace. Further—"

"Never mind," Ferret cut him off. "Happen I've other ideas than watching in the walls."

"But I could—" Mouse began.

"No," he said firmly. "Mouse, they don't know your face; the Ghytteve don't even have a *description* of you. Elkhar's seen both Donkey and Squirrel, so they *need* to stay out of sight in the walls. But you could wander about openly, if we made an excuse for it."

"You mean I could pose as a maid?"

"Actually," he flashed a look full of meaning at Venykhar, "I had something else in mind."

The old lord nodded. "You would have the run of the Palace, Mouse, if you were thought to be my adopted niece. The Ykhave do that: adopt people of talent into the clan. No one would doubt you, once they saw your drawings."

"But I canna talk like a noble," the girl protested.

Venykhar Ghobhezh-Ykhave smiled wryly. "Neither could I, when I first came to House Ykhave. Will you do it, Mouse?"

She nodded. "But it had better be 'Amynne.' Elkhar knows the name, 'Mouse.' And, Lord Venykhar, is this truth or pretense? I need to know."

"Truth—if your parents will agree to it."

She smiled, then, an expression full of radiant hope. "Oh, they'll agree when they see how much it matters to me."

"Well," Arre said into the brief silence this exchange engendered. "Perhaps we should study these maps."

"Wait," Sharkbait said. "Ferret, I'd like to know what your 'other ideas' include; and do you see a role for me?"

Ferret feigned wide-eyed innocence. "As if I'd *presume* to plan for you." At his silent challenge, she shrugged. "Seems to me that if the Ghytteve are fool enough to hunt in the midst of a Guild war, we might make use of that. It's a lawless place, the Slums, at the best of times. Happen if we were clever, we could lead some of Ycevi's hounds into Khyzhan's or Ybhanne's wolves."

"That sounds—" Arre began, but Ferret cut her off.

"Dangerous?" Some of her suppressed anger colored her tone. "So am I. Are you with me, Sharkbait?"

He nodded once, sharply. "Very well, my sweet thief; let's go hunting."

As the thief and the longshoreman departed, Arre unfurled her sheaf of papers and laid out the map on the table. The others crowded around. "This is the Ghytteve complex," Arre told them, pointing. "See the listening holes and passages? And here—look: a way to go secretly from the Ghytteve complex to the Ykhave quarters. That may be really useful."

Squirrel and Donkey exchanged perplexed looks. "But how do you tell which is what?" Squirrel asked.

"The symbols are identified in the key," Arre explained, then broke off, as pain contorted her features for an instant. "None of you can read," she said flatly.

"We're not *stupid*," Mouse responded sharply. "Once Squirrel and Donkey get their bearings, they *never* get lost; and if you explain what the signs mean, I'll remember the turnings."

They spent the next hour poring over the map. When they were done, Kerigden sent the children off in the care of some of his people to be scrubbed clean and made presentable. Venykhar went back to his apartments to fetch livery for the boys, and Arre went into town to find Mouse a decent dress. Much later, washed, brushed, trimmed and dressed, the three friends studied one another's transformation, before Venykhar took them up to the Palace.

Zherekhaf, the Prime Minister, poured coffee for his nephew, eyebrows arched inquiringly. "So you've a plan for the removal of the Emperor's foreign witch?"

Rhydev Azhere waved a dismissive hand. "Nothing so— mmm—*elaborate* as a plan, merely the skeleton of a notion." He paused to gather his thoughts under Zherekhaf's intent scrutiny. "We *know* the Ghytteve are conspiring. In my experience, they are rather—mmm—*intolerant* of interference, prone to leap to conclusions, and swift and ruthless in their responses."

"Swift, *rash*, and ruthless," the Prime Minister put in.

"Precisely." Rhydev fingered his beard reflectively. "I thought we might exploit such proclivites. If we—mmm— *encourage* the Ghytteve to belive that the Emperor's foreign witch is involved in a counterplot to thwart them, it might be enough to convince them to eliminate her."

"Thereby doing our dirty work for us," Zherekhaf said, smug. "I like it. Go on."

"If they *were* to kill Arre, and if we were able to—mmm— *implicate* them, I think it likely the Scholar King would bring Ycevi down over it."

Zherekhaf raised his eyebrows. "You amaze me," he murmured. "She's not even his wife; surely he wouldn't risk strife in his realm over a doxy."

"He loves her," Rhydev responded. "And perhaps he would—mmm—*underestimate* the resentment such an unreasonably harsh reprisal would engender."

"Still," the Prime Minister said, assessing his nephew inscrutably, as he considered. "It might serve nicely—though, frankly, I would not have expected you to see the possibility."

"It *will* serve," Rhydev responded, outwardly ignoring his uncle's comment while treasuring it for later analysis. "If we can pull this off (and you must realize, Uncle, that the timing is—mmm—*delicate*), we would be rid of Arre and Ycevi, and Khethyran's political position would be seriously—mmm—*undermined*. All to the good; how best to effect it?"

Zherekhaf arched his eyebrows. "Use the boy."

"The—the boy? You mean Owl?"

The Prime Minister permitted himself a tiny, superior smile. "The Ghytteve are not sure of him. Weren't you at Ycevi's latest soiree? I could taste that brute Elkhar's suspicion."

"Elkhar is suspicious of *everything*, Uncle," Rhydev protested. Owl was key to his other, unspoken, plan; he disliked the idea of risking him. "It's hardly sensible to impute similar excessive caution to the Lady."

"I watched her watching him. I tell you: the Ghytteve are not sure of him. With care, he could become the fulcrum to move them against the foreign witch."

Rhydev thought fast. It was true: and to protest overmuch might raise suspicions in his uncle. But still…He wet his lips. "Indeed he could; but remember, Uncle: I *want* that boy—alive and unharmed."

"As things stand, my dear Rhydev, you'll *never* get him. It merely amuses Ycevi to taunt you. If we shake her tower down, you may be able to rescue the boy from the rubble."

Rhydev thinned his lips and flared his nostrils in a skillful play of suppressed anger; then he eased his expression into a sigh. "You are right, alas. But we must move cautiously; and if we can—mmm—*implicate* the Emperor's foreign witch without the boy, let us do so."

"Of course, of course," the Prime Minister soothed. He hefted the coffee pot. "More, while we plan?"

Chapter Twenty-four
Hunting

The Trollop's Smile was quiet though not empty. Arkhyd surveyed the collection of refugees without enthusiasm. They
had ceased even to pretend to be normal tavern patrons—
which was just as well, as he was nearly out of ale, and food
stores were getting low. If the Guild war didn't cool soon,
hunger would join them in the taproom.

At these uneasy thoughts, the common room door swung
open. Two men came in, fast: well dressed and sleek as mas-
tiffs. Arkhyd noticed the dangling silver earring each of them
sported as they circled to pen him behind his own bar.

"We're looking for the child, Kitten," one of them told the
tapster. His handsome face was marred by a scar like a whip
cut sharp across one cheek.

"She's not here," Arkhyd replied, Sharkbait's warning upward in his mind. "She ran an errand for some foreigner last
night and didn't return. Happen she took shelter outside the
Slum; Guild war's bad, here."

The other man raised eyebrows. "Is the foreigner here?"

Arkhyd shook his head. "Slipped out," he replied with
unfeigned annoyance. "Stiffed me, too." Calculation showed
on his face. "Friend of yours?"

With a derisive smile, the first man spun a silver coin
across the polished wood. "We'll ask; you answer. Do you
know a man, scarred face?" His forefinger traced the line of
Sharkbait's scar.

"Happen I do?" Arkhyd was suddenly painfully aware of
the silence in the common room; his clients were listening hard.

Several coins followed the first; the glint in the man's eyes
grew hard. "You had better remember."

"You want to discuss it here?" he asked, casting a wary
eye at the gathered people.

"*We've* nothing to hide," the first said pointedly. "The
scarred man?"

Arkhyd gave in; he tried not to imagine how it would seem to his guests. "Longshoreman. Name of Sharkbait. He uses my kitchen as a meeting place, sometimes—and pays me well." The second man drawled, "Buys your silence, does he?" Arkhyd shrugged. "Doesn't pay *that* well."

"How often does he come? What time of day?"

Arkhyd shrugged again. "No set pattern—and no warning. He comes and goes when he chooses."

"With whom does he meet?" When Arkhyd hesitated, more silver chimed against the wood. *"With whom does he meet?"*

"It varies, and I dinna know them all. Some Guild thieves."

"Names."

Arkhyd shook his head.

"Names."

The tapster shook his head again. "You canna pay enough to make ratting on Guild thieves seem like sense."

The scarred man hooked talon-like fingers into Arkhyd's tunic and yanked him across the bar. Nose to nose, the tapster found himself gazing into hard, black eyes. "You've a choice," his captor gritted. "Risk the anger of the Thieves' Guild, or fatally offend House Ghytteve. Now: names."

"Ferret," he gasped. "She's Khyzhan's. I dinna know the others."

"Ferret," the Ghytteve repeated, twisting the tunic tighter. "And Kitten? Squirrel? Donkey? Mouse? Owl?"

Arkhyd shook his head helplessly. Over the thudding of his heart, he was aware of the tense attention of Mouse's parents. He willed them to silence, to calm.

"Did you know," the other Ghytteve drawled while his avid eyes scanned the tavern guests, "Sharkbait is selling children?"

"No!" It was Mouse's mother; her husband's hand closed warningly on her wrist, but too late.

"Yes." He pinned her with his eyes. "Sharkbait sells them to the Council Houses, for unspeakable things. Not a nice man."

Not true, not true, Arkhyd thought at her. His world wavered as the Ghytteve's grip constricted his breathing. Mouse's mother looked from the Ghytteve to Arkhyd, to her husband; puzzlement colored her face. "But I know those children. I can imagine someone paying for Owl—he's pretty. But *Donkey?* He's a half-wit; and yon Mouse? Happen she should be named 'Shrew.'"

Mouse's father hunched one shoulder. "There's no accounting for noble tastes, clearly. If I'd known there was a market for those little beasts, I'd have sold them myself."

The Ghytteve holding Arkhyd eased his grip fractionally, while the other man eyed Mouse's father. "You want to sell someone, Ghytteve would buy this Sharkbait."

"How much?" several voices asked.

"Alive: one hundred Royals. Dead: he's worthless to us."

There were low whistles. It was all Arkhyd could do to keep dismay off his face. With a price like *that* on his head, Sharkbait would be wise not to trust his own mother. For all that Arkhyd didn't much like the man, he owed him a favor for his help with the Ghytteve bodyguard's corpse.

The man holding Arkhyd released him. "House Ghytteve wants Sharkbait," he murmured. "Find and hold him for us; earn our gratitude and enjoy our money. But don't imagine you can betray us. We'll be watching; we'll be back."

Ferret and Sharkbait found Arkhyd in the Trollop's kitchen, worry in every line of his pudgy body. As they entered, he shook his head bleakly and gestured for quiet.

"The Ghytteve were here," he whispered.

Sharkbait arched eyebrows. "Are they still?" he breathed.

The tavern master shook his head.

"They posted no watchers?" Ferret prodded quietly.

"They've filled the Slums with watchers," Arkhyd said. "They set a price on your head, Sharkbait. A hundred Royals."

"*A hundred Royals?*" Ferret demanded in an urgent whisper. "*A hundred Royals?* Sharkbait—"

He stilled her with a raised hand. "Thank you for the warning, Arkhyd. Was there anything else of moment in your encounter with the Ghytteve?"

The tapster shuddered. "I thought Mouse's parents would give the game away when one of the Ghytteve said that you'd been selling children; but happen they covered well enough.

She pretended to have been surprised that anyone would want the children. 'Donkey? He's half-witted!'" he mimicked her. "'And yon *Mouse!* Happen she should be named 'Shrew.'"

"You told them I used the Trollop as a meeting place?"

"Aye," Arkhyd confirmed. "They wanted to know who you met; I told them Guild thieves and others, and when they pressed for names, I gave them yours, Ferret."

The thief nodded shortly. "Happen you'd like me to square that with Khyzhan; I'll do my best."

The tavern master looked grateful. "But Sharkbait, be careful: a hundred Royals is an emperor's ransom. Not many hold friendship that valuable."

"I know," Sharkbait said. "And I realize I'm in your debt. Can you describe the Ghytteve who were here?"

"There were two. One has a whip cut scar on his face; black eyes; a strong grip."

"Cezhar," Sharkbait supplied a name. "One of the lieutenants. The other?"

"Sandy haired; insolent tone; a bit shorter."

Sharkbait frowned. "Rhan—I think. It could be Ynteth, though he never spoke much when I knew him. Did they say when they'd be back?"

"No."

Sharkbait turned to his companion. "Well Ferret? Now what?"

"Happen you should lie low."

"Do you trust Khyzhan enough to enlist his aid?"

The thief shook her head. "He'd split the reward with me. A hundred Royals—that's money enough to start more than one Guild war." An idea struck her; she smiled wryly. "How well do you trust your longshoremen?"

Sharkbait nodded once. "Let's go. Arkhyd, I won't forget."

Shouting and thumps from the tap room interrupted them before the tavern master could reply; almost reflexively, he bustled into the front room. Ferret and Sharkbait headed for the door to the alleyway, but before they went out, Ferret halted him with a gesture. Using every bit of her skill, she slipped into the alley. Sharkbait waited, toying with something tucked into his tunic. When she returned, her face was gray.

"There's a watcher," she breathed. "If we leave, Arkhyd's dead."

"Did he see you just now?"

"No." Sharkbait's grim desperation crystallized resolve around Ferret's stuttering heart. "Shall I take him out?" she asked, matter-of-fact.

Sharkbait produced the thing with which he had been toying. "Can you use a garrote?"

She took it wordlessly and eased back into the street. Sharkbait leaned against the kitchen wall, pressing the heels of both hands to his mouth. Time stretched endlessly. Then Ferret popped open the door, gestured urgently, and they sprinted off through the Slum's warren. Neither of them hesitated as they leapt the crumpled figure in the alley mouth.

They took refuge in a warehouse in the waterfront district. For several minutes they sat silently, savoring their narrow escape. Sharkbait rested one hand on the young thief's shoulder. As Ferret's breathing slowed, Sharkbait realized she was shivering. He drew her close, comforting, but offered no words.

"It was so easy," she said with a violent shudder. "It shouldn't have been so easy. How can we be frightened of people who are so *careless?* He didn't even have a wall behind him."

"They are arrogant," Sharkbait offered. "The Ghytteve are unused to resistance; and they dismiss the poor as powerless and thus underestimate the strength of desperation." With two fingers he lifted Ferret's chin so that she met his eyes. "It won't be so easy again, my sweet thief."

"Meaning that they learn from their mistakes?" she asked. "But this makes *three*, Sharkbait; three of Ycevi Ghytteve's precious bodyguards dead. How many deaths before she learns? How many are there? Do you know?"

He shrugged. "Even if I thought I knew their number, it would be unwise not to suspect her of holding others in reserve. The Lady is devious indeed—and no stranger to intrigue or violence. And it isn't the Lady who will learn from her minions' deaths, but Elkhar. Ycevi is a ruthless *khacce* player."

Ferret raised eyebrows. "But these pieces *think*. How much to overturn their loyalty?"

Sharkbait shook his head. "Ycevi's hold is strong."

Ferret sighed and rested her head against his shoulder. "So what next?"

The longshoreman smiled wolfishly. "Is there any chance, do you think, of getting Khyzhan to help you find that foreign Temple Watchman?"

She turned ideas carefully in her mind, examining intricate facets. "Happen he would, if he thought it might lead to *you.*"

Concern knit his brow. "Doesn't it worry you to mislead Khyzhan? He's your Master—and the Guild has severe strictures about loyalty."

"If I'm sly, he'll leap to conclusions without my help. It's hardly my fault if he misconstrues."

"And it will keep me out of harm's way while you're running into danger. Ferret—"

"Out of harm's way? When the Ghytteve knew enough to throw Kitten's body *on the wharves?* Happen there's plenty of danger to share, Sharkbait."

His arm tightened around her so suddenly that she looked up in alarm. His face was anguished, vulnerable. "Ferret," he whispered. "I *need* you. Please be careful."

"I promise," she said, solemn. "So: dinna do aught stupid."

With his mask of cool self-mockery back in place, Sharkbait murmured, "Anything stupider, you mean." He added airily, "Oh, I'll be careful, my sweet thief. I've played this game before."

"I can tell," she retorted, gently sarcastic, as she brushed his scarred face with her fingertips. "Farewell."

His eyes followed Ferret's purposeful departure; he stared at the door through which she had gone as though it could show him the future.

Chapter Twenty-five
Whispers

Company was sparse at the Beaten Cur. Ferret found her Master at a table beside the empty hearth. The guttering oil lamp cast more shadows than light. Khyzhan didn't look well. A feverish glitter lurked in his eyes. And the pick of his bravos seemed lean, too; some of his favorites were conspicuously absent. Too late, she wished she hadn't come.

"Ho, Ferret," her Master greeted her. "On your own? I hear you've been keeping company with a certain longshoreman."

"News travels, apparently," she replied, then gave him his opening. "Happen I can look after myself without Sharkbait's help."

"Sharkbait, Master?" one of the bravos queried, eager.

Khyzhan held up one hand. "No. I've told you: I dinna care who wants him or what they're paying. Leave him alone."

"Master," one of the bravos began, wheedling. "You owe him naught—and we're your faithful servants."

"No."

Ferret watched the exchange, wondering if it were a ruse to lull her. "A word alone, Master?" she asked.

He dismissed the others. Ferret waited until she was sure they were all out of earshot, then she shook her head. "This Guild war—by now it should have burned to embers. I'm back safe; Ybhanne's organization is destroyed. But the streets are still littered with dead—and they're not all thieves. Happen you'll tell me what's really going on."

Khyzhan slipped his stiletto out of his wrist sheath and toyed with it. "Happen it would be dangerous for you to know."

His tone jangled something in her memory. "It's dangerous already," she answered. "Master, I'm up to my neck in Council House intrigue; happen I've learned to recognize the smell. Why isn't the Thieves' Guild letting the war burn out? Gods and fish, Master! *Who stands to gain?*"

Ferret glared at Khyzhan's opaque face; he held the tip of the stiletto against the lamp wick, splitting the flame like a serpent's forked tongue. "Ferret," he whispered finally. "Tread carefully."

Her mouth dried; he was trying to tell her something, trying to warn her. "I need your help, Master. I'm looking for someone: a foreigner; Temple Watch; name of Dedemar. A Ghytteve tool. They've dropped him; I need to talk to him."

"*Ghytteve,*" Khyzhan breathed. "The signet was Azhere."

Ferret cast her mind back to the signet ring she had stolen from her flash mark. "A ruse to shift blame. It's been the Ghytteve from the start."

Khyzhan balanced the stiletto on the forefinger of his right hand, while he tugged his earlobe with the other hand. He was silent so long that Ferret began to fear he would say no more; but finally, he flipped the knife off his finger, caught it by its point and nodded. "You're right about the Guild war," he offered. "It's not just the Thieves Guild fighting any longer. I'd thought it was the small drug runners using our troubles to hide some reapportionment of their trade. You make me question that, Ferret. This Dedemar. Why do you want him?"

She mimed a throw of *ysmath* bones. "I'm gambling he knows of the Ghytteve's plans—and is ready to tell."

"Council Houses dinna make careless discards," he warned.

"No. But happen they do make mistakes."

The stiletto spun upward out of Khyzhan's fingers, end over end in the fitful light; he caught the knife and sent it spinning again. "Dedemar." The knife spun a third time. Ferret noted that he caught and threw it with alternating hands. The pattern dredged her memory. "Dedemar." He repeated the name, while the knife spun hypnotically. "He's Frefrentian." The memory surfaced: a company of jugglers, spinning knives and torches. Fytrian jugglers: not Frefrentian, *Fytrian*. Ferret waited. Khyzhan's knife thudded into the tabletop, beside the lamp. The patterned hilt gleamed. "The ship, *Kakamyrrat* is in port. Happen its master, Momontar, knows something."

"Thank you, Master Khyzhan," she said, turning away.

He halted her with her name. "Ferret. Beware of Anthagh."

"The slaver?" She could almost hear his voice: 'The closest thing the Slum has to a Council Lord: independent and untouchable.' What *was* Khyzhan hinting at?

The Master Thief inclined his head. "Rumor ties him to Ghytteve. Watch your back."

Ferret bowed and moved away. "Well?" Khyzhan said softly.

A slight stir in the shadows by the chimney resolved itself into a figure: a hard faced woman with the silver Ghytteve ear-ring glinting in the lamp light. Her narrowed eyes challenged the Master-thief. "Why mention Anthagh?"

"Distraction," Khyzhan offered. "What more could I have given you? You wanted a lure for Sharkbait; I sent her to the wharves. And since she will watch her back—with or without my advice! —I'd rather have her looking in Anthagh's direction than mine, or yours."

"Dedemar's Fytrian."

"Is he? Well, no matter: *she* won't know the difference—an ignorant Slum-rat. Now, Ghytteve: payment."

She shook her head. "Not until we have him."

"That wasn't the bargain," Khyzhan said, idly drawing the knife out of the tabletop. "Was it?"

"You will be paid for your help; but I must be sure it's help, first, thief."

"So suspicious," he chided. "Dinna you know of honor among thieves? It would be wise to keep your end of the bargain, Ghytteve. *Now,*" he snarled.

Khyzhan's bravos moved, then, ringing the Ghytteve woman, knives drawn.

"You wouldn't *dare,*" she said. "I'm *Ghytteve.*"

The hiss of thrown knives silenced her.

"You *were* Ghytteve," Khyzhan whispered, sheathing his stiletto. "And arrogant. But not invincible."

Ferret didn't go directly to the wharves; and she did watch her back. She had a tail—but it wasn't Anthagh's: it was a Ghytteve. She moved cautiously while she pondered. Khyzhan had been careful to hand her enough inconsistencies to make her wary. She sifted bits. If Dedemar was Fytrian, not Frefrentian, then perhaps she should look for him on a Fytrian ship. But if the Temple Watchman was really on the wharves, Sharkbait's longshoremen were the ones best suited to hunt there for him. And there was the mention of *Anthagh*—which was surely more than an excuse to tell her to watch her back. Khyzhan knew she would without his reminder.

Then it clicked. She knew Anthagh by sight: an exotic face with a fringe of sandy beard and round, gray eyes. Half-Fytrian, rumor had it. Had Khyzhan been telling her to look for Dedemar with *Anthagh?* Ferret took to the rooftops to give her tail a dangerous choice between treacherous tiles and gutters or the most violent of the Slum streets. When she was confident she had lost him, she made for the Slave Market.

Ferret wasted no time on Anthagh's close-mouthed toughs. Instead, she took a position near the pleasure house rumored to be Anthagh's headquarters and waited for the slaver himself. It required patience; but at long last, Ferret was rewarded. Master Anthagh, in the company of two others, alighted from a sedan chair not fifteen paces from where Ferret lounged.

"Master Anthagh," she called. "I've a message for Dedemar."

The slaver extended his hand. When she put nothing in it, he raised his eyebrows. "From?"

Ferret's heart started sprinting; this was the touchy part, the part where she gambled most. "Kerigden."

Master Anthagh showed no surprise. "Tell me."

"I am to deliver it myself."

The slaver gestured to his companions. "Bring her."

Ferret let them flank her, wondering desperately if she had been clever, or the worst kind of fool. They escorted her though the wide stone doors, past a court with a fountain and a fish pond, up two wide flights of marble stairs, to a cool, dim chamber. The windows were swathed in gauzy blue draperies which kept out the strong sunlight, and gave the room's light an almost watery quality. A balcony, its open door likewise draped, would face the distant harbor. Master Anthagh motioned her to a seat, while the two others went out, closing the double doors behind them.

"What makes Kerigden think I have Dedemar?" Master Anthagh asked, with the air of someone humoring a fool.

Ferret shrugged. "How would I know? Happen the wind told him. I merely go where I'm sent, sir."

"I see." His mockery grew more pronounced. "Kerigden is known to be quite—fastidious. When did he begin using dirty Slum-rat children as couriers?"

"When he decided to move against Ycevi Ghytteve."

Surprise erased all traces of amusement from the slaver's face. "Do *what?*" he asked.

"Move against Ycevi Ghytteve."

Anthagh crossed his arms and glared at Ferret. "The Kerigden I know doesn't meddle in politics."

"Just how well do you know the High Priest of the Windbringer?" Ferret countered. "I wouldn't think you'd have much in common—given your trade." A movement by the balcony doors caught her eye. The draperies were drawn back to reveal a man, silhouetted against the light.

"What message?" he asked.

She couldn't see his face. "Are you Dedemar?"

"Aye."

"Very well. The child you sent to your Ghytteve masters—Kitten—was tortured and killed by Elkhar Ghytteve. Happen you need an opportunity to atone."

"'Elkhar's killing children.' You would have me, perhaps, betray the Ghytteve? Their arms are very long," Dedemar said bitterly, moving into the room.

Ferret saw his face; her eyes widened. It was the foreigner she had saved from the bravos. "You!"

He looked closely at Ferret, then swore in his own language. After a moment, he said, flatly, "Tell me, then, what you would have me do." He collapsed into a chair. "I will not be of much use, I fear. I have nothing to give for your dead friend. I am not—deep in their whispering. They have little trust of me. They tell me watch; so I watch. They tell me listen; so I listen. They send me with a message; so I go."

"Even so, it would be useful if we knew who the Ghytteve want watched, and what you hear, and where they send you."

Dedemar's eyes widened. "You want me to return to them? I am not clever like Elkhar. They will hear lies in my words." "Think of Kitten," Ferret said, cold. "Your task isn't meant to be easy—or safe. We know the Ghytteve plan to kill the Scholar King and put Cithanekh Anzhibhar-Ghytteve in his place. What we dinna know is when—or how."

"*Cithanekh,*" Anthagh exclaimed—almost a laugh. "But that's mad, even for Ycevi. Cithanekh is twice as stubborn as the Scholar King. How does she mean to control him?"

"She will use the boy you sold her: Owl," Ferret said.

"*Owl,*" Dedemar whispered.

"But she told me," Anthagh protested, "she meant to dangle him in front of Rhydev Azhere—to leverage some concessions out of the silk clans."

"She lied. Does it surprise you?"

Before Anthagh could respond, Dedemar held up a hand. "But how can I return? I am absent without leave from my company of Temple Watch. Did I return, there would be—unpleasantness."

Ferret shrugged. "The Windbringer High Priest would excuse you, if you were committed to working against the Ghytteve."

Dedemar was silent; and Ferret's attention was drawn to Anthagh's face, contorted with alarm.

"Dedemar!" the slaver cried. "Do you seek to atone—or to die? Are you completely mad? Ycevi Ghytteve will *eat* you!" When Dedemar did not instantly respond, he rounded on Ferret. "Do you know what you are doing? Or are you merely a *khacce* piece in your betters' fingers?"

"Do you care?" she challenged.

He rang a table cymbal. "Not particularly. But I do wonder. If you are a mere piece on the gameboard, you are not much regarded; for to send you here is a sacrifice play. But if you know what you are doing, you are either very foolish, or very brave—or, I suppose, both." The door opened for two of Anthagh's men; one held a coil of rope. "Bind her." Then Anthagh turned to the Temple Watchman. "If you're fool enough to go back to the Ghytteve, my friend, then you'd best take them a gift."

"No," Dedemar said sharply.

But Anthagh ignored him. He moved closer to watch as his men bound Ferret. Suddenly, he stiffened. "What's this?" he demanded, gesturing to the healing burns on her forearm.

"What, squeamish?" she mocked. "It's betrayal and Guild war, Council House intrigue and secrets."

"*Anthagh*, let her go."

The slaver ignored him while he studied Ferret silently. She sensed the calculation behind his cool eyes, but she was not sure how to influence it. She answered his assessment with impassive patience. "Which Council House?" he asked at last.

She shrugged. "Azhere."

"Ah. Ybhanne's patron. Did you know?"

"I'd guessed," Ferret replied. "Patron, but not protector. Ybhanne's dead, Master Anthagh. Happen we're all expendable."

"What *are* you?"

Ferret shrugged again. "Loyal friend; Journeyman thief."

"Instrument of judgment and the keeper of my life and honor," Dedemar said, coming to the slaver's side. "*Let her go!*"

Anthagh looked up at him, shocked. "Keeper—"

"She saved my life, in the Guild war. Let her go."

Anthagh stared at the other man, motionless, until Ferret asked, "Who fuels the Guild war, Master Anthagh, and *why?* Ybhanne's *dead*, and Khyzhan's no fool."

"Who is fighting?" the slaver responded, coming back to life and movement. He bent to Ferret's bonds, his thin fingers working loose the knots.

Ferret thought back to her conversation with her Master. It wasn't thieves; and Khyzhan had intimated it wasn't merely another deadly turf-war among the small drug runners. "House Azhere controls the silk trade, no?" The slaver hinted at a nod. "What does Ghytteve control?"

"Coffee and liquor—*officially*."

"*Drugs*," Ferret whispered. "Then the *Ghytteve* are keeping the Slums in turmoil. But why?"

Dedemar answered her. "Among my people there is a saying: 'In chaos is change.'"

The knots holding her yielded. Anthagh straightened. "What will happen, do you think, if the Guild war fails to cool?"

Ferret considered. People were tense; supplies were short; tempers were frayed. "Riots," she breathed. She closed her eyes on memories: the choking ash, the trampling tide of people, the clatter of weapons, the pelting hail of stones, screams, terror, death; it had taken the Watch and finally the Army to restore, with brutal force, a cowering calm. Most of the burned out husks of buildings had been torn down or repaired in the intervening six years, but the fear was graven deep in Ferret.

The slaver and the Temple Watchman watched remembrance flit across the thief's face. When Ferret opened her eyes, there was something steely and determined in their depths. "'In chaos is change,'" she quoted softly. "The Scholar King willn't send the Army to quell a riot; he'll go himself."

"Presenting an irresistible opportunity for his enemies? His advisors would talk him out of such a suicidal course."

"Happen he wouldn't listen. He came down to the Slums once before, right after his coronation. I remember. He gave a speech about being all the people's Emperor. It was very stirring."

"Madness," Anthagh said dismissively.

"But such wonderful madness. We must avert this riot."

"*We*, little thief?" the slaver laughed. "Dedemar may have a conscience (and a debt), but I disposed of mine many years ago. *And I don't owe you a thing.*"

"You sold my friend Owl to the Ghytteve," Ferret accused. "Happen you'll not acknowledge the debt, but it's there."

Anthagh smiled wryly. "It's my trade, Journeyman thief. Perhaps it's not pretty, nor admirable, but it was certainly in my interests to sell Owl to the highest bidder. Even were I in a mood to do you a good turn, the fate of the Scholar King is nothing to me. Less than nothing. The Emperor Khethyran has discussed with the Council banning the slave trade. With the Ghytteve, I know I can bargain."

Ferret laughed. "And what's said in the Council is common knowledge? *Who told you* the Scholar King spoke against slavery? And was it *in their interests* to have you hostile to him? The Scholar King is idealistic, but not *stupid.*"

The slaver was silent, but Dedemar clapped his hands in slow, ironic applause. "You are lazy in your cleverness, Anthagh. The little thief makes you think." He turned to Ferret. "If it were 'we' to avert this riot, what would you have us do?"

Ferret chewed her lip, thinking fast. "If the Slums erupt into riot it will be over food and fear. The thing we have to do is get the Slum markets open, and the people confident enough to use them." She met Anthagh's eyes. "Happen we'd keep control if we organized people to keep the peace: maybe some of your people; the Thieves' Guild, certainly; and the other Slum-Guilds ought to be willing to help. The only people who could *want* riot are the Ghytteve, and they willn't have to live through it."

Anthagh studied her in silence. "Very well," he said at last. "I'll summon the Masters of the Slum-Guilds to a meeting; they'll come—albeit reluctantly—at my whistle. But it will be up to you, little thief, to convince them."

Chapter Twenty-six
Eavesdropping

"You know, Ferret," Anthagh said as the door shut behind the last of the Slum-Guild Masters, "I would never have believed you could get us all to work together like that."

"Happen it's the only way we can survive," she retorted.

"No. It's the only way we can *all* survive. The strong can weather even riots; and according to the commonly held mores of the Slums, the weak deserve to perish. Yet, by some feat of arcane reasoning, you've gotten us to agree to a rule of law—swift and brutal Slum-law, true, but still! I never thought I'd see Slum-denizens work together to open and patrol the markets, and to enforce a curfew."

"Curfew!" Ferret exclaimed, then swore passionately. "How will I get home?"

The slaver chuckled. "You're welcome to stay here."

"Oh, aye," she said with a glint of sarcastic amusement. "But will I be welcome to leave, come morning?"

Anthagh raised his hands in a warding-off gesture. "The merciful gods forbid that I should so court the wrath of the Thieves' Guild!"

"You've some idea they'd be angry? I'd have said the Guildmaster thinks I've overstepped."

"The *Guildmaster* no doubt does," the slaver agreed. "But Khyzhan will back you far beyond the dictates of his self interest; and he's a dangerous enemy."

A tap at the door interrupted their conversation. One of Anthagh's men looked in. "Master, Cezhar Ghytteve wants a word with you. Shall I tell him you're otherwise engaged?"

"No. But first, send Marrekh and Thozh to me—I'd rather not meet him alone." As the man bowed and departed, the slaver glanced at Ferret. "If you'd like to listen, hide yourself."

Ferret's lungs tightened; it smelled like a trap. But she dared not leave for fear she'd meet the Ghytteve on his way in.

She chose a draperied window. At least then, if the slaver betrayed her, she could chance an escape to the roof.

She watched, breathless, from her hiding place while Anthagh's two men—clearly bodyguards—took up their places at the ready. Then, Cezhar Ghytteve came in. He moved with the lithe grace of a fighter. His handsome face was marred by a whip-cut scar across one cheekbone.

"Why were the Slum-Guild Masters here?"

"We were negotiating to avert riots."

His eyebrows rose. "Ycevi Ghytteve *wants* Slum riots."

"Ycevi Ghytteve doesn't live in the Slums."

"Scuttle the agreement, Anthagh. She'll make it worth your while."

"I'm not convinced that she can."

He laughed, disbelieving. "Are you trying to imply you have a price in something other than gold?"

"I don't think you realize, Cezhar, that history was made here, tonight. The Slum-Guild Masters have never before agreed to work together, to share strengths and resources. Ultimately, the effort may fail; none of us has much practice cooperating. But I won't intentionally work against this."

Cezhar's dark eyes narrowed. "Ycevi will be displeased."

The slaver spread his hands, deprecatingly. "Ycevi is only one of my many customers. But this—this place, these people. It is where I both work and live. If the Slum-Guild Masters can overcome their antipathies to work together, then perhaps I am not as untouchable as I have always believed. You *do* understand, I'm sure."

Cezhar Ghytteve was silent for several moments, his face unrevealing. "Who dreamed up this—cooperation?"

"A Journeyman thief by the name of Ferret."

Ferret's heart slammed against her ribs, but an instant's reflection told her Anthagh could really have done nothing else. Too many people knew of her involvement for it to remain secret; and the Ghytteve were already displeased with Anthagh.

"*Ferret!*" he exclaimed. "*Journeyman* thief? Whose?"

"One of Khyzhan's."

He mouthed the Master Thief's name silently. "We'd buy this Ferret, if she happened to fall into your hands. Two hundred Royals."

Anthagh laughed. "Ghytteve would be bidding against Khyzhan—and he pays his debts in blood. If Ferret fell into my hands, Cezhar, the touch would burn me. Your Lady must catch her without my aid."

Cezhar gave a faint nod. "Then I have no further business with you, Master Anthagh."

The two men exchanged polite bows. Ferret did not breathe freely until the Ghytteve had left in the company of Anthagh's toughs, and the door was firmly shut behind them.

Mouse's charcoal stick flew along the smooth page. Her clever fingers froze the courtiers' interesting faces in lines on vellum. Venykhar was busy being the Ykhave Council Lord: talking to various courtiers in the great meeting hall. She had swiftly grown tired of trailing in his wake, and with his permission, had faded to the room's ornamented edges to sketch in the book he had given her. She had tucked herself into one of the recessed window seats, a vantage point which let her see much of the hall while she nestled, inconspicuous, among the draperies. As she worked, absorbed by the translation of reality to images, furtive voices caught her attention.

"News, Ghorran?"

"I've done as you asked, Lord. The Ghytteve have posted a reward of *a hundred Royals* for the longshoreman known as 'Sharkbait.' Ybhanne is dead, yet the Slums won't quiet; rumor has it the drug runners are reapportioning territory."

"You seem—mmm—*skeptical.*"

"There are two more dead Ghytteve in it: Gholekh and Mynekhe."

The first man laughed, a sharp, amazed sound. "Ycevi must be livid, and Elkhar—mmm—*dangerously* annoyed."

"Yes, Lord. But none of my contacts have found anything pointing to the Emperor's foreign witch—other than her association with the Windbringer Temple and House Ykhave."

"Yes. You understand, Ghorran, that we need only innuendo. Even an extremely—mmm—*circumstantial* attachment could rouse Elkhar to violence."

One of them snapped his fingers. "Lord. This is tenuous at best, but perhaps it will serve. The thief, Ferret: Cithanekh Ghytteve gave her into the hands of the witch—and Ghobhezh-Ykhave, and the Windbringer High Priest."

"Ah," the first man said with satisfaction. "*That* is useful. Very good. Do you know: does Ycevi know?"

"She may; I'm not sure."

"Well, if you can do it—mmm—*gracefully*, pass the information on. Ferret," he added, in a musing tone. "It seems we were both wrong about her."

"Indeed, Lord; and I do feel the fool. The fact she was Journeyman (young as she looked) and *Khyzhan's* (who's as shrewd as the Guildmaster, and several times more ruthless) should have alerted me. But I was taken in—you'll admit she was good. Elkhar Ghytteve let it slip that he believes she helped Sharkbait take Cyffe out."

"Elkhar lets *nothing* slip without cause. But this—mmm—*longshoreman*, 'Sharkbait?' Who is he?"

"He's been organizing the dock workers—trying to form a guild; he's made enemies. More rumors than Elkhar's link his name with Ferret's."

"Find out more. The link with Ferret sounds—mmm—*promising.*"

"Very good, Lord."

Mouse heard footsteps moving off. She edged around to get a good look at the speakers. If she drew recognizable portraits of them, Venykhar could tell who was plotting against Arre. She got a clear view of each, and added their faces to her page of courtiers' portraits. Then, she turned her attention to a robed man whom she supposed to be the High Priest of the Horselord's Temple. She was still fussing with the drape of his rich clothing when Venykhar summoned her away.

The network of secret passages, spyhole niches and listening places soon became familiar territory to Squirrel and Donkey. They quickly grew adept at manipulating the shuttered lanterns Venykhar Ghobhezh-Ykhave provided; and their natural caution served them well as they kept their secret watch on the Ghytteve. The only problem was, Donkey reflected sourly, that much of it was so dull. At the moment, he watched a woman who wrote in a leather-bound ledger. Occasionally she would sigh, raise her head and stare off into space. If you're bored doing the work, Donkey thought, think how I feel, watching you.

He heard the room's door open. The woman looked up, then set aside her quill. "Lady," she murmured.

Donkey squirmed cautiously to get the newcomer in sight. She was an elegant old woman: from Venykhar's description, Lady Ycevi herself. He strained to hear.

They discussed the accounts on which the younger woman—Myncerre, the Lady called her—worked. Donkey's attention snagged briefly on the phrase: "payments to the small runners," but he could make no sense of it. After several minutes, the Lady turned away and Myncerre picked up the quill again.

"Where's Owl?" the Lady asked.

"In the library," Myncerre said. "Rhan is guarding him."

"And Cithanekh?"

"He went out. Evvan will report his movements when they return. Lady, has Cezhar returned?"

She nodded. "He's sleeping. He made his report, first. You'll never guess who is behind the Slum-Guild's cooperation: Ferret! It has become evident that she is not as innocent as our little Owl seems to believe. Cezhar offered Anthagh two hundred Royals for Ferret, if she should fall into his hands; and do you know what he said? Anthagh said, 'If she fell into my hands, the touch would burn me.' *Anthagh*—who I would not have said was afraid of *anyone*. Well," she added, in an effort to banish her temper. "With the price we've set on his head, I daresay it is only a matter of time before someone betrays Antryn—"

"If it *is* Antryn," Myncerre warned.

The Lady smiled; it wasn't a pleasant expression. "Always the doubter, Myncerre. In any case, it is only a matter of time. Slum friendships won't withstand the temptation of a hundred Royals." She shrugged. "And even if this Sharkbait *isn't* Antryn, he may still be useful."

Myncerre went back to the accounts.

After a moment of indecision, Donkey crept along the passage, trying to keep the Lady under surveillance. He flitted from spyhole niche to listening place, always on the edge of losing her. The secret way branched twice; and at each fork, Donkey took careful note of the symbol carved on the wall. It slowed him down, but it would keep him from losing his way.

At the next spyhole niche, he looked in on a spacious room lined with books. A slight figure in Ghytteve livery sat alone at the *khacce* table, fingering the carved pieces. With a start, Donkey recognized Owl. He heard the door open. As the Lady entered, Donkey saw Owl's expression change to wariness. She studied Owl, her back to Donkey. Whatever Owl saw in her expression turned his wariness to fear. "Lady?" the boy whispered.

She was silent for several heartbeats; then she said, "Your little friend Ferret is causing me difficulties. Can you imagine why that might be?"

Owl raised his head, his face pale and set. "Elkhar killed Kitten," he said steadily. "I expect that earned her enmity."

Donkey couldn't see the Lady's face, but she stiffened. "Kitten was a Slum-rat."

"I was a Slum-rat—gods, Lady! *Ferret* is a Slum-rat; but she has friends, and loyalty, and feelings; and she's brave and determined, and no doubt angry."

"And are you angry, and brave, and determined, Owl?" the Lady asked; the silken threat in her voice made Donkey tense.

"I'm frightened," Owl whispered, bitterly. "And I am your slave."

The Lady turned her back on Owl. Donkey shivered as he caught sight of her face: cold; utterly ruthless. "My little Owl," she said, mockingly. She whirled back to face her slave. "*What do you most fear?*" Her hands were raised like talons.

Owl cringed away from her, but did not speak.

She seized him, shook him. "Answer me!"

Visibly, Owl mastered his fear. "Lady, I am your slave; I have no choice but to dance to your piping. What I fear most is that I will forget to resent it."

Donkey held his breath. He was sure the Lady would strike Owl. But to his amazement, she began to laugh. It was a chilling sound. She brushed Owl's cheek with a claw-like finger. "No fear," she promised in a tone which froze blood. "I will find ways constantly to remind you to hate me." Then she went out.

The color drained out of Owl's face. He staggered to the *khacce* table, gripping the table until his knuckles whitened. His eyes were wide and staring, as though he saw things no one else could see. "No," he whispered, anguished. "Oh Lady, no." Then he crumpled to the floor.

While Donkey was riveted with shock, he heard—altogether too close—a breathless curse, then hurried steps: *approaching* hurried steps. He pressed into the spyhole niche, cursing silently as he remembered the woman Myncerre's mention of a guard for Owl. The steps drew closer; he held his breath. He felt rather than saw someone rush past. The faint click of a latch heralded a blinding oblong of daylight. The watcher had opened one of the secret access panels. He pushed into the library and shut the panel behind him. Donkey wanted to stay to see whether Owl was all right, but this might be his best chance of escape, while the watcher was busy. The memory of Ycevi's face decided him; as silently as he knew how, he fled.

Owl lay on his back, staring at the ceiling over his bed. The room was only dim; Myncerre had drawn the curtains, but the afternoon light filtered stubbornly in. He wasn't tired; he was lonely and frightened. After he had fainted in the library, the Lady had brought him back to himself with nasty smelling-salts (every bit as effective as cold water, but not as messy, the Lady had said with satisfaction); then, she and Rhan had grilled him about what he had seen in his dreaming fit. He shuddered. Among other things, he had seen riots. He had told the Lady that—it seemed safe enough; and riots were enough of a nightmare for a Slum-rat that he thought it would explain his distress. He hadn't dared to tell her the rest: that he had seen— in the strangely hazed visions he was coming to dread—a big man going after Ferret with a spar, or Mouse sinking her teeth into Rhan's wrist. (*Rhan*—who was there, questioning him!) He had managed not to vomit, this time, but when the Lady was appeased, she had banished him to his bedroom and instructed Myncerre to drug him into sleep. He had refused the drugged wine, even though the steward had promised it wasn't *haceth*, and had promised to sleep—or pretend—if she didn't force him.

Tears crept across his temples and into his ears. He *needed* to know whether his friends were safe; he wanted someone to talk with; he wished Cithanekh were here. The visions alone were bad, but coupled with Ycevi and Elkhar, and the constant danger, he felt frayed as an old rope. He wanted Cithanekh. Why couldn't he touch *Cithanekh's* mind, instead of two foreigners he barely knew and a goddess?

A *goddess*. Wonderingly, he touched the gem; Cithanekh had found him a leather pouch on a string, so he could wear her token around his neck. But what did it mean? He wished—

He only barely stopped himself from exclaiming aloud. Kerigden might be able to tell him what it meant. He made himself concentrate on the dreaming haven; and then he called.

Owl! The answer was almost immediate. The High Priest's attention blazed across Owl's inner vision like a falling star. *What is it?*

Quickly, he explained what he had done: how he had used the calling which Kerigden had taught him to summon Talyene, what she had said, and what she had given him.

When he had finished, the priest's mind-voice sounded puzzled. *But that was after she bid me into this; oh Lady, what moves you in this? A wager? And with whom? Owl, listen: keep the stone with you. I suspect my Lady means it to protect you.*

I will. Can you teach me a way to control my dreaming fits? They come on me so suddenly; and they make Ycevi suspicious.

She knows you're Sight-Gifted? Kerigden demanded, alarmed.

I had to tell her something after I fainted at her party. But now, when I have a fit, she questions me afterward; it frightens me. I dare not tell her much, but I mustn't let her realize I'm hiding things from her.

I wish I could help, Owl; but control on that level takes years to learn. Some of Owl's desperation must have been apparent to the priest, for he added, *I can tell you that your friends are well.*

Mouse (that is, Amynne) is at the Palace with Venykhar; you might see her. He's adopted her into House Ykhave.

Owl's heart lightened a bit. *Lucky Mouse. Doubtless I won't see her (Ycevi keeps me shut up and under guard), but tell her I'm glad for her. And Kerigden, my thanks.*

As the mind touch dissolved into memory, Kerigden raked his fingers through his fiery hair. "Lady, why?" he murmured. "What do you see in this which makes you act?"

A distant wisp of harpsong teased his memory, but he couldn't place the tune. "If that is a hint, I'm too thick to catch it," he said, rueful. When he heard no more distant harping, he shrugged and straightened. "Ah, well. You will make it clear, in time—or you will not."

Chapter Twenty-seven
Confrontations

To Ferret's secret amazement, the Slum markets opened the next morning, just as planned. Contingents of peacekeepers moved among wary Slum-dwellers, but trade was brisk. Ferret watched the activity for a while before she went to find Sharkbait.

One of Sharkbait's men was reporting on the situation in the Slums when Ferret entered the warehouse headquarters. She listened to his terse recital with embarrassment; credit for the peace in the Slums was being entirely ascribed to her intervention. When the man finished his report, Sharkbait sent him off and beckoned to her.

"So," he murmured. "You promised to be careful."

She thrust her chin in the air. "I *was* careful: it *worked.*"

"But the *risk*...Ferret," he added, beseechingly.

She gestured sharply. "The time when being careful meant staying out of sight is long gone, Sharkbait. Our best chance is to play this out boldly. Happen we've kept the wolf of riot from the Slums; odds are the Ghytteve aren't best pleased. You and I, we're both marked. Cezhar Ghytteve offered Anthagh two hundred Royals for me." At Sharkbait's wordless protest, Ferret's smile went feral. "Anthagh wouldn't take it. Told the Ghytteve they'd have to bid against Khyzhan, who pays his debts in blood. Happen we can trust the slaver—for now. It would have been very easy for him to give me to them; I was hiding in his draperies."

"Ferret, the Ghytteve don't know how to accept defeat. If they can't spark riot in the Slums, they'll try the wharves. And late or soon, they'll find someone whose greed outweighs his fear and you and I will be taken."

"Happen it's so," she agreed. "But I'll toss the *ysmath* bones on the chance you're wrong. Sharkbait, the stakes are high— but there's no safe retreat. Later, I'll go up to the Temple District and tell Kerigden what I've guessed: that the Ghytteve plan to create turmoil among the commoners in hopes of luring the Emperor someplace where it would be easy to assassinate him. If the Scholar King has any sense, he willn't allow himself to be drawn by their ruse."

"He *hasn't* that sort of sense—even warned. He's idealistic to the core."

"Well, I'll not leave him the excuse of ignorance!" she retorted. "If he chooses to act anyway, it's on his head. What will you do in the meantime, Sharkbait?"

The longshoreman sighed. "I've my work cut out to keep peace on the docks. There've been a number of—apparently—random beatings; my guess is that the Ghytteve have begun to foster unrest along the waterfront."

Ferret raised eyebrows. "Where are the Watch in this?"

"The Watch are curiously absent," he told her.

She caught his wrist, squeezed it. "Happen the Ghytteve mean to smoke you out, Sharkbait. Have a care."

He covered her hand as he arched a sardonic brow. "Such sage advice, sweet thief. Mind *you* heed it."

She managed a laugh. "Me? I'm always careful."

Arre was being followed. The Palace was full of watchers, but this was different: specific attention to her movements, not the watchfulness her presence generally caused. She laid a trap for her shadow, leading him ever deeper into the maze of inner Palace corridors, away from the galleries and gardens full of courtiers. She eased into the mouth of a narrow spiral staircase and waited. When the man came within reach, swift and unexpected, Arre pounced; she levered his arm painfully up his back.

"Now," she said evenly. "Why?"

"Why what? Let me go."

She twisted his arm a bit tighter. "Why are you following me? For whom are you working? Answer."

But the man shook his head. "You won't hurt me—not like my employers would, were I false to them."

"I don't need to hurt you," Arre said in a soft, almost purring sing-song. "I have other means of arriving at answers." Still holding him, she slipped half into her dreaming trance.

His fear was foremost: bright and pulsing like a caged hare's heartbeat. "For whom are you working?" she asked again.

"Not likely I'll tell you, is it?" he said. Beneath his words an image formed in her mind: the Azhere Council Lord.

"What do you hope to find by following me?" she asked.

"Give it up. I won't tell you anything." Again, under his words an image formed: a baited snare.

"Am I the bait or the trap?" she whispered.

A spurt of pure fear answered her; then, several rapid, confusing images: Elkhar Ghytteve; Owl; Ferret, bound and disheveled, facing the glowing point of a heated awl; Rhydev; the Prime Minister; Ycevi Ghytteve.

"I have an idea what the Ghytteve are after, but what's Azhere's stake in all this?"

"Witchcraft!" His mind was pure white with terror. *"You're taking answers out of my mind!"*

"Yes," she replied, matter-of-fact. "It's far more effective than heated implements, and does no lasting harm. What does Rhydev Azhere hope to gain from me?"

The image that answered her question was a building in roaring flames; she bit her lip in frustration. The man had summoned some childhood terror to deflect her questioning. She jerked his arm upward; the inferno vanished in a scarlet spurt of pain. "What does Rhydev Azhere hope to gain from me?"

There was a flash of bright image: a hand spinning a lure for a hawk; then the raging inferno reappeared. There were shadows moving within the smoke and flames. "A lure for a hawk," she mused aloud. "A hold on the Ghytteve." As though in answer, Elkhar Ghytteve's face, savage with fury, was superimposed on the fire scene.

"Who are you?" she asked him. But only the blazing building answered her. "Was it your home that burned?"

The white of terror blanked everything again. Arre strained to hold her half trance; this was tiring her. Suddenly, the approach of footsteps intruded on her concentration. She yanked her captive into the spiral stairway and, with the last of her strength, imposed silence on him. The walker passed, a man in the livery of House Mebhare: not a threat. Spent, Arre

abandoned her half trance. She searched her captive and relieved him of a brace of throwing knives and a garrote. Then,
she pushed him roughly into the corridor. Briefly, she regret-
ted that she was too spent to impose forgetfulness on him.

The man regarded her for a moment; then he touched the
hollow at the base of his throat. "This is the easiest kill with
a thrown knife," he told her, calm.

"I don't kill," she said, disgusted.

"Then how will you keep me silent?"

She laughed. "You're perfectly free to tell your master
Rhydev anything you choose—but none of it reflects well on
you, does it?" Then with a flick of her wrist, she sent his weapons spinning down the stone corridor away from them both; as
he went after them, she sprinted up the stairs and away.

Mouse sat on one of the stone benches in the garden. The
sketchbook Venykhar had given her was open on her lap; the
Ykhave Councilor was deep in conversation, ten paces away,
with the Council Lady of House Ambhere. Something to do
with mining and raw materials for House Ykhave. Venykhar
had promised to ask one of his kinsmen to help her experiment with paints, but she knew she would have to wait until
he had finished his business. She suppressed a sigh, and began
to sketch the Palace itself. There was a series of windows on
the third floor...

After several minutes, the book was taken from her. She
glanced up, expecting Venykhar; but the man flipping through
the pages was a stranger. He looked down at her, a mocking
smile on his lips; she noticed the dangling silver earring he
sported.

Mouse wanted to stamp her feet and demand that he return her book; but the way he looked at her warned her off.
She knew he would be suspicious of her Slum accent. She
eyed him with outward calm, as she listened in her mind to
the accents of the nobles and remembered the mannerisms
of the people she spent so much time watching. She extended one hand in an imperious gesture, and said, in the
crisp consonants and rounded vowels of the privileged, "If
you're quite finished..."

His eyebrows rose. "But I'm not. There's quite an amazing collection of portraits, here. Do you know who they are?"

"No," she lied. Venykhar had identified almost all of them.

His smile shaded toward condescension, which stung Mouse's temper. "What are you called, small Ykhave?"

"Amynne. Please return my book."

"Oh, I shall," he drawled, "when I am quite finished with it. I mean to show it to my Lady, first; she is *intrigued* by curiosities." He shut the book and started away.

Mouse's temper escaped her. She leapt up. "You canna do that. Yon book's mine. Give it over, do."

He turned back to face her, his smile broadening into triumph; but Mouse didn't notice. She stamped hard on his instep and used the surprise she gained to snatch the book out of his hand. He moved then, fast, and caught her by the wrist.

"I'll take you along, too. My Lady is *interested* in children."

"Let me *go!*" Mouse cried; but when he merely towed her along, she bit him.

A knife glinted lethally. Mouse froze.

"Now come quietly," the man purred.

"You canna knife me in a garden full of courtiers."

"Try me—and you're dead. My Lady will back me. Come along, *Mouse*—or is it 'Shrew?'"

At his insistence, Mouse stepped toward him, playing the cowed child; then, with desperate strength, she butted her head into his stomach. She yanked free of him, and dove into a roll. She scrambled to her feet in time to see him, his face contorted with rage, preparing to spring at her.

"Rhan Ghytteve, *drop the knife!*" The command in the voice silenced the courtiers' murmuring. Rhan Ghytteve, in a fighting crouch, spun toward the voice. Mouse looked on, horrified. The Scholar King and the Ghytteve bodyguard faced each other across an empty stretch of lawn. "Bare steel in your Emperor's presence?" the Scholar King demanded. "Drop the knife, Rhan, and perhaps I'll be lenient with your treasonous behavior."

Mouse pressed a fist against her mouth. Couldn't he see it? The Ghytteve's eyes were narrowed like an animal's; there wasn't much human reason behind their maddened glitter. But the Emperor stood with perfect calm, unarmed in the face of an assassin.

The garden was utterly hushed, frozen in precarious balance. No one was close enough to intervene; no one dared move. Only the Scholar King seemed unperturbed, his hand held out as expectantly as a schoolmaster confronting an errant boy. Rhan Ghytteve rose out of his fighting crouch, closed the distance between himself and the Emperor with two, fluid strides, and thrust the knife, hilt first, into the Emperor's hand.

"Thank you," the Emperor said softly. "Now, get out. I don't want to see your face again at Court."

Rhan Ghytteve stared at the Scholar King for a full half-minute. Then, he made a profound bow, turned on his heel, and sauntered off. The Emperor turned his attention to Mouse.

"Are you hurt, child?"

"No, Your Majesty."

"*Amynne*," Venykhar said, hurrying to her. "Are you all right? What happened?"

At the sight of the Ykhave Councilor, the Scholar King understood. "Ah. 'Mouse's nobleman,'" he said, very softly.

"He took my book," Mouse explained, "and it made me angry. Then he tried to drag me off to see his Lady. So I bit him, and he lost his temper. I'm sorry I caused a fuss."

"Don't apologize," the Emperor said, trying to hide a smile. "Someone has to make things interesting. But I think, young Ykhave, we need to make it quite clear that you're not to be threatened in the future. Come with me," he said, putting a hand on the girl's shoulder and including Venykhar in the invitation. "You're too young for brandy, but I need a drink."

Mouse looked up at him, suddenly, a question in her dark eyes. "Did you know it was dangerous, what you did?"

"Oh yes," he replied, a little bleakly. "I knew."

The Prime Minister Zherekhaf tapped his steepled forefingers against his front teeth as he studied his nephew. Rhydev poured the coffee, doing his best to ignore his uncle's obvious scrutiny. The Prime Minister took the proffered cup, sipped appreciatively, and sighed. "You know, Rhydev, I begin to doubt the wisdom of colluding to topple Khethyran."

Rhydev stifled irritation with a bland reply. "It is Ghytteve, uncle, against whom our—mmm—*energies* are directed."

"Indeed," the Prime Minister snapped. "But Ghytteve's fall will affect the Emperor's position, however indirectly. I begin to see more profit in open alliance than in devious opposition."

"*What?*" Rhydev laughed. "What could have brought on such a mad fancy?"

"Were you in the garden when he faced down Rhan Ghytteve?"

Rhydev waved a dismissive hand. "No. But I heard he let the man off with banishment. Such—mmm—*leniency* fairly shrieks of weakness."

"No," Zherekhaf countered. "It was demonstration of pure, unalloyed strength. *He stole Rhan Ghytteve's loyalty*—in front of the whole Court. I've never seen anything like it. Rhydev, if he lives, that young man may grow into an Emperor worth serving."

"Worth *serving!* Uncle Zherekhaf! If I did not know you better, I would suspect you had slipped—mmm—*inexplicably* into your dotage. Surely it is—mmm—*preferable* to control the Emperor than to serve him."

"One controls the Emperor, Rhydev, when one is convinced that one can rule more efficiently and better through him than he can rule by himself."

"One controls the Emperor, Zherekhaf, in order to safeguard one's own interests. Never lose sight of that. I will grant you that Khethyran is—mmm—*charismatic*, even inspiring; but he is also at heart—mmm—*egalitarian*, and a threat to the old order and to our very livelihood. During his stay at the Kellande School, he absorbed far more of Kalledann than mere arts and literature."

"No doubt. But is that altogether a bad thing? The Empire of Bharaghlaf is decadent to the core; perhaps the old order has outlived its usefulness." Zherekhaf turned a twisted smile on his nephew's shocked face. "I'm not seriously suggesting that we do anything differently, Rhydev. Ghytteve will certainly pursue their ambitious ploy to its conclusion; and we can so easily be on hand to pick up the pieces. Perhaps I *am* on the threshold of my dotage for wishing, even briefly, that the outcome might be different. Tell me, Rhydev: have you found the link to chain the Emperor's foreign witch to Elkhar's murderous madness?"

"Yes, Uncle. However," he raised one finger warningly, "the timing is—mmm—*delicate*. Elkhar must reach the conclusion she is—mmm—*dangerous* without obvious prompting from us. There are several Ghytteve—mmm—*objectives* with which we might arrange to have Arre interfere."

"For instance?" the Prime Minister prodded.

"You remember that I told you of the thief Ferret? Ycevi wants her, and some of her—mmm—*associates*. These are people for whom Arre might be—mmm—*induced* to risk herself."

The Prime Minister nodded. "So. Timing is everything. Well, do your best, Rhydev; and we shall see."

Squirrel had felt a little surge of triumph when he had drawn the night shift—sundown to sunrise—for watching in the walls. He had imagined that the plotting would occur in the stealthy hours of the night. In truth, he had found himself watching Ghytteve bodyguards tossing the *ysmath* bones and bragging about conquests, or guarding Owl's restless slumber, or observing the Lady's late night games of *khacce* with Myncerre. But the night after Rhan had been banished by the Scholar King, things were different. The Lady raged. It was difficult to tell whether she was angrier with Rhan or the Emperor. Rhan, who was packing his things preparatory to slipping away from the King's City by cover of night, merely gritted his teeth in a humorless grin at the Lady's diatribe.

"I don't understand why you didn't follow through after you'd been stupid enough to bare steel in his presence in the first place," she accused for the fortieth time.

Rhan shrugged. "Lady, I can neither explain nor excuse myself. But if I'd killed him, you'd berate me for imperiling the House."

"You warned the girl, Mouse—and let her escape! Such *clumsiness!* Such—"

"He's clumsy, useless, stupid, inept, incompetent, slip-shod, bungling, and inefficient," a new voice put in: Elkhar. "We've heard the litany, Lady. Why not concentrate on salvaging the situation?"

"*Is* there anything to salvage?" Lady Ycevi demanded passionately. "They've deprived me of another of my bodyguard—though admittedly, this one is merely rendered useless, not dead. Can you seriously suggest there is anything to salvage of such a—a rout?"

"We've identified another of the children: Mouse. We ought to be able to make use of that," Elkhar offered.

"How?" the Lady asked.

"Listen," her henchman said. "I've a mind to set a trap for our Owl. I think he should be permitted to *overhear* an unsettling little plan for Mouse. Only talk of course, but he needn't know that; we don't *dare* move against the artist after Rhan's foolishness and the Emperor's intervention. But as I said, Owl needn't know that. All we need is for him to *think* Mouse is in danger; then we watch, and let him show us how he reports to his allies."

In the wall, Squirrel caught his breath. He had to *warn* Owl—let him know that it was a trap, and assure him that he, Squirrel, would carry word to the others. Owl was sleeping; he'd checked on him not long ago. He made a rapid mental survey of the turnings to reach the secret panel in Owl's bedroom, and satisfied he could find his way without even the faintest betraying glimmer of light, he set out.

Blue moonlight filled Owl's bedchamber. Stealthily, Squirrel entered by the secret way and crept to Owl's bedside. The boy moaned in his sleep, rolling his head against the pillows.

"Owl," Squirrel breathed, shaking him gently. "Wake up."

Owl's eyes snapped open. He caught his breath in a little gasp. "Oh, no, Squirrel. You shouldn't be here!"

"I've an urgent message: they want you to *think* Mouse is in danger, so you'll betray yourself trying to warn us. It's a ruse—and I'll carry word to the others. Just act unconcerned— or worried but helpless. Got it?"

Owl shook his head, his eyes shadowed with pain. "No. It was a ruse for *you*. I dreamed it: Cezhar figured out you've been spying. Squirrel, they watch me constantly; by now, someone will have seen you."

"Oh, no," Squirrel breathed, thinking of Kitten. "Oh, Lady Windbringer, no!"

"Windbringer!" Owl whispered, something like hope animating him. "Here—take this. Kerigden said it was protection." He shoved a gleaming gem into Squirrel's hand. "Now, hurry."

Clutching the gem, Squirrel turned toward the secret panel; but the sound of the door latch froze him. With a faint, despairing moan, he dove under the bed. Elkhar stormed in, flanked by two of the other bodyguards. All bore lanterns.

"Where is the boy you were talking with?" Elkhar demanded.

"What are you talking about?" Owl asked. "What boy?"

"Search the room." Elkhar crossed to Owl, his face contorted with rage. "How stupid do you think I am?"

"I don't think you're stupid at all, Elkhar; I think you're obsessed. There's no boy here—but me."

Cowering under the bed, Squirrel prepared for capture. Steps neared his hiding place; lantern light flashed across him and he saw—with disbelieving clarity—the Ghytteve guard's eyes skip over and through him as though he didn't exist.

"There's no one here," the searchers reported; and relief, terror, and hysteria wrestled with Owl's sense.

Elkhar gripped the boy's nightshirt one-handed, thrust the lantern into his face. "What did you do with him, Owl?"

"Do with whom?" Owl replied wildly, laughter bubbling in his tone.

"*Owl!*" Elkhar growled, shaking the boy.

"You've been dreaming!" Owl persisted. "Your obsession is driving you to imagine things."

Elkhar let go of the nightshirt and slapped Owl's face. "What did you do with him? Tell me, or I'll break your neck."

Owl laughed hysterically. "I gave him a stone sacred to the Windbringer and he vanished, Elkhar; what do you think I did with him? *There's no boy here, Elkhar:* just me."

Elkhar was silent, but his eyes glittered dangerously. Beneath the bed, Squirrel did some rapid figuring. Owl's door was open, but the secret panel was closed and latched. Even if he were invisible, no one could fail to notice the panel opening. He edged out from under the bed, crept along the wall toward the open door. When Squirrel reached the door, he slipped out, and—gem clutched in his fist like his sole hope of redemption—he fled.

Chapter Twenty-eight
Raising the Stakes

Rage, barely contained, lit Elkhar Ghytteve's eyes. He frog-marched Owl to the library and left him with the Lady and Myncerre while he fetched Cithanekh. When the young lord, looking sleep-rumpled and alarmed, made to join Owl, Elkhar yanked him back. Cezhar and two other guards came in behind them and closed the door.

"Cezhar saw the spy," Elkhar told the Lady.

"He came through the panel and went to Owl's bed," Cezhar said. "I did not stay to listen to their conversation, but Owl called him 'Squirrel.' I barred the secret way and reported to Elkhar. The spy was not in the room when we returned."

Elkhar spoke then. "At first, Owl denied any knowledge of the spy; when I pressed him to tell me how the spy had escaped, he said: 'I gave him a stone sacred to the Windbringer and he vanished, Elkhar; what do you think I did with him?'"

"A stone *sacred to the Windbringer?*" the Lady repeated.

"I just said it for something to say, Lady," Owl protested. "Elkhar *hit* me; he said he'd break my neck. He wouldn't believe me that there was no boy but me."

"But why Windbringer?" the Lady pressed.

"It was something to say: something fantastic and impossible. There was no *reason.*"

"Just something to say, Owl? Is that what you want me to believe?" She pinched his chin and made him look at her. When he nodded, she turned to Cithanekh. "Cithanekh, remember the little thief—Owl's friend, Ferret? When you let her go, did you just turn her loose, or did you give her into someone's hands?"

"I don't recall," Cithanekh said.

The Lady raised an imperative eyebrow at Elkhar, who crossed swiftly to Owl and twisted the boy's wrist. Owl hissed.

"Lady, I don't recall," Cithanekh repeated, pleading.

The Lady shook her head. "Break his wrist, Elkhar."

For an interminable moment, there was a breathless hush. Anguish wrenched Cithanekh's face, but he said nothing. There was an ugly, splintering snap, and Owl cried out.

"Has your memory improved?" the Lady asked.

He shook his head, beyond speech.

"Break his other wrist, Elkhar."

"*No!*" The word was torn out of Cithanekh. "No more. I've remembered." He met Owl's streaming eyes. "I'm not strong enough for this, Owl. I gave Ferret to the Emperor's foreign witch; I thought she might be sympathetic."

"The Emperor's foreign witch," the Lady repeated. "And was she alone, Cithanekh?"

"I don't—" he began, but Elkhar jarred Owl's broken wrist and he cried out, again. Cithanekh's eyes were wide in his colorless face. "No more," he gasped. "She was making music with Venykhar Ghobhezh-Ykhave, and the Windbringer High Priest."

The Lady studied the young lord. "It would have been better, Cithanekh, if you had begun with the whole truth," she said in a voice like a serpent's warning hiss. "You see, I already knew. But even in the midst of your touching capitulation, *you still sought to conceal the truth from me.*" She went, then, to Owl's side, lifted his chin and gazed down at his tear-stained face. "Look at him. He's so vulnerable. But can we trust him? Cithanekh, Owl makes Elkhar nervous; he wants me to kill you both and start over with your brother. I think that would be a waste, and so for the moment, I have forbidden it. *Are you trying to force me to reconsider?*"

"No," Cithanekh whispered.

"Then you must tell me what I ask." She looked down at her slave. "Owl, do you want me to kill Cithanekh?"

"No, Lady."

A mocking smile touched her mouth. "You hate to be used; and you doubly hate to be used against your friend. But understand me: if I can't control Cithanekh through you, you are useless to me. If I cannot trust you, you are useless to me. *I do not keep useless things.* Do you understand?"

"Yes, Lady."

"Good. Now. Tell me what your friend Squirrel wanted and how he managed to escape."

Owl had known this was coming, and he had forced himself to come up with a plausible lie. "I don't know what he wanted. Whatever message he had, there wasn't time for it. I knew I was guarded and he would have been seen. I told him to hide on the window ledge, while I distracted whoever came. I didn't think anyone would look for him, there; it's such a long fall, and there's not even any ivy to climb. And then, when everyone came, I thought if I made Elkhar angry enough, he would haul me off to you, and Squirrel could escape."

"Why, you wretched—" Elkhar began, tightening his grip on Owl's injured arm.

The Lady stopped him with a gesture. "Why *Windbringer?*"

"She likes children."

"Perhaps. But you would indeed be a fool to expect her to protect you from *me*, child. Elkhar, did you tell me that Dedemar had reappeared?" The bodyguard nodded, and she smiled. "Good. I've a use for him." She turned to Myncerre. "Make up a lethal dose of *ghyar* and mix it with some of our finest coffee. I think it's time to send the Windbringer a message—in case she (or her priest) is of a mind to interfere." As the steward moved toward the door, the Lady added, "When you've done, come back and set the brat's wrist." Then, Ycevi swept her minions into her wake and sailed out of the library, leaving Cithanekh and Owl alone.

The young lord cradled the boy gently in his arms. "*Gods*, Owl. I'm sorry, I'm sorry, I'm sorry..."

Owl covered Cithanekh's mouth with his good hand. "Never mind. Cithanekh, I—"

"I should never have tried to resist her! I—"

"Cithanekh, *please!*" The undisguised pain cut off the young lord's self-recriminations. Owl continued, whispering through his tears. "I *did* give Squirrel the Windbringer's stone; and he *did* disappear. And I don't understand it; and I'm *frightened*."

"Oh, Owl," Cithanekh murmured, holding him. "It will be all right; it will be. She likes children; maybe she *will* protect us. But it's good you didn't tell my cousin."

"Cithanekh, what are we going to do?"

The young lord's expressive eyes were bleak. "Whatever Ycevi requires."

"No, I mean about the *ghyar*, about Kerigden. We must warn him. I can—" He shook his head, then. "No, I can't; I couldn't begin to concentrate. What are we going to do?"

"Owl, we can't risk it. Didn't you *hear?* She'll kill us."

"She'll kill him."

"He's Talyene's; she'll protect him. Owl—" he added as he felt the boy tense; but further discussion was cut off by the steward's return.

Myncerre probed Owl's wrist while Cithanekh held him still; then she wrapped it securely to a wooden splint. By the time she was done, Owl was white and sweating. Myncerre searched the boy's pain-shadowed eyes, read the mirroring anguish in Cithanekh's expression. Her face was stiff as plaster when she spoke, the words the merest whisper, the tone wondering. "I did as my Lady bid, as I must," she murmured. "But I mixed the *ghyar* with quinine." Then she went out.

Cithanekh leaned his cheek against the boy's hair; after a moment he breathed into his ear, "My dear, amazing Owl. *Ghyar* is nearly tasteless—but quinine is extremely bitter."

In the gray hour before dawn, Venykhar Ghobhezh-Ykhave finally gave up on sleep. Without disturbing his valet, he rose and dressed, intending to take a turn around the dark, empty gardens. He always found a measure of peace in the plash of water, so it was perhaps no wonder that he ended up sitting on the cool marble curb of his favorite garden fountain.

The fountain was a fine piece of statuary, carved several generations ago by an Ykhave artisan; it depicted two twining sea-serpents, one of creamy, pale marble and the other of black stone veined with pink. Water issued from a spout in the center of their writhing coils, curtaining their struggle—or was it play? —in silvery mist. The fountain sat at the center of a paved court bordered by sprawling yew bushes and dogwood trees. Venykhar folded his hands over the head of his walking stick, leaned his forehead against his hands, and let the gardens' peace and the soothing water-noise ease the tensions that had kept him wakeful.

Perhaps the old lord nodded off; quite suddenly, he realized the gardens were no longer silent nor empty. He heard low voices beyond the dark yews and footsteps crunched on the raked gravel paths.

"...don't mean to reproach you any further, Rhan. To tell you the honest truth, I wish I were going with you. You should have seen the look on Elkhar's face when he broke Owl's wrist. Gods. He's hardly sane—"

"Cezh! Be *careful*. It was hard on him, losing Cyffe. At least it sounds like you'll get the fellow who killed her."

"Aye. *That* trap should hold." The speaker gave a short, bitter laugh. "Poor Antryn—if it is Antryn. He's been swimming against the riptide for longer than I care to think. I almost hate to admit it, but you know, I've a sneaking admiration for that little thief, Ferret. I'd have given a great deal to see how she persuaded the Masters of the Slum-Guilds to work together." He sighed. "Lady wants her dead."

"She has plucky friends if Owl and that little artist are any indication."

"'Plucky,'" he laughed. "Admit it; the small Ykhave made you angry enough utterly to forget discretion."

"I never had much to begin with. But I'd best be off. It will be light in an hour. Cezhar, guard yourself."

"Oh, aye. And you: take care, little brother."

Footsteps crunched away. Venykhar remained immobile, though his thoughts roiled. After a moment he heard a sigh; and then, more footsteps, returning the way they had come. The sound changed to the faint scuff of shoes on paving stones instead of the crunch of gravel underfoot. With effort, Venykhar did not look up, but continued to rest his forehead against his hands.

"So," Cezhar Ghytteve breathed, adding more loudly, "A peaceful resting-place, Council Lord of Ykhave."

"Hrrmph-huh." As Venykhar jerked upright, his cane slipped from his hands to clatter on the pavement. "Gracious, you startled me, boy. I must have dozed off." Stiffly, the old man bent to retrieve his cane. His eyes never left the Ghytteve's knees. As his hand closed around the metal shod foot, Venykhar saw him tense to spring. He brought the weighted head of his cane up sharply, cracking the younger man viciously under the chin. Cezhar staggered.

With a spurt of adrenaline-born agility which would cost him dearly, Venykhar followed up his advantage with a hard rap to the temple. The Ghytteve crumpled.

Venykhar limped quickly away, thinking feverishly. His mouth was chalk. *Antryn.* But the Ghytteve hadn't told him anything specific enough to be helpful. They thought they had him—'*That* trap will hold'—but how? What use to send Ferret or one of the others hot-foot to tell Antryn he was in danger? They were *all* in danger. Even his own reputation for disinterest in Court intrigue was jeopardized—destroyed, actually, if that Ghytteve hound were only stunned. It wouldn't take a mastermind to make a plausible connection between Antryn Anzhibhar-Ykhave and the Ykhave Councilor. And *what* was happening to Owl?

"Ven!"

"Arre," he greeted her.

"Are you all right?" she asked, her eyes full of visions.

"I knocked him out: Cezhar Ghytteve."

She released pent breath. "I dreamed more than one ending to that encounter. Oh Ven, thank God you're all right."

"Antryn's in trouble. The Ghytteve think they have him trapped."

Arre pressed three fingers to her forehead and closed her eyes; but after a moment she shook her head, defeated. "I can't make it come clear." She closed her hand around one wrist, rubbing it as though it ached. "I don't know what's *wrong* with me. I can't concentrate."

The old lord's gaze sharpened on her hands. "Owl," he said, touching her forearm. "Elkhar broke Owl's wrist."

"*What?*" Her eyes unfocused briefly; when clarity returned to her gaze she shook her head ruefully. "He's *strong*, Ven. He's not even awake and he's projecting his pain. Ven, we mustn't stand about, talking. It's not safe."

"You've a notion what we should do next?" At her nod, he gestured grandly. "Then lead on."

Cezhar Ghytteve, with a discolored lump on the side of his face and a mien grim as winter, stood stiffly upright while Elkhar's tirade roared over him like surf. His head thrummed like a struck anvil and his eyes didn't want to focus; and the way the Lady studied him, as though he were some repellent curiosity, made him almost wish Ghobhezh-Ykhave's blow had finished him. He forced himself to pay attention; Elkhar was winding down. If the Lady started in, she would expect sensible answers.

"It does rather cast Venykhar Ghobhezh-Ykhave in a different light," Ycevi remarked. "I would never have thought him enough of a fighter to best one of my hand-picked, specially trained bodyguards. How indiscreet *were* you and Rhan, Cezhar?"

"We spoke mostly in generalities, Lady. I do remember mentioning Antryn's name; Ghobhezh-Ykhave might well have deduced his kinsman's danger, but we gave no hint from what quarter the threat would come."

"Was his attack unprovoked, or were you going to kill him?"

"I had that intention."

"Why—if you hadn't been dangerously indiscreet?"

"Because of the *connection*," Cezhar explained. "It had never occurred to me, until I saw the Ykhave Council Lord so suspiciously *there*, that Antryn Anzhibhar-Ykhave could be involved in anything but a lone-wolf plot or counter-plot. And as there was no one else in the gardens, no way to link his death to House Ghytteve, it seemed a perfect opportunity. My mistake was speaking to him first; but it was dark. I couldn't see his face. I didn't want to risk a dangerous error."

"And you thought him old and feeble," Ycevi said. "Did he know who you were? Did Rhan use your name?"

Cezhar thought back. "Yes. I think he did."

"Gods," Lady Ycevi snarled. "At least you didn't wound him—or did you?"

"No, Lady."

"Then he's unlikely to make formal charges, since we have such a clear line of defense: he struck you unprovoked. Remember that, Cezhar."

"Yes, Lady."

"And Elkhar? Be *extremely* circumspect. Spring the trap on this 'Sharkbait,' but be careful. I'm not looking for elegance: wring him dry and kill him."

"I had thought," Elkhar offered, "to use him as a lure for the thief, Ferret."

"I *do* want them both," the Lady admitted. "Very well, use your discretion, Elkhar—*but take no unnecessary risks.*" She rose, and with a last, exasperated shake of the head at Cezhar, left the chamber.

Cezhar braced for another round of recriminations, but Elkhar merely rolled his eyes at his lieutenant. "Go. Mend your head—but send Evvan and Ynteth to me."

Chapter Twenty-nine
Parry and Riposte

There was no sign of Venykhar Ghobhezh-Ykhave, when Mouse rose to greet the day; and none of his servants knew where he was. Though no one else seemed concerned, his absence worried her. After breakfast, she took her sketching case and went into the garden to look for him.

The garden hummed with gossip. Mouse scanned the crowd searching for Arre or Venykhar. She found neither of them, but she recognized Cithanekh Ghytteve, gray with strain, parrying the gibes of an assortment of court ladies. The haunted desperation in young lord's eyes made Mouse angry on his behalf. She rendered, in charcoal, a viciously satirical version of the scene: Cithanekh, looking noble and patient, at the center of a pack of silly lapdogs—each of whom resembled, with unflattering clarity, one of the ladies. When the drawing was done, she walked idly past the group; as she passed Cithanekh, she let the paper fall. With reflexive courtesy, he retrieved it. "Young Ykhave," he began, then spluttered into helpless laughter. Curiosity piqued, a lady twitched the page out of his fingers. Mouse serenely ignored the outraged yapping in her wake.

Mouse settled on a bench and began another drawing: a detailed sketch of one of the garden's flowering shrubs. A gentle touch interrupted her concentration. It was Cithanekh.

"That was clever," he said. "You've badly offended a third of the marriageable daughters of the Council Houses, but no one will wonder at my speaking with you. You must be Mouse; Owl's told me of you."

She nodded. "Amynne Ykhave. And you're Cithanekh Ghytteve."

He bowed slightly. "What with yesterday and this morning, you are fast becoming the Court's latest sensation." He gestured toward snickering courtiers knotted around a sheet of paper. "Be very careful."

Concern lit her eyes. "Is aught wrong? You look troubled."

Cithanekh told Mouse of Squirrel's near capture and its aftermath. Mouse shared her concern over Venykhar's absence, and the young lord promised to find out what he could.

After Cithanekh left, Mouse had no quiet, for the courtiers plagued her for sketches. She patiently obliged them with polite little portraits until her hand ached. Even after she was sure she'd drawn every face in the garden at least twice, they would not leave her alone. With vexed determination, she began to put away her things. "That's all," she said firmly.

"But no," a cool voice responded. The speaker was an elegant old woman, whose dark eyes were burningly intent. "You absolutely must not stop until you've done my portrait."

"No," Mouse said bluntly. "I've been drawing all morning and I'm tired."

The woman shook her silvery hair back with a laugh like shattered crystal. "Have I failed to make my wishes clear? You will make my portrait."

Her arrogance wound Mouse's temper. "Very well," she said crisply. She assessed the woman swiftly, then drew: not a simple likeness, but a stunning drawing nonetheless. Mouse captured her vibrant, unbending pride in a creature more hawk than woman: sleek feathers in place of coifed hair, aquiline features subtly exaggerated, posed with one arm raised imperiously, the hand a raptor's hooked talons. The likeness was inescapable, and anything but flattering. As Mouse wordlessly gave the sheet to the woman, she noticed the heavy, gold chain of office around her neck. Belatedly, she recognized the stooping hawk of House Ghytteve blazoned on her Council medallion.

Ycevi Ghytteve studied the page; the courtiers who stole glances at the drawing tensed to anticipation. A contagion of silence spread from Mouse and the Lady. Cithanekh, hurrying to tell Mouse what he had gleaned of Venykhar's encounter with Cezhar, froze in consternation.

"Why insult me?" Lady Ycevi whispered.

"You annoyed me," Mouse responded steadily.

"*Annoyed* you?" the Lady repeated, with real puzzlement.

"You canna even bring yourself to say 'please.'"

"*'Please?'*" Outrage rattled Lady Ycevi's tone.

Supporting hands gripped Mouse's shoulders; the Scholar King's voice, bright with irony, said, "Permit me to define it for you, Ycevi: the word 'please' is used to express politeness or emphasis in a request."

Lady Ycevi regained her composure. "Thank you, Your Majesty. But have you *seen* the drawing this horrible child made of me?"

The Emperor studied the drawing, then said seriously, "Oh, Amynne. That was terribly naughty of you."

Mouse studied one toe in contrition. "Yes, Your Majesty." She looked up at Lady Ycevi, winsome. "I'm sorry, Lady Ycevi. Please forgive me."

Their eyes met; cynicism stole into Lady Ycevi's face. "What sort of a monster would I appear," she remarked, "were I to reject such a winningly offered apology?"

An answering sardonic spark caught in Mouse's smile. "And in front of the whole Court, no less."

"*Amynne,*" the Scholar King warned under his breath.

"Precisely," Lady Ycevi said, wry. "You wretched child. I think I shall choose to find you amusing."

Mouse inclined her head. "My Lady is most gracious."

"Indeed," she replied, moving off. She had not taken three steps before she spun back. "Is he your brother: Owl?"

"No," Mouse answered calmly. "I dinna have a brother, gracious Lady. Has a Healer seen his wrist?"

Ycevi's eyes widened. "I beg your pardon? Waste a Healer's talents on a careless slave's injury?"

"Was it Owl who was careless, Lady Ycevi, or Elkhar?" Mouse persisted. The Scholar King's grip tightened on her shoulders.

Lady Ycevi made the two-fingered gesture of one conceding a hit. "I would send the Healer with your compliments, child, if only I knew your name."

She met Ycevi Ghytteve's sly challenge squarely. "It's Mouse," she said. "At least, that's my nickname. Happen you'll know me as Amynne Ykhave."

Ycevi studied the girl in silence before she smiled very faintly. "*Definitely,* I shall choose to find you amusing, Amynne Ykhave." Then she glided off in a whisper of silk.

Only Mouse was near enough to hear the Emperor's slowly expelled breath. She looked up at him curiously. "Do I make you nervous, Your Majesty?"

"You take such appalling risks," he said softly as he guided her out of the gardens. "You do know that, don't you?"

Mouse nodded. "Happen it's only a bold stroke will save us, now, Your Majesty. Lady Ycevi guessed who I was—else why mention Owl? She canna bear to look the fool. There was no hiding. At least now, she knows I know she knows who Mouse is—and so do you."

The Emperor gave a lopsided smile. "And to think I once believed it was only the Council Houses who had intrigue bred in their bones. But Mouse, knowledge is not enough to protect you—nor even my interest and favor—if Ycevi finds you alone and vulnerable."

"I know it. I'll be careful."

"See to it, child, that you are careful *enough*."

Sporadic violence raged in the waterfront district. Brawls broke out in more than one dockside tavern; three of Sharkbait's longshoremen were mobbed and beaten by Shippers' Guild goons; and then, toward evening, a Guild warehouse was torched.

Ferret saw the smoke from the fringes of the Slums, where she was taking her turn at peace keeping duties. She eyed the smudges which marred the sunset with deep misgiving; fire on the waterfront was likely to mean the loss of property: Shippers' Guild goods. Destruction of property would embroil the Watch in waterfront troubles. Further, the Shippers' Guild was the principal opponent of Sharkbait's organization. They would use this opportunity against him.

When Ferret spied one of Khyzhan's bravos, she hailed him. "Ho, Akhenn. Did you come from the wharves? What's burning?"

"Ho, Ferret. A right mess, it is. Shippers' Guild warehouses: fire's spread to three of them. Loaded with exports, to hear Master Ghankh tell it. Mobs willn't let the bucket brigade through. They've called out the Watch."

Ferret cursed. "Happen I'd best get down there. Take my watch, Akhenn?"

He shrugged. "Go. But you owe me."

The waterfront was in seething turmoil. Ferret followed the smoke and crowds and was soon in the thick of the tumult. People armed with buckets milled aimlessly in the face of a thin line of cudgel-bearing toughs.

"Let the cursed goods burn!" one of the toughs harangued. "Let us pay the bloodsuckers in their own coin! It is *they* who grow fat on our toil! *They* eat richly while *our children* starve!" At the alarming growls of agreement, both from the toughs on the line and from some of the watchers, Ferret's mouth turned to dust. "We've been patient with them. Even now, we're *too gentle* with these merchant scum!" he railed on. "*Gentle!* It's only their *goods* which burn now, but it's our *children* who burn up with fever!"

As his diatribe went on, the mob's responses grew angrier. Ferret realized if she didn't act quickly, events would escape her entirely. She pushed into the open space before the cudgel wielders, fists on her hips. "If you've lost a child to hunger, happen I'll eat my tunic," she challenged the leader. "You speak like a *noble*. What *are* you after starting? A riot? Happen you've no idea the damage *that* does! Happen you've never lost a family member to mob violence—or to *fire!* There's tenements—*where people live!*—not half far enough away from here. I dinna give a damn about merchants' goods, either— but there are *people's lives* at stake." She turned away to gather the onlookers into her outrage. "There canna be more than thirty toughs—and there's hundreds of us. We canna stand idle while people burn!"

A few growled agreement; but most shuffled awkwardly. With a sinking heart, Ferret realized her reasoning wasn't volatile enough to inflame them. For most of the bystanders, it was neither their homes nor their families at risk. They needed more to stir them up, more to enrage them. Before she could dream something up, her thief's instincts flashed danger. She spun to face the leader of the toughs, and by sheer luck, dodged the blow he had aimed at her head.

"For shame!" a voice cried. "She's a child!"

The man's return swing connected crushingly with her ribcage. Though she tried to ride the force of the blow, she landed winded and gasping on the cobbles ten feet away. Through dizzying pain stars, Ferret saw the start of his rush; but she couldn't even scramble away. Dimly, she heard a voice raised in fury: a familiar voice, a dear voice. And even more dimly, she realized that somehow, the mob had surged between her and her attacker. Strong arms hoisted her away from trampling feet; but the new pressure on her punished ribs pushed her into darkness, and she remembered nothing more.

Milling chaos, surging crowds, anger, smoke and shouting resolved finally, under the direction of Sharkbait and his longshoremen, into a ruthlessly efficient bucket brigade. As soon as it was possible, Sharkbait began to search for Ferret. But for all his frantic effort, he found no sign of her.

"She must have crawled out of the crowd," Sharkbait said for the tenth time—as much to reassure himself as for any other reason. "She *must* have."

"A brave lass, yon Ferret," his man said. "Happen you'd planned yon mob-turning, the two of you—it went so slick."

Sharkbait tried to smile. "She's reckless and rash, if you want the truth—but she has the Windbringer's own luck. By the names of all the gods, let her be safe."

"You ought, more properly, to be concerned for your own safety, Antryn."

Sharkbait spun: Elkhar—and a lot of men. Sharkbait grabbed his boot knife, but Elkhar's gesture froze him. "You wouldn't want harm to come to your companion, now, would you?"

Another Ghytteve bodyguard held a knife across the throat of Sharkbait's man. Sharkbait hesitated. If he fought, he might force them to kill him; but a fight would doom his man. He dropped his knife and spread empty hands in surrender.

They were efficient and took no chances. When Sharkbait was disarmed and bound, Elkhar turned to the Ghytteve holding his man. "Leave no traces for that little thief; she's damned clever. Kill him."

Sharkbait flinched as they opened his man's throat. Elkhar smiled nastily. "You should have fought, Antryn. You might have forced us to kill you cleanly. Death won't come easily, now."

Sharkbait said nothing. Around him, the crowd worked to control the fire; *hentes* of Watch moved through the mob tensely, but without drawn weapons. He could shout for help— but the waterfront still tottered on the brink of riot. His capture might overturn the balance. Two of Elkhar's men unrolled a stretcher; they pushed Sharkbait down onto it and covered him with a blanket. They made jostling progress away from the noise and the smell of burning.

Donkey leaned his broom against the wall of the Windbringer's Temple and sat down on the stone step. Though it was daylight—his hours of vigil in the walls—after Squirrel's near capture, Kerigden, Venykhar and Arre had unanimously forbidden the usual watches. The two boys had been sent to the Temple District for safety; Donkey had taken on chores to keep busy. He stifled impatience with his dullest, most obtuse face.

While he sat on the steps, the picture of a lazy dullard, he watched the Temple Watch on their rounds. One of the men looked familiar; it was Dedemar. Donkey remembered that Ferret had persuaded the Fytrian Temple Watchman to spy on the Ghytteve. Suddenly, Donkey realized Dedemar was coming toward him up the great stone steps. He rose, retrieved his broom and—the image of someone caught at his loafing— went back to work. As Dedemar approached, the guard regarded Donkey with a frown of concentration. Donkey moved into the Temple Watchman's path, gaped at him, then said, in the blankest tone imaginable, "Ma sent you flowers."

Dedemar's eyebrows shot upward and his lips shaped a silent 'o.' "Do more than gawk, foolish boy," he said aloud, making exasperated shooing motions. "Move along."

With idiotic delight, Donkey mimicked Dedemar's gestures. When he made to push by, Donkey refused to budge. Dedemar seized the boy's shoulders, shook him, and said, in a whispered rush, "Windbringer grant you are cleverer than you appear. There was coffee in the morning tribute: a 'gift' from the Ghytteve; it was poisoned. Warn the High Priest."

When Dedemar released him, Donkey shrank away as though cowed. "Ferret," he whispered as the man passed, to reassure him; Dedemar made no sign. As soon as the Temple Watchman had gone, Donkey went inside. Kerigden must be warned.

Owl's restless sleep worried Cithanekh. The Healer had said the boy should sleep quietly 'til morning; but through the long afternoon, Owl tossed more and more fretfully. The young lord smoothed the boy's hair, but nothing calmed him.

Owl thrashed against the young lord's restraining hands. "Oh Arre, no!" he cried.

"Owl, Owl. Be easy. You'll hurt yourself," Cithanekh pleaded; but when the boy showed no sign of relaxing, Cithanekh grew resolute. He shook him gently. "Wake up. You're dreaming."

Owl's eyes fluttered open, were wide and sightless, blinded by images. Then, he focused on Cithanekh's face. "I dreamed," he whispered in the toneless voice Cithanekh had learned to dread. "Arre's in danger. Rhydev Azhere set a trap for her. He wants Elkhar to kill her."

Cithanekh shivered. "Gods, Owl. What should we do?"

"Tell the Emperor," Owl said softly. "Have him send a few of the Imperial Guard to Ycevi's Upper Town house. If they're fast, they can warn Arre." The strange tonelessness had faded from his voice. Owl looked very young and frightened. "Please hurry, Cithanekh. There isn't much time."

"Owl," he protested, "we dare not."

"We *must*. Trust me."

Cithanekh rose, then looked down at his friend, hesitant, biting back questions.

"There isn't much time," Owl repeated. Cithanekh gently squeezed Owl's foot through the covers, willing some meaning into the touch; then, he went out.

Chapter Thirty
Rescue

Word of Sharkbait's capture spread outward like ripples on a pool. The news reached Rhydev Azhere's man, Ghorran, well before the Ghytteve litter bearers had gained the safety of their Upper Town house. Ghorran nodded with satisfaction and set the stage for the next act of his master's elaborate plan.

A seedy man accosted Arre as she headed toward the Palace. "Lady Arre! One of Ferret's friends sent me."

Arre paused. "Oh? Couldn't Ferret come herself?"

"The waterfront's on the brink of riot. It's madness there. I couldn't find Ferret, but Khyzhan told me you'd want to know this: Sharkbait's in bad trouble. The Ghytteve took him."

Images, clear and definite, filled Arre's inner vision: an Upper Town house, and its location; Sharkbait, bound to a chair; Elkhar, satisfied and lethal; and a knife, heated to a baleful red, resting in a brazier. "Merciful God," Arre whispered, horror in her voice. "Let me get help."

"Lady, there's no time; and if we're not quick and careful, they'll kill him, certain. The Ghytteve expect naught of trouble. You and me, and Khyzhan's others—happen it's enough."

"Others?" she asked, looking for reassurance.

"Aye: a scatter of his bravos. And I know he's still got eyes out for Ferret; happen she'll join us before we move."

Arre hesitated; the habit of caution was strong. But the image of the glowing knife seared away indecision. "Come, then," she said, turning unerringly in the direction of the Upper Town house. Her informant, without another word, followed.

Though the afternoon was fast fading, the Palace gardens were still bright with courtiers. Mouse sighed. She had found Venykhar, but now he was discussing business: a courtier with a commission. She wanted to get away from all these nobles, to hide in the Ykhave apartments; but the old lord had warned her about wandering through the Palace corridors alone.

"*Hsst!* Amynne!" The furtive voice startled her; it was Cithanekh. He relayed Owl's warning, giving careful directions to Ycevi's Upper Town house. "Can you get word to the Emperor? Owl said there wasn't much time," he ended anxiously.

Mouse glanced around the garden; the Emperor wasn't there, but she recognized one of his Imperial Guard. She nodded. "I'll tell him—but Cithanekh, you go to Kerigden. Ven said Arre was with him, earlier."

Indecision knit his brow. "If they're watching me," he began; and then he recalled an inconsistency. No one, not even Myncerre, had seen him leave the Ghytteve complex; there had been no guards on duty in the hall. What with the deaths, banishment and injury, Ycevi's complement was thin. It was possible no one was assigned to watch him, especially since Ycevi might easily expect the warning she had delivered last night still to be strong in his mind. "All right; I'll risk it." He sketched a farewell and faded into the milling courtiers.

Mouse walked over to the Imperial Guard and tugged at his sleeve. "I'd like to speak with the Emperor. He said I might."

The guard had no specific orders, but he had heard accounts of the young Ykhave's exploits; it was likely the Emperor had told the girl she could seek him out. "Come, then," he told her and led her into the labyrinth of the Palace.

Ferret stirred. It hurt to move. She groaned. It hurt to breathe. She opened her eyes and found herself nose to nose with another denizen of the waterfront: a rat. She started. It hurt to do that, too, but the rat scuttled off. Cursing, she sat up. She was in an empty warehouse, smaller than the ones Sharkbait typically used for his headquarters. It was dim; the air was musty, tainted with smoke. Cautiously, she got to her feet; the world spun sickly, pain stars stinging in her vision.

"What, leaving already?"

The voice made her jump—a bad mistake. Ferret sat down quickly to keep from falling over. "Clearly not," she said when she could manage speech. "Khyzhan?"

The Master Thief came near, a lamp in one hand. "Who else?"

"It was you, then, who pulled me out of the brawl?"

"Who else?"

She shrugged—and winced. "Sharkbait, or one of his men. I thought I heard his voice."

Khyzhan set the lamp on the floor and sank down beside her. The odd shadows on his face made his expression harder than usual to read. "Watch out for yon Sharkbait. He's flash, Ferret."

"I know. Noble. Happen it's not worth aught to him. Did he turn the mob?"

The Master Thief nodded, then added pensively, "I could envy your Sharkbait."

The comment surprised a painful laugh from Ferret. "Envy? But why? It's not as if he were rich or powerful. Did you see him? Is he all right?"

"Happen it's not wealth or power I crave, Ferret," Khyzhan remarked. "But never mind. He's not all right. He turned the mob well enough—he's slick, and you'd set it up nicely—but after, he ran afoul of the Ghytteve."

"*Gods*," Ferret responded. "Was he alive? Do you know where they took him?"

"Yes. They took him to a house in the Upper Town. Ferret, you can barely walk. You canna mean to go after him!"

"Happen I've no other choice."

"Wash your hands of him."

"Dinna be ridiculous. Where's this house?"

Khyzhan didn't answer. Finally, he turned both palms upward in an odd, relinquishing gesture. "I'll take you. Come on."

"Cithanekh Ghytteve," Kerigden greeted him, surprised. "If you're here about the tainted coffee—"

"What? No. Is Arre here? It's urgent I find her."

Kerigden shook his head. "She left a quarter of an hour ago." At the younger man's look of pain, the High Priest gripped his forearms. "What is it?"

"Owl dreamed. She's in danger: a trap. Azhere is trying to force Elkhar Ghytteve to kill her. Owl told me to see that the Emperor sent his Guards to the Ghytteve Upper Town house; I gave that message to Mouse, and she sent me to you."

The High Priest rummaged in his desk, then produced a large scroll. Before he unrolled it, he struck his table cymbal and sent the acolyte who answered his summons to fetch Squirrel and Donkey. Then he turned his attention to the map—a map of the Maze, Cithanekh realized as he came closer to look.

"There," Kerigden said, pointing to a passageway.

"Oh. The underground way? I could take you—but they always bar the cellar door from within the house."

"A barred door is no problem if my Lady is with me," he said calmly. "Can you take us there without alerting Ycevi or her minions?"

"Who knows? For all I know, I was followed *here*. I'm willing to try."

Just then, the two boys hurtled in at a dead run. "Lead the way, Cithanekh," Kerigden said. "There's no time to waste."

The knife in the brazier heated slowly. Elkhar watched it, ugly anticipation in his expression. Using a padded glove, he removed the knife from the coals and went to Sharkbait's side. He lowered the glowing point toward the sensitive skin of his wrist. "For whom are you working?"

Sharkbait was silent. The heated blade hovered above his wrist, scorching it with its nearness.

"For whom are you working, Antryn?" Elkhar asked again. This time, when Sharkbait did not answer, he pressed the flat of the blade hard against his wrist. Sharkbait gave a strangled cry, fighting his own rebellious voice. "For whom are you working?" Elkhar purred.

Sharkbait said nothing.

"Useless resistance," he remarked. "I can be far more persuasive, Antryn." He replaced the knife in the brazier. Elkhar fingered the fabric of Sharkbait's shirt meditatively. He tore the shirt from neck to hem and peeled the rags back, exposing Sharkbait's chest—and his healing knife wound.

"Ah. Cyffe's signature." Elkhar poked his knuckles into the still-tender flesh and twisted ruthlessly. Sharkbait's face knotted in pain. "Perhaps I should rephrase my question: Who are your allies, Antryn?" When Sharkbait did not respond, Elkhar fetched the knife. The pain was worse this time; Sharkbait did not bother to stifle his screams. It continued to get worse for an interminable span; and though he shrieked in agony, he managed to keep his tortured voice from shaping names.

Owl lay against the pillows and tried to summon back his dream. The dream had been so confusing, full of pieces of different endings; he felt as though he had been shown an instant of decision, fixed in time but surrounded with hundreds of branching choices. He breathed deeply, stilling his thoughts. As he drifted, images scoured his eyelids: a glowing knife; Elkhar, eyes vivid with triumph; Sharkbait, bound, contorted in agony; a stealthy figure scaling an ivy covered wall; a brief, violent scuffle in a wide, Upper Town street. Then, a haze of silver muted the searing quality of the visions, though they continued to spin past his mind's eye with dizzying speed. Elkhar and Ferret, dancing the feint and lunge of a desperately unequal knife fight; the Lady and several of her bodyguard, cornering Kerigden, Cithanekh and Squirrel against an iron-bound door; two *hentes* of Imperial Guard; Ycevi opening the veins of Cithanekh's wrists; Myncerre's face twisted with pain; Arre, her odd colored eyes open and lifeless; Donkey, weeping; the Scholar King obdurately holding out the black wand of death-judgment to Ycevi before the full Council; Rhydev Azhere, smug and knowing.

"No!" he cried aloud; his eyes snapped open. He sat up. Waves of dizziness pounded him, but urgency overrode his nausea. If the Lady caught Cithanekh there by the door, she would kill him; he knew it with the same unshakable certainty that he knew his own name. He fought free of the entangling bedclothes. With his injured wrist restrained in a sling, movement was awkward. He struggled into a dressing gown and went to his bedroom door. It was unlocked. "Lady!" he cried, making for her library. "Lady!" He had to delay her, to buy time for his friends. Somehow, beyond his panicky need, his mind spun tales to tell her: *anything* so long as it kept her here, away from Cithanekh, away from Elkhar. It had to be enough! There had to be a way to prevent what he had seen. There might still be hope. There *must* still be hope.

As Arre and her informant neared the Ghytteve's Upper Town house, her steps slowed. The garden wall would not be hard to scale, she thought. Her keen ears caught the muffled sound of a man's screams.

"Antryn! Oh God, Antryn! Where are you?" The cry—a fair approximation of her voice—startled Arre; she turned in time to see her informant sprinting away. Half-seen movement spun her back to face assailants scant moments before they struck. *Trap!* she thought, preparing to fight. But she was outnumbered, and they were ruthless. A blow to the head sent her into darkness.

Ferret and Khyzhan froze in the shadows; there were too many Ghytteve. The scuffle was brief and decisive. The two thieves exchanged glances while the Ghytteve bound the unresisting Arre and disappeared into the dark garden.

"Six," Khyzhan breathed, "not counting those inside. Long odds, Ferret."

She bared her teeth in a feral grimace. "The only kind I play, Master."

Khyzhan unwrapped a length of fine cord from his waist, then fitted together the pieces of a metal grapnel and tied it to the cord. The implement hissed through the air, landed with a faint thump and slithered to its hold. He pulled hard; it held. He gave the rope to Ferret. "Try the attic window. It's shuttered, but happen it's not barred."

She gritted her teeth against the pain of her abused ribs and scaled the wall of the house. Not only was the attic window not barred, the shutters were weak with dry rot. She braced herself between the inadequate window ledge and the overhanging gutter with one hand, while she worked the shutters open with the other. She slipped into the large, airless attic and gave the sleepy dove's coo which passed for "all clear" among Khyzhan's thieves. A moment later, her Master joined her. He dismantled the grapnel and coiled his cord. By the fitful candlelight which came up from the hall below, they fastened the shutters from the inside before, stealthy as training and care could make them, they crept to the stairway that led to the rest of the house. A hoarse cry, like a warning, drew them down.

"Owl!" Myncerre intercepted him. "You shouldn't be up."

"I must speak to the Lady. Myncerre, I *must!*" His manner was thick with urgency. "Please, Myncerre. Let me see her."

"She's going out, now. She'll see you when she returns."

"No. Now! *Now!* It must be *now!* She's in *danger,* I dreamt it!" As his voice spiraled upward in panic, he began to cry; the Lady appeared in the doorway.

"What's this?" she demanded.

Myncerre spread her hands. "He's hysterical. He says you're in danger."

"I heard that," she snapped. "Bring him inside. Owl, control yourself and talk sensibly."

Myncerre herded Owl inside. The Lady stood nearby, clearly fidgeting; two of her bodyguard exchanged impatient glances. As the library door clicked shut, Owl began the performance of a lifetime. If he just cried and babbled, she would send him to bed in disgust. He had to tell her *something* with enough truth in it to hold her attention; but he couldn't betray his friends, or alarm her into immediate action. "I—I had a dream: a terr—*terrible* dream. Rhy—Rhy—Rhydev—" He lapsed into sobs.

"What about Rhydev Azhere?" the Lady prodded.

"He promised—He promised me you wouldn't be hurt, that none of you would be hurt, *but he lied!*"

"Lady, have we time for this?" one of the men asked.

She raised one finger. "*What about Rhydev?*" she demanded.

Owl blended lies and truth with unwary speed. Ycevi's interest was snared. All that mattered now was that she *stay here* long enough for his friends to get out of danger. He answered question after question—with a heady mixture of twisted truth and pure imagination. Myncerre, standing behind the Lady, at first looked surprised; then alarm shaded her expression. Finally, she began to make small shushing gestures at the boy, but Owl, full of compelling need to keep the Lady interested, ignored her.

Donkey ran through the streets. It had been Cithanekh's idea to send him in case, the young lord had said, the Scholar King's guards *didn't* succeed in intercepting Arre. If she were already in the snare, the arrival of the Imperial Guard would be more likely to result in her immediate death than in rescue. He reached the Ghytteve house; the streets were quiet: no sign of the Emperor's foreign witch; no sign of the Guard. Then, Donkey froze. There! A figure crouched on the ledge of an attic window; it disappeared inside and the shutters were stealthily closed. Ferret. He'd bet money. But where was Arre?

Then, the measured tramp of footsteps disquieted the night. Donkey hurried toward the Imperial Guard with his warning. Stay still, Cithanekh and Kerigden had said; when we've assessed the situation, we'll send Squirrel with instructions.

"Barred from within," Kerigden breathed. "As you said." He pressed his cheek and palms against the door. A faint sheen of sweat dampened his brow and a single musical note, thrumming like the deepest string on a harp, stirred the air. Kerigden's jaw clenched and pain spasmed across his features. As the door swung open beneath his touch, they heard distantly a man's cry of pain. Squirrel flinched. Without speaking, Kerigden indicated that Squirrel—the Windbringer's protecting gem clutched in his fist—should come, but that Cithanekh should wait. The young lord shut the door, set the bar back in place, and waited.

Time stretched endlessly, punctuated with tortured cries; but it was really only a few minutes before the Windbringer's High Priest returned, alone. "I sent Squirrel out through the garden," he whispered. "The Ghytteve have Arre; she's un-conscious, so there's no help there. I think I can immobilize the extra guards; but I'll need your help with Elkhar."

They slipped up the basement stairs. Guards' chaffing and the click and rattle of the *ysmath* bones came from the large kitchen. The two men crouched in the shadows by the door; Kerigden took up his harp. At first, the music could hardly be heard over the talk and laughter, but it gained in power, throb-bing on some nearly unheard level against the young lord's temples. The talk within the kitchen slowed, words slurred, sentences left hanging. The rattle of the *ysmath* bones ceased; and a voice—not Kerigden's, but a clear, rich contralto—sang repetitively: "Sleep...sleep...sleep...dreamless and deep ...sleep..."

The music stopped. The world was utterly still. The cries of pain had ceased. Kerigden crept into the kitchen; a mo-ment later, he emerged with Arre's lute case and a wrought iron key. He locked the kitchen door.

They went upstairs. By the light of a sconce of candles set in the wall they saw that several doors opened off the hallway; all were silent, all shut. As the two men hesitated, there was a heavy thump against the nearest door. Moved by some instinc-tual reflex, Cithanekh sprang forward and yanked the door open. Two fighting men spilled into the hall: a stranger, with Elkhar's fingers gripping his throat; as they tumbled, the stranger rammed his knee into Elkhar's groin. They struck the ground rolling. Cithanekh, with strength born of desperation, aimed a punish-ing kick at Elkhar's head. The Ghytteve crumpled.

"Quick, quick, quick!" That was *Ferret's* voice. She had a half-conscious Sharkbait unbound and nearly to the door. "Get Arre." She stared at Kerigden and Cithanekh for an instant, then smiled. "Well met; let's move."

Kerigden scooped up Arre while Cithanekh helped the stranger to his feet. "Out through the garden. The Imperial Guard are there. We left Donkey and Squirrel to delay them."

Ferret swore as the implications sunk in. "Go! Get out!"

Cithanekh hesitated. He doubted he'd killed Elkhar, and if he hadn't, the man would cause trouble; but he wasn't sure he could kill him in cold blood.

"*Cithanekh*," Kerigden hissed. "If the Imperial Guard come, Khethyran will have a Council House *war* on his hands. Move!"

They moved. The scruffy party burst through the garden gate just as the last of Donkey's stalling tactics failed and Commander Bhenekh had drawn breath to order his men to break the door down. Commander Bhenekh took them all in train and set a rapid pace back to the Palace. Somehow, halfway between the Ghytteve's house and the Palace gates, Ferret's accomplice almost magically eluded his escort and vanished into the night.

"I should go, too," Cithanekh said to the Commander. "I am not skillful enough to escape you, but why give Ycevi Ghytteve something to use against the Scholar King?"

"That Ghytteve bitch is guilty of treason," he growled.

"Do you honestly think, Commander, the *other* Council Houses will support a trial for treason over something which is—from their point of view—as commonplace as *breathing?* If Arre had been *murdered*, the Emperor might survive such a move. *Might.* She's not even seriously injured. As for Sharkbait, to the Council Houses' way of thinking, he's riffraff—and they do what they please with riffraff."

"*Thank* you," Sharkbait commented, acidly.

"I'm speaking as a noble, cousin," Cithanekh retorted with a glint of sardonic humor.

"I can tell," Sharkbait jibed. "Commander, it's sense. Our best course is to *forget* this incident. Send Cithanekh off into the night. If it gets out that he was in the custody of the Imperial Guard—however briefly—it will make trouble."

"What if Elkhar saw him?" Ferret asked anxiously.

Cithanekh looked bleak. "There's no help for it. Believe me, Ferret: it will be worse if I'm found with the Imperial Guard."

"The damage may be done already," Commander Bhenekh said grimly. "My men are solid—but money's money; and intrigue's a way of life. Even if I order this night's work forgotten, it may not stay secret."

Cithanekh nudged Kerigden. "Might not 'forget' work as well as 'sleep?'"

The Windbringer's High Priest smiled slowly. "Now *that's* brilliant. It should. Go—and good luck to you. And Commander? When we get back to the Palace barracks, do you think your men would enjoy a little music?"

Chapter Thirty-one
Aftermath

Having utterly exhausted his inventiveness, Owl retreated into passionate hysterics. When everything failed to calm him, one of the bodyguard was sent to fetch Cithanekh, but Ycevi remained with her slave. Owl hoped it was enough. Prolonged hysterics were tiring. He had subsided to mere gasps and sobs in response to intermittant queries or slaps when the bodyguard returned with Cithanekh.

The young lord took in the situation with alarm. "What's *wrong* with him?"

"He had one of his dreaming fits," Myncerre replied. "I don't know what's the matter, now."

"Owl!" Cithanekh hugged him. "Stop! Whatever frightened you: it's just a dream. Never mind." And then, knowing the risk but needing to reassure his friend, he breathed into his ear, "They're safe: Arre and Sharkbait. Safe."

Owl nodded against his friend's shoulder and began to ease out of his hysterical performance. Not too suddenly, he knew, or they'd be suspicious. Cithanekh was safe. He took a deep breath which ended in a tiny, almost soundless sob. Safe.

The Lady watched, one eyebrow raised speculatively, while Cithanekh calmed the overwrought boy. Then, with a sniff of disdain, she gathered her bodyguard with a gesture. "Shall we go see what Elkhar has for us, now?"

As she spoke, the door to the library crashed back on its hinges. Elkhar—bruised, rumpled and raging—stormed in. "They've escaped: Antryn *and* the Emperor's foreign witch!"

"*Escaped?*" the Lady cried. "The *Emperor's foreign witch?*"

"Yes. We found her snooping on the street—but no doubt it was part of some larger ruse. My whole complement of extra guards were *sound asleep*—five locked in the kitchen, and the sixth on duty in the garden. It *reeks* of heathen magic."

"Report in an orderly fashion," Ycevi demanded.

Elkhar clasped his hands behind him and recounted events in a clipped tone. "Antryn's capture went smoothly. We returned with him to the Upper Town house. Once he was secured, I ordered the others to guard the perimeter. Some time later, the guards brought in the Emperor's foreign witch. She had been lurking in the street. She appeared unconscious—but perhaps that was, as I suggested, a ruse. In any case, I had the guards leave her, bound and unconscious as she was, with me and the other prisoner. They posted one guard in the garden and returned to the kitchen. A short time later, two intruders interrupted my interrogation of Antryn: a girl—probably Ferret; and a better than competent grown man. There were two other accomplices in the hallway, one of whom was (I *think*) the Windbringer's High Priest—at least, he had that unnatural hair. The other (not the priest) kicked me in the head, and when I came to myself, they were gone."

"The Emperor's foreign witch," Ycevi repeated, her fierce eyes searching Owl's face. "The Emperor's foreign witch *and the Windbringer's High Priest?*" Ycevi's voice shrilled with outrage. "Was that hysterical taradiddle *true—or was it purely intended to delay me? Owl?!*" Then, in a manner reminiscent of Elkhar at his most terrifying, the Lady's anger was replaced by deadly calm. "Haven't I made it clear to you, brat, that it is *dangerous*—perhaps even *fatal*—to lie to me?"

Owl pressed his lips with his good hand and nodded.

"Wait," Elkhar purred, matching his Lady's frightening coolness. "I haven't told you the best thing: the one who kicked me? *It was Cithanekh.*"

Mouse delivered Owl's warning. Without delay, the Scholar King called out the Imperial Guard. Then, he sent a servant to fetch Venykhar to the Imperial Apartments to await word of their friends. Though it seemed like years, it was less than an hour before Arre, Sharkbait, Ferret, Squirrel, Donkey and Kerigden—some looking a little the worse for wear—filed in and collapsed into chairs to an eager chorus of greeting.

"So what *happened?*" Mouse demanded.

"And where's Commander Bhenekh?" the Scholar King added.

"As to that," Kerigden offered diffidently, "I fear his report would have been rather garbled. I took the liberty of clouding the memories of the Guards; we thought this matter might best be forgotten."

Mouse, Venykhar, and the Emperor exchanged glances at this, and then said, together, "*So what happened?*"

It took some time tell all sides of the tale. By the end, Khethyran looked troubled. "You were right; this matter is best forgotten. But I fear for your friends in Ghytteve hands. What chance, truly, that Cithanekh's blow killed Elkhar?"

Sharkbait groaned. "It will take silver weapons and a spell to kill that bastard."

"So I'd wager," Ferret put in. "And unless he's dead, he'll have seen and recognized Cithanekh. So the question is: what now? Happen we canna send the Imperial Guard to the rescue, but I'll not sit idly by wringing my hands."

"Hear, hear!" Squirrel affirmed. "But what shall we *do?*"

"Into the walls, I think," Ferret said softly. "Happen we'd best get Cithanekh and Owl out of Ycevi's power—and soon. From all that's been said, I dinna believe she's one to accept the kind of meddling Cithanekh's done."

"Ferret, they know we know about the secret ways," Donkey reminded.

"True, but Squirrel escaped, so they'll know that we know that they know—and they'll not expect us to risk it."

Venykhar laughed. "That makes sense—or rather, it sounds like Ycevi's reasoning, which isn't the same thing. But not all of us, surely, Ferret. Won't too many become a danger?"

Ferret nodded.

"If you think to leave me behind, my sweet thief, think again," Sharkbait warned.

"You're hurt," she said, but he raised his eyebrows.

"I know my limits," he told her, and she nodded.

"So," she began, "Sharkbait and I will go." She scanned the others, plans roiling in her head. "And Donkey?" She touched his gaze, watched him nod. "Mouse?" The girl nodded vehemently. "And Squirrel?" He jerked his head in assent.

"*Mouse?*" Venykhar protested.

Before the girl could bristle, Ferret explained. "For messages. She can draw; Owl canna read."

"What about the rest of us?" Venykhar asked. "Do you have some plan for us?"

"Actually, Ven," Kerigden put in, "I have a plan—unless Ferret has something in mind? No? I could use your help, Ven—and yours, Arre, if you feel well enough."

As they murmured agreement, the Scholar King spoke ruefully. "Leaving me—as always—to await word in safety."

Arre responded, as though to an old argument, with a pained smile. "If you insist on being useful, Kheth, get Rhydev Azhere drunk."

The Emperor kissed her palm. "As you wish. Or rather, I'll do my best. That man can drink a soldier under. Are you set on drunk—or will it do if I just keep him out of the way?"

"Keep him out of the way," she said. "He seems to think it will advance his position if he can persuade the Ghytteve to murder me. I finally remembered where I'd seen that informant before: one of Rhydev's sneaks."

"Come on, troops," Ferret said. "Let's move."

"Squirrel," Kerigden asked. "Do you still have that stone?"

The boy nodded. "You want it?"

"No. But if you have the chance, give it back to Owl. I've a sense he may need it."

"*Cithanekh*," the Lady repeated. She stared at him as though she could flay him with her gaze. "No doubt you'll try to convince me you were safeguarding my interests."

"He *was*," Owl insisted. "I dreamed it: if Elkhar had killed Arre—*and he would have killed her*—the Emperor would have had you executed for *treason*, Lady."

Ycevi gave a short, outraged laugh. "Executed for treason over a foreign whore? Don't be ridiculous."

"He loves her," Owl persisted. "Don't you understand? He doesn't weigh the costs the way you do."

The Lady lapsed back into silent scrutiny. After a moment, she gestured to Elkhar. "Take the boy to the gallery; there's no sense in staining a perfectly good carpet. Bind him to a chair." Two of the men restrained Cithanekh while Elkhar took Owl away. Ycevi studied her kinsman as though reading secrets in his eyes. "You are of no use to me unless you are malleable, Cithanekh. You *do* understand that, don't you?" She spat the words with vicious precision.

"Yes, Lady."

"Then *why* do you persist in flouting me? Do you think I won't kill you?" At his headshake, she narrowed her eyes. "Do you think I won't harm your boy?"

"You've made it abundantly clear that you will!" he cried desperately.

"Then *why?* *Why* involve yourself in this? You must have known it would anger me."

"Lady, *I trust Owl.* He told me Khethyran would destroy you if the woman Arre died."

Ycevi glared at Cithanekh in disbelief. "Do you think I'm *stupid?* I know perfectly well *you'd dance on my grave*—both of you. No. If you saved that woman Arre, it was for your own reasons; *and I will know what they are!*"

"I *told* you," he insisted.

"Very well: be stubborn. You won't enjoy this—my solemn word on it, Cithanekh." She gestured with her head. "Take him him up to the gallery and bind him. Myncerre? Fetch my case of implements—the one with the tongs—and the supply of *ymekkhai* from the stores; and have the servants bring a brazier to the gallery."

Worry marred Myncerre's impassive face. "Lady, what—"

Ycevi rounded on her savagely. "*No questions: just do it!*"

The steward bowed and went out.

Rhydev Azhere set the note down on the silver salver and motioned the servant out. He turned a frowning visage on his uncle. "Now, this I *do not* like, in view of other—mmm— *considerations.*"

Zherekhaf inclined his head. "Oh?"

"An Imperial invitation—nay, command—to a game of *khacce* tonight."

"Oh."

"Is that all you can say?"

The Prime Minister shrugged. "It's all that's warranted,

surely. My dear Rhydev, you're thinking like a *conspirator.*
In your position, there's *nothing* more dangerous. Chances
are, the Emperor's invitation is completely innocent; and
even if he has some suspicion, he'd hardly invite you—in
writing and before witnesses—to your own assassination.
Go, my dear boy, and don't keep His Majesty waiting. I'll
find my own way out."

Donkey led, for he knew the hidden ways best; and Squirrel
took the rear, his keen ears straining for the sound of pursuit.
Mouse, with her drawing case tucked firmly under her arm,
gripped the back of Donkey's tunic with sweaty fingers.
Sharkbait kept a hand on Ferret's elbow, but whether to support her or steady himself, not even he could have said.

The Ghytteve complex seemed strangely empty. No
guards loitered in the kitchen or their common room; in the
light of the lone table lamp, the *ysmath* bones lay silent and
neglected. A half-finished *khacce* game graced the board in
the library, but no one was there. They crept carefully past
all the usual haunts of the Ghytteve, and found no one
worth watching until they came across the steward,
Myncerre, in her Lady's dressing room. The woman was
seated at Ycevi's dressing table, a lamp at her elbow, her
steepled forefingers against her lips, and a look of tremen-
dous abstraction on her face. Ferret studied the scene
through the spyhole. On the table before the steward lay
an ebony case, open; nestled in the dark silk lining were
silver implements with carved wooden handles. The thief
suppressed a shudder of recognition. Beside the open case
was a squat stoneware jar with a large round of cork shoved
into its mouth. Suddenly, the steward unfroze. She stirred
the tools in the case with her fingers until, with a faint sigh,
she withdrew a stiletto knife. She pilfered two ribbons from
the clutter on her Lady's dressing table and strapped the
blade to her left forearm. She fussed with her concealing
sleeve; then, taking the case and retrieving the jar and lamp,
she went out the door opposite the spyhole.

Donkey cursed softly. "Canna follow, now," he explained
on a breath, "without going into the room—which is unwise."

"Never mind," Ferret replied. "Just keep looking. Happen we'll find them, late or soon."

When Venykhar, Kerigden and Arre arrived in the safety of the Ykhave apartments, the old lord turned to the priest. "What, exactly, do you have in mind, Kerigden?"

"A form of mind work," Kerigden replied.

"I thought you said you needed me," the flute-maker said a little reproachfully.

"We do. I want you to play while we work. We need an anchor."

Worry knit Arre's brow. "Kerigden," she protested. "Work with an anchor is beyond—" She broke off as she remembered the feel of his mind: banked coals; power waiting for some enlivening touch. "I cannot balance you," she whispered, painfully. "My gifts are not as strong as yours."

The High Priest touched her shoulder gently. "Trust me. I will not hurt you; but I need your help."

Venykhar looked from one to the other, mystified. "What are you talking about? What are you planning to do? How dangerous is it—and, gods above and below, what good will it do? Arre, you're as brave as a lioness; if you're afraid of whatever Kerigden has in mind, it *must* be dangerous." As the priest turned toward him, he added, waspishly, "And don't just say: 'Trust me.' I do trust you, but I want to *know*."

Kerigden sighed. "My Lady Windbringer has some *interest* in the outcome here. She required me to help; she appeared to Owl in a dream and gave him a warding stone; and she aided me with the Ghytteve and the Imperial Guard. But there is more she wants, more at stake—*and I need to know what!* When she appeared to Owl, she mentioned a wager and said perhaps she had nothing to fear from her brother. It puzzles me; and it makes me tremble. You know the histories of the gods. My Lady Windbringer has not always fared well in the company of the gods; perhaps in this matter, she is in some danger, or facing some threat. Owl told me *he summoned her*, that he used the focus Arre and I taught him and *called* Talyene. With a human anchor instead of merely a focus stone, Arre and I might be able to do that, or to read more fully the future, using

Arre's Sight Gifts, or—possibly—to link with Owl and persuade him to summon the Windbringer."

Venykhar looked uncomfortable. "Wouldn't she tell you
if she wanted you to know?"

"Only if asked, I think," Kerigden replied.

"Very well. And how dangerous is this?"

"There is a risk," Kerigden admitted. "Not as much for
you, Ven, as for Arre and me. But there are also possible ben-
efits. By our asking, my Lady Windbringer may be empowered
to act directly, to help us save Owl and to defeat Ycevi. It
seems to me that is worth a considerable risk."

Venykhar glanced at Arre, who nodded agreement. "Very
well," he said. "Tell me what I must do."

It was Arre who answered him. "You must play your
flute—and you must not stop, no matter what. Think of your
music as a beacon which will show us how to return if we
should travel too deeply into the country of the mind."

"Just play? Play anything?"

Despite her own uneasiness, she smiled. "Play melodies
to call us home."

Venykhar was silent for a moment; then, he bowed his
head in acquiescence. Arre and Kerigden seated themselves
at the table while the old lord locked the door and got his
flute. He began to play, the thread of melody sweet in the dim
room. Together, the priest and the seer entered their trance;
and the flute both held them anchored and gave their minds
the courage and freedom to range far.

It was like nothing else Arre had experienced. Kerigden's
mind swept her up, into such a sea of feelings and images that
she was bewildered. Power gathered in their joined minds: a
river in spate, fire driven by wind, souls in ecstasy: harmony,
union, power. The power built; their minds strained to con-
tain it. Then, Kerigden called: *Talyene. Talyene!*

There was nothing, no answering power. It wasn't enough.
And then, like a glimmer of inspiration, Arre knew what lacked.
Carefully, she used a little of the power they had gathered to
make the illusion of sound: music to answer and incorporate
the voice of the almost unheeded flute.

Yes, Kerigden cried, and he twined his music into theirs.

It was beyond explaining, beyond words. They poured love and need and power into the crafting, and the music answered them. Of their minds and the gathered power they wove a music so yearning, so entreating that even a stone would answer. Kerigden began to sing: an ancient song in an ancient language, which repeated, each time more beseechingly, the goddess's ancient name. Talyene. Talyene. Talyene.

And she came.

Chapter Thirty-two
Retribution

Owl, bound to a chair in the shadowy gallery, couldn't stop shivering. Elkhar stood behind him, tense and eager. Later, others brought Cithanekh and tied him to a chair opposite the boy. When Owl greeted his friend, Elkhar snapped: "Keep still." So he held his tongue, but still shivered.

Ycevi joined them. Her gown kissed the tiles as she ghosted to Owl's side. Silent, she traced the planes of his face with a fingertip; she smiled when she noticed his shivering.

Servants brought a small table and a glowing brazier on a wrought iron stand. "Put it near the boy," Ycevi told them with a secretive smile. "I think he's cold." Owl felt the brazier's warmth on his skin, but he couldn't stop shivering.

Finally, Myncerre came. She laid a long wooden box on the table and put a squat stoneware jar down beside it. Then, she took a folding wooden tripod and a small metal bowl out of her pocket and set them up beside the other things. The Lady surveyed the preparations and nodded. She went to Cithanekh's chair, touched his face in the same way she had Owl's.

"Can you guess what I intend?" she asked in a voice brittle as frost. When the young lord shook his head, she smiled. "Then it will be a surprise." At the table, she opened the wooden box and removed a silver skewer which she placed in the brazier.

Owl's throat dried; his visions had shown him what atrocities to expect, with Kitten's murder. Across the span which separated them, he sought Cithanekh's eyes; but though Owl's terrified face was limned in firelight, Cithanekh's was shadowed.

"Don't hurt him, Ycevi." Cithanekh's voice came, broken, out of darkness. "Please don't hurt him."

"Don't hurt him, Ycevi. Please don't hurt him." Through a trick of the secret ways, the voice—*Cithanekh's* voice—

sounded impossibly close. Ferret's hand closed warningly on Donkey's shoulder. They were near a series of spyhole niches that gave a view of a seldom used gallery.

Swiftly but silently, they found places from which to watch—all save Mouse, who was not tall enough comfortably to reach these spyholes. Stifling irritation, the girl crouched beside the secret entrance. The panel was thin enough to conduct sound reasonably well. She strained to catch Ycevi's answer; they had to be talking about Owl.

"Please don't hurt him," Cithanekh repeated.

"His fate is in your hands. Tell me: why did you save the Emperor's witch?"

"I told you! Because the Scholar King would have brought you down over Arre's murder!"

She stalked to the brazier; seizing the skewer, she drove it into the boy's thigh. Unable to stop himself, Owl screamed.

"But I'm telling the *truth!*" Cithanekh cried.

Ycevi returned the skewer to the brazier. "Truth?" she laughed scornfully. "Perhaps that's a part of it, a part of the truth. But truly, I don't care. How did you know where Antryn was? How did you know when Arre was taken? How did your accomplices find them? *Who told you?* Was it Owl?" She rounded on the boy, suddenly. "*Who owns you*, body and soul? *Who commands your loyalty?*" She seized the skewer and advanced. "*Answer me!*"

"Cithanekh," he said, half-wonderingly. Ycevi drove the skewer into his leg again and he screamed.

"Cithanekh," Ycevi repeated. "*Cithanekh?* What kind of clever double game are you playing, my fine young puppy?"

"It's not like that," Owl protested, desperate. "It's no game we play, Lady; it's real. It's not politics, nor power; I'm not his tool, nor his toy. It is true that I would cut off my arm if he needed it, but he would also cut off his own for me. Don't you understand? We're *friends.*"

Ycevi looked from one to the other. "Do you still seek to play me for a fool? *Friends!*" She spat the word as though it were an obscenity. "I have no patience with fairy tales, boy." Then she turned to her steward. "Make ready the *ymekkhai.*"

Myncerre took an elegant pair of silver tongs out of the wooden case, opened the stoneware jar and extracted several long strips of a light colored substance. She laid the strips in the metal bowl then set the tongs down and moved aside.

"A useful substance, *ymekkhai*," the Lady said in a terrifyingly objective voice. "It burns with a particularly intense white light; it is unwise, however, to watch it burn, as it can do irreparable damage to one's vision. Elkhar, hold his head."

Elkhar's fingers found Owl's eyelids and peeled them open; he held him firmly but not ungently, while Ycevi picked up the tongs and chose a glowing coal from the brazier.

The reddish glow from the brazier lit Ycevi's terrible smile. Her voice was soft as the whisper of steel from scabbard. "You said you would cut off your arm for your *friend*, little Owl; would you pluck out your eyes?"

The goddess loomed through the music as though she were parting mist. Kerigden's song ended, though the power hummed like an echo.

Lady Windbringer, he began. But she held up one hand.

I am constrained. I have come, for you have summoned me with power, need and music; but your questions I am not permitted to answer without forfeit; and I can afford no forfeitures.

Arre's music wound down to silence. *Could you answer for me, Lady Windbringer? I am no priest, but a Kellande Seer.*

They must be your own questions. Kerigden, I bind silence on you. He bowed his head in submission, then picked up the threads of power which Arre had let fall and wove them back into the music. *Ask, Seer, three questions*, the goddess commanded, *and I shall answer.*

Arre cast her mind over all that had gone before. *What is your wager?* she asked at last.

Talyene smiled faintly. *I argued with my brother over hopeless causes. We wagered that I could not prove that loyalty, idealism and determination could triumph against self-interest, power, privilege and ruthlessness. He chose the proving ground: the court of Bharaghlaf; and I the players: a hente of Slum children.*

What are the stakes? Arre asked.

If I lose, I relinquish any right to the hearts of the people of the Bharaghlafi Empire; if he loses, he forfeits his right to their power.

Arre hesitated, weighing the third question carefully. Kerigden might want to know which of the other gods opposed her, though he might already be able to guess; or he might wish to know what specific effect losing would have upon his goddess; or—Suddenly, Arre remembered what the Windbringer had said: that they must be her questions. *How can I best aid your cause?* she asked.

Keep the boy Owl alive and sane, the goddess answered, her mental voice bleak. *If you can.* Then, posing her hands like a temple painting, she vanished into the music.

The coal in the tongs glowed like a baleful eye in the dim room. Ycevi drew it to hover over the bowl of *ymekkhai.*

"*NO!*" Cithanekh cried. "Stop! Whatever you want to know, I will tell you. I'll tell you; I'll tell you!"

Ycevi replaced the coal in the brazier; Elkhar released Owl who blinked fiercely stinging eyes. "So. You want me to believe you are at last ready to be reasonable. Very well. Proceed from the beginning."

"I never wanted to be part of your plan; you knew that. I chose to work against you as best I could; I've been aiding Rhydev Azhere. At the time, he seemed to offer the best chance of foiling your plans and freeing me. Recently I've come to see he only wants you out of the game so that *he* can be the one to make me Emperor and pull my strings. I got Arre away from Elkhar more to foul Rhydev's scheme than yours, truly. I didn't *know* you'd finally caught Antryn—I thought it was just Arre. So I told the Windbringer's High Priest; he and Arre are friends. I thought he'd help me rescue her."

"And Ferret?" Elkhar interjected.

"I had nothing to do with Antryn's escape—or at least, I didn't mean to. Those other people's presence was as much a surprise to me, I think, as to you, Elkhar."

"And little Owl is completely innocent, of course," Ycevi scoffed. "Never mind that he kept me and my bodyguards out of the way while you effected your rescue. Come, come, Cithanekh; I thought you were ready to tell me whatever I want to know. You haven't yet; your *explanation* is as full of holes as *myrakke* lace."

"Lady, please believe me: I've learned something from all this. Truly I can't bear to have Owl hurt. I can't possibly work against you any longer when it means risking harm to my friend." He leaned forward, straining against the bonds that held him. Firelight caught in the tears on his face. "Please, Lady. I dare not ask you to forgive me—but do *believe* me: you've won. I'll cooperate. I'll do whatever you require in exchange for Owl's safety." His face twisted with bitterness and defeat. "I'll be your obedient hound, just—*please*—don't hurt Owl."

The Lady gazed at him, then brushed his wet cheek with her fingers. "Tears, even. How impressive. I never knew you were such an actor. You plead very convincingly, Cithanekh—but I cannot fail to notice *you still evade my questions.*"

"*What more can I tell you?*" he demanded, anguished. "Owl told you why he came to you: his visions showed him what would happen to you if Elkhar killed the Emperor's lover. Perhaps he also saw what you would do to me if you found me trying to thwart your plans. Even if you don't believe that he would act to protect you, you must understand that he would risk a great deal to protect me."

"Why would he risk himself? Why would he court pain and mutilation?" she cried; then she rounded on Owl. "*Why?*"

Owl's eyes brimmed with tears. He said, despairingly—for he knew she would not understand, "Because I love him, Lady; and I do not reckon the cost the way that you expect."

Lady Ycevi studied him, her expression inscrutable. "And does he love you, boy?"

"Yes."

"And I suppose that means that he will forever be counting costs in unexpected ways, as well?"

"I daresay," Owl admitted.

"And do you expect me to use *unpredictable* tools, then?" she hissed.

Before Owl could respond, Cithanekh said, "Please, Lady; listen to me. I meant it when I said you've won. I promise I will be your obedient hound; I will do whatever you require. But please, don't hurt Owl."

She half turned toward Cithanekh; something in her posture told him that she was not convinced. She did not believe the young lord. As he watched her obdurate profile, he realized that she meant to kill them both.

"You have displeased me very deeply," she said, starting toward Cithanekh. "But you plead so pitiably, so touchingly. Perhaps I should give you a last chance. But you must first be punished, Cithanekh; I cannot allow you to flout me so and escape with a scolding."

"Punish *me*, then," he begged. "Not Owl."

A gloating edge shaded her voice; Owl could hear her poisonous smile. "But it will hurt you so much more if I use the boy." She turned suddenly to Myncerre. "Blind the boy."

"*Me?*" Myncerre protested. "Lady—"

"Do you *dispute* me? Do it." Warning thrummed in her tone.

For a moment, Owl thought Myncerre would refuse. Her face, usually so impassive, showed horror and denial. The Lady didn't see it; she had issued her order and turned away. Myncerre looked across at Owl, and he saw the shadow of some irrevocable decision in her expression. Then, the steward bowed her head. "As my Lady commands. Elkhar?"

As Owl's eyelids were forced open again, Elkhar growled, "Ready." Owl watched Myncerre's steady hand on the tongs, followed the path of the glowing coal from the brazier to where she held it over the metal bowl. On the edges of his vision, Owl saw the Lady covering Cithanekh's eyes with her hands. As she held the coal, its light gilded the track of tears on her face. Then, Myncerre opened the tongs. The coal fell like a meteor, and the world exploded in searing, white fire.

Arre screamed. White fire exploded in her vision, seared away control, loosed the power; a maelstrom of images drew her down, pulled her deep. She was inundated with visions, trapped in a firestorm of prophecy, buried in foresight. It was like trying to breathe fire, or walk on the wind; nothing made sense. Despair avalanched over her, crushing and battering. Madness leered and gibbered. Her soul fled— and was caught.

Kerigden's mind was there, its banked embers flaring to life. He gave her his power, invited her to take it, to remake order, sense, sanity with the strength of his mind. She steadied herself and set to work. It was a heady feeling; a temptation. Her own poor gifts were as nothing to this; and he gave it freely. She could take it, strip him of it, build the kind of powerful gift Owl bore and for which she had often wished. But no; there was something else that needed doing. There was Owl, and he was screaming.

Owl screamed. Images blazed in his mind. It was too much. Too much! The past, present and future jumbled together like beads in a box; the fragmented dazzle filled his mind. The tides of prophecy thundered over him, pelting him with their vivid flotsam, dragging him further and further from the shore of sanity. And then, like an exhausted swimmer, he ceased to struggle. It didn't matter; nothing mattered. It was too hard to impose order on this chaos. He would let go, strip his sense from his inner vision and lose himself in the depths of history, possibility and immediacy. He let go; his soul fled—and was caught.

Arre felt him: Owl, snared in the web of power and order she had built with Kerigden's strength. She held him, channeled his raging visions into the framework she imposed, trying, ruthlessly, to force him back to sanity. He fought her with all his despairing might. But he was untrained, and she had her own and Kerigden's strength.

Owl! Owl, listen: she cried, though he gave no sign of hearing her. *This will pass; I know what they've done, but this impossible madness will pass. You were unprepared and unwilling, but you can master this!*

Her knowledge outstripped her mind voice. She knew her history. The ancient Khyghafe nomads had ritually blinded their shaman to bring him to his full power. It had required preparation, for the rite would loose a fearful storm of visions in the seer's mind. Some of them died, or went mad. Then, Arre remembered the words of the Windbringer: Keep the boy alive and sane. If you can.

* * *

Owl's screams broke off as he slumped against his bonds. Startled, Ycevi went to his side. "What's this? Elkhar, what's wrong with him? Owl? *Owl!*" She patted his unresponsive cheeks.

"Has he fainted?" Elkhar suggested.

Across the room, Cithanekh repeated his friend's name over and over, a quiet litany of anguish. Myncerre looked from the young lord to her mistress, then to Owl's hunched figure; and with unhurried precision, she filled the metal bowl with more *ymekkhai* and set the tongs down beside the brazier. Then, she slipped the stiletto from its hiding place into her hand.

"Lady? Would you like some smelling salts for him?" She pantomimed holding something out to Ycevi.

As the Lady reached for what the steward seemed to hold, Myncerre grabbed her wrist and gave a hard yank. She pulled Ycevi to her in a deadly embrace and slid the stiletto between her ribs. The Lady's startled exclamation was abruptly cut off. Holding the Lady's inert body upright with one arm, she snatched up the tongs and took a coal from the brazier. "*Elkhar*," she said, with enough real alarm to draw his gaze. Then she dropped the coal into the *ymekkhai*.

She shut her eyes against the fierce flash; she could feel the heat of the burning on her face. Then, Myncerre shoved the Lady's body into Elkhar's oncoming rush. His stumble bought her the time to move from the place he'd last seen her. She could tell her ploy had worked: Elkhar was relying on sound more than sight, his night vision disturbed by the brilliant *ymekkhai* flash. She slipped her shoes off and tossed one to land just beyond Elkhar's left shoulder. As he spun toward the sound, she sprang.

She made her strike, high up on the left side of his back. Not the clean kill she had been taught; a fatal wound—but too slow. She swore, softly. Writhing in her hold, Elkhar freed his knife hand for a counter thrust. His blade found, unerringly, the heart thrust. Life left the steward's face.

"Gods, Myncerre. *Why?*" Elkhar demanded, uselessly: his breath rattled unpleasantly. He started toward Owl with a snarl.

"*Why*, Elkhar?" Cithanekh challenged from the shadows. "Because, in the end, Myncerre reclaimed her own will. She broke Ycevi's control at the last; and she died free. Will you?"

He advanced on the bound man with deadly purpose. "I'll kill you, Cithanekh. *You're my meat now!*"

"Exactly as Ycevi would have wished," he responded acidly. "She meant to kill us both; I'm certain. Myncerre must have guessed."

"I am loyal to my Lady," Elkhar cried. "*Loyal!*" He laid his knife against Cithanekh's bare throat. "Can you say the same?"

Cithanekh's voice was grave and rather sad. "But was she loyal to *you*, Elkhar? To be genuine, loyalty must run in both directions—else one is either the puppet, or the puppeteer. I have been—tried to be—loyal to my friends."

After the second flash, Mouse quietly slipped the catch on the secret entrance and crept cautiously into the room. She was the only one of her companions who was not blinking stupidly at black and green afterimages when Myncerre killed Ycevi. During the fight between the steward and Elkhar, Mouse stole along the wall toward Cithanekh; but she was too slow. Before she was in position to loose the young lord's bonds, the bodyguard was towering threateningly over him, a knife pressed to his throat. She took a running leap at the bodyguard, flinging her slight weight against his chest.

Startled and still half-blinded, the knife flew out of Elkhar's hand as he rolled with the force of Mouse's attack. His hands clutched her tunic; with a wriggle, she left it in his fingers like a reptile's shed skin and pelted out of reach. He started toward her; but after two strides, he dropped to one knee, coughing wetly.

Mouse saw the glint of light on metal and dove for Elkhar's knife. She came up, clutching it, and found herself facing the man across a span of ten feet or so. He knelt, bewilderment on his face. "Who?" he gasped. "Who are you?"

"I'm Loyalty," Mouse said clearly, "and Retribution." As she watched, Elkhar's eyes dulled and his face began to relax. "And Peace," the child added more gently. Elkhar fell, then, slow and heavy as a tree. But Mouse was sure she saw him smile, just before he died.

* * *

"Mouse?" Cithanekh said wonderingly. "I can't see you."

The girl scurried to Cithanekh and cut his bonds with Elkhar's knife. "Quick, quick, quick," she whispered. "Take my hand—I'll lead you."

"Owl," Cithanekh protested.

"Half a moment," she snapped. "I canna do it all at once."

By the time she got Cithanekh inside the secret passageway, Donkey and Ferret had untied Owl and hauled his curiously inert form to the secret panel.

"What's the *matter* with him?" Ferret demanded. "I dinna think he's unconscious. Owl!"

The boy rolled away from her touch, curling into a ball. "*Owl!*" Mouse, Ferret and Squirrel cried.

Cithanekh took the boy from the thief. "Owl." It was plea, and pain, and endearment. "*Owl*," he repeated, but the boy was unresponsive. "Owl, come back. Don't leave me. I *need* you. *Owl!*"

Squirrel took the Windbringer's stone out of his pocket. In the close darkness of the passage, it coruscated with imperative light. In the eerie glow, Cithanekh watched with reckless hope, as Squirrel pressed the gem into Owl's palm and wrapped his fingers around it. For an instant, Owl gripped it; then his hand went limp. The stone shattered. Rain-scented air gusted in the passage. They watched for some change in the boy, but Owl made no sign. Cithanekh bowed his head in unspeakable pain.

Ferret touched his shoulder gently. "We canna stay here."

The young lord lifted Owl's motionless body and followed numbly. They were halfway back to the Imperial Apartments when Owl raised a questing hand to his friend's cheek.

"Cithanekh?" he asked plaintively. "I can't see you."

"I'm here, Owl," Cithanekh assured him; relief quavered in his voice. "And you're safe."

Chapter Thirty-three
Tidying Up

Owl sat quietly before the window of the guest room of the Imperial Apartments. He felt the sun on his face; it was too warm, but the air from the gardens smelled sweet. Behind him, he heard the door open.

"Cithanekh?" he asked without turning. It did no good, anymore, to look.

The door closed. Footsteps approached: not Cithanekh's tread. A face crossed his inner sight. "Your Majesty."

Hands took his shoulders, gentle, as the Emperor spoke. "You're hard to surprise, Owl. Oh, lad," he sighed. "I hardly know how to ask you this: it's so unfair. I had a letter from the Duke of Ghytteve; he flatly refuses to serve as the Council representative for his House. He named three possible successors: one's so corrupt he makes even Zherekhaf blanch; the second is gullible and venal; and the third is Cithanekh."

Owl swallowed tears. "Kerigden says it is imperative that I train my gift. You say I'm hard to surprise, Your Majesty, but my inner sight is very unreliable, yet. Arre says I can learn control, but both she and Kerigden think I should attend the Kellande School on Kalledann. Cithanekh was going to go with me. What did he say when you appointed him?"

"I haven't appointed him. Owl, I *won't* appoint him without your permission."

"*My* permission? That's absurd. You're the *Emperor*."

"True. But I am also very deeply in your debt, Owl. Without your help, Arre would be dead. You and your friends have saved my kingdom, my crown and my very life. And it has cost you dearly. Perhaps you can imagine how much I'd like— how much I *need*—an ally on the Council: someone intelligent, and moral, and compassionate. But I owe you so much, Owl, that I cannot—*I will not*—take any more from you than you can freely give. So: may I appoint him, Owl?"

As Owl considered, a silver-tinged image filled his inner sight: Cithanekh, a little older, laughing over a *khacce* board with the Scholar King and *wearing a Councilor's chain of office.* Something twisted inside Owl. He bowed his head to hide his tears. "As you will, Your Majesty."

Khethyran's hands tightened suddenly on the boy's shoulders. "*Owl,*" he protested.

Owl raised his head. His cheeks were wet but his voice was steady as he sketched a sign in the air. "With my blessing."

Owl couldn't see the pain in the Emperor's eyes; but he heard the tremor in his voice. "Thank you, Owl."

The death of Ycevi Ghytteve at the hands of her steward caused a seven-days wonder even at a Court as jaded as Bharaghlaf's. It was not so much that Ycevi had been murdered (many pundits quipped the real mystery was that she had ever *survived*); but most had thought Myncerre utterly loyal to her Lady, and few could imagine the quiet woman outwitting Elkhar's single-minded suspicion.

But if the murder of the Ghytteve Councilor caused a stir, finding a successor to her seat caused a tempest. Contrary to every expectation, Ycevi's son the Duke declined to step into his mother's shoes. So the Scholar King appointed his own first cousin (and arguably his heir) Cithanekh Anzhibhar-Ghytteve. Cithanekh promptly shocked everyone by making three outrageous proposals at his first Council meeting: first, that the informal organization of dock workers be recognized as a legal Guild, and its chief proponent—a man known as Sharkbait—be named Master of the Longshoreman's Guild; second, that a token of royal favor and the right to display the Emperor's Crest be granted to a seedy Slum tavern known as the Trollop's Smile; and third, that a sum of 9,000 Royals be levied from the nine Council Houses for the establishment of schools in the Slums and the waterfront district, so that the children of families too poor to afford private tutors might be taught to read and write.

No conclusive action was taken on Cithanekh's proposals,

though a lively discussion ensued. After the meeting, Khethyran and Cithanekh found Arre and Mouse helping Owl with his packing. Their laughter preceded them into the room.

"So," Arre smiled. "What *is* so funny?" When they recounted Cithanekh's first Council meeting, Arre raised her eyebrows. "You must have set them utterly at odds. What *were* you thinking of, Cithanekh?"

Owl smiled wryly. "That's easy. He's just making it abundantly clear to the entire happy family of Council snakes that they are far better off with the Scholar King for Emperor than they would be with *him*."

Cithanekh put a companionable arm around Owl's shoulder. "Found out!" he said. "Gods, but I'll miss you, Owl."

Choking down tears, Owl leaned against the young lord, and nodded. "I'll miss you, too," Owl told Cithanekh softly, after a moment. "But Arre says they'll let me come home for a visit at the end of the first year. And if I study really, really hard, perhaps I won't need to go back."

"Study really, really hard, then, lad. I can probably survive a year—but I don't think I can spare you for two."

In the end, the Council voted down the proposed schools; the argument over the Longshoreman's Guild, though tabled for the moment, promised to reemerge periodically. But the Trollop's Smile was granted the right to display the Emperor's Crest. An Ykhave artisan painted a new sign, the Emperor's Crest (with the Emperor's permission) flaunted brazenly on the saucy lady's red dress. Royal favor aside, Arkhyd found himself (courtesy of House Ghytteve) with a reliable source of excellent spirits at reasonable prices. The ale at the Trollop was still swill, but for those who knew to ask for it, the brandy was superb.

Ykhave artisans painted a second sign (which also displayed the Emperor's crest, though in a more conventional manner) for a new flower shop slated to open in the waterfront district. The shop was purchased with the help of Venykhar Ghobhezh-Ykhave—Amynne Ykhave's adopted uncle—and Squirrel and his father looked forward to regular employment with Mouse's parents.

The night before Arre and Owl sailed for Kalledann, the

Trollop's Smile was the site for a comprehensive celebration. Arkhyd—when he got over dithering and settled down to tending his patrons' needs—outdid himself. Sharkbait cheated shamelessly at the *ysmath* bones and won (he said) enough money from Cithanekh and Venykhar to finance his operations for half a year. Arre, Kerigden and Venykhar (when he could be pried away from the fickle *ysmath* bones) made music; Owl got Commander Bhenekh tipsy enough to recite some of his own poetry (which, for a wonder, wasn't bad); Squirrel and Donkey persuaded an Imperial Guard to teach them a variant of the Bharaghlafi Sword Dance; Mouse drew irreverent sketches of *everyone* for Arre to take with her to Kalledann; and the Emperor challenged Ferret to a game of *khacce* which (amazingly) she won.

As the Emperor was putting his *khacce* set away, he fixed the thief with an unsettlingly direct gaze. "Ferret, I want you to think about something for me." As she raised eyebrows encouragingly, he went on. "You've seen what Council House intrigue is like. Most Houses have their people like Azhere's man, Ghorran. I have Bhenekh—a good man, mind, but not precisely subtle."

Ferret laughed. "Even out of uniform. Happen I know what you mean. Right now, he looks ready to have kittens at the mere thought of escorting Your August Personage home through the Slums. But Your Majesty, I've a shameless ambition to be the youngest thief ever promoted Master, before I'm done in this Guild. Happen that will take me a year or two."

"And once you're Master?"

"We'll talk again; but in the meantime, speak to Donkey."

It was late when Ferret returned to her lair. After the party, she'd run an errand for Khyzhan. She climbed wearily up to her rooftop—and froze. Someone was there before her. "What are *you* doing here?" she demanded of Sharkbait.

He shrugged. "I made some coffee. Would you like some?"

She spent a moment deciding whether to be outraged or amused. Amusement won. "Thanks. How'd you get up here?"

"The same way you do."

Ferret thought of the treacherous ascent and shuddered. Sharkbait was quite a bit heavier than she was. "You must be braver than you look—or more a fool."

Sharkbait laughed. "Brave; drunk; determined; foolish; desperate. Take your pick." He poured coffee into one of her battered mugs. "Would you like sugar? I brought some." At her nod, he added sugar and held the cup out to her; when she came over to get the cup, he took her hand and drew her down beside him. "What took you so long?"

"Guild business for Khyzhan. Sharkbait, it's late. Are you just making conversation, or are you coming to some point?"

He shifted so that his shoulder was under her head. "I'm coming to a point," he murmured into her hair. "Trust me."

"*Trust* you?" she laughed. "After watching you cheat *despicably* at the *ysmath* bones?"

"Ferret," he chided. "Despicable cheaters get *caught.*"

She yawned and leaned against him. "It's hardly fair to bandy words with me when I'm this tired."

He smiled with mock nastiness. "That, my sweet thief, was the plan. It's my only hope of winning an argument with you."

"What a thoroughly ungentlemanly attitude!"

Very slowly, Sharkbait reached out to rest his fingers on the sides of her face. "I never claimed to be a gentleman," he pointed out. He gently drew her closer. When they were nose to nose, he spoke again. "Would you mind terribly if I kissed you?"

Laughter found its way around a breathless flutter in her throat. "I thought you weren't a gentleman. *Why are you asking?*"

"Good point," he acknowledged, and kissed her.

Author Bio
Beth Hilgartner

Beth Hilgartner has published five previous books: three fan-
tasies, a historical fiction novel, and a picture book. She is an
Episcopal priest, an award-winning author, a musician, a flower
farmer, an equestrian, a maker of historical instruments (re-
corders), and chronically short of sleep. She lives in Orford,
NH - no, not OXford - with her husband and their four seriously pampered cats.

The titles of her previous works are:

Great Gorilla Grins (the picture book)

A Necklace of Fallen Stars

A Murder for her Majesty (winner of the Golden Pen Award
1987 - Mystery category and a Notable Children's Trade Book
in the Field of Social Studies)

Colors in the Dreamweaver's Loom

The Feast of the Trickster

Artist Bio
Charles Keegan

Charles has painted covers for Tor, Del Rey and Baen Books. Between other projects Charles does poster and card art for Five Rings' "Doomtown" Collectable Card Game. He was a 1998 Chesley Award nominee and saw his first international publication in December 1998. Four of Charles' paintings were accepted into *Spectrum 5: the Best in Contemporary Fantastic Art*, one of which won a Judges' Choice Award at the 1998 World Con Art Show. One piece has been accepted into *Spectrum 6*.

In January 1997, Charles appeared fighting with live steel in Discovery Channel's *Deadly Duels: Duels of Chivalry* with internationally recognized edged weapons expert Hank Reinhardt, and is a member of Hank's fight team.

Charles Keegan is a member of the Association of Science Fiction and Fantasy Artists (ASFA) and is an affiliate member of the Science Fiction & Fantasy Writers of America (SFWA).

Trained at both the National Academy of Design and Art Students' League of New York, he lives in Atlanta with his wife Heather.

His web site is:

http://www.KeeganPrints.com

Come check out our web site for details on these Meisha Merlin authors!

Kevin J. Anderson
Edo van Belkom
Janet Berliner
Storm Constantine
Diane Duane
Sylvia Engdahl
Jim Grimsley
George Guthridge
Keith Hartman
Beth Hilgartner
P. C. Hodgell
Tanya Huff
Janet Kagan
Caitlin R. Kiernan
Lee Killough
George R. R. Martin
Lee Martindale
Jack McDevitt
Sharon Lee & Steve Miller
James A. Moore
Adam Niswander
Andre Norton
Jody Lynn Nye
Selina Rosen
Kristine Kathryn Rusch
Michael Scott
S. P. Somtow
Allen Steele
Freda Warrington

http://www.MeishaMerlin.com